RA ~~MPAGE~~

Land of the Elementals
Book One

AARON OSTER

To Jerry
From Ari

(AO)

For myself. Yeah, I dedicated this book to myself. I did all the work, so I've earned it!

1

Arbor swung his ax into the tree with a resounding thud, the blade biting deep in the trunk and lodging there. He pulled the blade out with a grunt and swung again. Sweat beaded his brow as he worked, swinging the ax methodically until the tree came down with a splintering crack. Arbor left the ax in the tree stump, wiping his brow with a rag as he sat down, leaning against what was left of the tree. He leaned to the side and grabbed his waterskin, taking a long draft. Keeping the water in the shade had kept it cool despite the heat of the day, and Arbor enjoyed the feeling of the liquid running down his parched throat.

It was a beautiful day. The sun shone brightly overhead, and he breathed in deeply, the scent of the forest around him relaxing him in a way that nothing else could. A breeze wafted through the clearing, rustling the treetops and making sunspots dance on the ground. It was always nice this time of year, and Arbor loved spending his days outside. In his mind, there was nothing like the peace and tranquility that came with being alone in the forest. It always made him feel small, but also as if he were part of something greater than himself.

It was nearing the end of the summer- at least that's what his mother had said. She said that the summer moon would only shine for another week or two before the dark moon came. The thought made him shudder, and a chill ran down his spine, despite the warm weather. He didn't know why, but the four months between the summer and winter moons always made him feel uneasy. He wasn't the only, one of course. Four months when the night was so dark that you couldn't see a foot in any direction was quite disconcerting. The lack of a moon in those months gave rise to all sorts of superstitions.

His mother said that the four months with no moon was the Almighty's way of reminding them to pray. Arbor didn't believe in that, but he just nodded whenever his mother talked about it. She was a hard woman to argue with.

He looked at the pile of logs, grimacing. He knew that he was only halfway done for the day. He also knew that if he wanted the house ready by next week, he would have to get up off his lazy ass and put in the work. He got up, his muscles groaning in protest and he stretched his arms and back, trying to work out the stiff muscles. He put the stopper into his waterskin and pulled the ax back out of the stump. He looked around for a moment, before finding one of the trees he'd marked and headed over to it.

He adjusted his grip and was about to take his first swing when he saw a deer wander into the clearing, not five yards from him. He stood stock-still as the deer watched him calmly, its ears flicking slightly as it bent down to begin grazing. The tranquility was ruined instantaneously by the loud voice of his sister. "Arbor!" she yelled, coming into the clearing, "Mother wants to know when you'll be home!"

The deer bolted at the first sound of her voice and Arbor sighed, setting his ax down again. Karria was fourteen, just two years away from adulthood, but he swore she still acted like a child sometimes.

Despite his annoyance at having the tranquility of the forest ruined, he couldn't help but smile as she came into view. At just over five feet tall, she was a pretty young girl, with bright green eyes, a small nose and lips, and long brown hair falling in curls down her back. She had a small splash of freckles across her nose and a mischievous smile that got her into trouble on more than one occasion.

"You don't need to yell, you know. It's very unbecoming of a proper young woman," Arbor said, laughing as she came running up to him and launching herself at him. She wrapped her arms around him and planted a kiss on his cheek.

"Propriety can kiss my ass. I don't see any proper women, do you?" she asked, letting go of him and flashing him a grin. "You'll be gone in a few days, and I'll never see you again, so I have to take every opportunity I have left to tease you." She ended her sentence with a faux pout on her face.

"First of all, language!" Arbor scolded, "And secondly, I'm getting married, not moving across the kingdom." He laughed. "The house is less than a mile from here. I bet that it didn't even take you ten minutes to walk over."

"I know," she said, still pouting. "It just feels like I'm losing you. You only seem to have time for Florren now." She wrinkled her nose when she said Florren's name, as if she had smelled something unpleasant.

"Florren is a wonderful woman. You know I love her, but that doesn't mean that I love you any less," Arbor said sternly. "And just because we will no longer live under the same roof, doesn't mean that I won't visit. I'll be over at least once a week."

"Promise?" Karria asked, looking up at him, her eyes watering.

Mother really has taught her well in the art of guilt-tripping, Arbor thought to himself, suppressing a grin.

"I promise," he said, patting the top of her head. "Now, you can either help me chop down trees, or you can tell Mother that I'll be home before sunset."

Karria stuck her tongue out at him. Then, giggling, she ran towards the edge of the clearing. "I'll let mother know that you'll be back for dinner! I'm a proper young lady, remember? I'll leave all the hard, sweaty labor to the big, strong men like you!"

Arbor sighed and shook his head as he watched her go. She had a serious mouth on her, but that was a problem for his parents to deal with. He picked up the ax and grimaced again. He still had a lot of work to do before night fell.

2

The sun was already beginning to set when Arbor felled his last tree. He tiredly slung the ax on his shoulder and headed down the path leading back to his house. Long shadows stretched out in front of him, and he could see the orange summer moon already rising.

As he walked, he couldn't help but marvel at the colors in the sky. There were always beautiful sunsets in the summer, but this one was especially spectacular. Streaks of red, orange, and purple lit up the sky, and he almost tripped over a tree root as he walked. He laughed to himself and decided that keeping his eyes on the path ahead was probably a good idea.

It got noticeably darker as the canopy overhead thickened as he walked, until he was squinting at the path ahead and stumbling every now and then as he made his way through the woods. His parents lived in a clearing and he was only about a quarter-mile away, but the thick tree cover let in almost no light.

Arbor sighed and resolved himself to bring a torch the next time he decided to work late. He stopped suddenly, his ears picking up a faint rustling in the undergrowth. He quickly turned around, scanning the nearby trees and trying to pierce the darkness. He kept looking, his heart racing as he imagined all sorts of wild beasts coming out of the darkness to attack him.

There had been reports of some unusual activity in the area as of late, and he didn't want to be caught unawares. He stood motionless for a few more moments before letting his shoulders relaxed.

"Must have been the wind," he muttered as started down the path again.

***

Just a few yards from the path, a man dressed in black leather let out the breath he'd been holding. It wouldn't do to get caught so close to the operation, and his boss was not someone to trifle with. The man shivered at the thought of what would have happened had he been spotted.

Probably a swift death, if he'd been lucky. A long, drawn-out one, if he wasn't. He stood up slowly, backing into the brush, careful not to make any sound this time. As soon as he was back on the game trail behind the main path, he turned to head back to their camp. He had a report to make.

***

A few minutes later, Arbor could see the faint flicker of torchlight coming from the clearing where his parents' house stood. With a sigh of relief, he left the forest and entered the clearing. He laughed at himself for getting so worked up and imagining wild beasts attacking him. It was considerably easier to do, now that he was out of the surrounding forest.

"I'm home!" he called out, opening the front door and coming into the entryway.

"Wait! Don't come in yet!" he heard his mother cry, frantically. "Florren is here. Go back out and come around the other side!"

Arbor exited in a hurry when he heard that and walked around to the back entrance. It was a tradition as old as time in the settlement of Woods' Clearing. A husband and wife-to-be could not see or speak to one another the week before their wedding. Arbor thought it was a stupid tradition and he missed Florren dearly, as he had not seen her in the last six days.

"Is she gone?" he asked as he cracked the back door open. "Wouldn't want to call the wrath of the gods down upon us for breaking tradition."

"Yes, she's gone, my boy," he heard his father's deep voice call out in answer. "And there's no need for that snark. It's tradition!"

He came in, hiding an eye-roll and headed into the dining room. His father and Karria were both sitting by the table. Karria was trying to hide a smile behind her hand but was not doing a very good job of it.

"You could have warned me that she was here," Arbor grumbled as he sat down across her.

"But what fun would that be?" she asked, not even trying to hide her smile now. "You should have seen her face when she heard

7

you come in! She just about crapped her dress!" Karria said, now laughing so hard that tears were coming out of her eyes.

"Language!" both Arbor and his father yelled, at the same time.

Karria just waved her hand, continuing to laugh at his future wife's expense.

"I don't think I've seen someone go that red since the first time you two met!" Karria was laughing so hard at that point that she started wheezing and trying to catch her breath.

"I'm glad you thought it was so funny," Arbor deadpanned.

"That wasn't very nice of you, Karria," his father said, but Arbor could see the corner of his mouth twitching.

He heard the front door close, and a few seconds later, his mother came bustling in. Karrin was a slightly plump woman standing at around five and a half feet. She had sparkling green eyes and brown hair, now slightly graying at the temples. She was still beautiful, of course, and it was easy to see where Karria had gotten her looks, though where she'd gotten her sense of humor was still a mystery.

"Why did you come into the house?" His mother placed her hands on her hips and stared at him with a disapproving glare. "You knew that Florren was going to be here! You were supposed to knock first and then go around back so I could get her out!"

"How was I supposed to know? No one told me anything about this!" Arbor retorted.

"Karria told you! I sent her over earlier with a message!" His mother returned, just as loudly, then stopped. She looked from Arbor's outraged face to Karria, who was still laughing, and sighed.

"I suppose the next time I want an important message sent, I'll have to do it myself," she said while shooting Karria a glare. "Don't think you'll be getting away with this, young lady. I'll have to think up a suitable punishment for you."

She turned back to Arbor then, her tone softening. "Go wash up. Dinner will be ready soon, and you look filthy. I won't have that at the dinner table." With that, she bustled into the kitchen and started stirring a pot sitting on the stove.

Arbor headed up into his room and closed the door. There was a small wooden bed frame with a straw-filled mattress on top. His sheets were most likely still hanging out on the line, as they weren't on his bed. He grabbed a chair and sat down heavily. Leaning down, he began unlacing his boots, wincing as he noticed the mud clinging to the bottom. His mother would give him an earful for tracking it through the house.

Tugging them off, he placed them in a corner. Then he stripped down to his underclothes. He dropped the dirty clothes into a bin beside his bed, then grabbed a rough towel and a clean set of clothes. He opened the door to his room and headed to the washroom at the end of the hallway.

He was going to miss this room most of all. Arbor's parents had apparently known a Mage in their earlier years, a person capable of using magic, and he had done them a few favors when they'd moved in. He had enchanted the waterspout in the wall, to ensure they always have hot water. Sitting down on a low bench, he turned on the spout. The entire room was made of stone, unlike the rest of the house, and there was a small drain near the far wall to allow the water to run out.

Steam quickly filled the room, and he grabbed a bar of soap and lathered himself up. He immensely enjoyed the feeling of washing off the day's dirt and grime, feeling the hot water ease the tension in his sore muscles.

Once he'd finished drying himself, he walked to the looking glass hanging on the far side of the room. This was another thing that most people didn't have, and they were considered to be lucky to have one. Arbor looked into the glass and turned his face from side to side. He was being neglectful and definitely needed a shave. He walked back to where he'd left the soap and grabbed it, along with a small bin. He filled the bin with steaming water and brought it back to the looking glass.

Lathering up his hands, he spread the bubbly substance across his face and picked up his razor. He dragged the razor across his cheeks and chin, dipping it in the steaming bucket from time to time. Then when he was finished, he washed his face vigorously and examined his work.

Not too bad looking, he thought.

He had the same dark brown hair as his mother and sister, and light gray eyes. He had a straight nose, a strong jaw, and well-rounded shoulders. He turned his face a little to the side to see if he had missed anything when he heard a pounding on the door.

"Stop staring at yourself in the mirror; I'm sure you're pretty enough! Mother said that supper will get cold, so you better come down!" Karria yelled into the crack between the doorframe.

He could hear her sniggering, even through the door and sighed yet again. Karria's teasing was one thing he definitely would not miss.

3

The next day was a hectic one, with everyone rushing to get ready for the wedding. Arbor was forcefully shaken from his slumber before the sun had even come up, only to be rushed around getting his hair cut and his wedding coat fitted. When he finally got back to his family's home around midday, he felt about ready to drop from exhaustion.

The clearing around the house had been transformed while he'd been out getting ready. Tables were now set up in neat rows, white cloths adorning each. The tables were decorated with vases of wildflowers, and rows of candles sat in small glass bowls filled with water. There was a raised stage on the far side of the clearing with a row of chairs neatly arranged before it. The chairs were split down the middle, and a long white cloth stretched through the center. He could see torches spread throughout the clearing to provide light for the long night of celebration.

He decided to sit down and relax for a bit. After all, the wedding ceremony wouldn't be starting until just before nightfall. He put his back against a tree on the edge of the clearing and closed his eyes. Arbor was exhausted. He'd had a difficult time falling asleep last night. The excitement of the following day had kept him up, tossing and turning for hours. Now that he was sitting down for the first time all day, he couldn't help but begin to nod off and was soon fast asleep.

"Wake up, sleepyhead! That is, unless you want to sleep through your own wedding!" Arbor slowly cracked his eyes open. The sun was already beginning to set, and he could see that torches were being lit around the clearing as night fell.

Karria stood in front of him with her hands on her hips and a look of amusement on her face. She was already dressed for the wedding, in a long blue dress with white lace stitched around her wrists and neckline. The neckline dipped, in his opinion, just a bit too far for a girl her age. The was also a large white bow tied around her waist, and her usually curly brown hair had been braided with white and red lilies.

"How much longer to the ceremony?" Arbor asked, standing up and rubbing his eyes. "Guests are already arriving, but the ceremony isn't for at least another hour," Karria said, then narrowed her eyes at him.

When that failed to prompt a response from him, she rolled her eyes and prodded, "Well?" She gave him a meaningful look.

"Well, what?" Arbor asked, covering a wide yawn and blinking a few times.

Karria sighed loudly, then did another exaggerated eye roll. "My dress," she said with obvious annoyance, "How do I look?"

She did a twirl for him, her skirts swishing and billowing out as she completed the turn. She looked at him with an expectant gaze.

"You look beautiful, Karria. You'll be the envy of all the other young women here tonight. And I'm sure you'll have those boys fawning over you non-stop," he said with a smile.

"You really think so?" she asked in a small voice, her cheeks going slightly pink.

"Yes, I do. But if I catch any of them trying to make a pass at you, I'll break their legs and make them crawl home!"

Karria snorted out a laugh.

"I'd pay good money to see that!"

Arbor snorted out a laugh as well.

"Oh, come here, you bloodthirsty excuse for a lady!" he said, then wrapped his arms around her in a tight hug. He held her for another minute until she began squirming.

"Let go of me!" she said, struggling in his grasp. "You'll wrinkle my dress!"

Laughing, he let her go, and she stood back from him, smoothing out imagined wrinkles. She was quiet for a moment, then she spoke, her voice low and all hints of playful cheer gone.

"I'm going to miss you, you know."

Arbor saw her look up then and could see her eyes beginning to water. "Don't cry now. Your eyes will get all puffy, and everyone will see," he said, getting down on one knee and pulling a kerchief from his pocket to dab at her eyes. "I'm not leaving forever. I'll still be around," he said, trying to be reassuring.

She sniffed a few more times before composing herself. "You promise?"

"Yes, I promise. Now run along, I think I hear Mother calling your name." He handed her the handkerchief and watched her dab at her eyes a few more times before tucking it away.

She smiled then and leaned in to kiss him on the cheek. "Thanks, Arbor. You always know exactly what to say."

She straightened the front of her dress one more time before heading towards their mother. His father approached him then, holding his wedding coat, a long blue jacket with silver trim and shining bronze buttons.

"She's been having a hard time adjusting to the fact that you'll no longer be living at home. You are her only brother, after all," he said, holding the coat open for him.

"I know, but we all have to grow up and leave sometime, and one day soon, it'll be her turn to go," Arbor said, turning his back to his father and allowing him to slide the coat on over his shoulders.

"Just give her some time. She may try to hold on a bit tighter for a little while," Darver said, as his son turned around. "And show a little extra compassion, hmm?" he said, smoothing the front of his coat.

"I'll do my best," Arbor replied, though inwardly, he thought that it was he who would need to adjust.

Moving away from home was a lot more difficult than he was letting on, and if he were being honest with himself, it scared him more than he wanted to admit.

"That's all a person can ask for," his father said, snapping him from his thoughts.

He then reached out, putting a hand on his shoulder. He paused for a moment, as if trying to gather his thoughts.

"You know you've made me prouder than any man has a right to be, and you've found yourself a fine woman."

Arbor was slightly taken aback by the sudden show of emotion from his usually stoic father, and it made him feel a bit uncomfortable.

"Here, I'd like you to have this," Darver continued, pulling a pendant from his coat pocket.

Arbor took the pendant in his hands and stared at it in wonder. It was unlike anything he had ever seen before. It was slightly larger than his palm, and it was a deep, almost blood-red in color. Light sparkled off five small stones around the edges and an oak tree was etched into the surface. He turned it over and a lion's head roared back at him, almost seeming to be alive. The detail was unreal, and he knew right away that this was an extremely valuable gift.

"What is this?" Arbor asked, entranced by the beauty of the thing.

"It has been in our family for generations," his father said. "My father told me that this once belonged to a great king and that it was gifted to one of our ancestors thousands of years ago for a great personal deed. My father entrusted me with it on my wedding day. Now, I give it to you, my son."

Arbor looked into his father's eyes then and saw pride. He felt emotion try to claim him but quickly tamped it down. It wouldn't do for the groom to cry on his wedding night.

"Thank you for entrusting me with such a wonderful gift. I will treasure it always." He then slid the pendant over his neck and tucked it under his shirt.

"Now come. The ceremony will be starting soon, and Florren will be here at any moment," Darver said, taking him by the arm and steering him towards the house.

Arbor heard a wagon pull up a few minutes later as he sat inside the house. He could hear all the people outside begin to sing the song of greeting, and he knew Florren had arrived.

His mother came in then, and Arbor stood up. He embraced her and she wept silently into his shoulder. She stood back after a minute, tears in her eyes as she held his face in her hands.

"I can't believe that this day is finally here!" she sobbed. "You have no idea how proud you have made me, and a mother could not have asked for a more wonderful and caring son."

Arbor felt his eyes start to water then. He bit his lip, and with a monumental effort, he forced himself not to cry. His mother let go of his face, and he could hear the song of the bride as she walked down the aisle.

They sat in silence, waiting for the song to end, and when it did, both his mother and father picked up the two burning candles sitting on the table before them.

"Are you ready for this?" his father asked, holding his candle aloft.

Arbor squared his shoulders. He could feel his heart racing in nervous anticipation.

"As ready as I'll ever be."

They each took one of his arms, and together, they walked out of the house. The first thing he saw upon exiting were all the people seated on either side of the aisle. All eyes were on him as they began to sing the song of the groom.

He approached the aisle with his parents escorting him on either side. Looking around at all the familiar faces, all singing for him, he once again had a hard time controlling his emotions. He could see Karria near the front, dabbing at her eyes with the kerchief he'd given her earlier. Then he looked up to the approaching platform, and there she was.

Florren was dressed in a long, flowing white gown, a bouquet of white lilies clutched between her hands. She was standing at the very center of the stage. He couldn't see her face as it was veiled, but he could just imagine her under it; her large dark eyes and full lips, her bright smile, and long dark hair. The entire thing felt surreal to him, as if this was all just a dream.

He could see Florren's aunt and uncle standing behind her, also smiling brightly as he approached. Florren had no parents of her own. They had died when she was very young, so her aunt and uncle had taken her in.

Arbor remembered their first meeting like it had only happened yesterday.

She'd moved to Woods' Clearing just four months ago with her aunt and uncle. He had been in town that day, doing some repair work on the blacksmith's shop roof, when he'd seen her ride in for the first time.

He remembered staring at her, his eyes drawn as though by a magnet, to her curvaceous figure. Until she'd looked at him. He'd flushed a deep red when she did, realizing that he'd been caught staring. Instead of looking away or yelling at him, though, she'd just smiled and winked, then blown him a kiss. Her actions had shocked him so much that he'd almost fallen off the roof.

She'd laughed then, covering her mouth with a delicate hand as she rode away. It was that laugh that had made him fall in love with her. With that laugh and her brazen attitude, he resolved himself to make her laugh like that again.

All these memories and more came to him as he approached the platform. He had eyes only for her. He could imagine their life together, and all the wonderful years they had ahead of them.

Life was never so kind, however, and Arbor was about to receive one of life's harshest lessons.

With no warning at all, the trees around the clearing exploded with sounds of galloping horses and screaming men. The guests stopped singing immediately and stood from their seats, some gasping in surprise and others with feelings of dread, as the horsemen moved to circle them, cutting off any path of escape.

4

Arbor could hardly believe his eyes.

What the hell are armed men doing here?

Whatever the reason, he knew it was nothing good. He felt his mother's grip tighten on his arm as three men detached themselves from the front of the force and rode forward.

The man in the middle dismounted, swaggering forward with an authoritative air, while the other two stayed on horseback.

"My name is Ramson," he said, eyes sweeping over the gathered guests.

He was tall, a little over six feet, with dark hair and a hooked nose. His eyes were what caught Arbor's attention. They were black as night, and the flickering torchlight seemed to make them glimmer with malevolence.

This is not a man to cross, Arbor thought, taking an involuntary step back.

He wore a curved sickle sword at his waist, balanced on the other side by a heavy bladed dagger. The rest of his body was covered in heavy leather armor interwoven with black-painted metal plates.

"Don't mind me," he said with a smile. "I seem to be interrupting an important moment here, so I'll be quick. Would you be so kind as to tell me who among you is Darver?"

A tone of hushed whispers went through the gathered guests at that, though none spoke up. Ramson's lips turned down at that, and he took another step forward.

"You see, he has something of mine," he continued, "And I'd very much like to have it back."

When he still failed to get an answer, he started to become annoyed, but he quickly schooled himself and allowed his easy smile back on his face.

"Oh, come now, this shouldn't be hard. I just want to have a little…chat with him," he said, his lips twisting into a cruel smile. "No takers? Someone must know who Darver is."

"What is he talking about?" Arbor asked under his breath. "What did you take from him?"

"I don't know," his father answered.

Aaron Oster

He looked pale and shaken, and Arbor felt the hand he had wrapped around his elbow quivering.

"I've never seen this man before, but if I had to guess…" he paused here and gave Arbor a grim look. "I'd say he's after that pendant you've got hidden under your shirt."

"Should I just give it him then? Maybe he'll leave if he has what he wants."

"No!"

Arbor was shocked at his father's vehemence. "No matter what happens, do not give him that pendant! Do you understand?"

"This man looks very dangerous. Are you sure you want me to keep it from him?"

Arbor was doubtful that his father was thinking too clearly. After all, it was a family heirloom, so it would be hard for him to give up. But when he nodded once again, Arbor agreed to stay silent. As soon as he gave his confirmation, he felt his father's grip relax.

Ramson had been moving forward while they were talking, swaggering down the aisle and staring down the various gathered guests. He singled one of them out, placing a hand on her shoulder.

"Tell me, Miss, would you happen to know who Darver is?" he asked in a pleasant voice. The woman just shook her head, quivering in terror.

"What a shame," he said, letting go and turning around as if to leave.

The woman seemed to relax a bit, letting out a shaky breath.

Ramson spun then, pulling his sickle sword from his belt and decapitating the woman with a single, well-placed blow.

Several people screamed, and a couple even fainted, lumping to the ground in undignified heaps. The rest stared in horror and disbelief as the corpse fell to the ground with two distinct thuds.

"I can see that no one is willing to help," he said, still using the same conversational tone as he had been before, seeming completely unfazed by the body now lying at his feet.

He whipped his sword through the air, sending droplets of blood spraying the ground. He turned to one of the bandits still on horseback, a small, greasy-looking man with a smashed nose.

"Smit, kill them all. Maybe take a few of the prettier ones. I bet we can get a fair bit for them in Fivora."

18

Then, turning to the podium where Florren stood, he smiled cruelly then bowed at the waist, pointing at her with his sword.

"Oh. And kill that one first. It is her wedding night, after all, and we wouldn't want to be rude."

Arbor whirled in place, seeing that Florren had uncovered her face and was standing huddled between her aunt and uncle. He watched in horror as the realization of what was about to happen hit her. Tearing himself free of his parents' arms, he ran for the podium. It was as though he were running through quicksand, the stage seeming to be miles away.

The world seemed to freeze in that moment, and she met his gaze as the loud thwack of over a dozen crossbows sounded through the clearing. A sad smile touched her lips, and she mouthed something at him. He couldn't make it out as half a dozen bolts seemed to sprout from her at once, slamming into her slim frame one after the next. She staggered back, her white gown already beginning to turn red as she fell.

A scream tore itself from his throat as he launched himself onto the stage, shoving her aunt and uncle out of the way. He bent down next to Florren and lifted her in his arms, but he could see that it was too late. Her body had gone limp and cold, glassy eyes stared back at him, and she had a trickle of blood running from the corner of her mouth.

He felt tears streaming down his face as he hugged her limp body. He screamed, burying his face in her bloody chest, and rocked back and forth with her. He dimly heard people in the background, but all he could do was hold Florren and cry.

Someone was tugging on his shoulder, shouting urgently, but he ignored them. The hand then went limp and slid down his back.

This couldn't be happening. She couldn't be dead.

This must all be a horrible dream. It has to be!

He heard a scream then, and it finally pierced through his grief-stricken mind. Ramson was standing in the center of the aisle, holding his mother by the hair, his sword at her throat. His father was on his knees in front of him, his hands clasped in supplication.

His leg bumped against something soft and Arbor felt something soaking into his pant leg. Turning his head to the side, he saw Florren's uncle lying next to him, crossbow quarrels sticking out of the man, and he finally understood why his pant leg was wet.

It was slowly soaking up the pool of blood spreading from the man's body. He let go of Florren's body, his heart beginning to race, and bile rising in his throat.

Florren was gone.

His future in-laws were gone.

He couldn't lose his parents as well!

"Let her go!" Arbor yelled, staggering to his feet and running towards them.

"Stop him," Ramson said calmly, and Arbor stumbled as a hard blow connected with the side of his face.

His vision swam, and he tasted blood. His arms were roughly seized by two of the men, and he was dragged before Ramson.

"So, which one of you is Darver?" he asked again, holding Karrin by her hair. "One of these lovely people were nice enough to point you out. Unfortunately, there were two of you in the direction he was pointing, and he tragically died before he could clarify which one of you he meant."

His lips turned down as the screams around him rose in pitch and volume – clearly, the bandits were having their way with some of the guests before killing them. After only a moment, they fell ominously silent.

"Finally. I can't abide people who take forever to die," Ramson continued, turning his attention back to them. "Now I'll only ask once." He jerked violently at Karrin's hair and pressed the sword to her throat, hard enough to draw blood. "Which one of you is it?"

Seeing his wife in pain was apparently too much for his father because he finally cracked.

"I'm Darver! Please don't kill her. I'll give you whatever you want. Just please…!"

"Are you now?" Ramson asked in a conversational tone. "Then tell me. I've heard of a wonderful pendant that happens to be in your possession. Would you happen to know where this pendant may be?"

"I've never heard of such a thing!" Darver said vehemently. "Now please, let her go! She hasn't done anything to you!"

Karrin's throat bobbed in terror, tears streaming down her cheeks as the blade was pressed just a bit harder, a line of red now welling around the sharpened edge.

20

Arbor looked on in helpless rage.

He had the pendant around his neck. All he had to do was tell Ramson, and he would let his mother go. But he'd promised his father not to give the pendant up under any circumstances.

Indecision warred inside him as he stood there. He opened his mouth to speak and then closed it, gritting his teeth in frustration.

Ramson stared down at Darver for a long moment, then let out a snort.

"What a pity. It seems you wife isn't worth much to you."

He drew his sword across Karrin's neck, kicking her forward and spraying her husband in a shower of blood.

Karrin gurgled, her eyes bulging wide, hands clutching at her neck, as blood pumped out from between her fingers. Then she went limp.

Arbor screamed in helpless rage as his mother's lifeless body dropped to the ground, blood pouring from her open throat and soaking into the once-white carpet rolled between the aisles.

"You bastard! I'll kill you for that!" Darver roared, throwing himself at the man, hands outstretched as he reached for the man's throat.

Ramson stood back calmly as Darver ran at him, his sword held loosely in his hand. One of Ramson's men stuck from the side, burying a spear in his throat, twisting it and ripping it free. Darver was dead before his body even hit the ground, blood pumping from the ragged tear in his throat.

Arbor stared as both his parents were brutally murdered in front of him. His mind was numb with shock, but something was quickly beginning to take its place. Rage.

First, Florren and now, my parents. I have nothing left to lose now, Arbor thought to himself, feeling almost surreal, as though he were walking through a dream.

But this wasn't a dream.

Arbor felt something welling up inside of him, and it suddenly burst forth, manifesting itself in a scream of rage. With a mighty heave, he tore himself from the men who were holding him, sending them staggering back in surprise.

Ramson was cleaning his blade when he saw Arbor running at him. "Oh, good. Another one. Kill him as well," he said to the spearman who had just killed his father.

21

The man stepped forward, thrusting his spear at Arbor's throat. Something odd happened then. Arbor could somehow *feel* where the spear was going to be.

He didn't question it and following that feeling, he managed to duck the blow, coming up inside the spear's reach. Drawing his fist back, Arbor used the momentum of his forward movement and caught the man's nose with a vicious cross punch.

The bones beneath his fist crunched, sending a spray of blood across the man's face. His spear clattered to the ground as he fell back, clutching at his ruined nose and howling in pain.

Arbor bent quickly and snatched up the fallen spear.

Leveling the weapon at Ramson, he screamed, making a clumsy thrust, which Ramson easily side-stepped. The strange feeling that had warned him of the spear-strike earlier was now gone, leaving him devoid of any idea of what to do.

"You have no idea how to use that weapon, do you, boy?" Ramson said with a sneer. "I bet you've never held a weapon in your life. Think you'll be a hero and avenge your parents and your bride?"

He moved forward swiftly, swinging his sickle sword in a wide arc and Arbor stumbled back, clumsily attempting a parry. He felt a sharp pain burn across his cheek, and when he touched it, his fingers came away bloody.

Ramson's men had surrounded the two of them, cutting off any path of retreat. One of the men moved forward to grab Arbor, but Ramson just waved him off.

"Leave him be. I want to kill this one myself. After all," he said with a wicked smile. "I may as well get the whole set!"

Arbor attempted another clumsy lunge at that remark, but Ramson nimbly dogged back. He looked at Arbor and laughed, his cruel eyes boring into him, mocking him. Arbor knew that he stood no chance of winning. He was clearly outmatched and had no idea how to use a weapon, but he was past caring about his own life.

There was nothing left to lose and if he had to die to kill this man, so be it.

"Is that the best you've got, boy?" Ramson asked.

He took a step forward and began a complicated series of slashing blows, forcing Arbor to stumble back once again, trying to avoid the glittering blade. He tried to use the spear defensively, but

Ramson knocked it to the side, stepping into his guard and smashing the pommel into his face, right below one of his eyes. Arbor stumbled back, clutching his face in pain.

This is it, he thought in resignation.

That last attack had forced him to drop his spear and now he was defenseless. He closed his eyes, waiting, but instead of the expected blow, Ramson just stood back.

"Go ahead," he said with a sneer, "Pick it up."

Arbor looked at him in horror. Ramson was playing with him.

When he didn't move to pick up the spear, Ramson started to become impatient.

"How about this," he said in a mocking tone. "I will give you one free blow. I will not attempt to block or parry. All you have to do is strike me down and my men will let you go free. What do you say?"

There was a collective roar of laughter from the men surrounding them as Ramson made his declaration.

Arbor bent down slowly and picked up the spear, keeping his eye on Ramson the entire time. He only had one chance, so he needed to do something unexpected. He took the weapon in a double-handed grip and stepped forward.

Ramson smiled as he did so and opened his arms wide, exposing his chest. His men laughed even louder at this. It was great entertainment.

Arbor stepped forward and thrust towards Ramson's chest. Then, the strange feeling came back and with a grunt, he changed his thrust to a swing, slashing the spear in a narrow arc.

Ramson, expecting the thrust, was already moving back when Arbor attacked, but his sudden shift caught him off guard and he inadvertently stepped right into the path of the incoming spear blade. The spear tip sliced cleanly into his left eye with a spray of blood. The blade bit deep, hitting the bone in his nose and being forced upward, leaving a bloody trail across his face.

Ramson howled in pain, dropping his sword and clutching his ruined eye. Arbor tried to capitalize on the opening, but he was mobbed by Ramson's men. They beat him, knocking him to the ground and pummeling his body with vicious kicks. Arbor was sure he felt a few of his ribs crack and he gasped out in pain. Finally, mercifully, it stopped, and he was hauled up on his feet.

Ramson now had a red-stained cloth wrapped around the left side of his face, the makeshift bandage hiding his ruined eye. His face was twisted in anger and pain as he walked up to him.

"I'm going to enjoy killing you," Ramson said in a low voice tinged with hate.

"Go ahead and kill me," Arbor croaked through a split lip. "You're a coward — a man without honor. I'm not afraid to die. You've already killed everyone I care about, so go ahead and kill me."

Arbor closed his eyes then, waiting for the blow. "I'll be with you soon, my love," he whispered.

The blow never came. He opened his eyes and saw that Ramson was looking at him with a thoughtful expression. It was somewhat marred by the heavy bandage, but Arbor felt his heart drop as he began to speak.

"No. I'm not going to kill you," he said, sheathing his sword. "I think you want that, don't you? Everyone you love is dead, so why go on living, right?" he asked, grabbing Arbor by the hair and pulling his eyes up to meet his remaining one.

"I'm going to let you live. Live with the knowledge that I took everything from you. Live with that every day. Live! Until the day you find the courage to end your own miserable life."

Ramson turned his back on him then and walked away.

"Come on, men. We're done here. Finish up with your fun and gather up the rest. We're heading to Fivora!" he roared as he got onto his horse.

His men answered back with a cheer, finishing off the few remaining villagers. The men holding Arbor let go of him then and without their support, he fell to the ground in a limp heap. He saw hooves passing by as he lay on the ground, hearing the screams of the dead and dying, weeping quietly and lost in his misery.

5

The sun was beaming down, and Arbor woke with a start, opening his eyes. He was lying in the same spot they'd left him the night before. He quickly closed his eyes as the sun directly overhead nearly blinded him. Everything hurt. He lay there for a few minutes, trying to gather his wits. His head was pounding, it hurt to breathe, and it felt like his throat was full of cotton.

He rolled onto his stomach with a groan, keeping his eyes closed for the moment. His ribs ached with the movement, pain flaring up as tried to get his feet under him. He finally managed to stand, swaying drunkenly as he attempted to orient himself.

What happened last night?

He tried opening his eyes again but found that only one would obey. He gingerly brought his fingers up to his eye and winced as he felt it. The eye was swollen shut.

He looked around the clearing. There were bodies everywhere. His confusion cleared up in an instant and he felt tears try to work themselves out of his eyes, but they wouldn't come.

I can't even cry anymore.

He felt hollow inside, as though his entire world had ended, and nothing mattered anymore. He did feel one thing, though. Through all the misery and pain, one emotion stood out in stark contrast - hatred. He'd never thought he could hate someone as much as he did right now, but it burned within him like a raging inferno.

That was the only thing that kept him from collapsing on the ground right now and waiting to die. He hobbled over to his house and pushed the door open. It swung loosely on a single hinge, the rest having been torn off by the bandits the night before. As he suspected, the place had been ransacked.

Probably Ramson's men looking for the pendant.

He stumbled up the stairs to the washroom and turned on the spout; hot water immediately began pouring out.

At least they left this room intact, he thought bitterly.

He slowly and painfully worked himself out of his wedding clothes. They were muddy, torn, and covered in blood. They were difficult to remove with his injuries, but he managed to get them off with a bit of effort.

He was surprised to still see the red pendant hanging around his neck. He felt an unexpected rage overtake him at the sight and tore it from his neck, suddenly having the overwhelming desire to toss it as far as he could and never look back. After all, it had cost over a hundred people their lives.

In the end, though, he decided to keep it.

If Darver had been willing to give his life for it, he wouldn't throw it away. He sat down under the spout and just let the water wash over him, wincing as the steaming water hit his bruised and battered body. He turned his head to the side, catching some of the hot water in his mouth and swallowing.

The water burned his throat on the way down, and he coughed, leaning forward and retching. His stomach heaved a few times as bile rose in his throat. After a while, his stomach settled and the heaving subsided. He rose shakily to his feet and dabbed at his body with a ripped towel.

Leaving the washroom, he stumbled to the room to where his parents had slept. This room, too, was completely destroyed. The bed frame was cracked, the sheets and blankets were torn, and clothes littered the floor. All his mother's jewelry was gone, along with his father's savings.

It wasn't enough to kill them. Of course, those bastards would rob them blind as well.

He felt his anger rise once again at the injustice and had to take a few deep breaths not to start screaming and start rampaging through what was left of their family home.

After calming down somewhat, he began to search the room for what he'd originally come for. A few moments later, he spotted some of rags on the floor that his mother used as bandages, along with a cracked jar of salve to ease pain and prevent infection.

At least they didn't think this was valuable enough to take, he bitterly thought to himself.

He picked them up and headed back to the washroom. Bathing the cloth strips in warm water, he spread some of the salve on them, before winding them around his ribs. He winced as he worked, sure that at least three or four of them were broken. He hadn't gotten a good look at them earlier, but now he could see that his entire side was a mass of cuts and splotchy bruises. He quickly looked away from the horrible sight and finished tying off the last of the bandages. Next, he used some of the salve on the cut Ramson's sword had left on his cheek and dabbed some over his swollen eye as well.

He could feel the warm tingling coming from where the salve had been applied and sighed in relief as the pain began to abate slowly. He headed to his room next to find some clothes. This room hadn't been spared either. His clothes littered the room and the box where he'd kept his money had been cracked open and emptied.

Gritting his teeth, he bent and began salvaging what he could. There were a few good pairs of pants and a shirt or two left over. His boots still sat in the corner and appeared to be untouched.

He dressed quickly, being careful not to aggravate his injuries any further. Once he was done, he headed to Karria's room. This had been ransacked as well, and all her valuables had been taken.

Deciding that he'd rather not see any more, he headed outside instead. He went straight to the work shed in the back of the house, trying not to look at all the dead faces staring back at him. He grabbed a shovel and headed a small way into the forest to a clearing under a massive oak tree.

The shovel sank into the earth easily enough and he grunted as his ribs flared in pain. He ignored it, digging methodically and allowing his mind wander a bit. This was where his parents had wanted to be buried, and Arbor would make sure they got to their final resting place.

It took him many hours, but eventually, four graves sat side by side at the base of the tree. He planted the shovel in the ground and went into the forest to look for stones. It didn't take too long to find, and he grunted with effort as he rolled them over to the graves. He wiped his sweaty brow and straightened, nodding to himself as he examined his work.

He had been dreading this next part. Slowly, he made his way through the clearing to where his parents lay. The blood had already dried on their clothes, and there were flies buzzing around their corpses. The stench was horrific, and he did his best to block it out. Shooing the flies away, he lifted his mother's body and carried her over to the first grave. Setting her down gently, he went for his father next.

Finally, he went for Florren. His feet dragged as he approached the stage where they were supposed to have been married, trying not to look at her lifeless face again. Her dress was stained almost black with the dried blood, a few spots of white peeking out.

He didn't cry, didn't wince in pain, keeping a hard expression on his face as he carried her to the grave he'd dug for her. He then began to look for Karria. He wandered around the clearing for over an hour, checking each body, but he didn't see her anywhere. He checked the surrounding woods, seeing a few more bodies littered about, but his sister's was not among them.

Then a memory came to him, something Ramson had said. He had said something about taking some of the villagers to Fivora. He'd never heard of Fivora, but he assumed that it was a town or city.

Dare he hope that his sister was still alive?

Taking a deep breath, he tried to quash any feelings of excitement. He would see in a moment. Running quickly through the woods, he soon came to the path that led to the main road. Sure enough, there were wagon tracks there, heading in the direction of the main town. He bent down and examined them. He wasn't much of a tracker, but even he could tell that the wagons were laden quite heavily.

A small glimmer of something shiny caught his attention then. Straightening and walking over to the spot, he saw a small necklace half-buried in the dirt. He brushed the dirt aside and stood up, holding a small silver chain with a lily hanging from the end.

This was Karria's necklace! He'd given it to her on her last birthday, and there was no way the men would have left behind something so valuable, had she been dead.

He felt a small glimmer of hope, real hope, that his sister may have survived the attack. Then his hopes were once again squashed.

If she was still alive, she was most certainly a captive of Ramson's, and he would never be able to get her back. He shook his head reproachfully at himself then. If his sister was still alive, he would do whatever it took to get her back.

No matter the consequences.

He walked back to where his parents and Florren lay. He'd closed their eyes, and if he ignored the horrific injuries, it almost looked like they were only sleeping. He clutched Karria's necklace tightly between his fingers, then slipped the chain around his neck, tucking it next to the pendant.

Lifting the shovel again, he began pouring dirt over them, their faces and bodies soon obscured from view. Tears fell as he worked, pain and sadness combining in an all-consuming whirl of misery. The graves were soon filled, and he rolled a stone over each of them.

"I'm sorry that you died because of me," he said as tears streamed down his face. "If I had only given up the damn pendant, none of this would have happened!"

He took a deep, shaky breath and continued. "Karria is still alive, and I will do whatever it takes to find her, that I promise you."

He bent down, touching the stone over Florren's grave, his voice becoming steely.

"When I find the man who did this to you, I will destroy him. I promise this, before the Almighty himself! This way, you can rest in peace, knowing that your death has been avenged."

Arbor felt a strange tightness in his chest as he spoke, as though his vow had been witnessed and he would be held to it by a higher power. He then placed a small stone by each of their graves, remembering what his mother had once told him.

"Some people place flowers at graves, but we don't do that. Flowers eventually wither and die, but stones will endure forever."

He agreed with that sentiment. The thought of the stones he'd placed staying here forever was oddly comforting. He finally wiped his tears and straightened to his full height. No matter what happened now, no matter how miserable he felt inside, he would not die.

Not until the promises he'd made had been fulfilled.

With that thought in his mind, he left the small clearing behind and headed towards the town.

6

Arbor followed the trail that led into town. He wasn't sure what he could do against that many men, but he would come up with something. After all, his sister was counting on him, and she was the only reason he still had to keep going: that, and his vow of vengeance.

He followed the trail for a little under an hour, the dirt trail slowly transforming into gravel as he neared the town. Emerging from the forest, Arbor looked around. The town was still, not a sound was to be heard.

He wondered at the quiet. Normally at this time of the day, the town would be alive with people doing their daily work. Then it came to him. The entire town was back in the clearing. They'd all been there for his wedding the previous night. Guilt wracked him as he thought of all the people that were dead because of him.

If only I'd just handed over the pendant... He shook his head.

It would do him no good thinking about what-ifs. They were all dead, and blaming himself wouldn't bring them back.

He headed down the main road towards the grocer's shop. His stomach growled, reminding him how hungry he was. Walking in, he could see that Ramson's men had been here as well. Cracked jars of flour and sugar littered the floor. Bags of beans had been torn and scattered, and preserves were smeared against the walls.

What could have possessed them to do this?

Arbor was horrified at the blatant waste of good food. Farmers had to struggle night and day to produce that flour. It took months of work for it to reach the shelves, and here were months' worth of provisions, carelessly tossed on the ground.

He went up to the front desk. The money was gone, of course. The safe box had been torn open and looted. Arbor stooped, picking up one of the storage sacks with only a small hole in it and tied it shut. He then began walking around and started salvaging what he could.

There were some unspoiled beans and a few jars of dried fruit they hadn't bothered with. He also found a small pouch of salt on one of the bottom shelves. Everything else was spoiled. Chewing on some of the fruit, he left the store and headed to the baker's.

Every store he visited was in a similar state to the grocer's. Ransacked, all items of value taken, and the rest, scattered all over the store.

All but one, Arbor noticed as he walked past the last store. The blacksmith's shop stood alone and untouched in a sea of wrecked goods. Arbor was a little surprised that they hadn't gone in. The blacksmith was bound to have plenty of money, as well as valuable goods.

He walked up to the door and tried to open it, but it wouldn't budge. The blacksmith, a grumpy old man by the name of Sedrin, was very paranoid and had apparently reinforced his locks with iron bindings on the inside. He had even placed metal shutters over his windows.

Arbor went around the side and could see that the glass was cracked, but the shutters had held. It was then that he realized something.

Ramson's men couldn't get in, but he could.

After all, how would Ramson's men know that Sedrin's brother was the grocer and that he would most likely have a key to the shop stashed away in his store?

Arbor had remembered seeing a key on the floor behind the counter, near the money chest. The men had most likely just thought it a spare to the shop and had left it there. He ran back to the first store and, fetching the key, rushed back to the smith's shop. The key slid in smoothly and Arbor heard the distinct click as the door opened.

Pushing the heavy door aside, he entered the shop. It was dark and smelled of charcoal and smoke. Heading past the rack of unfinished items, he walked over to the counter. Sure enough, there was an iron-bound chest bolted to the floor. He tried the door key. No luck.

"It must be around here somewhere," he muttered as he stood.

He hunted around behind the counter but couldn't find it. He then walked around to the front, frowning to himself.

If I were a paranoid blacksmith, where would I hide the key to my money chest?

Arbor then began sliding his hands over the surface of the counter. He had helped his father install more than a few hidden compartments for the townsfolk over the years. And he suspected that the blacksmith would definitely have one as well.

"There you are," he muttered as the counter beneath his searching fingers gave slightly, and he heard a faint click as part of the counter popped open, revealing a small wooden box.

Sure enough, when he opened it, a small steel key sat within. He wasted no time fitting the key into the chest. It slid in without any effort. He turned it, holding his breath, and it opened with a soft click. Arbor lifted the lid and was more than a little disappointed. There was just one small bag sitting on the bottom of the heavy chest.

He opened the bag and his mind was quickly changed once he saw the contents in question. Small glittering stones peeked back at him from the opening, and he quickly pulled it shut, stuffing it into his pocket. He didn't know much about jewels, but he knew enough that these were probably worth a small fortune. He was getting ready to leave when a thought occurred to him.

If he was going after Ramson and his men, he would probably need a weapon.

Putting the sack with all his gathered items to the side, he walked back to the entrance and looked at the rack of half-finished items. He looked and looked but could not find any weapons. He found this quite odd until he realized that there would be no need for weapons in a small peaceful town like this. People in his town didn't even hunt. They would trap the animals and then slaughter them. He did find a small knife, however, and tied that to his belt.

He was about to leave when something caught his eye. Sunlight was now streaming in through the open door, and he could see a small crack outlined on one of the walls.

Walking over to get a closer look, he was once again surprised.

The old man was far more paranoid than he'd originally thought.

He ran his hands over the wall until he found a small keyhole hidden by charcoal dust, made to look like part of the wall. Praying that it would work, he slid the chest key into the slot and held his breath as he turned it. He was rewarded with a small click and panel in the wall swung outward revealing… Well, Arbor wasn't quite sure what it was.

A two-foot-long double-edged blade was mounted on the wall. The blade was attached to a three-foot iron-bound rod and capped on the bottom by a heavy looking steel spike. The blade was wider at the tip and narrowed slightly as it tapered down to a straight crossguard.

Arbor reached out and took the weapon from the wall mount. It was a lot lighter than he'd been expecting, and now that he held it, he could feel that the wider blade tip was balanced nicely by the spike on the other end.

He looked around the shop for a moment before finding a sheath for the weapon. It was a long leather strap that rested over one shoulder. There were two hooks in the back, and the weapon easily slid inside, the bladed end entering a sheath near the ground.

Heading back outside, he grabbed his small sack and slung it over one of his shoulders. By the position of the sun, he could see that he only had about an hour's worth of daylight. Had he really been wandering around the town for so long?

Debating whether to spend the night in town, he walked to the middle of the street. It felt unnatural standing there. It was just too quiet, and he quickly changed his mind about sleeping in town. He looked around for the wagon tracks he'd seen earlier but had no luck. He wasn't much of a tracker anyways.

He had never left Woods' Clearing, but his father had told him that the Endless Wood bordered the Dead Forest where the gremlin city of Grend was located.

Arbor didn't know much about gremlins, only what he'd head in stories as a child. What he did know was that the gremlins served the king and the king was a great and just ruler. So anyone serving the king would be able to help him. He was pretty sure that the city was due south from where he was, so all he had to do was watch the position of the sun, and he should have no trouble finding the gremlin city.

He walked down the empty streets, fighting down his emotions as he approached the tree line. Stopping before the thick foliage, he looked back one last time at the town that had been his home for the last eighteen years. Then he turned his back, saying goodbye to the life he'd once known, and headed into the Endless Wood.

7

He was lost.

Arbor could admit that much to himself. The journey had been fine at the beginning. He wasn't exactly hopeful, but he thought he could find his way by the position of the sun. What he hadn't realized was that the deeper into the forest he went, the thicker the tree cover overhead would be. He criticized himself over and over for making such a stupid mistake.

Now here he was, two weeks later and he was no closer to the gremlin city than when he had left. Worse, he was completely out of food and nearly out of water as well.

He had tried to climb a tree but had quickly dismissed that idea after his ribs had violently protested. Now he sat with his back to a tree, his stomach rumbling loudly and his head pounding, due to the lack of water. He took out his waterskin and removed the stopper. A few drops of leathery tasting water landed on his tongue as he upended it. He shook it a few times, trying to get more, but no more water was forthcoming.

Removing the skin from his lips, he replaced the stopper with a sigh. Here he was sitting in the middle of the woods with no food or water. How had he thought that this would be a good idea? The sun beat down from overhead, still somehow managing to reach him, despite the thick foliage.

The summer moon may be gone, but it's still hot as hell, he thought bitterly.

He looked around once more, trying to get some sense of direction. Everything looked the same. Shrugging to himself, he started walking again, hoping he was going in the right direction.

He walked for hours, the scenery never changing, and the leaves overhead never growing any sparser. It was all he could do not to drop, but he forced himself on, despite his growing thirst and never-ending hunger. He only stopped once the sun had set, and it had become too hard to see.

Dropping his nearly empty sack to the ground, he unslung his weapon from over his shoulder and dropped it to the ground. He slumped tiredly with his back to a tree and lifted the sack to see if he'd missed any food in his previous five searches.

He hadn't.

Sighing in frustration, he threw the sack to the ground. All it contained was some salt, his empty water skins and the small bag of diamonds he'd pilfered from the smith's shop.

If only I could eat diamonds, he thought sarcastically.

Closing his eyes, he resigned himself yet to another miserable night. His stomach rumbled again, much louder than before. He moved his tongue around, trying unsuccessfully to bring some moisture into his parched mouth.

The forest was pitch black, with not a glimmer of light to be seen. The first few nights in the forest, Arbor had jumped at every little noise, fearing bears and wild dogs were sneaking up on him. He had gotten over that quickly enough and now felt oddly at home. He had seen the occasional deer or fox, but when he'd tried caching them, they'd just run off.

His stomach rumbled again, and he growled in frustration.

The worst part was not being able to find any water. This he had found quite odd. Given that there were so many animals living in the Endless Wood, water should have been easy to find.

His back slid off the tree stump until he found himself lying on the ground, the smell of rotting leaves and earth filling his nostrils. That made him feel just a little better. He listened to the sounds of the forest, to the leaves rustling in the wind, the creaking of branches, the sound of crickets chirping.

Those bugs seem to be everywhere and nowhere at the same time.

Arbor wasn't proud to admit it, but if he could catch a cricket right now, he would most likely eat it. His mind wandered for a few more moments, but it soon surrendered to exhaustion and he fell asleep. The next morning, he awoke to begin his wandering anew. His stomach was growling non-stop now.

It's no wonder it won't shut up. I haven't eaten in three days.

He couldn't even feel any residual moisture in his mouth anymore. Yet he kept on going, knowing that if stopped, he would most likely not be able to continue. The only thing keeping him going at this point was anger and spite.

The forest could go to hell if it thought it could kill him.

He stopped for a moment around midday, feeling light-headed, and looked up to the canopy above. The wind rustled through the leaves overhead. It made the sunlight dance over his face, and he felt a spinning sensation, and then he was falling. He blinked a few times, trying to clear the fog from his mind.

How had he gotten on the ground? Wasn't he just walking? He should probably get up, but why did he have to do that? The ground was so soft. He'd just take a quick nap and then be on his way.

A voice in the back of his mind screamed at him not to fall asleep, that doing so was a terrible idea, but he just felt too tired to care. The world around him became fuzzy, and then blackness enveloped him.

Arbor woke up sometime later. Blinking a few times, he tried clearing his vision. Where was he?

Turning his head to the side, he could see that he was in some sort of clearing. He was lying on his back with his head propped up, and there was a sheet covering him. He tried to sit up, but his head swam, and he immediately fell back with a groan.

"Easy there," said a lighthearted sounding voice. "You were nearly dead from dehydration when I found you."

A man came into Arbor's line of sight and held out a full waterskin. Only then did Arbor realize his raging thirst. He quickly grabbed the waterskin and took a big gulp. His eyes bulged then as his throat unexpectedly tightened and he leaned over to the side, coughing and retching.

"Slowly. Drink slowly," the man said. "You can't deprive your body of water for that long and expect to be able to gulp it down like a fish. Take small sips."

Arbor did as the man instructed, and while he did cough a few more times, the water stayed down this time. He then sat up slowly, taking small sips and enjoying the feeling of life the water seemed to be giving him.

"Here," the man said, handing him a skewer of meat.

Arbor's mouth watered at the sight and nodded he his thanks. Taking the skewer from the stranger, he tore into it, ripping off a large chunk, hardly chewing at all before swallowing. He polished off the skewer in another two bites, and the man wordlessly handed him another.

He silently accepted the meat and tore into it, feeling the juices run down his chin. He finally stopped after the fourth piece, feeling a bit sick, but he wasn't about to complain about overeating.

"It's been quite some time since I've seen someone enjoy my cooking that much," the man said with a grin.

Arbor hadn't really looked at the man while he had been eating, but now he noticed how odd the man actually looked.

He was tall, over six and a half feet by Arbor's guess, with bright red hair that grew in wild spikes. He had bright purple eyes and his skin tone seemed off somehow. Instead of the usual pale or tan complexion he was used to, his skin seemed to be almost orange.

"Who are you?" Arbor asked. Then realizing that he sounded a bit rude, he quickly added, "You have my thanks for saving my life. My name is Arbor."

The man smiled brightly. His smile was warm and inviting and put him a bit more at ease.

Arbor didn't smile back, though. Since the night when his life had been ruined, he found that he no longer had much reason to.

"You can call me Silver," the man said, not at all deterred by Arbor's grim expression, "And you are quite welcome. I must say that it's nice to have a visitor. It's been quite some time since anyone has wandered into this part of the forest."

The man sat down across him, a questioning look in his eyes.

"So, tell me, if you don't mind, what you are doing here?"

Arbor didn't know how to feel about telling a complete stranger his story, but there was just something about the man that put him at ease. As though he could trust him with anything. He didn't like that feeling, but he couldn't see any harm in telling this odd forest hermit his story, so he did.

It took him well over an hour to recount his tale. He hadn't realized how much had happened in the last two weeks. Silver sat silent through his entire recounting and when he was done sat there in contemplation.

"I was wondering why a young man such as yourself was wandering through the woods with this," Silver said, holding up Arbor's pendant.

"That's mine!"

He must have taken it when I was unconscious! Arbor realized.

37

"Woah there, calm down!" Silver said, chuckling to himself. He flipped the pendant back to Arbor, who caught it deftly.

"That is a very valuable artifact you've got there. I'd find a better spot to hide it if I were you."

"Wait, you know what this is?" Arbor asked quickly, sliding the pendant over his neck and tucking it under his shirt.

Maybe I can find out why Ramson wanted this so badly.

"I do," Silver said, "But if I tell you, you'll throw it away and never look at it again."

"So you know what it is, but won't tell me?!"

Arbor was outraged. This man had the answers he was looking for but was refusing to give them to him!

"I don't care what you think!" Arbor yelled, throwing the sheet off himself and standing up.

He swayed a little but otherwise felt fine.

"Tell me what you know! A man killed my entire family and a hundred other people to get this. Now tell me what it is!"

Silver stood as well and calmly listened to his outburst. He waited for Arbor to take a breath and spoke.

"I'll make you a deal. If you manage to hit me with that big scary glaive of yours, I'll tell you whatever you want to know."

Arbor blinked at the man in confusion.

"What's a glaive?"

Silver stared at him for a few seconds, incredulity written on his face, then he roared with laughter.

"What's so funny?" Arbor asked, going red in the face.

Silver just kept on laughing, his deep voice booming out through the clearing.

"Answer me, dammit!" he yelled again.

Silver finally calmed down after a minute, small chuckles still coming every few seconds.

"You mean to tell me that you've been carrying that thing around for two weeks and you don't even know what it's called?"

Arbor looked over to see the odd weapon he had found in the blacksmith's shop leaning against a tree. He went red again, this time out of embarrassment.

"How was I supposed to know what it's called? I've never seen anything like it in my life," Arbor said, snatching up the weapon.

"Very well, very well." Silver said, holding his hands up in surrender.

He then bent down and picked up a length of polished hardwood.

"The offer still stands. Hit me with that weapon, and I'll tell you everything you want to know about that pendant."

Arbor just nodded once and then took up what he thought of as a fighting stance. He could beat this odd forest hermit, and then he would get his answers.

Taking a deep breath, he charged at Silver with a shout and swung the weapon, aiming for the man's hand – he didn't want to kill him, after all.

The next thing he knew, Arbor felt a blinding pain and was somehow left staring up at the trees above, his head ringing.

He stood up on shaky legs, feeling the back of his head and wincing.

How had he done that?

Arbor shook his head once more and picked up his glaive.

"Oh, good. You're not giving up. That's the spirit!" Silver said, flashing him a smile.

Arbor just grimaced and moved forward, slower this time. He swung the weapon again, this time at Silver's head. Since he was watching closely, he saw it what had happened.

Silver seemed to flow as he moved forward, neatly stepping out of the way as Arbor over-extended, then his hardwood staff came up in a blur cracking him across his knuckles.

Arbor screamed and let go of his weapon, the glaive falling to the forest floor as he shook his stinging hands.

"Is that all? Guess you don't want to know what that pendant is, after all," Silver mocked, that infuriating smile plastered across his face.

Arbor just scowled and picked the weapon up again.

He would hit this smug bastard if it was the last thing he'd do.

For the next hour, Arbor tried to hit Silver but was unsuccessful. Silver kept on goading him, smiling the entire time as Arbor threw himself at the infuriating man. Finally, Arbor had to give up, throwing the weapon away in disgust. He sat down and put his back to tree, panting hard.

Closing his eyes, he could feel the throbbing pain from the dozen or so new bruises Silver's staff had inflicted.

"Don't blame the weapon! After all, it's not the weapon's fault that you don't know how to use it," Silver called out, the ever-present smile still stretched across his face.

He wasn't even winded!

Arbor was outraged. Here he was, covered in bruises and this hermit looked as though he wasn't even trying!

"Yeah, what do you know about the glaive?" Arbor asked with a bitter, mocking tone.

Silver quirked his head, then bent down and picked up the discarded weapon. Spinning it a few times, he began moving through a form, the blade whirling in his hands as he spun, slashed and stabbed.

Arbor watched in fascination as Silver flowed effortlessly through the form, seeming to dance as he moved, the blade never stopping. As he moved, the weapon seemed to travel faster and faster, until it was little more than a silver blur.

Finally, he finished with a big overhead slash. He held the position for a few seconds before straightening. Looking over at Arbor, he smiled again.

"Oh. Nothing much."

8

Arbor walked through the forest, the leaves crunching underfoot as he went. The brown trees of the Endless Wood were slowly changing into the black, leafless trunks of the Dead Forest. He could feel a slight chill in the air as he walked.

The landscape had been slowly shifting over the last few hours, and he knew he was close to the border of the Dead Forest. He checked the map Silver had provided.

"Should be there by nightfall," he muttered, rolling up the map and placing it back in his pack.

He had ended up spending an entire month with Silver. He had protested at first, saying that he needed to get to Grend and find help for his sister. He quickly changed his mind when Silver asked if he knew where the city was. Arbor, much to his chagrin, had admitted that no, he didn't know where Grend was. He honestly didn't even know what part of the woods he was in.

Silver had then made him a deal. Arbor would stay for one month, and Silver would educate him. Arbor had scoffed at the idea, but then Silver had said that they would spar every day, and if Arbor could hit him just once, he would tell him whatever he wanted to know about his pendant.

Arbor had soon learned that there was a lot he didn't know. The main thing being the name of the land he lived in. He learned that the kingdom was called Laedrin and that the land stretched from the Red Ocean, hundreds of miles to the north, to the Goldenleaf Forest of the elves all the way in the south. There were also the Jagged Peaks, where the dwarves lived, to the west, and all this was connected by massive Flatlands, hundreds of miles of dry, cracked earth where nothing grew.

The capital city of Galmir was near the Red Ocean to the north. Arbor was shocked by all this information. He hadn't even known that there were dwarves or elves. He'd thought they were just myths. Silver also explained about another race, the race of the salamanders.

Arbor asked where they lived, and Silver had just shook his head sadly. He said they were mostly extinct, and the few surviving members were scattered all over Laedrin. Arbor was saddened by this news. He didn't know why, but he felt a sort of kinship with this unknown race. He had lost his family, and they had lost theirs.

He fought with Silver every day, the odd man teaching him stances and forms to better use his weapon. He tried every day but did not manage to so much as touch Silver, even once. Arbor had discovered another thing about himself while training, and this stuck most prominently in his mind.

He was sparring with Silver one day. It was the twenty-second day of his training, and Arbor was infuriated at not being able to hit him. As they circled each other, Arbor felt the same odd feeling he'd had during the bandit attack during his wedding. He didn't know how, but he was sure that Silver would move in and feint with an overhead blow, before dropping the staff and sweeping his feet out from under him.

Remembering how it had worked the last time, he decided to test this feeling, and when Silver came in for the blow, he had stepped in instead of back and swung his glaive in a downward parry.

Arbor was shocked when his block actually worked. He had correctly predicted Silver's move. He didn't get much of a chance to celebrate, though, as Silver's staff came around and cracked on the side of his head, dropping him like a sack.

"How did you do that?" Silver asked, holding his hand out to help him up. He had an odd look on his face, like he knew something but had to be sure.

"I don't know," Arbor had said honestly as he took the proffered hand. "I just had a feeling that the blow was a feint."

Silver looked at him for a moment, seeming to be lost in thought.

"Is this the first time you've had that feeling?" he asked.

Arbor shook his head, explaining the last time he'd felt the same thing. Silver nodded at that, taking up his fighting stance again.

"Let's try that once more. Tell me if you have that feeling again."

Arbor nodded and took up his stance, legs spread and balanced, the glaive held in a double-handed grip across his body, with the tip dipping slightly toward the ground. He waited for a moment, and then the feeling came again — a tight feeling in his stomach, along with a certainty of how Silver would attack.

The man would come in high, with a feint. Arbor would raise his glaive in a defensive parry, and Silver would spin his staff, knocking his glaive aside and crack him across the ribs. He could see the entire scene play out ahead of time, as though seeing into the future.

Following his instincts again, he turned out to be right. He tried moving in again after Silver's feint failed, but he danced nimbly backward. Arbor rushed to follow him.

If he knew where Silver would be, he could beat him.

Silver's staff caught his ankle, and Arbor went down again, hard. He groaned, rubbing his stinging leg and looking up at Silver with a glower.

"I knew where you would be! I should have beaten you!" he said with a scowl.

Silver just shook his head. "Your mind might know where I will be, but your body can't keep up yet."

He helped him up and smiled brightly again.

"More important than that, you have magic!" Silver said with a huge grin.

"I have what?" Arbor asked, not sure he'd heard the hermit correctly.

"Magic!" he said again, his smile not diminishing at all. "It's rare for humans to have magic these days, let alone your type of magic!"

He seemed very happy and moved around the clearing with excitement.

"What do you mean by, my type of magic?" Arbor asked, still a little skeptical about what the clearly crazy hermit was saying.

There was no way he could have magic.

Sure, he knew that it existed and that some people had the talent for it, but there was just no way he could have it. He would have known by now if he did.

"Well, I'm not quite sure yet. This is just a guess, mind you," Silver said, finally seeming to calm down. He looked at Arbor then, a shrewd look on his face. "What do you know about magic?" he asked.

"Not much," Arbor said with a shrug. "I know it exists, and that some people have it. That's really about it."

He slung his glaive over his shoulder and sheathed the weapon.

"Let me explain the origin of magic and how it will affect you," Silver sat down and motioned Arbor to do so as well.

"Magic is one of the great forces of this world," Silver began. "Long ago, the salamander race began to discover the gift of controlling the natural energies in the world. The salamanders soon decided to share their discovery with the other races, for this was a wonderful discovery indeed and they dare not keep it to themselves. It soon became clear to them that magic could not be taught to everyone.

"For example, the dwarves had almost no affinity for it, while the elves had a surprisingly high one. The gremlins and humans were in between, some being able to learn it, while others were inept."

Silver had stopped at that point to light a fire and put a kettle on for tea. He sat back as the water boiled and continued.

"As it is with all things, when people have power, they inevitably want to dominate others. Magic was a wild thing back then, and there was little control," Silver sighed sadly at this point, his usual smile slipping from his face.

"There was war. Hundreds of thousands of lives were lost, and soon it looked as though the world itself would be destroyed."

Silver stopped again to get the kettle off the fire. He poured hot water over the leaves in a cup and took a slow sip.

"Well?" Arbor asked impatiently. "What happened next?"

Silver put his cup down, the smile returning to his face. "No one knows. That part was lost to history."

"What was the point of you telling me the story then?" Arbor asked in frustration.

"The point," Silver said, putting his cup down. "Is that control is the most important thing a Mage can have. Without it, there's just war and death! Magic is much different now than it was back then. For example, magic is no longer a wild power to be harnessed; rather, it is a power born within oneself. It needs to be nurtured, trained, and honed like any skill."

"How do you mean?" Arbor asked.

The longer the man spoke, the more confused he was becoming.

"Magic is still in the world around us, but at some point, people lost the ability to control it. Now anyone who can use magic has the power inside of them — a small piece of the wild magic from their ancestors.

"Right now, you are only a Tier 1 Mage, the very weakest there is. In order to advance your magic, you will need to train, grow, strengthen your body, and so on. I can't teach you how to do this though, as it's something all Mages must figure out for themselves."

Arbor had no idea what the man was going on about. What the hell even was a Tier 1 Mage, and why couldn't he teach him how to get stronger?

"I'm still very confused," Arbor said, trying to wrap his head around the whole thing.

"That's not important for now," Silver said, waving his hand dismissively.

"I think I know your magic type. I believe that you have the rare gift of Perception magic," he said, expecting him to be excited by the news.

"What's that?" Arbor asked, his brow creasing in confusion. "And what do you mean by my type of magic?"

"Every person who has magic has a specific type of magic, unique to them. For example, someone who can control fire won't also be able to use healing magic."

Arbor finally nodded his understanding.

"As for Perception magic," he continued. "It's a special type of body magic. There have only been a few known cases, and fewer still have been recorded. The simple and very basic explanation is that Perception magic can boost your physical capabilities further than it would normally be possible. You will, of course, be constrained to what is possible at your Tier, but with time and training, your ability will grow."

"That doesn't sound like anything special," Arbor said. "And if my Tier limits my power, shouldn't it be important to know how to move to the next one? In fact, what does it even mean? You're not really doing a very good job of explaining."

"Fine," Silver said, rolling his eyes. "Mages gain power throughout their lives by practicing and honing their craft. But everyone needs to start at the beginning and to make sure you don't hurt yourself accidentally, limits are placed. These limits are what we call Tiers. There is no limit to the number of Tiers out there, but every Mage has their limit. This is a point at which they can no longer advance.

"But don't make the mistake of thinking that just because someone is a higher Tier than you, that they are automatically more powerful or vice-versa. Tiers only limit how much power can be safely used, without the risk of injury or death. That being said, those who can wield more of their power will usually come out on top in a fight. That is why training is so important."

Arbor slowly nodded, finally grasping the basis of what Silver was talking about.

"You still haven't explained what's so great about my magic though," he said, wrinkling his brows.

"I see you're still confused, so let me give you an example. Say a normal man can lift fifty pounds. At Tier 1, someone like you would easily be able to lift five times that amount!"

Arbor was shocked, but Silver just continued talking.

"There are, of course, many different types of Perception magic. While one man can lift five times more than another, a different man could move five times as fast. You were able to predict my actions after watching me fight. It may be that your magic can increase your perception or remember an opponent's movements and correctly predict where they will be. Only time will tell, but one thing is already abundantly clear. Your learning speed is far above that of a normal person."

He smiled conspiratorially at Arbor then. "Truth be told, there aren't many with your physical capabilities in the entire world. It's amazing how quickly you've taken to your chosen weapon, and I predict you'll only become better in time. Who knows? You might even be able to reach Tier 2 in a couple of months!"

"Is that fast?"

Silver nodded vehemently.

"It takes most new mages well over half a year to hit Tier 2, though, by your age, most are sitting at around Tier 4 or 5."

Arbor frowned at that. It seemed that he had a lot of catching up to do.

"So, can you teach me magic then?" he asked, hopefully.

Silver shook his head sadly at that.

"I'm sorry, but I can't teach what I don't know."

Arbor's face had fallen then. Of course Silver couldn't teach him. There was no way he had magic. The man must have been mistaken about him, and he wasn't nearly as special as Silver seemed to think him to be.

He was snapped out of his self-deprecating thoughts when Silver continued speaking.

"What I can tell you, though, is that there is a magic school in the Goldenleaf Forest. The elves are very knowledgeable when it comes to magic. They're not especially fond of humans, but they may accept you, as you have such a rare type of magic."

Silver grew very serious then. Any trace of a smile was now gone.

"Now I must warn about using magic. It may seem harmless at first, but all magic has a price. Push yourself too far too fast, and you will destroy yourself."

Arbor just shook his head.

"I don't have time for this elf school, and I won't use magic if it's that risky."

The smile had returned to Silver's face by then.

"Magic doesn't work that way. It will come, whether you want it or not."

With that last statement, he stood and picked up his staff to resume their training.

Arbor remembered the experience while he walked. Silver was right. Even now, he could feel it- a small pulsing from his center where he now knew his magic to be located. He was tempted to reach for it, but he quickly forced it down, remembering Silver's warning.

It wasn't all bad, though. His magic had somehow sped up his ability to heal. His ribs didn't even twinge anymore, and any bruises that Silver had inflicted had healed within hours. He frowned at that memory.

Sure, it was nice that his injuries were gone, but it disconcerted him that some unknown power had done it, and he was sure it wouldn't be the last time. Arbor walked until the sun was low on the horizon. The landscape had considerably changed over the course of the day, and he was now standing in a small clearing surrounded by black trunked trees.

This was as good a spot as any to make camp for the night.

He collected some dead branches from around the clearing and soon had a small fire going. He sipped from his waterskin, then bit into some of the dried meat that Silver had provided for him.

The dark, ominous trees made him feel uneasy, as though something sinister were lurking in the surrounding trees, hiding just out of view. There was no question in his mind now.

He had reached the Dead Forest.

9

Arbor was exhausted. He'd been walking for days, and even his new magic didn't seem to work on sore feet, not that he even knew what his magic could actually do.

His boots were worn out, and his clothes were barely holding up any better. He resolved himself to get new clothing once he reached Grend.

And a horse. Definitely a horse, he thought. *Maybe even two.*

All around him, black leafless trunks stood, creaking in the light breeze. Stopping for a moment, he pulled his map out once again. According to Silver, he should already have reached Grend or at least caught sight of it. He put the map back in his bag with a sound of disgust.

There was a hill up ahead. Maybe he'd get a better view from the top.

Arbor trudged up the hill, his aching feet crying out in protest. As he crested the hill, his eyes widened, and he gasped audibly.

A massive city sprawled out before him, surrounded by a huge stone wall. There was a road down below, and he could see small figures and carts moving along. He could also see an open gate, where people and carts were lined up. It seemed that he'd finally reached his destination.

With a sigh of relief, he began the long trek down to the road below. It took him the better part of an hour, but he finally reached the road. Upon reaching the road, he realized how tall the walls actually were. Made of massive stone blocks and piled atop one another, the wall stood over fifty feet tall. Walking towards the gate, he was soon forced to stop and wait his turn until a cart in front of him moved on ahead.

"What's your business in Grend?"

Arbor looked down in surprise. A short, red-skinned figure dressed in a guard's uniform was looking up at him with a bored expression on his face. The man, or gremlin, Arbor supposed, had deep red skin and short pointed ears. He had a long thin nose and a narrow face. His eyes were slanted and had bright yellow irises.

Green hair peeked out from under his helmet, and Arbor noticed short claws on the hand that gripped his spear.

The guard just sighed as if he were used to this.

"First time here, then. What business do you have here?" he asked again.

Arbor had prepared for this in advance. Silver had warned him that he'd need a cover story once he reached the city.

"Better not to let anyone know why you're there," he'd said.

When Arbor had asked why, Silver had replied in a tone that suggested he think before he speak.

"That man Ramson may have friends in the city. Best not to tip him off if he's there."

Arbor had felt a little annoyed at Silver's tone of voice, but in the end, had decided he was probably correct.

"I'm a jewel merchant, here to trade my wares," he said smoothly.

The guard gave him an appraising look. Arbor was dressed in tattered clothes and the heavy spike of his sheathed glaive peeked over his shoulder.

"It's been a long road here," he was quick to explain. "And one can't be too careful when carrying valuable merchandise."

Apparently, his story wasn't very convincing because the guard just snorted and shook his head, though he didn't seem to care either way, as he launched into what sounded like a well-rehearsed speech.

"There's an inn a bit down the main road called The Swan. They have decent rates on rooms and board. The local jeweler is in the market district on the east side of the city. If you are selling jewels, you will have to pay the standard thirty percent tax on all items sold in the city."

"Thirty percent? Are you nuts? That's highway robbery!" Arbor exclaimed.

He couldn't pay thirty percent of the diamonds' value! He needed every copper he could make.

"It's the standard tax. If you don't like it, you can leave."

The guard's eyes narrowed, and his grip tightened on the haft of his spear.

"No. It's fine," Arbor said quickly, not wanting to cause a scene.

"Good," the guard waved him past. "And don't go stirring up any trouble."

Arbor nodded, then headed through the massive open gates, trying not to gawk. It was unlike anything he'd ever seen before. There were people everywhere he looked, and for someone who grew up in a small town, it was a bit overwhelming.

The crowd seemed to be a mix of mostly humans and gremlins, but there were a few dwarves mixed in as well.

Silver's description of them is spot on, he noted.

The short bearded men seemed to move the crowd around them as they walked, their broad forms easily standing out from the red-skinned gremlins and the taller humans.

He kept walking down the main street until he saw a wooden sign swinging over a door with the word 'Swan' written on it. He was about to go in, when he remembered he had no money, only the jewels he had taken from the blacksmith's shop back home.

He walked past the inn and headed for the east side of the city, staring at the tall towers and all the people around him. The buildings ranged in size, from tall spired buildings to smaller family homes. Everything was made of stone and Arbor couldn't even imagine the amount of time it must have taken for this all to be built.

It took him a little under half an hour, but by constantly asking for directions from annoyed passers-by, he finally made it to the trading district. He wandered around a bit, looking at all the stores lining the street and marveling at the variety of different goods being sold. He finally spotted a small sign with the picture of a diamond painted on and guessed that that was the Jewelers.

He heard a bell tinkle overhead as he walked into the small shop. There was a dwarf behind the counter, looking at a stone through a small eyeglass. He looked up as Arbor walked in and slipped the stone into his pocket.

"How can I help you?" he asked.

The dwarf had an odd accent that Arbor hadn't heard before. He placed inflections in odd places, so the word 'you' sounded more like 'yee.' Walking up to the counter, he removed the small leather bag from his pocket.

"I'd like to exchange these for some gold," Arbor said handing him the bag.

The dwarf's eyes bulged as he looked inside.

"Are you crazy, lad?" the dwarf asked. "If you go flashing around that much wealth, you'll catch a knife the back!"

The dwarf was sweating and looked around the empty shop nervously.

"Are they really worth that much?" Arbor asked, more curious than afraid.

"Yes!"

He looked around once more, then walked around to the front of the counter.

"Follow me around back, and we'll get you sorted."

Arbor followed the dwarf to a small door on the side of the counter. He had to stoop a bit to enter through the low doorway, but the ceiling was high enough for him to stand once he'd entered.

"Have a seat, lad." The dwarf motioned to a chair by a small table. "This might take a few minutes, so best get comfortable."

Arbor nodded his thanks and sank into the chair as the dwarf emptied the small pouch onto the table. There were sixteen gems in all. Five were blue, six red, four yellow, and one clear. They varied in size, with the yellow being the largest and the clear one the smallest. The dwarf took his looking glass out once again, and muttering to himself, began examining the stones.

After a while of looking, muttering, and note-taking, the dwarf looked up.

"You really do have quite a lot of money here," he said.

"How much are they worth?" Arbor asked with interest.

"Well, the yellow ones are worth roughly fifty gold apiece, the reds are seventy-five, the blues are around two hundred, and the clear one is around three thousand."

Arbor had to suppress a shout of glee when the dwarf said that. Back home, the average person only made between thirty and fifty gold a month! The crotchety old blacksmith must have been saving for years to have so much stashed away.

He'd never been any good at math, but even he could count these numbers. That was over four thousand five hundred gold! He said so out loud, and the dwarf nodded.

"Four thousand six hundred and fifty to be accurate. I can give you a hundred gold in coins, the rest I can give you in traders notes."

"What are those?" He'd never heard of trader's notes.

"Traders notes can be exchanged for coin at any trading guild or bank owned by the kingdom. I would recommend the guild, though, as their taxes are far less than the king's," the dwarf said with a wink.

"So, do we have a deal?" he asked, holding out his hand.

Arbor reached out and shook it. The dwarf smiled, then swept the gems back into the bag and placed them in his pocket. He opened a drawer and began counting notes. He placed six notes in front of Arbor.

"These are each worth one thousand," he said, pointing to four of the larger notes. "This one is five hundred, and this one is fifty," he pointed to two smaller notes.

Arbor picked them up. They felt odd in his hand, not like paper at all, more like cloth. There was an official-looking seal on all of them, with numbers declaring their value. The dwarf then placed a small sack of glittering coins, containing copper, silver, and gold on the table as well.

The way currency worked in Laedrin wasn't too complicated. The lowest denomination was the copper coin. There were ten copper to a silver and one hundred silver to a gold. There were also larger gold bars that banks and merchants used, worth anywhere from one hundred to one thousand gold, depending on the weight.

Arbor picked up the small sack of coins a tied it to his belt.

"I thank you for your business, lad. Now, is there anything else I can help you with?"

Arbor thought on that for a few moments, before nodding.

"Do you know where I might be able to buy some horses?"

Arbor now stood inside the stables. The dwarf hadn't just told him where he could buy a horse but had also told where he could find trail rations and new clothes as well. The stable master was a nice enough man and gave him a fair price on two horses and a full set tack for both. He also showed him how properly saddle and care for them after a day's ride.

He directed him to where he could buy feed for the horses. It took Arbor another hour, but at last, he was done with his shopping spree. His coin purse was now sixty-three gold and six silver lighter, but he had everything he would need for a month-long journey. He also bought a small metal cylinder on a thin chain where he could store his trader's notes. This he slipped over his neck and tucked under his shirt to rest near his other valuables.

The light was starting to fade as he headed back to the Swan to see if he could still get a room for the night. He was passing a narrow alley when he heard a scream echo from within.

He looked around quickly, trying to see if anyone was going to help. He was shocked though, when everyone just turned the other way, ignoring the obvious sounds of distress. Arbor felt his blood boil as he watched this.

How could people so callously ignore someone in need?!

Quickly dismounting, he tied his two horses to a nearby post, then ran into the alley. The light was noticeably dimmer inside the alley, and it took a few moments for his vision to adjust. What he saw disgusted him even more than the people outside who were ignoring the cries for help.

Four male gremlins were standing around a single female gremlin and beating her. The female was on the ground, trying to cover herself as they mercilessly kicked her, pleading for mercy. Her face was tear-streaked and he could see she wouldn't last much longer.

"Leave her alone!" Arbor shouted, running up and grabbing one of the gremlins by the shoulder.

The guard turned around, a sneer coming to face.

"This is official city business," the gremlin said, pointing to a patch on his chest. "Now move along unless you want to get hurt."

The other gremlins had stopped beating the girl and were now watching him in obvious interest.

"You're supposed to be city guards?" Arbor asked, appalled.

Why were city guards beating an innocent girl?

Arbor didn't care who they were. He couldn't stand bullies. So, drawing his glaive, he took up a fighting stance.

"I won't ask you again. Leave or die. It's your choice."

"Look at this. The little shit thinks he can beat us," the ringleader said, drawing a sword from his belt. "Let's show him what we do to lawbreakers around here."

Arbor took a step back and widened his stance. The alley was narrow, so they would only be able to come at him one or two at a time, though they would still outnumber him. As the first gremlin approached, Arbor quickly stepped forward, thrusting the heavy blade towards his midsection. The blade sunk a few inches into the red creature with a sickening squelch, and he looked at Arbor in shock.

Arbor quickly pulled the blade out and spun it, knocking the second gremlin's sword to the side with a loud clang. Bringing the spiked end around in a wide sweep, he cracked him over the head, knocking him to the ground, where he lay dazed.

Arbor was shocked that it had worked at all. All that time with Silver and he hadn't managed to hit him once. Now he'd taken down two opponents in a matter of seconds!

The other two approached, more wary now that half their number was down. One tried to get around him, but Arbor shifted his stance and slashed his weapon, intending to take the gremlin's head off. But the nimble bastard jumped back, cursing and narrowly avoided the blow.

Arbor sensed it then, the light thrumming in his chest and he knew what would happen next. They would both rush him at once, thinking to overwhelm him. One would slash at his legs and the other at his head. It seemed that the gremlins didn't know much about taking on someone with a two-handed weapon, as it wasn't a very good plan.

They both charged at him and slashed at the same time. Arbor turned his glaive in a half-circle and neatly knocked both to the side at once. Then allowing his grip to slide up near the blade, he pulled it back and thrust forward, stabbing one of them through the eye. He pulled the blade free and turned to the last gremlin, who'd already begun stepping back.

"Looks like all your friends are gone. Care for a fair fight?" Arbor growled, taking a threatening step forward.

The gremlin's eyes widened in terror, then he dropped his sword and ran from the alley, throwing dire threats over his shoulder.

"The guards will be here for you soon! You'll be hanged for this!"

Arbor just sighed and sheathed his weapon. He went over to the gremlin girl and bent down.

"It's okay. They're gone. They won't hurt you anymore. My name is Arbor, by the way. What's yours?"

55

The girl looked up at him then and he finally got a good look at her face. Arbor was slightly taken aback. She was pretty in a weird, alien sort of way. She had a lighter red complexion than the gremlins he'd seen so far. Dark blue hair hung to her shoulders, and small, pointed ears peeked out from within.

She had bright blue eyes that looked back at him from under slanted brows. She had a small pert nose, and full lips colored a darker red than her face. She also a rather impressive bust with just a hint of cleavage showing. A narrow waist and wide hips completed her rather fetching figure. Now that she was standing, he could see that she was slightly taller than the other gremlins, standing a little under five and a half feet.

"Thank you for saving me."

Her voice was lighter than he'd expected.

"My name is Grakvine, but you can just call me Grak," she said, wiping her tear-streaked face.

She had some visible bruising on her face and arms, and he was sure that her long dress hid further injuries.

"Can you tell me why they were hurting you?" he asked.

"I didn't have enough money to pay my taxes this month," she said, with a sniff. "The city guards are awful, constantly raising taxes and claiming them in the name of the king. And when you can't pay them…"

A loud horn blared, interrupting Grak in the middle of her explanation. Then an alarm began ringing, and Grak's face paled.

"We need to leave now!"

"I take it we've been found out?" Arbor asked.

Grak nodded, then grabbed his hand and ran for the alley entrance.

"You killed three city guards. They'll hang you for that, and likely me along with you!"

"Well, that's not good," he muttered to himself.

Dying wasn't an option right now, at least, not until he managed to save his sister and avenge his family. They came running out of the alley and Arbor stopped, looking for his horses.

"Why are you stopping? We need to run!" Grak said, pulling his arm.

Finally spotting them, he pulled her towards them.

"I have horses! Which way is the fastest out of the city?"

"That way, there's a small gate on the south side that might still be open," she said as the two of them mounted up.

The alarm was now ringing louder and Grak spun her horse to the south gate, kicking it into a gallop. Arbor followed behind her, yelling for people to get out of the way. Men, dwarves and gremlins alike dove out of the way, cursing at them as they galloped through the crowded streets.

Finally, the gate came into view, but what he saw made his heart skip a beat.

They were closing the gate!

Arbor spurred his horse faster, kicking its ribs and shouting. He overtook Grak and bolted towards the gate guards at what was surely a dangerous pace for his horse. He drew his glaive and threw it like a javelin at one of the guards. He was only trying to distract the gremlin, but the blade actually hit him, sinking deep into his shoulder, causing him to spin away from the gate.

That was all they needed.

The gates stopped closing and they galloped past the guards, Arbor reaching out as they passed and ripping the glaive free. He heard a scream of pain follow him and did his best to block out the deaths he's just caused.

He heard shouting behind him and looked over his shoulder to see one of the guards shaking their fists at him. Grak pulled up alongside him as they came onto the main road.

"Why aren't they chasing us?" Arbor yelled over to her.

"They will, but probably not until morning."

Arbor figured she was right. There was barely enough light to see by, and going out now would be a bad idea. Even with torches, the dark moonless night would be treacherous for the horses. They rode off the path and into the woods, deciding that it would be safer that way, continuing until there was just the barest glimmer of light left to see by.

Once they'd dismounted, they tied the horses to a tree and collected some deadwood. Since no one would be following, it was safe to light a fire. Arbor struck a few sparks into his tinderbox and soon had one going, though he made sure to keep it small.

Grak sat across from him, shivering and wrapping her bare arms around herself in an attempt to stay warm. The nights were becoming colder as the dark months passed. Soon the winter moon would be rising and it would be truly cold.

"Here," Arbor said, handing her a cloak from one of his saddlebags. "I bought an extra one in case it got too cold."

Grak took the cloak and wrapped it around herself with a nod of thanks.

Arbor then dug into his pack, removing a few strips of dried meat and some hard bread. Not very appetizing, but it would be filling nonetheless.

He handed Grak a few pieces and passed her a waterskin as well.

"Where do we go from here?" Arbor asked.

"Well, we can try to head deeper into the kingdom, towards the capital, though I don't think they'll let us in," Grak said sadly.

"We can also try braving the Flatlands. I hear the Jagged Peaks are welcoming, though I'm not sure if they'll want a gremlin staying there."

"Why? What's wrong with gremlins? You all serve the king, don't you?"

Grak just shook her head.

"Yes, we serve the king, but we're outlaws now. Besides, gremlins aren't exactly treated well in the capital, at least not ones like me."

"What do you mean, ones like you?"

Grak fidgeted for a few moments and Arbor could see that he'd touched on a sensitive topic, so he decided to change the subject.

"Do you know where Fivora is? As far as I know, my sister was taken there by a group of bandits to be sold."

Grak nodded, seemingly relieved at the change of subject.

"I do know where Fivora is, but I don't think you'll find any help from the king's men. If she's being sold, there's nothing you can do. She's now the rightful property of the men who took her."

Arbor felt his anger begin to boil at that.

"What do you mean, rightful property?! Those bastards killed my parents and my future wife, and took my sister as a slave! The king wouldn't stand for that!"

Grak sighed sadly and shook her head once more.

"I'm afraid you've got it wrong there. Who do you think makes these laws? Fivora is in the kingdom of Laedrin. These laws were made by the king himself."

Arbor felt his blood run cold.

"What do you mean?" he asked, shooting to his feet. "The king is a just ruler and a good man. He protects us from bandits and thieves and hangs men like Ramson for their crimes!"

Grak flinched when Ramson's name was mentioned.

"I'm afraid not. The king is not the kind and just man you believe him to be. The slave trade is one of the crown's most profitable sources of income. And that man, Ramson, is well known in that market."

Arbor sat down, feeling numb shock threatening to overtake him.

"What can I do then? How can I save her?" he asked quietly.

Grak looked at him, pity in her eyes. She opened her mouth once or twice, then closed it again. The two sat in silence for a while, the only sounds coming from the crackling and popping of the small fire. Finally, Grak spoke up, her shoulders straightening as she seemed to come to a decision.

"You saved my life, and I owe you a debt. I will help you find your sister, and we will rescue her together."

Arbor was slightly taken aback at the sudden declaration from the gremlin girl.

"You don't owe me anything. I just did what any decent man would do."

Grak's red face went slightly redder as he said this, and she looked down in embarrassment.

"All the same," she said. "I will stay with you. I have nowhere else to go."

Her voice softened at touch, "And I'm sorry to hear about your family. I understand the pain of losing someone."

She wrapped the cloak a bit tighter around herself, staring into the fire with haunted eyes. Arbor had to wonder just what types of horrors this girl had to have seen but kept his questions to himself. If she wanted to talk about it, she would. Until then, he wouldn't pry.

"Well, better get to sleep," he finally said, shifting uncomfortably.

"They most likely won't come looking tonight, but it wouldn't hurt to keep a watch just in case. I'll take the first one and wake you in a few hours."

Grak nodded, not about to argue and rolled up in the cloak. Within minutes, her chest was rising and falling in an even pattern that meant she'd fallen asleep. He hunkered down against a tree, staring into the fire and pondering what his next moves should be. His plans had fallen through, so what should he do now?

He woke her a few hours later for her turn at watch and rolled up in his own cloak. Grak yawned tiredly and blinked sleep from her eyes, but hunkered down in his spot to take her turn. It took him a while to fall asleep, despite how tired he felt. All his hopes for getting help from the king's soldiers had been dashed and now he didn't know how he'd be able to save Karria. He rolled over again, trying to banish these thoughts from his mind.

It would do no good worrying about that now. He needed sleep if he wanted to live through the following days.

"Arbor, wake up!" Grak was shaking him hard.

"What is it?" he asked sleepily.

He didn't remember when, but he'd finally managed to fall asleep. Judging by how tired he felt, it couldn't have been more than four hours ago.

He cracked his eyes, slowly blinking away the fog of sleep. The sun was just peeking over the horizon, and he could hear birds chirping. Then he heard it- the sound of hunting horns coming from the city. He sat up quickly then, shivering as the cold morning air bit into his skin.

He and Grak moved swiftly, saddling the horses and mounting up.

"How long have the horns been blowing?" Arbor asked as they started to move.

"I woke you as soon as I heard the first one," Grak said, coming up beside him.

She had torn her skirt down the middle and tied the ends, forming rough pants so she could sit in the saddle more comfortably. She also had his heavy cloak draped across her shoulders, protecting her bare arms. Her thin dress was really not suited to the wild.

"Do you think we can outrun them?" Arbor asked.

"It's about two hundred miles over the flatlands to reach the Jagged Peaks," Grak said thoughtfully. "We're around twenty miles from the flatlands now. So long as we keep a good pace and the winter moon doesn't rise, we should be able to keep ahead of them."

They wheeled their horses to the west and kicked them into a run. The chase was on, and Arbor could only hope they would live through the experience.

10

Karria slowly came to. The ground beneath her was rumbling and seemed to be moving. Cracking her eyes open, she was greeted by the sight of metal bars and slowly passing trees. It seemed that she was in some sort of wagon, but how had she gotten here?

Examining herself, she could see she was still in dress she'd worn to the wedding, but it was now torn and muddied. She could feel a headache coming on, so closing her eyes, she tried to gather her wits.

What was the last thing she remembered? She was at the wedding when a bunch of men had come riding in. Tears began welling it the corners of her eyes as it came back to her. The screams, the fire, the blood. All that death. There was a chance that her family was dead. It was all she could do not to break down right then and there.

She'd run into the woods once the men had started butchering people. But her dress had caused her to stumble and fall. When she'd looked up, a greasy looking man was standing over her. He said something about her fetching a nice price, and then there was nothing.

"Looks like you're finally up."

Karria jumped at the sound of that voice, not expecting anyone else to be with her, wherever with her was. Turning her head, she saw a boy sitting across her, but he was the strangest looking boy she'd ever seen. First of all, his ears were all weird and pointy, his eyes were slanted like a cat's and his face was too thin.

"What are you?" Karria asked, shrinking back against the bars and wiping her eyes.

She was scared, alone and she didn't know where she was. Apparently, she was locked in a cage with some creep.

The boy only smiled, seeming not at all deterred by her reaction.

"To answer your first question, I am an elf. My name is Sylvester. I'd shake your hand but..." He trailed off, showing that his wrists were cuffed in front of him.

Karria stared at him for a moment. An elf? But elves were a made-up fairytale- something parents told their children to help them get to sleep at night. Yet she couldn't deny what was sitting right in front of her and she couldn't really explain away the pointy ears.

"I'm Karria," she said, slowly leaning forward and shaking one of the elf's hands.

She decided to see if the elf knew anything about their current predicament.

"Do you know where we are?"

"We," said the elf, "are in a slaver's wagon, headed for the city of Fivora to be sold at auction."

The elf seemed quite relaxed as he made this statement, as though he didn't have a care in the world. Karria sat there, still trying to understand what was going on.

"I was at my brother's wedding, then these men attacked. That's the last thing I remember," she said. "How long have I been in here?"

"Two weeks, give or take a day," Sylvester said nonchalantly. "I have to say, I'm glad you're awake. It's dreadfully boring just sitting here with only the slavers for company. They don't talk much, only grunt and spit at me when I try to make conversation. I have to wonder if they have a single brain cell between the lot of them," he said with a grin.

"Two weeks!" Karria exclaimed. "There's no way I could have been out for that long! How am I still breathing?"

"See that greasy man there?" Sylvester pointed through the bars to the man in question. "He fed you every day, pounded up some berries, and poured them down your throat."

Karria shuddered at the thought of that greasy man touching her and clutched instinctively at her necklace. But it was gone!

She began frantically looking around, but it was nowhere in sight.

"Have you seen a silver necklace with a lily on the end?" she asked frantically.

"I didn't see anything around your neck when they tossed you in here," Sylvester said with a shrug.

She must have dropped it when the slavers had taken her from her family.

"My family!" she exclaimed, remembering the slaughter back home. "Do you know what happened to them?"

"Sorry, can't help you there," the elf said. "If you want to know, try asking one of the slavers. I wouldn't ask Ramson, though."

"Why's that?" she asked, remembering the man well. He was the leader of this group and had decapitated a woman for no apparent reason.

Sylvester leaned in with a conspiratorial smile.

"Before he left to raid your town, he had both of his eyes. When he came back though…" he covered once of his eyes in an approximation of an eyepatch, then leaned back against the bars and burst out laughing.

Karria couldn't help herself. The elf's laughter was contagious, and soon she was laughing as well.

"That's the spirit. Keep your chin up. We'll find a way out of this."

"You in there, keep it down!"

One of the slavers passed by and jabbed the butt of his spear through the bars, hitting Sylvester in the back. He grunted in pain and hunched forward.

"You'll get a lot worse if I hear you again, freak," the man threatened before riding further down the line.

"Are you alright?" Karria asked worriedly as the man moved away.

Sylvester nodded, wincing slightly.

"They do that from time to time. It makes them feel powerful."

"What a bunch of heartless bastards!" Karria exclaimed angrily. "What kind of man feels powerful by picking on others? Doesn't sound very manly to me."

Sylvester just sighed.

"This world is full of people just like him. My parents warned me not to go too far from the Goldenleaf Forest, but I just had to go looking for adventure. I only wish I'd listened to them. I could be in school right now, enjoying three square meals a day, going to sleep in my nice, soft bed and having fun with my friends. Instead, I'm here, getting beatings and dried bread once a day."

He sounded bitter, and Karria couldn't blame him. She decided to try and distract the elf. She had only just met him, but already felt better after talking with him.

64

"You mentioned a school? What kind of school?" she asked.

Sylvester smiled wistfully.

"The Goldenleaf School of Magic. The finest magic school in all of Laedrin. According to the brochures, anyway."

"School of magic?" Karria asked, ignoring the snide comment at the end. "If you know magic, can you get us out of here?"

Sylvester just held up his shackled wrists in answer. "These block my magic. Damn slavers know their stuff and made sure to slap them on me as soon as I was captured."

Now that he'd mentioned it, Karria had an idea.

"If I can get the key, could you get us out?" she asked in a hushed voice.

"You can try, but they never come near me with the keys. Otherwise, I'd have tried by now."

Karria only smiled at that.

"I've gotten my brother to do loads of things for me when he didn't want to. And the boys around the village were always doing nice things for me. I'm sure I can trick one of these slavers without too much trouble."

Sylvester looked skeptical at this.

"You do realize that these are slavers, right? They won't fall for any tricks."

Karria didn't hear him. She was already making her move.

She schooled her face, then cried out in pain. It didn't take long for the greasy man who Sylvester had pointed out to come riding over.

"What's all this fuss about?"

He had a thick and slurred way of speaking that made it hard to understand.

Karria leaned forward against the bars. She could see keys swinging from the man's belt. All she had to do was get them. She put on her best smile, cringing inwardly as the man's eyes flicked to her neckline.

What a creep!

"My foot hurts quite badly. I think I twisted it," she said, sticking her bottom lip out in a pretend pout and rubbing at her foot.

The bandit stared at her for so long that she felt the urge to cover up. He was seriously creeping her out.

"Don't worry, love," he finally said. "I'll fetch you some bandages, and you can wrap it up. After all, lame salves fetch a lot less at auction."

He cackled as he headed off for the bandages.

"So, what exactly is your plan?" Sylvester asked with a raised eyebrow.

"I'm going to try and steal the keys when he brings the bandages," Karria whispered to him as she kept an eye out for the greasy man.

It only took a few minutes, but he soon came riding back with a roll of bandages. Karria expected him to come into the cage, but instead, he shoved them through the bars at her.

This wasn't good. He was supposed to come into the cart. She would now have to improvise a way to get those keys. Cringing inwardly at what she was about to do, she got shakily to her feet.

"Thanks for your help," she said, reaching for the bandages and giving him her most dazzling smile.

She then pretended to slip, and her arms went through the bars and struck the man in his face.

"You little bitch!" the man screamed as his hands flew to his injured face. His horse reared at the sudden excitement, and the man had to fight to get it under control.

Karria took the opportunity to grab the keys from his belt and stuff them down her dress. She sat back down and plastered an apologetic look on her face.

The greasy man finally managed to calm his horse down and glared at her through the bars.

"Are you alright, sir?" Karria asked in a voice laden with concern.

"No. I'm not alright!" he yelled. "You just whacked me in the face!"

Karria pretended to look puzzled at that statement.

"Surely a blow from a little girl like me couldn't hurt a big, strong man like you."

She layered her voice with as much sarcasm and scorn as she could. She couldn't physically hurt him for being a creep, but she could at least try and hurt his ego.

He opened his mouth to reply but saw that they'd attracted the attention of some of the other men. He straightened his jacket and glared at her one more time.

"No, I'm sure you couldn't," he muttered.

With that, he spurred his horse on ahead, and Karria breathed a sigh of relief.

"Well, did you get them?" Sylvester asked.

Karria dug her hand down her dress and brought it back up clutching the ring of keys, a grin of triumph on her face. She moved forward, fumbling slightly, and started trying each one on Sylvester's restraints.

"Better move quick. He'll notice sooner or later that they're gone," he said as she worked. "I do have to say though, that was quite a masterful performance."

"Just be quiet. I'm trying to concentrate here," she admonished him.

Finally, she found the right key and the cuffs came away with a click.

"Oh, that feels nice," Sylvester said, rubbing his wrists.

"Now which one of these will open the door?" Karria asked, holding the keyring up to him.

"None of them will," Sylvester answered. "Only Ramson has the keys to the wagons. It's the only way he can stop his men from stealing his stuff and running off with them in the night."

"How are we supposed to get out then?" Karria exclaimed, throwing the keys away in frustration.

"I can feel my magic now that the restraints have been removed," Sylvester answered calmly.

Karria glared at him for a moment as he continued rubbing his wrists.

"Well, then hurry up and get us out of here!"

"Give me a minute. I've been wearing those things for the last month!"

"You'll be wearing them for the rest of your life if we don't get out of here now!"

"Alright!" Sylvester said. "Just give me a few seconds."

The elf closed his eyes, a look of concentration coming to his face. Karria wondered what he would do and soon found out. Long vines crawled up the sides of the wagon and began winding around the bars. There was the sound of creaking wood as they constricted. Soon there was a muffled crack, and a hole opened in the wagon floor. The vines quickly receded, and he opened his eyes.

"Ladies first," he said, motioning to the hole.

Karria didn't need to be told twice, hopping through the hole and rolling a few times as she hit the ground to lessen the impact. There was a muffled thump, and she saw Sylvester rolling to his feet behind her. They were fortunate that no one had spotted them yet, but they wouldn't escape notice for long.

"Into the trees!" he whispered, motioning the thick cover on the idea of the road.

They ran quickly into the cover of the forest and headed deeper in, running for all they were worth. Just a few moments later, Karria heard the distinct sound of shouting voices.

"Damn it all," she muttered under her breath.

They'd already spotted the empty wagon. This wasn't good. She couldn't run that quickly due to her long dress and weeks of inactivity. Sylvester didn't look any better. The weeks of malnourishment had weakened him as well, and he was already flagging.

Sylvester stopped suddenly, by the base of an enormous tree.

"Karria, come here quickly!" he said, leaning up against it.

Karria ran over to him. He was pale and shaking.

"We have to keep going! They'll catch us if we stay and I doubt we'll be able to get away a second time!" she said trying to pull him away from the tree. But he didn't budge.

"Lean against the trunk. Just trust me!" the elf said.

Karria didn't know the elf all that well and was tempted to just keep running. She heard a shout, much closer this time. After a moment of indecision, she pressed her back to the tree. Sylvester then closed his eyes and vines flowed over the two of them, the thick ivy soon hiding them from view.

Karria didn't move, holding her breath as she heard the men come crashing through the underbrush and then move past her.

A voice suddenly rang out, and she felt her blood run cold in her veins.

"I want those two found. Do you have any idea how much an elf is worth?!"

It was Ramson. Karria froze in terror, remembering the man brutally murdering people in cold blood. She closed her eyes and tried calming down.

They were hidden. Ramson couldn't find them. They would be alright.

She kept repeating this herself until she managed to calm down. She looked over at Sylvester, noting with worry that he didn't look too good. The elf was deathly pale and visibly sweating.

"How long can you hold this?" she hissed in an undertone.

"As long as I have to," the elf replied, his voice clearly strained.

There was nothing much to do now but wait, so Karria slid to the ground and searched around until she found a sharp stone. Lifting the hem of her skirt and wincing a bit, she plugged the stone into the fabric just below her knees. It was an expensive dress, so it really hurt to ruin it like this, but she wouldn't be able to run with the long skirt hampering her movement. She slowly worked her way around, cutting with the sharp stone, until the extra cloth fell away.

Finally, after a few more minutes of waiting, the sounds of pursuit receded. Sylvester relaxed, releasing his hold on the magic and letting out a sigh of relief.

Karria stood quickly, her eyes scanning the surrounding forest.

"Do you think we lost them?" she asked, looking over at the weary elf.

"I don't think we're in the clear just yet," he said panting. "They're not likely to give up so easily with a prize like me on the line."

"So how do we escape?" she asked.

She didn't hear anything, but she was sure they'd be close by. If Sylvester couldn't hold their cover for more than a few minutes, they would need to be really careful.

Sylvester stood, brushing himself off. He seemed to be recovering, albeit at a slow rate.

"For now, let's just get moving. Sitting still will likely get us captured again."

He looked around for a moment, then took off at a jog, dodging between trees.

Karria was quick to follow, glad now she'd taken the time to cut her skirt. They went on like that for the next few minutes, before Sylvester slowed down.

Karria came up next to him and he put a finger to his lips, indicating for her to be silent. He then pointed down a small slope, to where two men were searching the underbrush, poking with their spear points.

"What do we do?" Karria asked in a hushed whisper.

"Go that way," Sylvester answered back, pointing in the opposite direction.

They quietly turned and headed the other way, moving quickly through the brush. They'd only been running in that direction for a few minutes when Sylvester once again stopped. Karria was about to ask what was wrong when she once again heard gruff voices from up ahead.

Sylvester put a finger to his lips, then took off in a different direction. Karria looked back one more time, before rushing to keep pace with him.

It soon became clear that they were being hemmed in. But Karria had no idea how they knew where to look. They had just narrowly avoided another patrol, and Karria was growing frustrated.

"How do they keep closing in on us? It's not like we're making a lot of noise."

"They must have a tracker with them," Sylvester answered as they ran. "This is really bad. Even if I can manage to make another hiding spot, our tracks will lead them right to us."

"How many trackers do you think they have?" Karria asked as a plan began to form in her mind.

"Likely only one. They don't come cheap, and Ramson wouldn't want to cut too much into his profit."

He was slowing down and his breaths were becoming ragged.

"Why does it matter, though?" he panted. "One tracker is all they need to find us."

Karria grimaced, already knowing what they would need to do.

"Then we need to find the tracker and kill him."

Sylvester blanched at the suggestion and opened his mouth to protest when Karria cut him off.

"I don't like the idea of taking a life any more than you do," she said, "But in order to survive, we need to do whatever it takes, even if it means killing a man."

Sylvester went pale, but he nodded his assent. Even if he didn't much like the idea of killing someone, they would have to get rid of the man if they had any hopes for survival.

"So, how do we go about killing the tracker?"

His voice shook as he asked the question. Just because he agreed they had to do it, didn't mean he wasn't terrified of the idea.

"We set a trap for him," Karria answered. "If anyone will find us, he'll be the first. So, use your magic and hide against a tree. I'll let him spot me. Once he sees me, he likely won't go looking for any more tracks. I'll run past your hiding spot. Once he passes, use your magic to kill him."

Sylvester didn't like the idea of Karria using herself as bait, but there were no better alternatives.

"Please be careful," he said, putting his back to a tree. He closed his eyes, and after a moment of concentration, he was soon hidden from view.

Karria walked forward about a hundred paces and then stopped. She took a deep breath to steady her nerves. Her heart was racing, and it took every ounce of willpower not to bolt right then and there. It went against her own survival instincts to just sit still and let herself be spotted, but she balled up her fists and forced herself not to move.

Sure enough, just a few minutes later, a small man came into view, his eyes peering down at the ground. Karria took a deep breath, her heart just about stopping, and then let out a small scream.

Just as she had hoped, the man's head whipped up at the sound, and a sneer crossed his face. Karria turned around and took off running. She could hear the man crashing through the undergrowth behind her and put on another burst of speed.

Her breath was coming in ragged gasps as she neared the site of the trap. There! She saw the telltale signs that Sylvester had left for her, and with a cry of relief, she stopped a few feet past the tree.

She turned back to see the man come crashing into the clearing behind her. He stopped, whipping his head about for a few seconds until his eyes locked onto her.

"Finally decided to give up, my pretty?" he asked, drawing a small knife from his belt. "How about you come nice and quiet like now? I wouldn't want to scar that pretty face of yours." He stepped forward, passing Sylvester's hiding place.

Sylvester could feel his heart hammering in his chest as the man passed. He'd never taken a life before and the very idea terrified him.

"Now!" Karria screamed, and despite his fears, he acted.

"What the…" the man cried out, as the tree next to him exploded, vines flowing outward and wrapping him up in a crushing grip.

The knife dropped from his nerveless fingers as the vines flowed around him. Sylvester emerged from his hiding spot, concentrating hard as he tightened the vines even further. The tracker screamed in pain as the vines began crushing him to death.

Sylvester opened his eyes at the tracker's cry of pain and hesitated. The tracker, feeling the vines loosen their grip, turned his head to look at the elf.

"Never killed a man before, have you?" the man said with a sneer, as he felt the vines slacken a bit more. "Never looked a man in the eye as you watched the life bleed out of him, watched the light go from his eyes?" the man continued, a snarl coming to his face.

Sylvester took an involuntary step back as the man spoke, and the vines binding him slackened just enough for the tracker to escape. The man pounced on Sylvester as soon as he was free, his scrawny hands wrapping around his neck and driving him to the ground.

"You've never taken a life, but I have. I'm sure the boss won't mind too much. After all, a dead elf is still worth plenty!"

He couldn't breathe. The man on top of him was crushing the life out of him. His vision began to darken as he felt unconsciousness claiming him.

Suddenly, he felt the man's grip go slack, and he took a deep gasping breath, coughing hard as air entered his bruised throat. The man was slumped over him, a glassy expression on his face, as blood leaked from the back of his head.

Karria stood over him, the man's now bloody knife clutched in her shaking hands. She dropped the knife and fell to her knees, shock clearly written across her face. Sylvester rolled the man off of him and quickly ran over to her.

"Karria!" he said, shaking her shoulders, "Karria, look at me."

She looked up then, and he could see tears streaming down her face.

"We have to go," he said, "The tracker is dead, but more men will be coming soon."

She nodded, and he helped her stand on shaky legs, and together they took off at a run.

Karria ran along, her mind reeling. She couldn't believe what she had just done. She'd killed a man! She had never taken a life, nor had she ever wanted to. She replayed it in her mind over and over.

The feeling of the knife sinking in, the grating of bone through the handle. The man shuddering, blood pumping from the back of his head.

She was running now. Sylvester was holding her hand and leading her through the forest. It had to be done, though. Otherwise, they'd both have been captured or killed. Sylvester definitely would have died had she not intervened.

Sylvester!

Her thoughts came to a screaming halt and anger bloomed in her chest. It was his fault! The little coward couldn't do it, so she'd been forced to step in!

This thought snapped her out of her shock, and she tore her hand from his. He turned quickly, only for a stinging slap to rock his head to the side. He looked at her in shock, his hand going to his cheek.

"The next time you decide to spare an enemy out of pity," she said with a venomous glare. "Don't expect me to save you!"

She then ran on ahead of him, fighting to keep the rage alive. It was the only thing keeping her from collapsing on the spot and retching.

Sylvester stared after her for a moment, holding his face. Anger boiled inside him at the indignity. He opened his mouth to retort when another feeling slammed into him. Shame. He'd almost cost them both their lives, and for what? To spare the life of a man who would sell them as if they were animals?

He took off after Karria, resolving himself not to show that kind of mercy again. He couldn't afford to.

11

Karria was annoyed.

No, she thought, *I'm not just annoyed. I'm pissed!*

She looked over at Sylvester, who was trying, unsuccessfully, to find the position of the sun for about the thousandth time that day. After killing the tracker, they'd had a fairly easy time evading their pursuers, and had now made their way deep into the Endless Wood.

Sylvester had explained that the Goldenleaf Forest was on the other side of the Flatlands, all the way to the south. They just had to make it to the Flatlands, and from there, it should be just two weeks to reach the border of the elven territory. What he hadn't said was that he had no idea how to get there.

They'd been wandering the Endless Wood for over a month now as far as she could tell. Her clothes were dirty and torn, and her shoes weren't in any better shape.

She'd probably have found it pretty ironic had she known her brother had recently found himself in a similar situation.

Sure, they weren't dying of hunger or thirst. Sylvester's Nature magic made sure they could always find wild berries. And apparently, he was a Tier 3 Mage, so once he'd recovered somewhat, he had a pretty easy time finding them. He could also bring up vines filled with water to keep them from dehydrating.

What she didn't understand was why there were no rivers or lakes. How did the trees and animals stay alive?

Sylvester had explained that there was a massive underground river flowing beneath their feet, and though they couldn't reach it, the trees' roots could. He also speculated that the animals must have some way of getting water where they couldn't.

"Well?" she asked as he walked over. "Do you have any idea where we are, or how to get out of here?" She didn't mean to sound so rude, but she was beyond frustrated.

"No, I don't!" he answered back, equally as frustrated. "Why don't you try and find a way out of here? Everything looks the same!"

"I'm not the one with plant magic! How the hell are you even lost?"

"It's *Nature* magic! Not Plant magic! And that's not how it works!"

The two of them glared daggers at one another, both gearing up for a fight.

"I really seem to be getting a lot of visitors lately," a friendly sounding voice called out.

They both jumped at the sound of it, snapped from their argument, and whirled around to see who'd spoken.

"My, you two are quite jumpy!" The man laughed.

Karria stared. He had to be the oddest-looking man she had ever seen, and that included Sylvester. The man was tall, over six and a half feet, with bright red hair growing in wild spikes. He had purple eyes and… She blinked a few times. Was his skin orange?

Karria snapped out of her stupor and tried to curtsy, realizing that she'd been staring – her mother had always told her it was rude. She wasn't very good at it, seeing as she'd rarely met anyone she didn't know. It was always polite to curtsy to strangers – that was another thing her mother had said.

My mother sure did have a lot of sayings.

She realized that her mind had begun wandering and straightened quickly from the curtsy, her cheeks going a little pink.

"My name is Karria, and this is Sylvester." She wasn't sure why, but she felt oddly at ease, as though she could trust this man with anything.

"Who are you?" Sylvester asked, suspiciously.

He didn't seem at all relaxed around the stranger. He looked tense, as if he were preparing to run. The man smiled easily at them both.

"What a polite young lady you are," he said, sweeping into a formal bow. "My name is Silver," he said straightening.

"What are you doing here?" Sylvester asked, not dropping his guard at all.

His eyes were slitted, and he looked on in suspicion.

"I live here, of course!" Silver said, his smile just growing wider. "Come, my dear. You must come to my clearing. I can fix those clothes right up and get you a decent meal," he said, holding out an arm for Karria.

She took the proffered arm and shot Sylvester a smug look as the man began leading her away. They walked together, weaving through the forest until they entered a small clearing about five minutes later. Karria chatted with the man the entire time, while Sylvester just followed behind, glowering the entire time.

"Wow! It's amazing here!" Karria exclaimed as she looked around.

The branches overhead were woven together, forming a sort of roof. A small fire pit stood in the center, with a kettle boiling on top. The trees were tightly packed together as well, effectively hiding it from the rest of the forest. In fact, if she'd been standing outside, she wouldn't have even known it was here.

"Yes, it's quite the sight, isn't it?" Sliver said with a contented sigh.

He then went to a hollow tree and produced a long shirt.

"This is one of mine," he said, handing it over. "It should serve as a dress until I get yours fixed. You can change over there."

He pointed to an area where the leaves grew too thick to look through.

"Thank you, sir," Karria said, taking the shirt and draping it over an arm.

"Please, no formalities. You'll make me feel old," Silver said with a grin. "Just call me Silver."

Karria smiled at that and walked to the private area to change out of her dirty dress.

Sylvester walked up to Silver once she was out of sight.

"I know what you are," he said in a low voice. "And I want to know what you're really doing here."

Silver stiffened at this and looked down at the glowering elf.

"I would appreciate it if you kept your observations to yourself," he said quietly. "That girl has more magic potential than I've sensed from anyone in over a thousand years. Well, other than her brother, of course," he said as an afterthought.

Sylvester's sour expression changed to one of surprise at hearing that bit of news.

"You met her brother? He's alive?"

A wide grin spread across his face then. "I should tell her the good news!" Sylvester said, heading towards the trees.

He felt a hand on his shoulder and looked back. Silver's purple eyes were glowing now, and he had a very serious expression on his face.

"You will not tell that girl anything," he said, his expression grim. "They will meet again soon, but until that happens, she must go on believing that he is dead. She must go to the Goldenleaf School of magic. That is where she belongs. I've set her brother on a different path, and you will not interfere!"

Sylvester winced as he felt the hand on his shoulder burn white-hot before releasing him. He looked up in fear and bobbed his head vigorously. He'd heard the stories. He might not like the man, but he wouldn't interfere.

Not if I want to keep on breathing, anyway.

"Thank you for lending me this shirt," Karria said as came back into the clearing.

The shirt hung well past her knees, due to the vast height difference between her and Silver. The dirty dress was neatly folded over one arm, and her worn-out shoes dangled from the fingers of the other.

"Oh, it's my pleasure," Silver said, his serious expression from a moment before gone in an instant. "Here, let me take those," he said, taking the dirty dress and shoes from her. "Now sit and eat. There's plenty of food."

Karria squeaked in excitement as she saw skewers of meat roasting over the fire, and steaming cups sitting on the ground next to it.

"Thank you so much!" she said, immediately running for the food.

Sylvester looked at the meat with distrust. It hadn't been there a moment ago.

"I think I'll just stick to berries," he said, heading into the forest. "I'll be back soon."

Karria had no idea why the elf seemed to be in such a bad mood, but she honestly couldn't bring herself to care at the moment.

"Take your time," she called out through a mouthful of steaming meat.

She had never tasted anything so good.

It had been way too long since she'd had a decent meal, and she would enjoy this one while it lasted.

"My, you have quite an appetite for such a pretty young lady," Silver said, chuckling.

Karria swallowed and flashed him a grin.

"You'd be hungry, too, if you spent a month eating nothing but berries!"

She made a face, letting him know exactly what she thought of those berries. She then took another bite of her meat and chewed happily.

"Yes, I think I would," Silver said, his smile widening just a bit. "So, would you be so kind as to tell me your story? When you're done eating, of course."

Karria nodded and continued right on eating. After her third skewer, she had to slow down as she'd already started feeling quite full. Taking her fourth skewer with her, she sat in front of Silver, who had already managed to get all the dirt off her dress.

"How did you do that, and so quickly?" she asked, pleasantly surprised.

The blue color was showing as clearly as the day she'd first worn it.

"Oh, when you live in the forest as long as I have, you tend to pick up a few things. Mainly, how to get dirt out of clothing."

He pulled out a needle and thread and began working quickly on fixing all the holes on the dress.

"So, now that you've eaten, would you mind sharing your story?"

Karria felt that same feeling of relaxation wash over her again. She leaned her back against a tree, and she began recounting the events of the last few weeks.

It took her some time to retell her entire ordeal. By the time she was finished, Sylvester had already returned with a handful of berries, and Silver had finished repairing her dress.

"It sounds like you've been through quite a lot in the past few weeks," Silver said, handing her the repaired dress.

"It's been more difficult than I care to admit," she replied, taking the dress and marveling at the work he'd done in such a short amount of time.

Silver had washed out the dirt, sewn up all the holes and replaced the fraying fabric. He'd split the skirt down the middle and fashioned them into shorts that ended at the knees. Next, he handed her an overskirt, something she could wear over the pants to protect her modesty.

She was quite grateful for the overskirt. After all, wearing pants in public would make her feel uncomfortable, though she wasn't entirely sure why they should. She felt comfortable with the dipping neckline of the dress, so why did pants bother her? She shrugged to herself and decided that it was probably due to her upbringing.

"Thank you," she said, standing up and giving him a hug. "I'll get into this now and see how it fits."

That said, she headed back into the cover of the trees to change once more.

"I'll be escorting you to the Goldenleaf Forest," Silver said once Karria had disappeared from view.

Sylvester's head whipped up at this, his lips turning down in annoyance.

"What possible reason could you have to come with?"

"I have my reasons. Foremost among them, is that you won't make it there without me," Silver said his tone calm and measured. "I'd also like to be there when the girl's power awakens for the first time. I'd like to know what type of magic she has."

Sylvester just glared at him but didn't dispute his decision. Once again, he had to admit that the man was correct. He had no idea how to get out of the Endless Wood, let alone survive the harsh Flatlands. Plus, there was always the chance of running into another group of bandits. Best to take precautions, even if he didn't like the present company all that much.

"I'm glad to see that we understand one another," Silver said as Karria came back with a light bounce in her step.

"Thank you again," she said, handing Silver his shirt. "The clothes fit perfectly!"

She sat down on a log, smoothing the front of her new skirt, humming under her breath. The sun was beginning to set now, and darkness was creeping in. Though she was loathe to do so, Karria knew they couldn't stay around forever. They had to be on their way.

"Would you happen to have a map that we could use?" she asked, "You've already done so much for us, but we don't know the way out of the woods. I would really appreciate any help you could give."

Silver just laughed and waved her compliment away.

"It was my pleasure to help such a polite young lady, and if you don't mind, I'd like to escort you to the Goldenleaf Forest. I've been there a few times and know the way quite well."

The air whooshed out of Silver's lungs as Karria barreled into him and wrapped her arms around him. Silver was a bit surprised at the show of affection but soon hugged her back.

She pulled away after a moment, wiping her eyes and sniffing.

"I'm sorry," she said. "It's just been so long since anyone's been this nice to me."

She stopped for a moment in an effort to hold back her tears, as memories of her family suddenly flooded in.

"I know my family is gone now, but I just don't want to believe it! Someone must have survived. They can't all be dead, right?"

She sounded as though she were pleading, hoping for someone to reassure her that at least one family member was still alive. Sylvester wanted to speak then, to reassure her and tell her that her brother was alive. But a warning glance from Silver made him bite his tongue.

"Don't worry, my dear," Silver said, taking her small hands in his. "The world is a large place, with many wonders. And who knows? You may just find that you're not as alone as you believe."

Karria smiled at that and wiped her eyes. She didn't know why, but what Silver said comforted her.

"It's been a very long and exhausting day," she said covering up a yawn. "I think I'll go turn in for the night."

She patted Silver on the arm once more, then rose from her seat and headed for an alcove near one of the trees.

"You should get some rest as well," Silver said, turning to look at the elf. "We have a long journey ahead of us, and we'll be heading out a first light."

Sylvester stood, and, shooting him one last dirty look, headed to his own alcove.

He would keep silent for now, but the moment Silver was gone, he would tell Karria everything. After all, he couldn't keep him quiet forever.

12

Arbor stared out at the empty, barren Flatlands, his eyes burning with exhaustion. The landscape stretched in all directions as far as the eye could see, and he knew that whatever he was seeing now was only a fraction of their true size and scale. His horse's hooves pounded beneath him in a constant muffled clatter, kicking up a cloud of dust in their wake.

After a long chase through the woods, they'd finally reached the plains a few days ago. According to Grak, the outline of the Jagged Peaks would soon become visible. He turned his head back and peeked over his shoulder.

Grak was riding a few feet behind him, and off in the distance, he could see a plume of dust rising in the air.

They've gotten closer since yesterday, he noted worriedly.

Arbor's entire body felt thoroughly bruised and banged up. They'd been riding non-stop since the previous morning and had both taken turns sleeping in the saddle. He wasn't the only one who was tired, though. Grak was exhausted as well, though she didn't utter a single sound of complaint. The horses were nearing the limit of their endurance though, not having been able to rest in over a day. Their flanks were covered with foam, and he could feel their pace flagging as the day wore on. They wouldn't last for much longer.

Grak pulled up alongside him as he slowed to a walk. It would give the horses some rest, thereby assuring they could ride for longer before the beasts inevitably collapsed and they'd be forced to continue on foot.

"How much further to the Jagged Peaks, do you think?" he asked, wiping dust from his brow.

"Probably another day or so," Grak replied wearily.

Now that he could see her up close, he could tell that she was worse off than he'd first thought. Arbor had his magic, and that somehow seemed to be giving him a bit of a boost to ward off exhaustion. Grak, however, looked to be half asleep in the saddle.

The winter moon had risen the previous evening, and the gremlin force had continued to chase them into the night, instead of resting. Consequently, they hadn't gotten any sleep and were forced to keep riding once the sun had gone down as well.

Even though the winter moon was in the sky, Arbor noticed that it had gotten noticeably hotter once they reached the Flatlands. Grak had explained that it was hot here year-round, and that was why the ground was so dry. It was a barren wasteland where almost nothing grew or lived. It rarely ever rained either and, when it did, it soon became treacherous to travel.

Arbor looked over his shoulder once again. For the first time, he could make out faint specs on the horizon.

"We need to keep moving," he said. "Just a bit more and we'll make it, right?"

Grak nodded wearily, then kicked her horse's flanks and rode out ahead of him. He followed, his horse moving sluggishly as they continued to ride towards the mountains.

After about an hour or so, Arbor could begin to make out the peaks of mountaintops on the horizon. The sun was already getting low, though, and their pursuers seemed to have shortened the distance between them.

Now only about two miles behind, he could hear their horns blowing, carried to them through the scorching and still air. The cries of the gremlins were now audible as they whipped their horses to move faster.

He narrowed his eyes, noting that the group seemed smaller than it should be. Only six of them to be exact.

Must be an advance party.

The thought gave him pause as he considered their options. If they kept going at their current pace, they would be caught within a half-hour, but their horses would be even more exhausted than they already were. If, however, they dismounted now and put up a defense, they could have a pretty good chance of escape. All they would have to do was kill them off, and then the others would have no way of following them. Or so he hoped, anyway.

"Grak, can you fight?" he asked, turning to the gremlin woman.

She looked at him as though he'd just lost his mind.

"You want to fight an entire city's garrison with just the two of us?!"

"No," he said quickly. "But the advance party will catch up to us any minute. There's only six of them as best I can make out. If we kill them now, we may have a better chance of escape."

Grak still looked skeptical but nodded her head in the affirmative.

"I do know how to fight. I can't use a sword to save my life, but I can use a knife if I have to."

"Good," Arbor said, unsheathing his belt knife and handing it to her. "Because I don't have any swords to hand out. Now, can you take care of two of them?"

The riders were now only a few hundred yards away and were whooping in excitement, thinking that they must have given up.

"I can try," she said, tying her long blue hair back to keep it out of her eyes.

She didn't sound too confident, but he would take what he could get. After all, two people were better than one. He drew his glaive and spun it a few times, getting the feel for it before settling into a fighting stance.

The gremlins quickly dismounted as they reached them, pulling swords from their belts in obvious glee. They were lightly armored, though- probably to give their horses a little extra speed.

The gremlins moved quickly to try and surround him, but Arbor would have none of that. As one moved to his left, he quickly stepped forward in a lunge, extending his glaive out in front of him and taking him in the gut. His sharpened blade easily punched through the light armor, sinking in until he felt it grate against the gremlin's spine.

Ripping the blade free with a savage twist, he quickly spun the weapon, just managing to knock aside an overhead blow. He then kicked the gremlin in the chest, sending him to the ground where he lay clutching at the massive wound. He quickly ducked, the strange sensation of his magic warning him of incoming danger. A blade cut through the area that his head had been just seconds before. He spun in a circle from his crouched position, tucking the shaft of the weapon close to his body, the blade glittering as it whistled through the air.

Two gremlins toppled with a howl, their legs cleanly cut below the knees and black blood spraying from the dissected stumps. He stood quickly, ignoring the fallen gremlins and stepped back to assess the situation. One gremlin was dead, two were down with missing limbs, and one was still standing before him. He chanced a glance back at Grak and saw that she'd successfully killed one of the gremlins but was now limping heavily.

He could see a deep gash on her inner thigh and a black stain swiftly growing from the spot, staining her pant leg. He felt a warning then and stepped quickly to the right. He grunted, as the sword meant to take him through the heart cut a line into his side, skating over one of his ribs, but not managing to cause more than a flesh wound.

Cursing himself for being so careless, he whirled to face his attacker. The fourth gremlin was looking at him in open amazement, as his seemingly easy victory was somehow thwarted. He was still staring when Arbor took his head from his shoulders with a wide sweep of his glaive. He then walked over to the two gremlins on the ground and put them out of their misery with two clean stabs to the head.

He looked around for Grak and felt his heart skip a beat. She was on her back, desperately holding the last gremlin's arms as he drove a dagger towards her throat. Arbor started to run towards her, but he could already tell that he wouldn't make it in time.

The feeling of helplessness threatened to overtake him as the vision of his dead parents and Florren flashed through his mind. He would be too late once again. Too weak to save her. Then he felt it again — his magic thrumming in his center. For a moment, nothing happened, then strength flooded his body.

His speed picked up noticeably as he pumped his legs and he almost tripped at the unaccustomed speed he was moving. His body thrummed with suppressed energy, and Arbor felt more alive than he ever had before. The feeling was intoxicating, like that one time he'd gotten drunk back home, only a thousand times stronger!

He released his glaive as he approached the struggling pair, and dove forward, catching the gremlin on top of Grak in a sideways tackle. The two of them hit the ground in a jumble of tangled limbs, rolling a few times due to his momentum.

When they finally stopped, Arbor quickly moved on top and struck the gremlin in the face. The gremlin was quick though and managed to pull his head to the side, turning it into a glancing blow. The gremlin bucked his hips then, and Arbor fell forward, throwing his hands out to stop himself from losing his position.

The smaller creature took the opportunity to wrap his arms around his neck, trying to pull Arbor's head down to his shoulder where he would have more control.

Arbor reached around, grabbing the offending creature's thumbs and wrenched them back, hearing a distinct crack as he did so. The gremlin howled in pain as he straightened up, trying to push back with his legs to escape. Arbor quickly shifted his position then, putting his knee into his ribs and driving the wind out of him.

He then brought his elbow down viciously, throwing his body forward as he did so. He struck the gremlin square across the face and caved his head in, spraying blood and brain matter all over the parched ground. The gremlin stopped moving, his body going limp, with only the small twitches of his nervous system not yet realizing he was dead.

Arbor got up then, his body trembling with adrenaline and fear. He had no time to break down though and ran over to the still prone Grak. He got down on his knees next to her, feeling a huge sense of relief that she was still breathing, though he could see it wasn't all good. The black stain on her thigh had spread, and she was now holding both hands over the wound.

"I think he may have nicked an artery," she managed to say in answer to his questioning look. "It won't stop bleeding and I'm afraid to move my hands."

She was clearly in a great deal of pain, and Arbor knew he had to act quickly to staunch the bleeding. He stood, grabbing his cloak from the saddle of one of the horses and tore a strip of cloth from the bottom. He took a waterskin, soaking the rag as he bent down next to her.

"Move your hands away, and I'll wrap it for you. I don't have anything to clean the wound, so we'll just have to hope that it doesn't get infected."

Grak nodded. She was clearly afraid and a bit embarrassed. The wound was pretty high up on her thigh, after all. But after taking a few deep breaths, she let go of her leg. Blood instantly began pumping from the wound, but Arbor worked quickly and wrapped the strip of cloth tightly around her leg. She was lucky that they weren't a regular pair of pants. Otherwise, he'd have had to cut them away, which would have taken precious seconds.

The only thing holding her makeshift pants in place were two knots near the bottom. Thus, he was easily able to work the bandage around under the cloth, tying it off tightly. Blood soaked the makeshift bandage when he sat back, but no blood leaked from under it.

Grak smiled at him in thanks, clear relief showing now that the bleeding had been stopped. Then a look of concern crossed her face.

"Arbor, you're bleeding!"

Arbor looked at himself then, only now noticing that his side was indeed soaked in blood.

"Must've cut deeper than I thought," he said, remembering the gremlin that had almost killed him before. "Don't worry about it. I've had worse."

Grak glared at him and got shakily to her feet.

"Don't give me that macho bullcrap! Take off your shirt. I won't have you bleeding to death on me," she ordered, in a tone that would brook no argument.

Arbor did so, grumbling under his breath that he didn't need any help and that it was no big deal.

Grak just ignored him and set about poking and prodding the wound. Once she was satisfied that it wasn't life-threatening, she washed it off with some water and wrapped it with some more strips torn from Arbor's cloak. After a few more minutes, she stepped back to admire her work and nodded in satisfaction.

Though she did take the time to admire his well-muscled chest, her eyes were inexplicably drawn upward to the pendant sitting around his neck.

"What is that?" Grak asked, pointing to the pendant.

Arbor looked down at his chest, where the pendant, Karria's necklace, and his wallet hung.

"You'll have to be more specific. Which one do you want to know about?"

He knew what she was referring to but didn't want to talk about the painful memories associated with the pendant.

Grak just rolled her eyes though and reached out to pull the pendant from his neck. Then she gave him a questioning look.

"My father gave it to me on the night I was supposed to be married," he said in a sober tone. "It's the only thing I have left of him."

Grak examined the pendant with wide eyes for a few moments before handing it back.

"Do you know what kind of metal it is? It's clearly not painted, and I've never seen metal that color before."

Arbor shook his head, taking the pendant back and sliding it over his head. He stood in silence, his thoughts grim as he relived the horrific night. Had it really been three months since that had happened? To him, it still felt like yesterday.

He was snapped from his thoughts as Grak held his shirt out to him, soaking wet. She'd rinsed the blood out as best she could with just plain water.

"Thank you," he said, taking the shirt from her, glad that he could occupy his mind with something else.

There was still a hole in the side, but he could always change later.

"We better get moving," he finally said, looking back to the horizon. "We've bought ourselves some time with this. Best not to waste it."

Grak nodded in agreement and headed over to her horse.

"Um, Arbor."

He turned his head as he heard her call out.

"What is it?" he asked. He started walking over, wondering if her bandage might have come loose.

She looked slightly embarrassed, and her usual light red complexion was a bit darker as she flushed.

"I can't mount up by myself," she said quietly. "My leg won't support my weight."

Arbor just nodded and, grabbing her by the waist, he hoisted her up onto her horse. Her body was soft and feminine, and he felt a pang as it reminded him of what he'd lost.

"Thank you," she said quietly.

Her cheeks were burning with embarrassment now, but Arbor had the good grace not to say anything about it.

"No need to thank me. After all, it was my idea to stay and fight. It's my fault you were injured, so this was the least I could do."

He then headed back to his horse and mounted up, and the two of them took off again. They rode on for another hour before Grak signaled him to come over.

"We're closer than I thought," she said in answer to his unasked question. "Another few hours of hard riding and we should be able to reach the Peaks."

The excitement dropped from her voice then and was replaced by worry.

"Though I don't know if the horses will be able to make it."

"We'll make it," Arbor said confidently. "We've come this far and I'm not about to give up now."

"It's not you I'm worried about," Grak said, patting the horse's side.

Arbor bit his bottom lip as he thought. She was right. At this rate, the horses would drop dead from fatigue before they were even halfway there. He'd been wracking his mind for a full five minutes when an idea suddenly came to him.

Silver had told him that his magic could affect his body and he'd experienced this first-hand during his fight with the gremlins. If he could enhance himself, could he do the same for others as well?

"Grak, I have an idea," he said tentatively. "I don't know if it'll work, but it may just save our lives."

She shrugged, her red-skinned shoulders rising and falling.

"If you think it'll help us survive, go right ahead."

He nodded his thanks at her trust and leaned over to place a hand on her horse's flank. He then closed his eyes and concentrated inward.

He'd never actively tried to access his magic before, so he imagined trying to feel the same sensation he'd felt while fighting earlier. It took a few minutes of searching, but he soon found what he'd been looking for.

A small blue sphere was sitting at the very center of his body, the Core of his power. If he concentrated hard enough, he could feel the power contained within. Five large streams extended out of his Core, and when he followed them, he could see that they connected to his arms, legs, and head. A few smaller streams broke off the main ones, but there weren't many. Going back to the Core at his center, he tried pulling on it, but nothing happened.

He tried next to push it outward, towards his hand, but once again, nothing happened. He was about to give up, when another thought struck him.

There seemed to be streams coming off the Core. Maybe his magic would only follow a specific path?

He tested out his theory and was rewarded when the magic responded immediately and began flowing along the streams. He idly wondered what would happen if he tried to force more magic through the streams. Would he be able to use more of his power?

Arbor once again tested his theory and was once again rewarded when the magic began flowing at an accelerated rate. He gasped as the electric feeling filled him, making him feel more alive than he ever had before. He increased the flow once again, trying to flood his body with the power.

He felt amazing, as though he could jump fifty feet in the air or destroy boulders with his bare hands! Why hadn't he tried doing this previously? They didn't need to run from the gremlins anymore! He could destroy them all with his bare hands!

"Arbor! Arbor, open your eyes!"

Who was talking to him? He could feel a small hand on his shoulder, shaking him hard. Couldn't they just leave him alone?

"Open your eyes! Whatever you're doing, you need to stop!"

The voice finally cut through the haze of power, and Arbor slowly opened his eyes. He was lying on the ground next to his horse and Grak was kneeling down next to him with panic written on all over her face.

"Grak? How did I get on the ground?"

His head was foggy and he shook it, trying to clear the haze from his mind. Grak wordlessly handed him a waterskin then held his head up so he could drink. He winced as he reached out for the waterskin, seeing that his hands and arms were red and blistered.

How the hell had that happened?

His muscles were shrieking in agony as well, and he had a hard time keeping ahold of the skin. He slowly raised it to his lips and took a long sip, then he upended it and quickly drained the contents. He didn't understand why, but he had a raging thirst that just needed to be sated. He handed back the empty skin and then rose painfully to his feet.

91

"What happened to you?" Grak asked, a worried expression still on her face. "One moment, you were sitting there with your eyes closed. The next moment, steam began pouring out of you in waves, your skin began to blister, and then you fell off your horse!"

"Is that what happened?" he asked, rubbing the back of his sore head.

Arbor now fully understood Silver's warning about using magic. He'd used too much before he was ready, and his body had been injured as a result. If he pushed himself too hard, he could end up killing himself.

"I have magic," Arbor said, unable to meet her gaze. "I know I should have told you earlier, but I've been trying to deny it ever since I found out."

He expected her to be mad with him for not telling her, but she surprised him by stepping forward and wrapping her arms around him.

She was careful not to squeeze too hard, as they were both injured, but he understood the sentiment all the same. It felt nice to have contact with another living being after so long, though he didn't say so out loud.

"Thank you," he said quietly, once she stepped back from him.

"You don't need to keep secrets from me, Arbor. We're friends, after all," she said, a bright smile lighting up her face.

He looked over the Flatlands then and could now see the main gremlin force. They were riding hard and only a mile and a half back. His heart sank.

"I was trying to pump the horses full of magic to give us a chance to escape. I guess it didn't work though," Arbor said with a sigh as he turned back to Grak.

"Oh, I wouldn't be too sure of that," she said, pointing to the horses with a grin.

Arbor turned to look at them and was momentarily struck speechless. Both horses were now at least a foot taller at the shoulder, as well as broader in the chest. They looked energized and pawed at the ground with their hooves as if they wanted nothing more than to run.

"I don't know how you did that, but you are definitely going to have to tell me!" Grak said, quickly running up to her horse and attempting to mount it.

Her injured leg was still giving her trouble, and she looked back at Arbor with a bemused expression.

"Mind helping me up?"

Arbor ran over and helped her into the saddle once again, noting that she held just a bit tighter to him as he lifted her. He then ran back to his horse and quickly mounted up. It was a little harder than it had been previously, due to the horse's new height, but he managed it on the second try.

"Let's get moving," he said and tapped his horse on the ribs.

The horse shook its mane a few times before it took off, and Arbor had to hold on for dear life as he was nearly thrown from the saddle. He looked back to see Grak clinging to her mount's neck and laughing wildly, her dark blue hair streaming in the wind.

He could understand the feeling well. They were now moving at least five times as fast as before, which was absolutely crazy. He wasn't sure how he'd done this, but some of the power he was exuding must have leaked into them while he was busy getting drunk off it.

As they rode, he concentrated on his magic once more. This time he could feel the power much more easily, the small blue Core pulsing lightly in his center. He noticed a small change to the magic streams as he looked on. There were two more of the smaller streams branching off the main ones in both of his arms, and the five main steams also seemed to have widened a bit.

Did this mean he was on his path to Tier 2? Arbor couldn't help but wonder at this, feeling a slight thrill as the wind whistled past his ears.

Magic was a wonderful thing indeed!

13

They ran on late into the night, the horses eating up the distance with their accumulated power. What would have originally taken them at least another twelve hours, now only took them around three. They had long since left their pursuit behind and were now approaching the base of the mountains.

The winter moon was shining overhead, its cold blue light giving the landscape an otherworldly cast. They had wrapped themselves in their cloaks once they crossed into the rocky mountain terrain, as the temperature had dropped noticeably the moment they'd left the Flatlands behind. Their breath now steamed in front of them as they breathed out.

Grak rode up next to him, her shoulders slumping and a weary grin on her face.

"The entrance to the dwarven city of Heart should be around here. Check the map you have to see if the location is marked."

Arbor nodded, kicking himself for not thinking of it earlier. Pulling the map from his pack, he could indeed see a marker for the city entrance. He looked around, trying to find a notable landmark to work off.

There! His eyes locked on to a large boulder with two small spikes protruding to either side.

"The entrance is only a mile in that direction," he said, pointing up the slope of the mountain. "We don't need to rush now, so best to let the horses walk."

He didn't know why yet, but at some point, the horses had started losing their gained mass. Perhaps the power he'd imbued them with had begun to wear off?

Yet another mystery about magic, he thought.

Grak moved up alongside him once more, and they began their ascent up the mountain slope. They rode on in silence for a few moments before Grak spoke up.

"Would you mind if I asked you something?"

Arbor was snapped from his contemplations on magic and looked over the gremlin woman. She uncomfortable and was squirming in her saddle.

"What would you like to know?"

94

She was silent for a moment as if trying to find the right way to ask.

"Why don't you ever smile? We've been together for the last ten days. I know there wasn't much reason to smile in that time, but I haven't seen you smile even once."

Arbor sat quietly for a few minutes, trying to think of the best way to answer her question as their horse's hooves crunched through the gravel underfoot.

"It's not that I don't want to smile," he finally answered. "It's more like I can't. I've told what happened to my family, how they were all killed on my wedding night?"

Grak nodded. She'd heard his story alright, and it had chilled her to the bone.

"Well, ever since that night, I've found that I just can't smile. No matter how much I try or how much I might want to, it just won't come."

He paused here once again and fought to get his anger under control.

"There seems to be little joy in this world. The only reason I haven't given up and died yet is that I need to save my sister, and I have a promise to keep."

Grak could hear the pain in his voice as he spoke. She could scarcely imagine what he had gone through that night.

"And what promise is that?" she asked quietly.

Here, a steely note entered his voice. It was a voice tinged with rage and hatred.

"I made a promise over the graves of my parents and my slain wife-to-be. A promise before the Almighty himself that I will find the bastard who killed them. And when I do, will destroy him."

Grak shivered when she heard that. Gone was the calm and measured tone she was used to hearing and gone was the Arbor she had come to know over the last week and a half. The man sitting next to her was someone else entirely.

"What will you do after you've gotten your revenge?" she asked in a quiet voice.

Arbor looked at her then, his angry expression replaced by one of sadness.

"Then, I can die in peace, knowing that Florren will be waiting for me."

With that statement, he kicked his horse into a trot and rode out ahead of her.

Grak felt immense sadness at his last statement. Arbor had saved more than just her life that day in the alley. He'd saved her will to live as well.

Life had hardly been worth living before he'd shown up. She'd lost her parents at an early age, and her only brother had been conscripted into the army. That day when the four soldiers had been beating her to death, she'd accepted her fate and was even happy to do so.

Then Arbor had come along and stood up for her when no one else would. He was a shining light that pulled her from despair, and even though they'd only known each other for a short amount of time, the thought of losing him was almost unimaginable.

"Come on, I've found the entrance," Arbor called from up ahead.

Grak felt tears sliding down her cheek and quickly wiped them away, steeling herself. She couldn't give up just yet. Arbor had saved her life and now was her chance to return the favor, even if she had to save him from himself. She was determined that no matter what, Arbor would not die.

14

Karria looked out over the same Flatlands that Arbor had just crossed. The only difference was that they were separated by several hundred miles. It had been interesting traveling with Silver, thought Sylvester seemed to have something against him. Karria wasn't sure why the elf disliked the odd man so much, but she wasn't going to pry.

"It's wide open as far as I can see!" Karria said, a touch of wonder in her voice as she looked out at the parched and cracked earth of the Flatlands.

Having lived in the woods her entire life, she was constantly surrounded by trees, so the wide-open Flatlands seemed almost unreal to her. There was so much open space! It was both frightening and exhilarating at once. How did anyone live where it was this open all the time?

"Yes, quite a sight, isn't it?" Silver said, walking up beside her. "Just two weeks by foot across this arid wasteland and we'll arrive at the border of the Goldenleaf Forest."

"The sooner we get there, the better," Sylvester grumbled.

Karria noticed that his mood was perpetually worsening as time went on.

"Well then, let's get going," Silver said. With that, he stepped out onto the dry, baked earth.

Karria followed with a small bounce in her step, and Sylvester just glowered as he followed as well. They walked in silence for the first few minutes, their feet crunching on the dry ground and small puffs of dust rising with each step.

The heat was something that Karria noticed almost immediately. The moment they stepped out of the cover of the trees, the temperature rose by at least thirty degrees. She felt sweat breaking out all over her body, and she fanned her face with one of her hands.

"You'll get used to the heat eventually," Silver called back when he saw her fanning herself.

Karria had to wonder how Silver seemed completely unaffected by the scorching heat. Not even a single drop of sweat appeared on the man's face. In fact, he seemed to be right at home in the arid wasteland.

"How about a little history lesson to pass the time?"

Karria blushed a bit as she was sure he'd caught her staring, but she ran up next to him all same.

"Why not?" she quipped. "Nothing else to really do out here."

"That's the spirit." He flashed her a grin. "It's always good when young people are willing to learn."

He then cleared his throat theatrically before beginning his tale.

"These Flatlands span most of the kingdom of Laedrin, covering hundreds of miles in all directions. But they weren't always like this. Once upon a time, this area was occupied by lush forests and flowing streams."

"So, what happened?" Karria asked, her interest now piqued. "How did it end up like this?"

Silver laughed. "Have a little patience, Karria. A good story needs a little introduction."

Karria stuck her bottom lip out in a pout.

"Come on, Silver! Don't make me wait. Just get to the good part. I don't need all the boring details!"

"Oh alright, if you insist," he said, shaking his head in mock disapproval.

"Thousands of years ago, when magic was still new to this world, the five races battled each other on a near-constant basis. You see, magic was a wild thing back then, and all who had it were drunk with power. They desired only one thing, to conquer the other races and rule the world.

"After years of fighting and thousands of lives lost, the gremlins and salamanders decided to retreat to their cities and wait the others out. The humans, elves, and dwarves, however, weren't so easily deterred. They fought on for another five years, costing thousands of additional lives on all sides. However, there was never a clear victor from any of their battles.

"A day came when all their forces met here for one final battle. This would be the last great battle any of them could afford. It raged on for weeks with hundreds of thousands of deaths, but no one was willing to give in. After all, this was what they'd been fighting for, for the last five years, and the winner of this battle would rule the world!

"After another week of fighting, they were forced to stop. Too many people were dying, and continuing to fight would no longer benefit anyone. All sides could see that neither of the other two would give up. So, they called a truce."

Silver stopped his story for a moment and pulled a waterskin from his pack. He took a long sip then passed it to Karria, who took in gratefully. She'd been so wrapped up in the story that she hadn't even realized how thirsty she was.

"The commanders of the three armies were set to meet the next day. Each force would send three of their top commanders, and they would all agree to sign a peace treaty," Silver continued his story.

"However, some of the commanders weren't so keen on giving up after fighting for so long. So, unbeknownst to the other races and even their own people, three commanders met in secret to make sure that the war would continue."

"That's horrible!" Karria exclaimed. "Three people decided that the fight had to keep going and screw what everyone else wants? What a bunch of rat bastards!"

Silver suppressed a grin and nodded in confirmation.

"Not all people are honorable, and this treachery would cost them their lives. Not only their lives but the lives of countless others. The three commanders each went to their forces and told them that the meeting was a trap, and that the other two races planned a betrayal. They were, of course, completely outraged by this and demanded retribution.

"So it was when the nine commanders met in the clearing, the three who had conspired against their races put their plans into action. Pulling daggers that they'd concealed before entering, they killed their fellow commanders."

Karria felt herself becoming angry with these unknown people. She was completely appalled by such treachery.

"Please tell me that they at least got what was coming to them," she begged.

"Oh, they were punished alright," Silver said.

"As it is with traitors, they never completely trusted one another, and each had set a trap for the other two. Once the deed was done, all three acted at once, calling their Mages to attack. As I said before, magic was a wild thing back then, and this blunder would cost them all their lives.

"The humans broke open the earth and brought molten rock to the surface. The elves called down meteors from above, and the dwarves triggered massive explosions. They soon lost control of their magic, as it grew in power and scale. And the results were catastrophic.

"The entire forest burned that day, killing hundreds of thousands from all races. The magic was so out of control that it continued feeding on the land for weeks on end. When the fires finally died down and the molten rock cooled, there was nothing left but dry, cracked ground. Not a single soul had survived."

"What an awful story!" Karria exclaimed. "All that death! And for what, a bit of extra land?"

"Alas, we cannot know what was going through their minds at the time, but there is a lesson in this story. Magic, if not properly controlled, can be the most destructive thing in this world."

"That is something I can definitely agree with!" Karria said. "If that's what magic is, then I'm happy not to have it. I wouldn't want something like that happening because of me."

"Oh, I'm sure that if you had magic, you wouldn't use it in the same way as those greedy people of the past," Silver said, patting her on the shoulder.

The next week and a half went by quickly as they walked across the Flatlands. It didn't take Karria long to see that Silver had been right about the heat. After the first day, she'd quickly become accustomed to it and now it barely bothered her at all.

She was constantly fascinated by what Silver had to say. He seemed so knowledgeable and told her about the world, magic and all the other races.

They were nearing the end of their journey now. Silver said they'd made good time and should be there in the next day or so. They'd stopped for the night to make camp when things finally boiled over between Sylvester and Silver.

"Well, if we're almost there, why don't you leave then?" Sylvester asked, sneering at the taller man. "I'm sure we can find our own way from here."

"Sylvester!" Karria said, appalled at his behavior. "What is the matter with you?!"

She placed her hands on her hips and glared at him.

"*He's* been nothing but gracious and accommodating and *you've* been acting like a total asshole! Now apologize to him."

Sylvester blanched at the open tirade but decided to stand his ground.

"I will not apologize to him! His kind are not to be trusted!"

"What do you mean, his kind!?" Karria thundered, "Do you mean nice men who give you food, clothes and escort you across a barren wasteland out of the goodness of their hearts?!"

Sylvester had never seen Karria so angry, even when he'd gotten them lost in the woods for a month or almost cost them their lives when he'd failed to kill the tracker. He decided to back off, but not without having the final say.

"You can stay here with him if you want, but I'm leaving."

With that statement, he scooped up his pack and left, skulking off into the night.

Karria stood still, quivering with anger, but then felt a hand on her shoulder. She looked up to see Silver, who was watching the elf's retreating form.

"Let him go, for now. I'm sure we'll see him again soon. For now, I think it's best we all cool off, don't you?"

Karria felt a calming sensation then, and she let her shoulders relax. She didn't understand why Sylvester hated Silver so much, but she would definitely be asking if she saw him again.

"Yeah, you're probably right," Karria said with a sigh. "I'm going to get some sleep. It's been a long day."

Silver patted her shoulder one last time before heading to his bedroll.

Karria headed to her own bedroll and bundled up. The nights were somewhat chilly, despite the heat of the day. She only hoped that Sylvester would calm down and be back in the morning.

15

A scream in the night tore Karria from her slumber, and she shot up from her bedroll, disoriented and alarmed.

What the hell was that?

"Calm yourself," she heard Silver's voice reassure her.

Taking a deep breath, she allowed her racing heart to calm down as she took in her surroundings. The moon was high overhead, casting a pale blue light over the cracked ground. Silver was crouching next to her, a long hardwood staff clutched in his hand as he scanned the open terrain.

She quickly got out of her bedroll and crouched next to him, shivering a bit in the chill night air.

"What was that scream?" Karria asked in a soft voice.

"If I don't miss my guess, that was your elf friend," Silver answered. "I imagine he's run across some of the local wildlife."

"What local wildlife?" Karria asked.

She wasn't aware of anything living on the Flatlands.

"Gila lizards," Silver said mildly. "Giant monsters that roam the Flatlands in packs. I spotted their tracks earlier today. It was why I was sure we'd see Sylvester again shortly."

Silver waited a few moments as he finished scanning the surrounding area.

"Ah, here he comes now."

Karria looked up, and sure enough, Sylvester was sprinting towards them for all he was worth. A few hundred yards behind him came a pack of vicious-looking lizards. Karria's eyes went wide in fear. They were huge! They were as long as two horses put together and nearly as tall at the shoulder. Their hides were a mix of brown and tan splotches, effectively camouflaging them and making them hard to keep track of in the uncertain light.

"What should we do?" Karria asked in a panicked voice. "Those things are going to eat us alive!"

She winced then at the onset of a throbbing headache and clutched at her head.

"Oh, I'm sure we'll manage," Silver said, flashing her one of his wide smiles.

It was at that moment when Sylvester came running into camp. He was pale and visibly shaking with adrenaline and fear. He hunched over, his hands on his knees, panting hard.

"I'm glad to see you! I'm sorry for what I said," he wheezed out. "Please let me stay!"

"Why didn't you use your magic on them?" Karria asked, keeping her eyes on the approaching monsters.

There were five of them in all, big, scaly and ugly, with mouths full of razor-sharp teeth. A row of spines ran down their sinuous backs, and they seemed to glide over the ground.

"I tried!" he said, panicked. "But there's nothing growing for miles around here! I'm basically helpless. Please help me. I don't know how to fight!"

"And why the hell are you looking at me?" Karria yelled back, equally as panicked.

She growled as her headache intensified, growing to near blinding proportions. Her legs could no longer hold her up at that and she fell to her knees, clutching at her head and moaning in pain. It was the worst pain she'd ever felt. It felt like her head would split open.

"Don't worry. Everything will be fine," Silver said calmly as he took up a fighting stance.

"What do you mean, everything will be fine?" Karria asked, now hunched over as she tried to fight through the pain.

What was happening to her? Was she going to die? Her ears were ringing, and she could see stars dancing in front of her eyes.

She then felt a pressure begin building behind her eyes. She tried to hold in her cries of pain by clenching her jaw. It wasn't working, and as the pressure increased, she finally let it out. Throwing her head back, she screamed.

Karria felt a rushing sensation, and then cool relief as the pounding behind her eyes finally abated. Then, her head swam and she felt suddenly very weak. Slumping to the ground, she fell into an unconscious heap.

The lizards were almost upon them when Karria fell to her knees. Sylvester watched her go down, his momentary fear deserting him. He took a step towards her, worried, and extended a hand towards her as she lifted her head.

"Karria, are you…?" He never got to finish his sentence, as something hit him from the side and knocked him to the ground.

"Stay down!" he heard Silver's voice yell from on top of him, right before a massive boom rocked the night air. It was followed moments later by a powerful shockwave that sent them tumbling end over end.

Sylvester rolled across the ground, feeling small pebbles and rocks digging into him as he continually slammed into the hard-packed earth. His momentum was finally halted as he slammed into something hard. The air left his lungs in an explosive gasp as he struck, and he lay there gasping for air, completely stunned. After a few moments of desperate gasping, he finally managed to get in a lungful of air.

He slowly got to his feet, gasping and coughing as he attempted to orient himself. His ears were ringing, his vision was fuzzy, and he stumbled as the world seemed to spin around him. He ached all over and could taste something coppery in his mouth. Bringing his hand up to his head, he winced as his fingers came away bloody.

He tried to take a step forward and would have fallen, if not for a firm hand that reached out to steady him. Looking back, he saw Silver, who seemed to be mouthing words at him.

"What?" he asked loudly.

His voice sounded strangely muffled and he couldn't make out what he was saying.

Silver seemed to glow with a soft light for a second and then his ears popped.

"Is that better?" Silver asked.

Sylvester nodded.

"What just happened?" he asked.

Then his eyes widened and panic set in as he remembered their precarious situation before the unexpected explosion.

"Karria! The lizards! Did they get her?"

Silver just pointed in the way of an answer.

Twenty feet away, at the center of a crater that radiated out for ten feet in all directions, lay Karria. Completely whole and unhurt. He looked around for the lizards and saw them some fifty feet away in a twisted, broken heap.

All five of them were completely still and unmoving. Sylvester rushed to the center of the crater to check on Karria. He was surprised to find her fast asleep with a small smile on her face.

He then turned at the sound of crunching gravel to see Silver approaching.

"What the hell was that?!" he exclaimed.

Silver smiled widely before breaking out into a rumbling laugh.

"That," he said, "was Karria's magic. It looks like we know what type she's got!"

"That's impossible, though! No one has so much power at their disposal right away!" Sylvester retorted. "She just displayed the raw power of a Tier 4 Mage!"

"Tier 5, actually," Silver replied smugly. "And it's entirely possible for her type of magic."

Sylvester's eyes flicked to the sleeping girl, and he felt an involuntary shiver run up his spine. A Tier 1 Mage with that much power? Just what kind of monster was she?

***

Karria awoke the next morning with a pounding headache. Her mouth felt dry and she had a nasty taste in her mouth. She sat up slowly, clutching at her head and wincing as she tried to get her bearings.

"That's what you get for overextending yourself," she heard Silver say.

A small cup was then shoved into her hand and she drank it gratefully. It hit her tongue, and she almost gagged on the contents.

It was the single nastiest thing she'd ever tasted.

"Drink it all," she heard Silver say again. "It'll help with the headache."

"As nasty as this tastes, it better!" she threatened.

She did as she was told and drank the entire thing. The headache immediately lessened to an almost imperceptible ache as she finished the nasty liquid. Silver handed her a waterskin next, and she took it gratefully. Taking a sip, she swished it around a few times before spitting it out. Then she took a longer and deeper sip, swallowing it this time with a sigh of relief.

"What happened last night?" she asked, looking first at Silver's smiling face, then to Sylvester's openly shocked one.

"And why are you both looking at me like that? And what happened to you?" she asked Sylvester with a raised eyebrow. "You look like you spent the night allowing a horse to drag you around on your face."

"Don't you remember what happened?" Sylvester asked, ignoring her comment.

Karria gave him a dirty look.

"If I remembered, would I be asking?"

Sylvester puffed out his chest, a cocky grin coming to his face.

"You should be thanking me for saving your life. After you passed out for some reason, I singlehandedly killed all the lizards," he bragged.

Karria looked over at Silver with a quirked eyebrow. "What really happened?" she asked, seeing Sylvester's shoulders slump.

She didn't know why, but Sylvester seemed to have a penitent for lying.

"What Sylvester said could have been true, for all you know," Silver said, the grin not leaving his face.

"Oh alright, I'll tell you what really happened," he said after a few seconds of Karria glaring at him.

He explained what had happened the previous night and who had really saved them all.

"You have magic. I suspected you did from the moment I first met you," Silver said as he finished recounting the previous night's events.

Karria listened to the entire story and when Silver finally finished, she looked between his excited face and Sylvester's downcast one and decided that he was probably telling the truth.

I have magic?!

The thought both astounded and amazed her. She turned quickly back to Silver, needing some answers.

"What kind of magic do I have?"

"It's only a guess, but I'm pretty sure you have the very rare and powerful Mythic magic!"

Karria raised an eyebrow and then placed her hands on her hips.

"Well, that explains *everything*," she said sarcastically.

Now that the initial excitement had worn off, she was quickly becoming annoyed with him for keeping it a secret.

"Keep your breeches on. I'll explain!" He held his hands up in a soothing gesture.

"Mythic magic is a very rare type of magic, only seen once every few hundred years. I don't know much about it, except that it's a form of mental magic. What happened last night was a good example of this. It seems that you built the power up unconsciously and let it out in a massive blast. The attack killed the lizards and, as a bonus, left that nice little hole in the ground," Silver said, pointing to the crater a few feet from them.

Karria's eyes wandered over to the five twisted lizard corpses.

Did I really do that on my own? she wondered.

She looked next to where the large crater sat in the parched ground.

I managed that as well?

"What else can Mythic magic do?"

Truthfully, she was afraid of what she saw. How could she do those things and not remember doing them at all? Would she start hurting people while she was asleep?

"I'm not too sure. Like I said, everyone's magic is different. Some Mythic Mages could use their magic to make things fly, while others could project creatures out into the world. Only time will tell what you may be capable of."

She bit her lip nervously, afraid to ask what was on her mind. Finally, she steeled herself and asked, "Is it safe for me to be around other people? Or will my magic attack them while I'm asleep?"

"Don't worry yourself about your magic acting on its own," Silver was quick to reassure her. "You were in danger when you used it last night and called upon it without realizing what you were doing. I do think you should attend the elven magic school to gain conscious control over it."

Karria paused at that. The thought of attending school with Sylvester excited her to no end. And thought of actually learning to control her newly discovered magic was even more exciting than that.

"A warning, though…"

She was snapped out of her excited thoughts for a moment as she heard Silver speak again.

"As I'm sure you already experienced this morning, using too much power too soon will have consequences. If you overuse your magic, you will destroy your mind and be left a drooling husk of your former self."

The thought of that quickly dampened her excitement as she remembered Silver's story about the people who had misused magic.

He stood then, brushing the dust off his pants and approached her.

"I will be going now. We're close enough to the forest that I feel comfortable leaving you. If you look off into the distance, you can already see the tree line of the Goldenleaf Forest."

Karria felt her bottom lip quiver slightly at his pronouncement. She could see the distant tree line, but she wanted him to stay.

He wrapped his arms around her then, and Karria hugged him back, her small arms squeezing for all they were worth.

"Thank you for everything you've done for me, Silver," she said, standing back from him. "I'll never forget the kindness you've shown me over the last weeks."

Sylvester looked on, awkwardly shuffling his feet.

"I suppose I should thank you as well," he said grudgingly and shook Silver's hand.

Silver then bent down in front of Karria and handed her a small dagger. The handle was inlaid with mother of pearl and shone brightly in the light of the morning sun. The handle was capped by a small piece of ruby red metal, carved into the likeness of a roaring tiger. Pulling it out of its sheath, she saw that the blade was the same red color as the pommel. She marveled at the gift and looked at Silver in open amazement.

"This is beautiful!" she said. "I can't take this. It's too much!"

Silver smiled at her, waving off her concerns.

"It's in the right hands. Now, you take care of yourself, my dear. I'm sure we'll meet again, one day."

He straightened then and turned to head back in the direction they had come, raising his hand in farewell.

Karria watched him go for a long moment. Then she turned around, facing the direction in which he'd pointed them. She could see a distant swaying tree line on the horizon and knew that they were near their destination.

"Come on!" she said to Sylvester with a grin. "I'll race you there!" Clutching her new dagger, she took off towards the Goldenleaf Forest.

16

Arbor and Grak were riding through a rough-hewn tunnel, their horses' clacking hooves echoing off the walls. Oddly enough, the tunnel was quite well lit, with small glowing stones set at intervals along the tunnel wall.

They rode in silence for a while. The tunnel was oppressive and seemed to discourage conversation. He looked back to Grak – she'd been acting strangely since their talk earlier and that worried him.

She was riding a few feet behind him and gave him a reassuring smile as he looked back at her. He turned to face forward once again and just shook his head. Whether human or gremlin, he would never understand women.

They continued riding for a few more minutes before the silence became too oppressive to bear.

"How much further do you think we'll need to go?" he asked, turning in his saddle once again.

He had to admit to himself that now that the earlier excitement had worn off, he felt quite exhausted. He could also feel his side throbbing where the gremlin had cut him and could only hope it wasn't infected.

"I'm not sure," he heard Grak reply. "Dwarves live deep in the mountains, so theoretically, we could follow this tunnel for days before we reach a city."

She sounded tired, and Arbor decided that it was probably best to make camp for the night. Or was it day now? He had a hard time keeping track when he couldn't see the sky.

The tunnel was relatively warm compared to the outdoors and falling asleep wouldn't be too difficult, especially with how tired he felt.

"I think we should stop and make camp," he suggested, bringing his horse to a halt.

Grak pulled up next to him and gave him a tired smile.

"Yes, I would agree with you on that."

Arbor quickly dismounted and then went to help Grak as she was still having trouble, due to her injured leg. She wobbled over to a nearby outcropping in the wall and sat down with a sigh of relief.

Arbor set about unsaddling the horses. His magic had fully worn off by now. Despite that, he could see the horses were far better off than they were. He loosened the straps on their saddles and slid them off, then dug around in the saddlebags for a moment, removing a brush and some heavy blankets. He rubbed them down, making sure to dry them thoroughly before draping the blankets over their backs, then went back to the saddlebags for the feed sack.

Pulling the bag open, he could see that there was only enough left for another week or so of travel. He really hoped they would make it to a city by then. Otherwise, the horses would begin to starve. He poured some feed into a small bag and tied one over each of their faces, stepping back and wiping his brow tiredly.

He looked over to Grak then, who had just finished rewrapping her leg. The wound had scabbed over, but it looked very painful. An entire day of riding with that could not have helped make it better, either. He pulled some dried meat and fruit from one of the bags, as well as a half-full waterskin. The horses weren't the only ones running short on food or water.

When he'd purchased food in Grend, it had been with only one person in mind. Now they had only three days' worth of provisions left. Arbor sighed. Nothing could ever be easy.

He walked tiredly over to Grak, who tried to stand up from her spot against the wall. Her leg buckled under her and she fell back with a small cry of pain.

Arbor put the food on the ground and helped to ease her back into a comfortable sitting position. Grak gave him a grateful look but seemed to grow upset.

"I'm sorry I've been so useless," she said, a bitter tone in her voice. "I can't seem to do anything right, and now I can't even walk."

Arbor didn't really know what to say. He put his hand on hers, trying to offer comfort as he wracked his mind of a solution. A thought occurred to him then. His magic could accelerate his healing, and he'd filled the horses with magic earlier. Maybe he could help her as well?

He bit his bottom lip for a moment as he thought it through.

"Grak, I want to try something with my magic. I know you're in pain, but I might be able to help you heal faster. I do have to warn you, I've never done this before, so it may not work."

Grak looked at him for minute, not saying anything. "I trust you," she finally answered in a quiet voice. "Just please be careful. I don't want you hurting yourself like you did earlier."

Arbor nodded, then closed his eyes. He found the Core of magic located in center – it was getting to be easier now – and concentrated on the streams flowing to his hands. He followed the path a few times, making sure to get a good feel for it, then slowly allowed the magic to flow towards his hands.

He soon found that he could feel a slight pressure building where he'd allowed the magic to collect. The magic seemed to want to disperse into his arms instead of staying bottled up in one spot.

He gritted his teeth and kept the magic there. Sweat beaded his brow as more magic concentrated, and finally, he allowed the flow to stop. He could feel Grak's hand in his, small and warm, her fingers curled tightly around his. He concentrated on his hands, on the power collected there, and willed it to move into Grak's.

The magic resisted at first, wanting only to stay and give him strength, but after a few minutes, it finally flowed outward and into her. He heard a small gasp as he did this and found that he could now sense her entire body through his magic.

He could feel her weariness, the aches and pains of a few bruises, and the burning agony coming from the wound. He took ahold of his magic and streamed it down to the area that was giving her the most pain.

He could feel the cut now. It was deep, and there was a nick in the artery, as she'd feared. The wound was still bleeding, despite the cut having scabbed over. Something like this would kill her if it wasn't treated right away. She'd already lost a fair amount of blood, so Arbor concentrated on coating the wound in his magic.

It was fascinating to watch. His magic seeped into the wound and began knitting it together. The artery closed up and the inflamed muscle and tissue knitted back together.

There was a sigh of relief so audible that he knew Grak could feel the difference right away. He poured more power into her, soothing all the aches and bruises. Once he was done, he started to pull his magic back, but something made him stop.

He could feel something else from her now, a kind of thrumming power that seemed to be emanating from the center of her back. He didn't understand what it was at first, so he moved his magic back to investigate. The thrumming seemed to be emanating from a small sphere located in the center of her spine. The Core was similar to his in many ways, except hers was a lighter blue and no streams were coming off it.

A wave of exhaustion washed over him then, and he was forced to pull his magic back in himself.

When he opened his eyes, he saw Grak leaning back against the wall. Her hand had gone noticeably slack in his and a small contented smile was plastered across her face. Her eyes were half-lidded and her body seemed to have an almost boneless quality to it in the way she was sitting.

"Grak?" Arbor asked.

"What is it?" she asked, in a drowsy voice.

She sounded like she was half asleep.

"How do you feel?"

"I feel wonderful," she said contentedly, her words slightly slurred. "The pain is all gone, and I feel so relaxed." She giggled a little.

Oh no! Arbor thought. He'd overdone it with the magic, and she seemed to be drunk.

It made a weird sort of sense to him. He remembered well the drunk feeling of power he had had while trying to re-energize the horses earlier. He'd wanted to tell her about the small Core he'd felt in her spine.

She definitely had magic, but it seemed to be dormant for some reason.

He figured that his magic must have looked like that up to a certain point. He desperately wanted to ask her about it, but he could see she was already nodding off and decided not to bother her. He released her hand then and straightened, groaning in pain as his cramped muscles stretched.

Digging his fists into his lower back, he leaned backward, hearing a satisfying number of pops. He then fetched a cloak and draped it over Grak. The red-skinned woman mumbled something as he did but didn't wake up when he pulled the cloak up to her chin.

He then picked up the discarded food and sat down with his back to the opposite wall, munching on the dried fruit and meat. The horses were nickering softly next to him as he ate, small crunching sounds coming from the oats in their feed bags. His mind began to wander as he ate, wondering how his life had become so complicated.

All he had wanted was to get married, settle down, and live a normal life. But fate had intervened. His family had been butchered and his sister had been captured. He'd been forced to kill other sentient beings and was now looking for help from dwarves. There was also likely a warrant out for his head at this point, as well.

He rubbed his temples as he felt a headache coming on. Leaning back against the cave wall, he closed his eyes. All these problems will still be here in the morning. Right now, though, he just needed to get some sleep.

Arbor awoke with a start, his heart racing. He wasn't sure, but he thought he heard a noise coming from further down the tunnel.

He looked over at Grak and saw that she was still fast asleep. He had a crick in his neck from sleeping at an awkward angle against the stone wall. Wincing slightly as he forced himself to get up, he made his way over to Grak, rubbing at the sore spot. He froze in his tracks, hearing the noise again. It sounded like a light scuffing of boots over the stone floor.

"I know you're there," he called out, his voice echoing off the tunnel walls. "Whoever you are, come out!"

He unsheathed his glaive and took up a fighting stance, preparing for a fight.

Grak started at this and began to wake up, rubbing her eyes sleepily. She looked around in confusion.

"Arbor?" She was still half asleep. "What's going on?"

Just as he was about to answer, a troupe of dwarves came around a bend in the tunnel. They were fully armed and armored in gleaming plate mail. It was a wonder that he'd only heard them when they'd gotten this close with amount of noise they were making. From what he knew, they were supposed to be friendly, so he relaxed his stance.

"Hello, we've been looking for the city of Heart. Could you be so kind as to direct us there?"

Much to his surprise, the troop took up a defensive position and leveled their weapons at the two of them.

"The two of you will come with us. Drop your weapons and come peacefully. Otherwise, we will be forced to attack. Not that I'd mind killing a filthy gremlin," the lead dwarf said.

Arbor noticed that the dwarf's face twisted in disgust when he said the word 'gremlin,' as though it was the worst thing someone could possibly be.

Grak was fully awake and on her feet now, but she looked frightened. Arbor decided that it probably was best to cooperate. After all, he didn't think the two of them could beat ten fully armored dwarves who were prepared for a fight. He leaned his weapon again the wall and held his hands out in front of him.

"We don't want a fight. We'll come peacefully."

The dwarf seemed to relax, just a bit. With a sharp command, his troop moved forward, surrounding the two of them.

"We will escort you to Heart. But if you so much as sneeze in the wrong direction, we will not hesitate to kill you."

Arbor just nodded. Two of the dwarves gathered their belongings and began to herd them down the tunnel. Grak walked beside him, and he was glad to see she was no longer limping. He could see grim and distrustful looks on the dwarves faces as they walked, and he couldn't help but wonder what they had in store for them.

17

Arbor and Grak were sitting in a cell.

They had arrived in the city of Heart just two hours ago and were immediately thrown in a cell with no food or water. When he tried to ask questions, the guards just ignored him.

He looked over to Grak. She was sitting on the opposite side of the cell and had pulled her knees up before her and wrapped her arms around them, hiding her face.

"Grak?" he asked.

She looked up with a start as he called out. He could see that she was very visibly shaking and that her face was pale with fear. He got up and walked over to sit next to her.

"Why are you so afraid?" he asked gently. "Those dwarves seemed to hate you for some reason. Can you tell me why?"

She shuddered at this, but then took a deep breath and began to speak.

"Gremlins," she began in an even measured tone, "are sworn to serve the king. We are his soldiers, his assassins, his to do with as he wishes. Gremlins have done many horrible things to all the other races over the years, and all in the name of the king. Five years ago, the gremlins were ordered to raid this mountain. They destroyed buildings, burned food stores, and killed thousands of dwarves."

She paused here for a second, and then added in a quieter voice, "They also killed the queen and her unborn child."

Arbor winced when he heard this but then thought back to his visit to Grend. Something wasn't sitting right with him. Hadn't there been dwarves in the gremlin city?

"I saw plenty of dwarves in my visit to the city, and they didn't seem to have any problems with the gremlins."

Grak just shook her head at this statement.

"There are many different tribes of dwarves. The ones you saw in the city had been living there for generations, long subjected to the king's rule. The dwarves of the Jagged Peaks, however, still openly defy the king and everything he stands for. That is why they hate me so much," she finished with a sigh.

"There's one thing I don't understand," Arbor said. "Why do the gremlins serve the king? Can't you just do what you want, like everyone else?"

Grak shrugged.

"No one knows why we serve the king. Only that we've been doing it as long as anyone could remember."

"Do all gremlins serve the king, even the women and children?" Arbor asked with a raised eyebrow.

"Yes, even the women and children," she replied sadly.

"That doesn't make any sense, though," Arbor argued. "You're a gremlin and you don't serve the king. You're actually in open defiance, as far as I can tell. You helped me kill others of your kind when they were chasing us."

Grak just shrugged once more.

"I don't like him. He's a total asshole, and I'd honestly prefer it if he just dropped dead."

Arbor had just opened his mouth to ask Grak to explain, when the bars on the door rattled as a dwarf slid a key into the lock.

"Come with me," he said, looking at Arbor.

He had a scowl on his face and eyed Grak with hatred.

Arbor and Grak both got up and headed towards the door.

"Not you! Damn filthy gremlin, just him," the dwarf said, pointing a finger at Arbor.

Arbor was about to protest when Grak just waved him on.

"Just go. Don't worry about me. I'll be fine."

He wasn't so sure about that, but seeing as he had no choice, he followed the guard, hearing the door clang shut behind him.

The guard led him through a low archway and out on to an open street. He looked up, seeing a high ceiling of stone at least hundred feet above his head. Glowing stones were everywhere, set in the walls and ceiling, lighting up the entire city. He stopped for a moment to gape, when the guard prodded him in the back with his spear.

"Quit gawking!" he snarled.

Arbor glared at him but continued down the street. Another guard soon joined them as they walked, presumably to stop him from running.

There were dwarves everywhere he looked, shouting greetings at one another and eating at open booths on the side of the street. He saw a plump dwarf woman leading two children to an open doorway, with the words 'Finest clothing in Heart' painted above the door.

He felt a prod in his back the moment he stopped and was forced to move forward once again. He gritted his teeth and had to restrain himself from punching the dwarf in the face. They continued walking until they left the main part of the city behind. Up ahead, he could see a massive stone building, with huge iron-bound doors set into the front and guessed that this was their destination.

As they approached the entrance, Arbor could see that a smaller set of doors had been built into the larger ones. This would allow people to move in and out without having to open the massive doors each time.

There were two guards standing to attention at either side, and they nodded at the dwarves escorting him. They gave Arbor curious glances but stepped aside and opened the smaller doors for them.

Arbor was roughly shoved forward, and he glared back at the guard who was seeming to take every opportunity to prod and poke him. The guard just sneered back and prodded him once again. Hard.

Arbor didn't move, instead narrowing his eyes at the dwarf as he thought of the best way to take his weapon from him.

"If you don't get a move on, I'll use the other end," the dwarf said, turning the spear around and leveling the point at him threateningly.

Arbor gritted his teeth and moved forward, inwardly seething at the unfair treatment. He was escorted down a long hallway, decorated with fine tapestries and marble carvings.

He could see another set of doors at the end of the corridor with two more guards standing at the entrance. One of the guards stopped them once they'd gotten within ten feet. Apparently, the dwarf behind him hadn't noticed, because he exclaimed angrily and prodded him with the spear butt once again.

Arbor whirled on the dwarf and pointed to the guards by the door.

"If you'd like me to keep going, I suggest you take it up with them. But if you just want a fight, I'll be happy to take you on."

The dwarf's face reddened as the door guards gave him annoyed looks.

"I'll teach you to mind your tongue, human!" he snarled, bringing the spear blade to bear once again.

"That's enough of that," the other guard said, placing a firm hand on his shoulder. "You will not attack an unarmed prisoner just because you don't like his traveling companion."

The angry dwarf looked between the other guard and Arbor for a moment, before angrily lowering the point of his spear and nodding once.

The guards relaxed as the situation was resolved and one of them pounded twice on the door.

"Enter!" a voice called out through the door.

The guard pushed the door open, and Arbor once again felt the spear butt prod him hard in the back to get him moving. Apparently, he wasn't about to let the insult go so easily.

Arbor stumbled forward and once again gritted his teeth as he felt rage begin to boil up within him. He would get even with the little bastard if it was the last thing he did!

He did manage to keep a clear enough head to notice the splendor of the room he'd just entered. The ceiling towered fifty feet over his head, and a long carpet stretched towards to a raised dais. An elaborate throne carved of blue marble sat atop the pedestal, and in that throne sat a dwarf.

The dwarf was quite handsome and a lot younger than Arbor would have expected. A long red beard flowed down his chest, and deep brown eyes looked back at him from under a stern brow. He was powerfully built, and knotted muscles rippled under his fine shirt. Golden rings adorned his fingers and a bright crown sat atop his brow.

Arbor couldn't help but notice that it was made of same blue marble as the throne. It was interwoven with glittering gems and bands of gold and silver.

"His royal majesty, King Akkard! King of the Jagged Peaks, killer of a thousand foes and bane of the Mythic Bear!" a dwarf next to the throne announced in, what Arbor thought, was way too loud a voice. He could see the king agreed as well, by the slight wince he gave at the volume.

"You should bow, peasant!"

He heard a whisper in his ear, right before he felt a sharp crack right behind his legs, forcing him to drop to his knees with a grunt of pain.

"There's no need for that," Akkard said, with a disapproving look directed at the dwarf who'd been tormenting him for the last few minutes.

"You may rise," he said, directing his gaze on him.

Arbor rose to his feet, hiding a wince as he did so. He was sure he'd just bruised his knees.

"Tell me, human, what is your name?" Akkard asked, not unkindly.

"My name is Arbor."

"Tell me then, Arbor," the king said, leaning forward in his throne. "What you were doing traveling through my tunnels, and in the company of a gremlin no less?"

For some reason, the king didn't sneer when he said the word gremlin. He seemed genuinely curious, so Arbor related his tale.

He told everything, from how his family had been killed, to his rescue of Grak and his subsequent run from the soldiers. He skipped over the part about Silver. He didn't know why, but he didn't think he should mention the odd hermit to the dwarf king.

Akkard listened patiently, not saying a word throughout his entire tale, then leaned back in his throne once Arbor concluded his story.

"It sounds as though you've had quite a number of hardships leading up to your capture here," he said in an even voice.

"You have my condolences for what happened to your family. I, too, know the pain of losing those close to one's heart." His voice seemed to soften for second, and an undisguised look of grief crossed his face.

"You can't really believe this human, Your Majesty!" the guard behind him exclaimed in outrage. "This filthy human is conspiring with the gremlins! He must die along with the filth we've locked up in the dungeons!"

"That's quite enough of that!"

The other guard stepped forward to try and intercede again, but the dwarf just shoved him aside. He then stepped forward and tried to jab at Arbor again, but this time, Arbor wasn't about to take it lying down.

Reaching for the pulsing Core at his center, Arbor pumped magic down the streams to his hands and feet. He could feel his muscles strengthening as the magic seeped into them. The process didn't take very long, just a second or two, but the dwarf had already jabbed him twice in the ribs before he felt ready to make his move.

The dwarf was pulling the spear back to poke at him a third time, this time with the spear point and not the butt as he had with the previous strikes when Arbor felt his senses sharpen.

He could now sense where the attack would land, his magic showing him a brief glimpse into the future. He took in a deep breath, then moving faster than anyone could follow, made his move.

The dwarf seemed to be almost standing still, and he easily sidestepped the incoming thrust. The dwarf, expecting to meet resistance, stumbled forward, completely off balance as his spear thrust through the empty air.

Arbor grabbed his spear then, twisting it out of his grasp and sending the offending dwarf stumbling back. He quickly spun, twirling the spear in his hands as he'd seen Silver do, and cracked the dwarf across the temple with all his might.

The haft struck the dwarf so hard that it shattered in his grip, sending splintered fragments flying in all directions.

Despite this, the dwarf was the true victim, not the spear.

His head was whipped to the side with the force of the impact and he was sent flying a good ten feet across the room. He smashed into the opposite wall so hard that stone chips flaked off. He then crashed to the ground in an unmoving heap, a small groan escaping his crumpled form. Arbor stood there, holding the remains of the shattered spear, panting lightly as steam poured off his body.

He'd overdone it again, but since it had only been for a couple of seconds, it shouldn't be too bad.

There was a sound of slithering leather on steel as every dwarf in the room drew their weapons. None of them were sure of what had just happened, as Arbor had moved too quickly for any of them to see. One minute, the dwarf guard was rambling and jabbing at him with his spear and the next, he was lying ten feet away and Arbor was holding the splintered remains of his weapon.

"Put your weapons down!" This cry came from the king.

Arbor looked at him and was shocked to see a broad grin across his face.

"Excellent show!" he boomed, clapping his hands. "I've never seen anyone move like that in my entire life! And I can't think of anyone more deserving of punishment than young Jek over there."

Akkard's grin turned into a full-bellied laugh, and the dwarves looked on in confusion as their king had seemingly lost his mind. Finally calming down, then king motioned his guards out of the room.

"You may leave us now. If he wanted me dead, none of you would be able to stop him before he took my head, anyway."

He said this in an oddly cheerful voice, and the dwarves still didn't move, unsure whether they should really go. When they didn't immediately move, the king's expression changed in an instant.

"Why are you still here? That was an order from your king!" he roared, and the dwarves quickly obeyed, tripping over themselves to leave the room.

Two of them bent down on their way, grabbed the unconscious Jek, and dragged him out of the room by his arms. Akkard waited until they were all gone, then he slumped in his throne, a tired sigh escaping his lips.

Arbor could now see that Akkard had been putting on a strong front for his subjects. Once they were gone, however, he allowed his true weariness to show.

"I apologize for the rough treatment you've been subjected to since coming here," he began. "Some of the younger dwarves are overzealous and believe they know better than everyone how the kingdom should be run."

He rubbed the bridge of his nose, as if trying to fight an oncoming headache.

"Truth be told, we are in a great amount of danger, more than most know."

Arbor was slightly taken aback at the sudden transformation Akkard displayed. This wasn't at all what he'd been expecting a king to be like.

"What kind of trouble?" he asked, wondering why the king of dwarves, someone with thousands of warriors at his command, would be admitting something like this to him, a human he barely knew.

It was as if the king could read his mind, as he gave him a weary smile.

"You must be wondering why I'm confiding in a total stranger. Don't worry about that for now. I assure you that I have a very good reason to be confiding in you."

"And what possible reason could that be?" Arbor asked, his curiosity getting the better of him.

"That," the king said, pointing at his chest.

Arbor looked down to see that the items he kept around his neck had somehow managed to slip out of his shirt.

It must have happened during the fight, he realized, tucking the items away.

"I'm guessing that you're referring to the red pendant, and not the necklace," Arbor said in a dry tone. "What is it you know about the pendant, and why do you trust me because I have it?"

He needed answers. His family had been butchered in the pursuit for this pendant. He had to know what was so special about it.

"Unfortunately, it is not my place to tell you about that pendant."

Arbor opened his mouth to protest when Akkard held up a hand to forestall him.

"It's not that I don't want to tell you. It's more that I can't tell you."

The king rolled up his sleeve to reveal a small red mark in the shape of a diamond, with a winding pattern of confusing lines surrounding it.

"This mark was placed on me by someone on the day I ascended to the throne. He told me many secrets that day, things that you could scarcely imagine. That pendant you're wearing, and its significance were one of those secrets."

Akkard rolled down his sleeve, covering the mark from view.

"He placed the mark on me then, a powerful bit of magic that prevents me from speaking of anything he told me on that day."

Arbor was excited at this revelation. There was someone out there who knew what this was, and its apparent importance.

"There has to be something you can tell me. Please!" Arbor begged.

The king was silent for a moment, as if contemplating whether to say something or not. He finally decided on something as he nodded to himself a few times before speaking.

"I can only tell you what he told me after the seal was placed on me. The man said that one day, my entire nation would be at risk from a terrible threat. He told me that someone wearing your pendant would show up in my throne room and perform a feat of magic I'd never seen before. He told me that he would be our salvation, and here you are."

Arbor was shocked. How could someone he'd never met know he would come here at a time when the dwarves were in danger? He didn't doubt the king for a second as to whether he was telling the truth or not. Whoever this mystery man was, Arbor was almost positive he would meet him one day. He didn't know why, but that feeling had cemented itself within him when Akkard had finished speaking.

He took a deep breath and looked up to the king.

"How can I help?"

Akkard breathed a sigh of relief as Arbor asked that question and began his tale.

"There is a beast deep in the heart of this mountain. I don't know where it came from, but it has already claimed the lives of over three hundred good dwarves. I have sent a number of patrols down after it, and out of the six I've sent, only one has come back. Even that patrol didn't escape unharmed."

His face took on a pained expression and he had to fight to keep his emotions in check.

"My younger brother went down with one of the patrols. He hasn't come back."

"Why did you let your brother go after it?" Arbor asked. "If he's your brother, wouldn't that make him the prince?"

"He's young and headstrong. Probably thought he could kill the beast on his own. Foolish boy," Akkard answered. "I will grieve for my brother alone. Right now, I must think of my subjects."

Arbor nodded. He respected a man who could put his own grief to the side when more important matters needed his attention.

"What kind of beast is it that has you so afraid? Can't you just swarm it with dwarves? Don't you have thousands of warriors?"

Akkard shook his head at the question.

"I could send thousands against it, and we would probably win in the end, but how many hundreds of lives would it cost? I cannot, as a king, order dwarves into combat, knowing that most will definitely die."

Arbor nodded. He hadn't thought of that.

"I apologize for my callousness. Please forgive me," he said, bowing his head.

"No need for all that bowing and scraping," he said, waving his hand.

"To answer your earlier question, the beast haunting our mines is a Mythic Beast, one of the five Mythic Cats. These are creatures steeped so deeply in magic, that they have been known to wipe out entire civilizations with their fury. The few scouts who made it back gave a description of the beast and I believe that this is the Roc-Jaguar."

Arbor listened carefully as Akkard related his story. He didn't want to believe that such monsters could really exist.

"How can I possibly succeed where so many have failed?" he asked.

He already knew the answer before the king opened his mouth.

"The man told me you would be the one to defeat the threat, and after I witnessed your power, I must agree with him. I won't ask you to do this for free though," Akkard continued. "You told me that your sister was taken to Fivora. Is that correct?"

Arbor nodded.

"Well, I just happen to know where the rebel alliance, directly opposed to the king, is currently located. I also know that they are planning on attacking Fivora in a bid to free the slaves and hopefully gain some new recruits."

Arbor could see where he was going with this but let the king finish.

"If you kill the Roc-Jaguar for me, I will write you a personal letter of commendation. Present this letter to one of the co-founders of the rebels and they will take you with them when they attack Fivora," the king finished. "What do you say? Do we have a deal?"

Arbor stood there, thinking for a few moments.

He'd already made up his mind to do it. The proposal set forth by the king was too good an opportunity to pass up. He also didn't think he could say no after the story Akkard had told him. Someone had prophesied that this would happen. He wasn't a superstitious person, but even he could sense that there was something more going on here.

Finally, he gave his answer.

"I'll do it, but on one condition. You give my friend a safe place to stay while I'm gone, and should I die in the attempt, you will make sure she has a safe place to call home."

"You have my word," Akkard said gravely.

"You will be given rooms in a nearby inn," he continued after Arbor nodded his assent.

"Anything you need will be provided for you. All you have to do is ask. A guard will come for you in the morning to escort you to the entrance of the tunnels. The Almighty guide your blade, Arbor."

The king stood then and bowed his head in a sign of respect.

"Thank you, Your Majesty," he answered back.

He then bowed his head once, and with that, he turned on his heel and headed out of the throne room.

18

Arbor was sitting on the bed in the room he'd been given by the king. A candle was the only source of light, the flickering flame sending weird shadows dancing across the walls. The dwarf who'd escorted him here had told him that Grak would be there shortly.

So now he waited, letting his meeting with the king replay in his mind. There was someone out there who could see into the future. They had predicted these events years before, when Akkard had first taken the throne.

He was brought out of his musings by a knock on the door. He stood to open it and found Grak standing in the hall, looking confused but happy.

"Can I come in?" she asked.

Arbor stood aside and let her walk in, closing the door behind her. She looked around the room before going to sit down in the only chair. Arbor, for his part, just went back to sit on the bed.

"I don't know how you managed to get me out," Grak began, "But it seems that I owe you my life once again."

"You don't owe me anything," Arbor said, waving it off. "Without you, I'd never have made it here, or been given the opportunity the king has offered."

"What opportunity?"

Arbor then explained what Akkard had told him, about the Roc-Jaguar, and about helping him find the rebels. He decided to leave out the part about a stranger predicting this would all come to pass. For some reason, he felt he should keep that particular piece of information to himself.

Grak sat quietly through his story, then sat up straighter in her chair once he finished.

"I'm coming with you," she said simply.

"No!" Arbor answered back. "I won't knowingly put you in that kind of danger. Not when you will be safe staying here."

Grak's face went a bit redder, and she seemed to bristle at this.

"Listen to me, Arbor, and listen well. I'm not some child or helpless maiden that needs to sheltered and protected! I can handle myself in a fight. I will be coming with you, and nothing you can say will stop me!"

Arbor sat back, shocked at the tirade coming out of the usually quiet woman. He just nodded dumbly as she got up. She approached him then and embraced him.

"You don't need to do everything alone," she said quietly.

He was surprised at the sudden show of affection but returned the hug in kind. She felt warm and reassuring, and he could distinctly feel her body heating up as she was pressed to him. He was also very aware that her heart rate had just spiked. When she pulled back, her breath was coming just a bit faster and her cheeks were flushed.

It was now very obvious to him that she liked him. He would have had to be denser than a brick not to realize that. And though he liked her as well and found her company enjoyable, he just couldn't bring himself to feel the same. Not after what had happened to him recently. He tried to give her a smile, though, to force his lips to turn upward, but it just wouldn't come. He still couldn't do it.

Instead, he settled for just thanking her.

"Thank you for that. I'm grateful that you're coming with me."

"Of course. I wouldn't leave you to face something like that alone," she said, her lips turning up slightly at the corners. "Now go get some sleep. Don't stay up tossing and turning all night. We have a big day ahead of us."

"I'll definitely try, but no promises," he said as she headed for the door.

"Do you need me to sing you a lullaby to help you sleep?" She turned from the open doorway, smirking at him.

Arbor shook his head and waved her off.

"I'll sing myself to sleep, but thanks for the offer."

He heard her giggling as she closed the door behind her and felt a pang of sadness. She had just reminded him of the way Karria used to tease him.

Despite his feelings of melancholy, he did feel a lot better about the day ahead. Grak just had a way of lifting his spirits, and he was glad she'd be accompanying him on this dangerous mission.

Despite what Grak had said, he still had a hard time falling asleep that night. All he could think about was failing to kill the beast and dying before he could save his sister. He tossed and turned, and worried into the late hours of the night until an uneasy sleep finally took him.

Arbor awoke the next morning with a sense of purpose. He was tired, as he hadn't gotten much sleep. He got out of bed and washed his face in the bowl of water that had been left on the small table for him. Next to the bowl, there was a plate with bread, cheese, and a pitcher of some sort of fruit juice.

Arbor found that he was ravenous after foregoing a meal the previous evening, and quickly devoured the food. He'd never had this kind of fruit juice. It had a sweet and tangy flavor, and Arbor found that he really enjoyed it.

He heard a knock on his door then and went to open it. A dwarf stood there, holding Arbor's glaive and a set of leather armor.

"I'm sorry we couldn't get you better armor," the dwarf apologized. "We don't usually have human guests, so we didn't have any mail that would fit you."

"That's quite alright," Arbor said, taking the armor and his glaive.

He was surprised at the relief he felt to be holding his weapon again. He hadn't realized it until now, but he'd felt vulnerable without it.

"I've given the gremlin girl a set of armor as well, along with the long-bladed dagger you requested."

Arbor thanked the dwarf and closed the door to get changed. He donned the armor, first putting on the hardened leather breastplate, then sliding the bracers over his forearms. Next, he slid on the hardened leather greaves and pulled the straps tight around his legs.

There were also heavy boots, some sort of skirt that went from his waist to his knees, as well as a helm. He opted to forgo these, as they would likely impede his movement. He slung his leather harness over his shoulder and, checking to make sure the blade was sharpened, slid it into the sheath on his back. He quickly laced up his soft leather boots and jumped a few times to make sure that he could move well in what he was wearing.

Satisfied with the result, he left his room, closing the door behind him. Grak was already waiting for him and flashed him a warm smile. She was adorned in similar armor, with the addition of a metal-studded skirt. It was divided in half and leather straps bound the loose ends to her legs to keep them from impeding her movement. A long, heavy bladed dagger hung from her waist, and Arbor nodded to the waiting dwarf in approval.

"Well, now that you're all ready, follow me, and I'll lead you to the entrance of the mines," the dwarf said.

Arbor and Grak fell in step behind the dwarf as they headed out onto the street. It was oddly silent outside, and the streets were completely empty.

"The king decided it would be best to leave before anyone was up. Humans are rarely seen here, and gremlins are only seen when they're attacking. Best not to cause a panic."

"What do you know of this Roc-Jaguar?" Arbor asked, quickly steering the conversation away from that sensitive topic.

He wanted as much information as he could get about their upcoming battle and figured the dwarf might know a few things.

"I don't know much, only from what little the surviving scouts reported," he said.

They left the city behind and headed down one of the many tunnels, walking deeper into the mountain.

"From what they reported, the creature is massive and much faster than you might expect. But the thing to really watch out for are its claws," he continued, his voice echoing off the walls. "The claws could easily shred through the steel armor the dwarves were wearing."

Arbor looked down at his own leather armor in bemusement. If the steel armor offered no protection, what was the point of wearing the inferior leather?

"Can you tell us anything else about it?" Grak asked. "Is there anything else to watch out for?"

The dwarf nodded his head gravely.

"This is one of the five Mythic Cats, so it should go without saying that this beast has magic. I don't know exactly how it will use it, but we do know that it uses some sort of earth magic."

Grak gave Arbor a look then. There was fear and trepidation in that look, but also excitement. How could she be excited to face such a monster?

They approached another tunnel and the dwarf stopped.

"I will go no further than here," he said. "Just follow this tunnel and it will lead you down into the mines."

He removed a rolled-up piece of parchment from his coat pocket.

"This map marks the location where the beast was last seen," he said, handing it to Arbor. "Good fortune be with you."

The dwarf clapped his fist to his heart in a sign of respect.

Arbor and Grak bowed their heads, then turned to the tunnel entrance. It was darker than the tunnel in which they were currently standing. Arbor could see regular torches lighting the way instead of the glowing stones he'd become accustomed to.

"Ready?" he asked, looking over at Grak.

She flashed him a fierce grin, her blue eyes shining brightly in the flickering torchlight.

"Then let's go kill a monster."

And with that statement, the two friends stepped into the tunnel.

19

Karria looked on in wonder as she and Sylvester approached the Goldenleaf Forest. Tall thin-trunked trees swayed before her. True to their names, the tops of the trees were all full of golden colored leaves and seemed to glimmer in the sunlight.

"Do they always look like this?" she asked Sylvester in awe.

"Yes, the leaves never change color in the forest. They never fall or die either," he said, looking at the trees with a smile on his face.

"It's always warm in the forest. Just like the Flatlands, winter never truly reaches this place."

"Wow!" Karria said, as they left the Flatlands and entered the forest.

Sylvester was right. Although the Flatlands were hot all year round, the Endless Wood and been becoming colder as winter set. It had become instantly hotter the moment they'd stepped out of the woods and onto the Flatlands.

The air cooled as they entered the shade of the trees and though it was cooler than the Flatlands, it was by no means cold. The air was pleasant and smelled of wildflowers and tree sap.

"So, how far is the magic school from here?" she asked, a light bounce in her step.

It was so nice to have shade again, after being out on the open Flatlands for so long.

"I'm actually not sure," he admitted. "I do know the way to the nearest settlement, though, and I'm sure they'll be able to direct us to the capital, which is where the school is located."

Karria nodded as she looked around. The forest was alive with sound, small rodents scurried through the underbrush and birds flitted about overhead. Sunlight shone through the leaves, painting the entire forest in a golden hue.

"So, tell me about the school. What's it like? I've never been to a school before. Are there lots of students there?"

"Slow down!" Sylvester said with a laugh. "One question at a time."

Karria blushed a little and smiled sheepishly.

"The school is in the outskirts of the capital city, which is called Srila. There are roughly seven hundred students, ranging from age thirteen all the way to twenty-two."

"Wow," Karria exclaimed. "They have students that old still in school?"

"Yes, though many don't stay that long," Sylvester said. "Only the truly gifted stay after the obligatory six years of training."

" I will have to stay for six years if I want to join?"

"I don't know," Sylvester shrugged. "You are the only human that I know of to come looking to be admitted. Most humans and gremlins go to the one in the capital city of Galmir."

"Oh," Karria said quietly. "Do you think they'll let me in?"

Sylvester gave her a reassuring smile.

"I'm sure you'll have no problem getting in."

Karria gave him a grateful smile, and they continued on in silence. After about an hour or so, she could begin to hear the sounds of civilization.

She heard the laughter of children at play and couldn't help but smile. They emerged onto a well-worn dirt path and she could see a village. A small cluster of houses built from the thin trunks of the Goldenleaf trees stood in a row, with the path winding through the center.

She could now see the children she'd heard earlier playing on the path ahead. They stopped playing as the two of them approached and stared with open curiosity at Karria.

Karria, for her part, just smiled and waved. They seemed hesitant at first, but soon smiled back and went back to playing their game. They continued down the path and into the village proper.

Approaching the first house, Sylvester knocked on the door. A young elf woman opened the door and they spoke for a minute. Finally, the elf gestured to a house in the center of the village, and Sylvester thanked her before returning to Karria.

"The leader of this village lives there," he said, pointing to the same house the elf woman had gestured to. "Just a warning- not everyone likes humans. Some elves have had their entire lives ruined by slavers, just like the ones who ruined yours."

Karria nodded soberly. If the only interactions she'd had with humans had been with people like Ramson, she would most likely hate them as well.

They approached the village leader's house and Sylvester knocked on the door. They waited in silence for a few moments before the door cracked open. An older elf stood in the doorway and looked at Sylvester, curiosity written on her face.

"Can I help you, dear?" she asked in a wary sounding voice.

"Yes," Sylvester said, putting on a winning smile. "My friend and I are headed to Srila to attend the Goldenleaf School of Magic but seem to have gotten lost. Would you by any chance have a map we could use?"

The elf woman's eyes narrowed as they fell on Karria, and she looked at Sylvester with suspicion.

"I've never heard of a human attending the school in Srila."

"This is a special exception," Sylvester answered. "They've already extended her an invitation. I was sent to guide her back, but I seem to have gotten lost."

There he goes again, lying right through his teeth, Karria thought, as she watched the exchange. She sometimes wondered how much about the elf was actually true.

The woman seemed to waver a bit but slowly nodded.

"I may have a map you can use," she said. "Just wait here and I'll go and get it."

She then closed the door in Sylvester's face, and he had to leap back to avoid breaking his nose.

Karria laughed loudly as he did so, but soon sobered as she noticed the distrustful gazes she was attracting from the other villagers. She tried to smile at them, but they just ignored the friendly gesture and kept watching her.

She had begun to fidget when the door opened again, and a map came flying out.

"There, you have it. Now leave!" She heard a voice from inside.

Not wanting to argue, and not wishing to stay a second longer, she scooped up the map and the two of them made their way quickly out of the village. Only once the village was out of sight did they slow to a more comfortable pace.

"I can see what you mean when you say they don't trust humans," Karria said with a frown.

"It is unfortunate, but the elves living the closest to the forest's edge are the ones most likely to be attacked. It shouldn't be nearly this bad in the capital," Sylvester said with a forced smile.

Karria wasn't so sure, but there was nothing she could do about it. She resolved herself to try and make a good impression on any further elves they might come across.

"Oh, here," she said, handing the map over. "I almost forgot."

Sylvester took the map and unrolled it, his brow furrowing as he looked it over.

"Good news," he said with a grin, rolling the map up. "Four days of walking, and we should reach the capital city."

That was good news. And it was about time too!

Karria was tired of sleeping on the road. She missed her bed, she missed normal food, but most of all, she missed her family. The thought saddened her and her good mood faded. She could have good food and a comfortable bed, but her family was another matter. She would never see them again.

She could feel tears beginning to form in the corners of her eyes but did not let them fall.

They walked on in silence. Sylvester, sensing that she would like to be alone with her thoughts, gave her space and focused instead on reading the map.

They camped for the night at the side of a stream. This cheered her up a little, as she hadn't been able to take a normal bath since they'd left Silver's clearing over two weeks ago. She went off to a more secluded part of the stream while Sylvester prepared supper.

It wasn't really what one would call a meal, just some dried meat and hard bread, but she knew it was only for the next few days. Once they reached Srila, they would have normal food once again.

She found a spot and quickly stripped out of her dust-covered clothes. Taking a deep breath, she plunged right in. The icy water robbed her momentarily of breath. After a few minutes of shivering, she became accustomed to it and was soon splashing about, enjoying the feeling of washing off weeks' worth of dust.

Once she was finished, she made sure to wash her clothes in the river as well. She wouldn't be able to wash all the dirt out until she had proper soap, but this would have to do for now. She wrung her clothes out as best she could and put them back on. They were still quite wet, but the air was pleasant and warm, and it didn't bother her too much.

She wandered into the camp and was surprised to see Sylvester turning a small animal on a spit over the fire.

He looked up at her approach and smiled. "I managed to snag this small forest rabbit with my magic. I used your knife to skin and gut it. I hope you don't mind."

"Not at all!" she said, sitting down by the fire. "So long as you plan on sharing."

"Well, I was going to eat it all myself, but…" Sylvester trailed off at Karria's deadpan expression and snorted out a laugh.

"Don't worry. I'll share it."

Sylvester then pulled the steaming meat from the fire and ripped it in half, hissing as the meat scorched his skin. He handed one of the pieces to Karria, juggling his own between his fingers. They both tore into the small animal with relish, ignoring the fact that the meat was still too hot. Karria burned her tongue more than once, but she didn't care. The two of them enjoyed the small animal immensely, and though it was not entirely filling, it was one of the best meals she'd eaten in weeks.

When the meat was all gone, she leaned back against one of the trees with a sigh of contentment. Looking up, she saw some sap oozing from a split in the bark. When she leaned in a little closer, she was surprised to find that it gave off quite a pleasant smell.

She mentioned this to Sylvester and was delighted when he explained that they used the Goldenleaf tree sap to make soap. Pulling the red dagger from its sheath, she scraped some off and went over to the stream to wash her face with it.

Karria lay down that night, more content than she could remember being in a very long time. Her face felt a little sticky from the sap, but she liked the way it smelled, so she didn't mind overmuch. She closed her eyes then and thought of Silver, wondering what the odd hermit could be doing now.

He had been so kind to her and taught her so much. She wasn't sure when, but at some point, she'd come to see him as a surrogate father figure and hoped to see him again soon.

She thought of her family next, of her mother and father. She hadn't had the time to think about their fates until now. Things had just been too crazy. She knew they were both dead. Sylvester had heard the slavers talking about how Ramson had butchered them both.

Then she thought of Arbor. She should be mourning for him as well, but she found that she just couldn't. Sylvester hadn't heard the slavers talking about him, so she still had hope he was alive. She felt the tears come then, hot and wet as they slid down her face. Silently sobbing to herself, she drifted into an exhausted sleep.

20

Arbor and Grak moved quietly down the torch-lit tunnel, careful not to dislodge any loose stones so as not to give away their position, should the Roc-Jaguar be nearby. They'd been descending into the mines for quite some time now and determined that, based on the map, they should be reaching an open area soon.

Arbor was on edge. The idea that a gigantic cat with razor-sharp claws could be waiting for him around every corner was extremely nerve-wracking. Grak didn't look much better. Her muscles were taut and she moved stiffly behind him, not at all like her usual graceful self.

He could see the tunnel widen up ahead and motioned for her to stay put. He moved forward, trying to be as quiet as he could, and peeked around the tunnel exit. The tunnel opened up into a wide-open space spanning several hundred feet in all directions. There were piles of ore in tall wooden bins, and the room was brightly lit by glow stones set in the walls.

Arbor breathed a sigh of relief when he didn't see anything out of the ordinary.

"You can come down now," he called up the tunnel.

The sound of shuffling feet and the creaking of leather marked Grak's arrival into the open cavern, and Arbor winced at the noise. It couldn't be helped, as he wasn't willing to tell her to remove the small protection the armor offered.

Grak leaned a bit closer as he unrolled the map, her warm breath tickling his cheek. Arbor ignored it as best he could, tracing a line down the path they'd taken, and finding where they were located. He could see that the Roc-Jaguar was last sighted in the next open cavern.

That didn't necessarily mean that it was still there, but it meant that it was likely to be close by. He rolled up the map and looked to his right. The tunnel that loomed before them would lead directly to the beast's last known location. He was about to step forward when Grak stopped him.

"Arbor, I have an idea."

He motioned for her to go on.

"You said that your magic could make you faster and stronger right?"

"It can," he confirmed.

"You also said, that in battle, you can sometimes predict an opponent's movements, is that correct?"

He nodded again, not entirely sure where she was going with this.

"So, it stands to reason, that your magic can heighten your other senses as well," Grak continued. "For example, you can improve your hearing, so the beast doesn't catch us by surprise."

Arbor had to think about it for a moment before giving her a grateful look. He hadn't even considered that his magic might be used in that way.

"That might actually work," he said excitedly. "Just give me a few minutes while I see if I can figure it out."

Grak flashed him a grin, her cheeks darkening at the compliment.

Closing his eyes, he felt for the streams of magic coming from the blue Core at his center. He could follow the lines more clearly now than he could previously and they stood out in sharp contrast against the black background of the rest of his body. He soon found the stream that connected to his head and concentrated very closely on it.

He tightened his focus, forcing himself to see only that one stream. Sweat began to bead his brow, but at last, he found what he was looking for. The main stream grew larger in his mind's eye, until he could see even smaller streams branching off that one. There were a lot more than last time, making him wonder if his magic was on its way to advancing to the next Tier. There were now at least thirty or so tiny streams flowing off the main one, and each connected to different parts of his head.

Following them carefully, he soon found a pair that connected to his eardrums. Working very slowly now, he allowed magic to flow from his Core, widening the smaller streams a bit to accommodate more magic.

The moment he did so, he hunched over in pain as sound assaulted him from every direction magnified many times over.

"Are you alright?"

He winced once more. Grak's whispered question sounded as though she'd screamed in his ear, but a hundred times louder.

He quickly cut the magic off and sighed in relief when sound returned to normal. He took a shaky breath and looked over at Grak.

"I'm going to try again, just please don't talk until I say so. The sound is just too overwhelming."

He waited until she nodded her understanding, then gathered himself and tried again. This time when he allowed magic to flow to his ears, he didn't widen the streams at all. He instead allowed only the barest trickle of magic to flow up to them.

He took another shaky breath. The smaller streams seemed to be a lot harder to work with than the larger ones.

His hearing suddenly sharpened, but not so much as to cause him pain. He could now acutely hear all the sounds around him. The sound of his and Grak's breathing, the small scuffs their boots made on the ground, the sound of their beating hearts.

Arbor froze and listened carefully. He counted to himself. *One... Two... Three!*

His eyes snapped open to see Grak's face just a few inches from his, her expression worried. Arbor took a moment to calm his racing heart and release the magic flowing to his ears. He then explained what he'd heard and what it insinuated.

"From which direction was it coming?" she whispered.

Arbor pointed to the tunnel, the one that led to where the Roc-Jaguar was last sighted.

"Then I guess we've found what we're looking for," she said, pulling the dagger from her belt with a soft hiss.

Arbor nodded. Drawing his glaive, he walked towards the tunnel with her in tow. They moved quickly, fearing the creature might be moving towards them even as they moved closer to it. It was often that the hunter became the hunted when one became careless.

They came to the end of the tunnel without being attacked. The two of them shared one last look, then, moving together, they entered the open cavern, brandishing their weapons and ready for a fight.

There was nothing there.

Arbor looked around in confusion. The cave was empty.

He looked up, but aside from the glow stone affixed to the ceiling fifty feet above, there was nothing up there. The cave was massive, spanning at least three hundred yards across with small ridges of stone extending from the walls, giving it a rough and uneven appearance.

Grak moved up beside him, her dagger still drawn.

"I don't understand," she said, looking around. "Didn't you say there was another heartbeat coming from this direction?"

Arbor didn't understand either. He closed his eyes and concentrated once again. It was a lot easier this time as his body seemed to have memorized exactly how much magic was needed. His hearing sharpened and he could once again hear another heartbeat. When he looked around, though, there was nothing to be seen.

"I hear another heart beating in this cave," he whispered back. "It has to be here."

They walked forward cautiously, making their way through the cave. They looked at the walls, the floor, and up at the ceiling again, but still saw nothing.

"Maybe you're doing something wrong?" Grak asked.

Arbor just shrugged helplessly as she walked over to a small protrusion of rock and sat down. The tension was draining, both physically and mentally. She jumped up with a very uncharacteristic shriek as the rock she'd just sat on cursed loudly.

"What the hell do you think you're doing, lass? Did I not suffer enough at the cruel paws of that overgrown excuse for a cat? Or do I perhaps look like a comfy chair to you? Maybe you thought you'd rest your weary gremlin behind on a poor dwarf's head for a laugh? Well, let me tell you something, missy. I will not be treated as furniture by anyone!"

The dwarf continued his tirade as Arbor and Grak looked on in shocked amusement. Now that he looked carefully, he could make out some facial features.

"I guess this explains the third heartbeat," Grak said as she eyed the dwarf.

Realizing that no one was responding to his rant, the dwarf stopped and glared at the two of them.

"Well?" he said, clearly outraged. "Are you gonna help me out or not?"

"My apologies," Arbor said as he moved over and got down on his knees near the dwarf's head.

As far as he could tell, the dwarf was encased in solid rock and Arbor had no idea how to get him out. He looked to Grak for help, but she just shrugged.

He looked to the dwarf instead.

"How am I supposed to get you out?"

"Well, obviously, you have to break up the surrounding stone," the dwarf replied, in a tone that suggested that he was an idiot.

"I can see that," Arbor replied, sorely tempted to just leave the dwarf there. "What I meant to ask was, how do I break up the stone?"

The dwarf sighed loudly and rolled his eyes upwards as if begging the heavens for strength. Arbor could hear Grak giggling behind him, but decided it was best to ignore her.

"If you look to your right, a small way across the room, you will see a hammer. Pick it up and use it to free me."

The dwarf spoke very slowly, saying each word with exaggerated care.

Arbor sighed and stood to get the hammer. He found it, exactly where the dwarf had said it would be. He lifted it, surprised at the weight of the thing and examined it closely. One side of the hammer head was broad and flat, while the other tapered off to a wicked spike.

He walked back to the dwarf, who seemed to be growing impatient.

"Well? Did you find it?" he asked.

Arbor had had enough of the dwarf at this point. It was time to put him in his place.

"From what I gathered from your earlier tirade, I'd guess the Roc-Jaguar buried you here for some reason, am I correct?" Arbor asked.

"Yes. Someone should give you a friggin' medal for figuring it out. Now get me out of here!" the dwarf yelled again.

"No, I don't think I will. All you have done since we found you is complain. You've also been treating me like I'm some sort of moron. I think we'll leave you for the giant cat, though I'm not sure if it'll even *want* to eat you. Thanks for the hammer, though. I bet I can get some good money for it. Come on Grak, we're leaving," he called over his shoulder as he walked away from the dwarf.

Grak looked surprised at this statement but shrugged and hurried to follow.

"Wait!" the dwarf called out in panic.

Arbor just kept on walking.

"I'm sorry!" the dwarf called again. "I've been down here for days without food or water. Please don't leave me here to die!"

Arbor stopped then and turned around.

"I will free you," Arbor said.

The dwarf opened his mouth to thank him, but Arbor cut him off.

"On one condition, though. You will formally apologize to my friend and I for all of your earlier comments. Otherwise..." He let the threat hang.

The dwarf was quick to agree and apologized profusely, going so far as to praise them for their bravery and good looks. Arbor just rolled his eyes and walked back to him. He worked swiftly, breaking up the stone around the dwarf. Once he was done, he grabbed him by the arm and hauled him out of the hole.

"Thanks for that, lad," he said as he dusted himself off.

He was about average height for a dwarf, around four and a half feet. He had a short beard, meaning he was quite young, though he couldn't tell what color the beard was, due to all the dirt. He had broad, wide-set shoulders and was quite muscular as well.

Arbor passed the dwarf a waterskin, and he took it gratefully, taking a long sip and swirling it around in his mouth, before spitting it out. He then took another sip, swallowing this time and smacking his lips. He took a few more sips and splashed a bit onto his face and hands.

Arbor could now see his features more clearly and thought he looked sort of familiar.

"I thank you for your timely rescue," he said, bowing slightly to the two of them. "Without your help, I'd have been that beastie's next meal. I owe you a debt."

Arbor nodded at the statement, agreeing wholeheartedly with him. He wasn't about to forget all the insults, even if the dwarf had apologized.

"The name's Hordvig," the dwarf said. "But everyone just calls me Hord."

"Well, I'm Arbor, and you already know Grak," Arbor said in the way of introduction.

"So, tell us, Hord. What are you doing down here?" Grak asked.

Here, Hord started to get worked up.

"Well, I was a part of the last patrol sent down to find out what kind of beast was haunting these halls. My entire patrol escaped, except for me, of course. Just ran and left me for dead! Cowards, all of them!"

Arbor was shocked that they could do such a thing. He couldn't understand how someone could leave a friend behind just to save themselves.

"Tell me, Hord," Grak said, walking over. "What would you do if you saw any of them again?"

"I would drag them all in front of the king as cowards and deserters!" he proclaimed angrily.

"But what would that accomplish?" she asked. "The king told us of all the people it already killed. Would you see more of your countrymen die, just to satisfy a grudge?"

Arbor was a little surprised that Grak, of all people, would care about the lives of dwarves. Most of them hated her kind with a passion, though there did seem to be a few exceptions.

Hord stood there for a moment, thinking.

"When you put it that way, it does sound a bit petty. I suppose I'd like to give 'em a good wallop, but I wouldn't want them killed on my behalf," he admitted grudgingly.

Grak nodded, satisfied with his answer.

"I think we should take him with us when we leave Heart," Grak said, turning to him. "I think he'd make a good addition to our team, and it would give us a better chance at rescuing your sister."

Arbor thought on that for a moment. He'd been skeptical about the dwarf at first, but anyone willing to put aside a personal grudge in favor of the greater good, was alright in his book.

"You know, I think you're right. That is an excellent idea."

She flashed him a grin and the two of them turned towards the dwarf, who looked outraged.

"Hold on now!" he began. "I never agreed to any of this! If you think I'll just go waltzing off on some hair-brained adventure, then you've got another thing coming!"

Arbor had been waiting for the dwarf to finish his latest rant and was opening his mouth to give the dwarf a piece of his mind when a loud roar shook the cavern. They all stopped talking and turned slowly, as a creature that even their worst nightmares would fear emerged from the opposite tunnel.

21

When Arbor had been younger, a traveling menagerie had come through Woods' Clearing. He remembered seeing all kinds of animals that day, from wildcats to deer to strange massive animals with leathery skin and huge noses, but a few really stood out to him. The jaguar they'd had was definitely one of those creatures.

The big cat had been just over six feet from nose to tail and was around three feet at the shoulder. It had had golden brown fur and black floral markings with small spots inside, over its entire body. Arbor remembered thinking that it was one of the most beautiful, and terrifying creatures he'd ever seen.

The Roc-Jaguar slowly stalking towards them looked just like the one he'd seen back then, but with a few major key differences. The first of which was the creature's size. The beast was at least eighteen feet from nose to tail and stood more than seven feet at the shoulder.

Its fur was a swirling mix of deep greens and browns, and the spotted floral pattern on its coat was white and red, instead of the usual black. Its eyes were a bright green and seemed to glow in the dim lighting of the cavern, and its muzzle was bunched up in a snarl.

The beast roared then, nearly deafening them and shaking the entire cavern with its rage. Arbor could see massive silvery canines as its mouth opened wide, and he could feel his heart rate increase yet again. He knew they only had seconds before the beast attacked, so he turned to Grak and Hord.

"I'll draw its attention," he said quickly as he began pumping his magic through himself. "While I've got it distracted, you two attack from the rear."

There was no time for argument, so the two of them just nodded. The giant cat roared one more time, then bounded forward, the mass of muscle along its body rippling as it moved. The solid rock beneath it cracked as it leaped into the air, the monster covering the three hundred-yard gap in a matter of seconds.

Arbor had expected the jaguar to be fast, but even with his body enhanced, he barely managed to avoid its first attack. He rolled quickly to the side, hearing the swish of deadly claws from above him. Holding his glaive close to his body, he completed the roll and came up in a defensive stance.

The beast turned on the spot, swiping out with its glittering claws once more and he barely managed to step back, twirling the glaive and slamming the spiked end into its jaw. The blow staggered the cat for a moment but didn't seem to do any real damage. The jaguar roared, its muscles bunching up. Arbor immediately dove to the side, his only thought on staying alive. As it turned out, he was lucky that he had, as the mass of muscle and tearing claws leaped through the spot he'd been occupying just a split second previously.

He turned, expecting to see the cat slam into the wall, but instead was surprised to see the jaguar was now *on* the wall, its razor claws easily slicing through the stone. The giant cat looked down at him, its gleaming eyes focused purely on its next meal. Arbor took a deep shuddering breath to calm himself, then as the jaguar lunged from the wall, dove out of the way once again, narrowly avoiding its deadly claws.

If they could slice through solid stone with such ease, he had no doubt that his squishy body wouldn't hold up much better.

He rolled to his feet, and the jaguar turned to face him, roaring in frustration at missing its mark yet again. Arbor swallowed hard and braced himself. This fight would not be an easy one, and if they survived, it would be a miracle.

Grak watched as the jaguar flew at Arbor and felt her heart flutter in fear as he narrowly avoided its first attack, then the second and third. She shook herself and charged forward, drawing her dagger as she went. Coming up behind the creature, she slashed out at its hind leg, attempting to cut a tendon. When she finished her pass, she looked back in triumph, expecting to see the cat crippled and falling to the ground.

Her mood quickly changed to one of dismay, when she saw the creature was completely unharmed. Worse, her dagger had lost its edge and was now looking more like a serrated and twisted hunk of metal.

"Arbor!" she called out in panic as he dodged around the cat, "the fur is too tough for me to cut!"

Arbor was doing his best to dodge the creature when he was momentarily distracted by Grak's warning. The jaguar roared as its paw extended out in a sideways swipe, its razor-sharp claws extending a full foot as it did so. It caught him unawares, as he hadn't been expecting the claws to give the cat extra reach, and now he was right in the path of the oncoming claws.

With a roar, Hord came barreling in from the side, his hammer crashing into its skull and sending the monster reeling. The Roc-Jaguar's claws just nicked the front of Arbor's hardened leather breastplate, but even that small contact was enough to tear massive gashes in the armor.

Arbor looked at his chest in shock where he could see four thin lines of blood begin to well up through the destroyed armor. That only seemed to underline the true danger they were in. One small mistake and that would be it. He looked at the stunned jaguar for a second, noting that it was down still down.

Now was his chance.

Arbor ran at the downed cat, letting his magic propel him forward at an incredible speed. He could feel his core thrumming as it sent the blue power racing through his veins, following the streams that seemed to be multiplying by the day. He leveled the blade at the jaguar's eye, intending to spear it right through. His reflexes had sped up to keep up with his heightened speed, and those reflexes were the only thing that kept him alive.

The Roc-Jaguar roared, its body seeming to glow with an inner light, and a shower of stone rained from the ceiling, falling with far greater speed than gravity should allow. He instinctively pumped a little extra magic to one of his legs, feeling the skin heat up and his muscles twinge in pain. All the same, he was fast enough, avoiding the shower of stone as he threw himself to the side. The rocks smashed into the ground, sending a cloud for dust into the air and shrapnel flying in all directions.

The stinging stone was mostly repelled by his armor, but a few hit his face and exposed arms. He was quick to scramble to his feet though, ignoring the pain and backpedaling towards Hord, who was looking both terrified and impressed.

"Well, that was something," Hord said as the dust cloud began settling.

"How are we supposed to beat that thing?" Arbor panted, keeping his eye on the dust cloud. "And how did you manage to hurt it when Grak's dagger didn't do a thing?"

"My hammer is enchanted so it will never break," the dwarf said with a shrug. "It could also be that since the beast is so full of magic, that only magic can really hurt it."

That made a weird sort of sense to him.

"Is there any way to stop it without magic?"

The dwarf was more knowledgeable than him in the art of battle, so his opinion would be invaluable at a moment like this.

"There are still has a few vulnerable areas, like the eyes and mouth. Aim for those and even a non-magical weapon should do the trick."

The beast was shaking off the effects of the blow and was slowly getting to its feet. The two of them backed away as the creature turned its head towards them and roared in rage, taking a stumbling step forward.

"Alright, then. Aim for the weak spots. Maybe we'll get lucky and hit one."

Hord nodded as the beast shook off its stupor and lunged at them once more. Arbor darted forward, far quicker than the stockier dwarf, and slashed at the beast's head, aiming for the eyes once more. The jaguar responded by somehow pulling a wall of stone up to intercept the weapon. His blade clanged uselessly off the stone and he was forced back, catching another glancing blow on his right bicep.

He grimaced as blood began seeping from the wound, but didn't have time to dwell on it, as the beast exploded through the wall of stone and leaped at him, its jaws gaping wide.

Hord slammed into it from the side once again, roaring as his crackling hammer sent the beast staggering back. The Roc-Jaguar was quicker to recover this time, sending a hail of stone at them and forcing them to take cover. It pounced, this time at Hord, and Arbor took the chance to hit it from the side, making sure to use the blunt spike instead of the blade.

As though it had eyes in the back of its head, the jaguar defended itself, pulling up a layer of stone in time to intercept. He growled in annoyance, leaping back to avoid those dangerous claws, when Hord's hammer slammed into it, shattering the stone and knocking the jaguar off its intended course.

"How you holding up, lad?" Hord asked.

The dwarf didn't look much better off than he did. His arms were covered in splotchy bruises from where the stones had hit, and he was bleeding from a cut above his temple. The Roc-Jaguar, on the other hand, seemed to still be perfectly fine.

This was not good. There was no way that just he and Hord could defeat this powerful beast on their own. They needed more magic. No one else was down here, though. It was just the three of them.

Arbor's thoughts came to a crashing halt, as he remembered the Core of power he'd felt in Grak's spine while healing her. He'd wanted to tell her about it, but there just hadn't been any time up until now. If he could somehow awaken her magic, they should have a fighting chance.

"I need you to try and hold the beast for five minutes. Do you think you can do that?" Arbor asked, turning to the dwarf.

Hord looked at him as if he'd lost his mind.

"I have a plan, but I'll need a few minutes," Arbor explained already turning away from the recovering cat. "This may just give us a fighting chance."

Hord nodded reluctantly. He must have also noticed their precarious situation and knew that if something wasn't done quickly, they would all surely die.

"I can't promise you five minutes, but I'll hold it as long as I can."

Arbor slapped him on the back and darted off towards Grak, who was hanging back and looking on in frustration at her inability to help. He tore the now useless breastplate from his chest as he ran, tossing it to the side. He could hear the dwarf cursing and the cat yowling behind him but didn't look back, hoping against hope that he could hold out. He came to a stumbling halt in front of Grak and began speaking in a rush.

"I have an idea of how you can help, but I don't have much time to explain, so just please hear me out."

She nodded, allowing him to continue without asking any questions.

"When I healed your leg on the way to Heart, I could feel something inside you. I'm not one hundred percent sure, but I think you may have magic, though it seems to be dormant at the moment. Will you let me try to awaken it?"

Grak's eyes had gone wide as saucers by the time he finished speaking and she seemed to have to think about it for a moment, biting her lip in indecision. A roar came from where Hord was battling the jaguar, and that seemed to make her mind up for her. Nodding her head, she extended her arm to him.

"Just try to be quick. I don't know how much longer he can hold out on his own."

Arbor nodded, then took her hand in his and closed his eyes, taking a deep breath. He concentrated hard on moving his magic through his hands and into her, pumping it through the streams in his body for all he was worth.

As with last time, he felt his magic resisting him and trying to stay in his body. And just like last time, he forced the magic through, enforcing his will over the power, and was soon sending it towards the center of her spine. He couldn't be positive, but the amount of power he was channeling seemed to be far greater than before. And if he wasn't mistaken, he was nearing the limits of Tier 1, pushing on the bounds of the 2nd Tier.

It didn't take him long feel the pulsing pool of energy located at the center of her spine and he had to wonder why her Core was in a different spot than his. He mentally shrugged at that, deciding to try and figure it out later, when their lives weren't hanging in the balance, and continued working.

First, he tried to pierce the Core with his own magic, but as soon as it came within a few inches, it was violently repelled by an invisible force. He grunted in pain as his body began straining with the effort of using so much magic at once. He tried next to surround the Core with his own magic, squeezing down as hard as he could. But he once again found that he was being blocked by that invisible barrier.

Grak squeezed his hand then - and pretty hard, too. He hadn't realized how much physical strength the girl had up until now.

"Arbor, whatever you're doing, hurry up. I don't think Hord can last much longer!"

151

He decided to try one last time to pierce the Core, but this time, poured a lot more power into it. He heard Grak gasp as he pumped as much magic as he could into her. He felt his skin grow hot and was sure that if he opened his eyes, he would see steam pouring off his skin in waves.

He concentrated all his power into one point, sharpening it to a needle-thin blade, and drove it into the Core. It resisted him at first, the invisible barrier holding him at bay. But just when he thought it would fail, the barrier finally gave, and his magic pierced the Core.

There was a massive explosion as the long dormant magic awoke in Grak. The force rippled out of her in a wave, blasting Arbor off his feet and sending him flying back, where he crashed to the ground. Luckily, he'd gotten a split-second warning of the incoming danger and managed to tuck himself into a ball, rolling to avoid any injury.

Getting slowly to his feet, Arbor watched the gremlin in amazement, as a cold mist began pouring off her body, coating the ground with frost.

She looked at him and he could see the disbelief in that gaze. Arbor felt the thrill of success as he got quickly to his feet and rushed over to her, feeling the chilly air surrounding her body as he drew near.

"You did it!" she said, as a wide smile spread across her face. "I never knew there was even a shred of magic in me."

She looked at him, her eyes shining with gratitude. And something else.

"No, really. It was nothing. I was happy to help," he said, trying to deflect her gratitude.

"No, it wasn't nothing. Thank you. Without your intervention, my magic would never have awoken."

She paused, her cheeks flushing furiously as she looked down at the ground and began fidgeting.

"I...Um..." She began, as though having a hard time saying what she wanted.

Arbor just shuffled awkwardly, unprepared at the amount of emotion pouring off the woman and afraid of what she would say next. He was saved from answering when Hord went flying across the room with a loud curse and slammed into the opposite wall.

That gave him the excuse he needed, and he drew his weapon once more, turning quickly towards the beast.

"Looks like we're out of time. I don't know if you have any idea how to use your magic, but you have to try."

"Don't worry about me," she said, seeming to have overcome her embarrassment

A devilish smile worked itself onto her face, and the cold intensified somewhat.

"I think I'll manage just fine.

He shivered at the sudden change in temperature and gave her an admiring look. It had taken him weeks just to use the slightest bit of magic once he'd discovered it. It seemed that she was talented after all!

"I'll distract the beast and you strike it from behind. Sound good?"

He waited for her to nod before dashing toward the giant jaguar, taking its attention off the unconscious Hord. As he ran, he could see that Hord had somehow managed to bloody the beast's head a bit, but that seemed only to enrage the creature instead of putting it down.

Arbor nimbly dodged a swipe from its claws as it closed with him and he darted forward, jabbing the spiked end of his glaive at its eyes and nose. He quickly pulled it back, as the beast snapped its jaws at the offending weapon.

Arbor spun the weapon and pumped magic down the streams in his arms. The blade came abound in a blur, too fast for the cat to dodge, and neatly sliced across its nose, drawing a line of blood. He was thrilled when the beast let out a howl of pain as the blade cut into it, thinking that he now had a real chance at success.

His happiness was short-lived, however, when the beast swiped back and he foolishly tried to block the attack, thinking his strength would be enough. What he forgot was that his blade wasn't nearly as strong as he was. The Roc-Jaguar's razor-sharp claws sliced through the blade as it if were made of paper, the blade falling to the ground in four neatly sliced sections, leaving Arbor holding a four-foot pole with a metal spike at the end. He stared in shock for a second, then quickly danced back, narrowly avoiding another swipe of its massive claws.

Arbor was extremely saddened at the loss. His glaive, the weapon he'd had since leaving his hometown, was now little more than an ironbound pole with a pointy end.

The creature slunk forward, teeth bared in a hateful growl and its eyes glowing malevolently. Arbor tried to step back, but the Roc-Jaguar roared again, using some of its vast stores of magic. Arbor felt the ground beneath his feet give out, and he sank up to his knees into the solid stone.

The beast pounced on him then, and Arbor quickly pushed the broken-off glaive haft between them in an attempt to stave it off. The monster's front paws landed on it, dropping its entire weight on him, its claws extending, but not quite reaching him. Arbor grunted and flooded his arms with magic, holding the beast's immense weight off himself, but he could already feel his body straining.

There was no way he'd be able to hold out for long. If he was at the next Tier, perhaps, but he wasn't quite there just yet. All his hope now lay in his gremlin companion. He just hoped she would be strong enough to take the beast down.

Grak could see that Arbor was in trouble and knew that she had to act immediately. She could feel her magic now, pulsing slowly through her. She had never dreamed that she, a weak and ostracized gremlin, would one day wield magic.

This was yet another thing Arbor had done for her. Her slowly budding attraction towards the handsome and sober man had turned to full-blown infatuation after what he'd just done. But all the same, she was becoming a little annoyed at how much she owed him already. How would she be able to repay this?

She shook herself from her thoughts, focusing on the task at hand.

Now was not the time to be thinking about this. She needed to concentrate and help him. Otherwise, she'd never get to tell him how she felt. Thanks to him, she now had power, and she would no longer be forced to watch from the side as others fought her battles. Arbor had saved her life on so many occasions. Maybe this time she could save his. That would be a great way to start evening the score and perhaps get him to cheer up a bit, or maybe even see her in a romantic light.

With that thought in mind, she closed her eyes and concentrated on finding the source of her magic.

She remembered what Arbor had told her about magic, about having to feel for the streams coming from her center. But despite feeling the power, she couldn't locate her Core, no matter how hard she looked. She concentrated harder, thinking she was doing something wrong, searching for the glowing sphere with the five streams extending out.

Where is it?!

It came to her then, and she remembered what Arbor had said about different types of magic. Maybe hers was in a different spot?

She concentrated once more, scouring her body until… There it was! A small pulsing Core at the center of her spine. She didn't see any streams coming off it, as Arbor had described his to have. Instead, the Core seemed to be sending pulses of energy up her spine and through her bones towards her hands. The power wasn't moving to the rest of her body, only to her arms.

This entire process only took around ten seconds, but in that time, the beast's body had grown noticeably closer to Arbor. Its claws already nicking his shoulder and drawing blood.

She growled long in her throat and started running towards the beast, thinking she understood now how to use her magic. She concentrated on her right hand, trying to make her Core pulse faster. She could feel the bones in her fingers growing icy cold as her power pulsed, and she grimaced at the unexpected pain.

Sharp icicles began to form over her fingers, making them claw-like, and the pain intensified. It felt like her bones were on fire. She pushed on, sprinting forward and leaping at the Roc-Jaguar's back, letting out a wordless howl.

Slamming into the beast, she buried her icy claws into its hind leg and felt cold radiate out of them in a wave. She screamed in pain as her arm burned with the cold pulsing through the bone. It was almost unbearable. She'd never hurt so much in her entire life.

She wasn't the only one in pain.

The jaguar howled as its limb froze solid within a matter of seconds. It kicked its leg violently, dislodging Grak and sending her flying back, slamming into the opposite wall. But even as she lay there, gasping for breath, she could see that the damage had already been done.

The beast was bearing down on Arbor, its wickedly sharp teeth only inches from his face. His shoulders were bleeding profusely now, as the sharp claws tore into the skin and even his magically enhanced strength was failing, unable hold that kind of weight for so long.

Steam poured off his arms in waves, and he screamed in pain as his muscles tore themselves apart from the overuse of magic. He knew that they would be giving out any second now, and then the beast would kill him.

Just as his arms were about to give out, the beast gave out a roar of pain and jerked back. Its paws left the shaft of his weapon, and its claws retracted, leaving him free, albeit exhausted. The jaguar's paws came back down on the ground with a thud, missing him by inches.

Arbor saw his opportunity and didn't waste a second, flooding his already tortured arms with even more magic. Then, screaming in pain and defiance, he lunged upward, burying the spiked end of his glaive a full two feet into the eye of the Roc-Jaguar.

A shudder ran down the massive beast's body as the shaft penetrated deep into its brain. Then, as though in slow motion, it crashed to the ground, its head landing on Arbor's chest. He stared back into the beast's uninjured eye for a full five seconds, feeling a sharp tugging at his center as his core expanded. He didn't know how, but he'd managed to make it to the end.

Despite the pain he was in, he let out a whoop of joy. The beast was dead, and he'd finally made it to Tier 2!

22

Arbor felt more exhausted than he ever had before in his entire life. He lay under the Roc-Jaguar's body, feeling his arms throbbing in pain. Despite his advancement to the next Tier, it seemed to have done nothing for his physical state.

When he decided that he'd spent enough time laying under the dead beast, he concentrated on the streams leading to his legs, flooding them with magic. After a few moments of work, he managed to free himself from the stone encasing them, pulling them out with a crack and a shower of rubble.

He got shakily to his feet, his arms hanging limply at his sides. The bleeding from the multiple lacerations the cat had inflicted were beginning to scab over, and seeing that he was in no immediate danger, he went over to check on Hord. Surprisingly enough, the dwarf appeared to be unharmed and began stirring after Arbor kicked him a few times.

The dwarf came to with a roar and launched himself at Arbor, who nimbly sidestepped the attack. Hord looked around wildly for a few more seconds, disoriented. His confusion cleared up when his eyes fell on the dead jaguar and a broad smile spread across his face.

He looked at Arbor, one eyebrow raised in an unasked question. Arbor simply nodded, and the dwarf let out a booming laugh that echoed off the cave walls.

"Killed that bastard right and good!" he boomed, seeming not even to have noticed the multitude of bruises covering his body.

Arbor went over to check on Grak next. She was sitting with her back against one of the walls, grimacing in obvious discomfort. She looked up as he approached and gave him a pained smile.

"You did it," she said, as he sat down next to her.

"No," Arbor said, giving her a meaningful look. "We did it. I'm not sure what you did, but you managed to hurt the beast badly enough to give me a chance to kill it."

Grak nodded, and then winced again.

Arbor noticed her hand then. Her body was shivering and her usually red skin had a blue tinge to it. What caught his attention most was her hand, which seemed to be missing a couple of fingers.

"Grak!" Arbor said in alarm, moving to examine the hand more closely.

"Don't worry about it," she said, trying to force a smile. "The price of winning and all."

"When did this happen? And what happened to your fingers?!"

"I used my magic to form ice onto my fingertips, but I didn't really know what I was doing. I stabbed the jaguar in one of its hind legs and froze it, but it kicked me off."

She grimaced again.

"The problem was that I froze my entire hand as well, and when I went flying back, two of my fingers cracked off. I think they're still stuck in the jaguar's leg."

Arbor took Grak's hand in his and examined it. Her second and third fingers were missing, and her entire hand was icy cold to the touch.

"Why is your hand so cold?" Arbor asked, concerned.

"I'm keeping it cold on purpose; otherwise the pain will be much worse," Grak said through clenched teeth.

Arbor stared at the hand for a few long seconds, his mind racing. There had to be something he could do about this. She couldn't go for the rest of her life without her fingers.

"I'll be right back. I want to check on something," he said, getting to his feet.

Grak just nodded and leaning her head back, she closed her eyes.

Arbor could feel his torn muscles and skin knitting itself back together as he approached the dead creature.

It was strange. His magic seemed to be a paradox. If he used too much, it would destroy him, but the moment he stopped, it would put him back together. And to top it all off, it would put him back, stronger than before.

He walked up to the massive hind legs of the jaguar, finding that one leg was indeed frozen solid. He marveled at what Grak had done mere moments after awakening her magic. She had paid a heavy price for using it though, but if he could find the fingers quickly enough, the price may not have to be permanent.

His eyes swept over the leg for a couple minutes, shifting the leg around until he finally found them. Two small, blue-tinged fingers were sticking out of the leg, and both were completely covered in ice. He carefully removed them from the leg, not wanting to cause any further damage. They were freezing cold to the touch as he carried them back, and he could soon feel them beginning to thaw.

Sitting down next to Grak, he shook her shoulder a few times as she'd started drifting off. This wasn't good. She was keeping herself too cold and her body was beginning to shut down as a result.

"Grak, wake up," he said, shaking her. "You have to release your magic. Otherwise, you'll freeze to death."

She blinked a few times, looking up at him in incomprehension. Her lips were tinged blue by now and she was shivering.

"You need to release your magic," Arbor reiterated. "Your body is too cold!"

She looked at him for another few seconds as she tried to clear the fog of pain from her mind. With a shudder, she started to regain her natural red color and Arbor took her injured hand in his once again.

He wasn't sure if he could reattach limbs, but he remembered his mother once telling him that if a finger was lost, it could still be reattached if done quickly enough. Holding the two severed fingers up to the stumps, he closed his eyes, feeling for the magic flowing through him. It seemed to be larger than before – a result of his advancement to the 2nd Tier – and he resolved to keep track and see if it was growing. There were many more streams flowing from the five main ones now, and smaller and smaller streams diverged off of them to form an intricate lattice work of magic pathways.

Arbor concentrated on the large streams to his hands and allowed the magic to flow down. He felt the familiar resistance, but forced it through, pushing his magic into Grak. He heard the expected gasp as his magic flowed into her and concentrated on where he could feel the greatest amount of pain.

He could see where the appendages had been severed, but he could feel that the nerves were all still alive. This would be very different than healing a cut or bruise. Those, he could feel. He couldn't feel where the severed fingers were, as they were no longer attached to her body. This would make it a lot harder for him.

Taking a few deep breaths to steady his nerves, he moved flows of his magic into the stumps. He then allowed his magic to leak out from the empty spaces at the ends and hoped that this would do the trick. His head soon began pounding with the effort, and a blinding pain began to form behind his eyes. Despite the pain, he just gritted his teeth and pushed on. His recently healed arms began twinging once more as he increased the flow of magic through them.

Finally, after what felt like ages, he began to feel a faint connection to the two missing fingers. The feeling became stronger as the time crawled by, and finally, he could fully sense them. He felt the thrill of success when his magic fully knitted the fingers back to her hand, and the nerves, bones, and tendons stitched themselves together.

He released his magic and felt the strain that had been building in his arms fall away. They still throbbed in pain when he opened his eyes, but at least they'd stopped tearing themselves apart. His eyes then moved up Grak's face, as he released her hand and allowed his arms to drop to his sides.

Her eyes were shining as she held it up, whole and unblemished. She flexed her fingers a few times, just to be sure she wasn't dreaming. A huge smile lit up her face. She threw her arms around him, laughing and crying at the same time.

"I can't believe it! I thought I'd lost them forever! Thank you! Thank you!" she sobbed.

Arbor, for his part, accepted it. He was aware of what he had just done, and he was glad to have helped her once more.

"It looks like I owe you, yet again," she said, pulling back with a small pout. "And I'd just evened the score by saving your life."

"You don't owe me anything. You are important to me, and if I have the power to help, I will."

Grak's face flushed a deep crimson, but she quickly covered it by sticking her tongue out at him.

"Easy for you to say. You didn't just have your fingers reattached."

Arbor just shook his head at her display.

"Is that any way for a lady to act?" he asked in mock annoyance.

"Who said anything about me be a lady?" she quipped.

Their banter was interrupted by Hord.

"Come over here. You'll want to see this."

He gave Grak an apologetic look, but she just waved him off.

"I'm fine. Go on. Go see what that lovely dwarf has to show you. And remind me to kill him for ruining a perfect moment."

This last bit was muttered under her breath, so Arbor didn't hear. As he approached the dwarf, who was on his knees before the dead monster, he could see that he'd been busy. He'd apparently cut all the claws out of the cat, as all sixteen were arranged on the floor before him.

"You cut out its claws?" Arbor asked.

"Indeed," Hord said with a wide grin. "Not many know this, but the claws of Mythic Beasts are made of a very rare metal, and the claws of one of the five Mythic Cats are the rarest of all!"

His grin seemed to widen even more at this, and he rubbed his hands together in glee.

"How rare is this metal really?" Arbor asked as he stooped to lift one of the claws.

As soon as he lifted it, he noticed how light it was. Way lighter than any metal of this size should be, in fact. It had to be magic of some sort.

The metal was deep brown in color with swirls of a deep green streaked throughout. He found this quite curious, as the metal had been a silvery color when they were still attached to the jaguar. Arbor felt at the tip with one of his fingers and winced as a small bead of blood welled up almost immediately. Gingerly, he handed the claw back to Hord, who took it with obvious care.

"Why is the metal green and brown now? Wasn't it a different color?" Arbor asked as he wiped his bleeding finger on his pant leg.

"The magic of the jaguar became infused in the claws once it was killed," Hord said as he examined one of them. "It really is quite fascinating!"

Arbor found it quite amusing that the gruff dwarf was becoming so excited over a few pieces of metal.

"So, would it sell for a lot of money in a city?" Arbor wondered.

"Sell it?! Are you crazy? This metal is one of the rarest and most powerful on the face of the planet! Is there some part of that you didn't understand?!" he asked, looking horrified at the very notion that he would want to sell it.

"No, I understood it just fine, but I have no use for it," Arbor said with a shrug.

The dwarf shook his head, wondering if Arbor's stupidity knew no bounds.

"This metal can be forged into the strongest magical weapons and armor in the world! I will not sell it!"

Arbor shrugged.

"Then don't sell it. By my count, five of those are yours," he said gesturing to the pile of claws. "There has to be at least fifty pounds worth of metal there, though it doesn't feel like it."

Hord nodded at that.

"Aside from it being the strongest magical metal, Mythicallium is also, by far and away, the lightest metal in the world."

"Mythicallium?"

"The name of the metal," Hord said waving his hand.

He stroked his beard for a moment as if contemplating something, then he looked at Arbor with a shrewd expression.

"Let me make you a bargain. I will make you any one piece of armor from this metal and forge you a new weapon."

He seemed to think for a second before nodding to himself.

"I'll throw in a weapon for the gremlin girl as well. In exchange, you'll let me have the rest."

Arbor could see a gleam in the dwarf's eye and immediately knew he was getting a really bad deal.

"Hord, you didn't answer my earlier question," Arbor said with a frown. "How much is that metal worth?"

Hord had the good grace to look embarrassed at this and sighed resignedly.

"The last time Mythicallium came to the market, it sold for just over five thousand gold an ounce," he grudgingly admitted.

Arbor gaped.

"So, what you're telling me," Arbor began in a tone threatening violence and severe bodily harm. "Is that each one of those claws is worth roughly eighty thousand gold. Is that correct?"

Hord nodded silently, taking a step back after seeing the expression on his face. It seemed that he now realized that he may have gone just a little too far in trying to cheat Arbor out of so much money.

"How about this," Hord said quickly. "I will forge you and the girl a weapon each. I'll also forge you one piece of armor, and I'll pay you six hundred thousand gold for the rest. What do you say?"

Arbor snorted out a laugh at that.

"And where do you plan on getting that kind of money?"

"Why, from the king, of course!" Hord said with a happy smile.

Arbor's disbelief turned to confusion.

"Why would the king agree to pay for all this metal?" he asked, already suspecting the coming answer.

"Oh, did I forget to mention?" Hord asked with a grin, "He's my brother!"

23

Arbor stood before the king of the Jagged Peaks, his hands clasped behind his back. Grak stood beside him and Hord was off to one side, quietly conversing with one of the guards.

Akkard had nearly broken down in front of everyone when Hord had come marching in, alive and well. The king had embraced his younger brother. Then he'd whacked him over the head and called him an idiot for going after the beast. Apparently, he'd been after the precious metals the beast naturally produced.

It had only then dawned on him that Hord was a prince, and since Akkard had no wife or children, he would be next in line to the throne, should the king die.

When Arbor had mentioned this to him, Hord just shrugged. He'd admitted that he had no interest in leadership and had said that in the event of Akkard's death, he would abdicate in favor of his cousin. He'd then wandered off with the metal to begin work on it, a look of unrepressed glee on his face.

After presenting themselves to the king with the good news, Arbor and Grak had gone back to their rooms for a well-deserved rest. Akkard had only seen them briefly but promised a longer meeting the next day.

Arbor had never been gladder to sink into a bed. He'd later found out from the dwarf who'd originally escorted them, that they'd been in the tunnels for two entire days.

He'd slept well that night. The cook had brought him a steaming bowl of beef stew and a loaf of warm crusty bread, along with a cold mug of beer.

Arbor had only rarely drunk alcohol. He always liked to be in control of himself but decided to ease up for the night and enjoy a mug or two. As soon as he'd taken his first bite, he'd found that he was ravenous. After using so much magic, it was hardly a surprise.

Grak had joined him in his room, bringing a chair with her, and the two had enjoyed a night of celebration for what they'd accomplished. Her eyes had nearly popped out of her head when Arbor had produced three hundred thousand gold worth of trader's notes and handed them over.

She'd insisted he keep it, saying that she had no need for money and that Arbor could make better use of it, but he would have none of it. After some argument, she'd grudgingly accepted the small stack of notes in denominations of ten thousand.

They'd spoken of their plans moving forward. Arbor wanted to leave as soon as possible and make for the rebel camp. Grak agreed with him, but they would have to wait for Hord to finish forging their weapons and armor before leaving.

So now they stood before the king five days later. They'd been confined to their rooms the entire time, and Arbor was already itching to leave. It would have been unwise for Grak to wander the city, and Arbor wasn't about to leave her alone to go exploring.

"First of all," began Akkard. "I must formally thank you for defeating such a mighty creature and saving my people." He stood and approached them. "Second, I must thank you for bringing my brother back, alive and well. I had not dared to hope that I would see him again, but you brought him back, and for this, you have my eternal gratitude."

Akkard embraced each of them in turn and went back to his throne.

"I am aware that Hord has been forging you each a weapon, but there is something I would like you to have."

A dwarf moved towards them, holding a soft pillow between his hands. He approached Arbor first, holding it up and presenting the contents. A shimmering brown and green armband sat on the pillow. It was exquisitely crafted, and Arbor lifted it up almost reverently.

There was a roaring jaguar's head engraved on the outside curve, and Arbor looked over to see that Grak had received a similar item, though hers was a wristband.

Arbor knew what it must have cost Akkard to make these precious gifts, and he bowed his head in thanks, sliding the armband over his left bicep.

"You honor us with such fine gifts, Your Majesty," Arbor said, and Grak mirrored his movement.

Akkard just waved away their thanks and smiled.

"You have given me something more precious than money can buy. This is but a small token of my appreciation."

He motioned another dwarf who was standing to the side.

"Now, to fulfill my end of the bargain."

The dwarf came forward, bearing a scroll with a wax seal.

"The rebels are located near the Giant Salt Lake in the Flatlands," he continued. "There is a secret entrance to their base, the location of which, I have had marked on your map."

Arbor took the proffered letter and the map with a nod of thanks.

Akkard continued to speak.

"I hear that my brother plans to accompany you on your travels. I am, of course, opposed to this idea, as I'm sure that you will be facing many dangers in the days ahead. However, this is his decision to make and I cannot force him to stay. I would ask you to look after him, though," he said with a sad smile. "He is the only family I have left."

Arbor nodded gravely.

"I promise we'll look out for him."

Hord approached then. He was carrying a bundle in his arms and set it down at Arbor's feet.

"Here are the items I promised you," he said with a grin, first pulling a long, slim sword from the cloth bundle.

Arbor's eyes immediately locked onto the weapon. He'd never seen a sword like that before. It was beautiful and deadly, all at the same time. The brown blade was long and slim, tapering to a wicked point at the end. The hilt, in contrast, was a deep green and was downturned and rounded.

"This is called a rapier," Hord said, handing the weapon over to Grak. "I figured you should have something with a little more reach than a dagger. It's light enough for you to use and strong enough to handle the toughest opponents."

"How did you manage to separate the two colors of the metal from one another, and why do it in the first place?"

Arbor was quite curious and Hord was more than happy to oblige, launching into an explanation with obvious glee.

"Well, that's the interesting part, isn't it? When I melted the metal down, the two separated all on their own! Once the metal cooled, I found that the green metal was a lot harder and more rigid, while the brown was softer and more pliable.

"Since a rapier has to bend and flex, I decided to forge the blade entirely from the softer metal, while I forged the guard from the much harder green. Wouldn't want you losing any more fingers!" he said with a chuckle as he slapped Grak on the shoulder.

Grak smiled back and took the sheath that Hord produced for the weapon.

"This is beyond amazing. Thank you!"

She hugged the dwarf, and he grumbled about her making a scene, but didn't push her away. Once she released him to admire her new weapon, he crouched down again, unwrapping the new piece of armor he'd forged for Arbor.

He'd asked Hord for a breastplate as the piece of armor he'd agreed to forge. He figured that he needed good protection and his chest did hold most of his vital organs, after all.

A softly shining breastplate was revealed as the cloth wrap fell away. The armor consisted of two pieces: the solid green chest plate adorned with another roaring jaguar's head, and the interlocking brown and green plates that would sit over his stomach. There was a backplate as well, attached to the front by leather straps. This piece, too, was made entirely of the dark green metal.

Arbor lifted the individual pieces of armor, still surprised by how light they were. The dark green metal of the chest piece reflected the light of the glow stones above, and Arbor could see a soft, swirling pattern in the metal that seemed to shift and dance when he turned it. The interlocking pieces were a mix of green and brown, and he could see how they would bend and flex as he did. Grak helped him buckle it on as Hord bent down to fetch the last item on the ground.

"Last but certainly not least, here is the weapon I promised," Hord said. "It took me all bloody night to finish, but I think you'll find it suitable."

He then handed Arbor his new weapon, treating it with obvious care.

Arbor held the glaive in his hands, staring down and marveling at the workmanship. The two-foot blade was a mix of the two metals, with the outer edge being a solid green and fading to a solid brown at the spine. The guard was made of the harder green metal and extended six inches to either side. The handle, to Arbor's surprise, was also made of Mythicallium, and was wrapped in leather in the center for a better grip. Finally, the four-foot pole ended in a solid green spike that balanced the weapon perfectly.

Arbor took a step back – he had to test this new weapon, after all – and moved through one of the forms Silver had taught him. The weapon was light as air and seemed to come alive in his hands. He twirled the glaive over the back of one hand, performing a sideways slash, then spun it to jab with the spiked end.

He then sprang forward, using the haft to shove an imagined foe back and spun it to deliver a finishing thrust, the blade extended outward. Then he leaped ten feet into the air and performed a downward spinning slash, light dancing off the whirling metal. He landed in a crouch with the blade held behind his back, point towards the ground. He held the position for a moment before relaxing and straightening to a standing position.

When he finally looked up, he noticed that the entire audience chamber was silent, and they all stared in open-mouthed amazement. Arbor flushed slightly as he saw that he'd drawn every eye in the room.

Then Hord roared with laughter, his booming voice echoing around the chamber and, after a few moments, Akkard joined in. Everyone else was too shocked to say a word.

"I've never seen a display such as that!" he exclaimed. "You were moving so quickly I could hardly follow what you were doing!"

Grak stared up at him, the same look of awe in her eyes.

"Were you using your magic to speed up your movements?" she asked in an undertone.

He was about to shake his head no, when he realized that he had been, subconsciously, speeding up his movements. Even more surprising was the fact that he didn't feel any pain or discomfort.

Now that he concentrated, he could feel the magic pulsing through him, flowing from his Core and making his body practically hum with energy and strength.

Is that a side effect of Tier 2 magic? Or could it be something else?

"I was using magic," Arbor sheepishly admitted as he released the flow of power. "I hadn't realized I was doing it until you pointed it out."

"I guess there are many things we have yet to discover about magic," Grak replied, her brow furrowed.

She then turning to Hord and gave him a bright smile.

"Thank you again for the rapier. I will cherish it as long as I live."

"Yes, thank you!" Arbor was quick to put in as well. "This weapon truly is a masterful work of art, and the armor is as well."

"These aren't just any weapons and armor you have with you," he said in a smug sounding voice. Apparently, he wasn't done bragging yet.

"We dwarves were never very adept at using magic ourselves, but the Almighty blessed us with the power of smithing and enchanting. Mythicallium is the single most magically charged metal in this world, and I've enchanted both your weapons and armor."

He turned to first to Grak.

"Your rapier will always strike its intended target, even if your aim is off. There is another perk to using Mythicallium as well. Since it is a magical metal, you should be able to conduct your magic through it."

He turned to Arbor next.

"I can't say this for sure, but it could be that you were subconsciously using magic due to the properties worked into your breastplate. It can – for a short while, anyway – take the strain of your magic upon itself. This way, you can use a lot more than would normally be advisable, without any risk of harm."

Arbor had to suppress the urge to cheer as he said this, already imagining how useful this would be, especially in a fight. With an enchantment like that, he could push his magic to unimaginable heights, drawing more magic from his Core than his body would normally be able to handle. It might even speed his advancement to the 3rd Tier.

"The blade on your glaive will cut through almost anything," the dwarf continued. "I didn't choose the enchantment, but with magical metals, it can sometimes happen. They have a mind of their own.

"The best part about this weapon is that you won't have to be afraid of the haft snapping like it did in your last fight. The metal is light enough that I was able to forge it from a single piece of Mythicallium, instead of wrapping it around a wooden haft like your last weapon."

Arbor thanked the dwarf once again as Hord handed him the sheath, noting that it was a little different than his last one. The blade slid into a sheath that hung down his back near the ground and two small hooks held the haft in place, with the spiked end protruding over his shoulder. Arbor drew it a few times and found he preferred this sheath to the last one. Once he was satisfied that he could draw the weapon at a moment's notice, he turned faced the king.

The dwarf bowed his head to the small group, keeping his features schooled, though Arbor could tell he was having a hard time of it. His brother, whom he'd thought dead, was now leaving once again. He could understand the king well. He only had one family member left as well. If he were in his position, he doubted he'd even be willing to let her out of his sight.

"Have a safe journey, and may you find what you've been seeking. Good fortune be with you."

The king stood then and placed his fist over his heart.

The three of them mirrored the movement, then Arbor and Grak turned to leave. It wouldn't be polite to stay and intrude on two brothers saying farewell.

24

Karria and Sylvester arrived at the gates of the elven capital, Srila, three days after leaving the small settlement. It was nearing sunset when they finally made it. As they approached the gates, they were stopped by two elves who were standing guard.

One of the guards moved forward, eyeing Karria with distrust.

"What business have you here, human?" he asked rudely, walking right up to her and leaning down to leer into her face.

Karria took an involuntary step back, but then Sylvester spoke up.

"She's with me," he said. "I hope you don't have a problem with that?"

The guard looked up at Sylvester, and the leer was instantly replaced by a look of fear and recognition.

"Of course not, My Lord!" the guard stuttered out, standing stiffly and saluting.

"Then we'll be on our way," he said, taking Karria by the arm and leading her past the guards.

"What was that all about?" she asked as he led her down a long winding street and into the city proper.

The city was nothing like she'd imagined it to be. There were tall, elegant buildings all made from the thin trunks of Goldenleaf trees. The streets were made of some kind of red stone that were laid out in patterns, and elves of all shapes and sizes moved about.

"Oh, think nothing of it, you'll find out soon enough," he replied, leading her deeper into the city.

Though she was curious about the guard's reaction, she decided to leave it for now. After all, there was just so much to see! Karria immediately noticed that Sylvester had been right about one thing. A lot fewer elves shot her dirty looks or purposely jostled her as she walked by. She did see the occasional look of distrust, but not nearly as many as she'd been expecting.

As they continued to walk, Karria looked around in wonder. There were all kinds of things to see in a city. Vendors shouted their wares from open storefronts, children laughed and ran through the streets, and delicious smells permeated the air. She stopped at one booth, where the smell was just too good to pass by. She could see small brown squares on thin wooden sticks lined up on the counter and her mouth watered at the scent.

Sylvester walked up next to her to see what had grabbed her attention.

"What is this? It smells so good!" Karri asked excitedly.

"It's called chocolate. It's a specialty of the city. You won't find it anywhere else in Laedrin."

"How is it made?" Karria almost demanded as the smell wafted over her again.

Sylvester laughed at that.

"There is a special bean that grows on the outskirts of the city. The trees can only survive here, due to the weather being warm all the time."

An elf came from the back of the stall, and a wide smile lit her face.

"First time in the city, dear?" she asked Karria.

Karria nodded vigorously.

"Yes, it's quite overwhelming, and there's just so much to see!"

Sylvester interrupted the two of them.

"I'm sorry to cut this short, but we don't really have a lot of time to hang around. We really should be going."

Karria glared at him, but the elven woman just laughed.

"Here you are, dear." She handed Karria one of the sticks of chocolate.

"But I don't have any money," Karria protested, but the woman waved her off.

"I hope you enjoy it, my dear."

She could hardly believe her good luck and wasn't one to turn down gifts when offered so generously.

"Thank you very much!" she said, as Sylvester tugged her away from the stand.

Karria glared at Sylvester one more time as she yanked her arm out of his grasp. Then she concentrated on the chocolate the woman had given her. Taking a small bite, her eyes went wide in delight. She had never tasted something so soft and rich before. The creamy chocolate was sweet and salty at the same time, but the opposing flavors complimented each other somehow. She finished it very slowly, savoring the chocolate until the very last bite.

Once she'd finished eating and could once again concentrated on her surroundings, she noticed that the buildings were changing around them, growing larger and more extravagant the longer they walked.

Sylvester led her deep into the heart of the city. She could see a tall wrought iron fence and a stone wall ahead, and inside was the largest house Karria had ever seen. She thought they would move around it, but Sylvester walked right up to the gates. Two guards stood here, but unlike the last time they'd run into a pair of guards, these ones broke out in wide smiles and opened them right away.

"It is good to see you back, Sylvester," one of them said as he passed.

Karria was growing more and more curious by the minute.

Just what was going on here?

They walked down a cobblestone path, moving through a sea of flowers, the likes of which she'd never seen before. Butterflies fluttered around the garden, and Karria watched with wide eyes as they flitted around from flower to flower. She could hear the sound of running water and figured there must be some sort of stream nearby.

They came to the end of the path and were greeted by a set of large ornate doors, carved with vines. She noticed that the walls of the manor were entirely covered by ivy, vines, and flowers.

She'd never seen a house like it, let alone one so big.

She heard Sylvester take a deep breath. Then he pushed the doors open. The silence was palpable as they entered the large manor, and there was a loud echoing boom as the doors closed behind them. They walked into a large, empty entryway with three corridors leading off in different directions. The ceiling towered more than thirty feet above them, and a large wooden fixture with thousands of tiny lights hung above their heads. They moved out of the entryway and into the main corridor, their footsteps echoing off the walls as they did so.

Paintings of nature and fine tapestries dotted the walls on both sides, flowers stood in tall vases along the walls, and a rich violet carpet ran the length of the corridor. There were doors dotting the walls every so often, but Karria could see they were heading to the ones at the far end of the hallway.

Four guards stood by this door, and when they saw Sylvester, they stood straighter, their expressions changing to those of shock and disbelief. One of the guards knocked and quickly entered the room as they approached. Karria heard a loud cry from inside and the guard quickly emerged, holding doors open for them.

Karria noticed that Sylvester looked tense as he entered, and she followed behind him warily, wondering just what could be going on.

Just who was Sylvester really?

The first thing she noticed upon entering were the two elves sitting in bright wooden thrones, which sat on a raised dais occupying the back of the room. The thrones were stained a light cherry color and shone brightly with polish.

Looking around, she could see more guards dispersed throughout the circular room, all standing to attention. Tall vases were dispersed about the room, all filled with an assortment of flowers, and long banners hung from the walls. They were a deep violet and bore a symbol of a Goldenleaf tree, outlined in gold stitching. There was also a large table with a set of high-backed chairs, one of which were occupied by a female elf around her own age.

All three of them turned to look as they entered, and the woman sitting on the throne stood abruptly. Karria could see she was shaking, and the man stood to help her down from the raised platform.

They both appeared to be in their early fifties, the woman tall and slender, and had light, straw-colored hair streaked with gray. She had high cheekbones, long pointed ears, and a refined air about her. The man was handsome, despite his face showing signs of age. His gray hair hung to his shoulders and was tucked neatly behind his pointed ears.

Just like the woman, he walked with a grace and dignity that Karria had rarely seen. They were dressed in flowing robes of deep violet with the Goldenleaf coat of arms emblazoned across their chests. Each wore a golden circlet on their brows, and the woman had a flower tucked behind one ear.

Karria had pretty much guessed what was going on at this point and stood back as they approached.

"Sylvester?" the woman asked, her hand reaching out to gently stroke his face. "Is that really you?"

Karria was shocked to see tears in Sylvester's eyes as he threw his arms around the both of them, laughing and crying at the same time.

The king and queen of the elves, for Karria had no doubt now to their identities, hugged him back, tears streaming down their faces as well. Then they were all talking at once, the queen asking where he'd been, the king wanting to know what had happened, and Sylvester trying to fill them in.

Karria felt embarrassed to be intruding in what was clearly a private family moment and was stepping back when the queen's voice stopped her.

"Who might you be, my dear?" she asked.

She'd let go of Sylvester and the three of them were now looking at her.

She felt a bit awkward but dipped into a small curtsy.

"My name is Karria, My Lady," she said, not knowing how to address a queen properly.

"Oh, what a polite young lady you are," she said with a warm smile. "Sit down at the table, dear. We just want to speak with Sylvester alone for a few minutes. We'll join you as soon as we're finished." She gestured to the table where the elf girl sat.

Karria nodded and walked to sit down next to the girl.

"My name is Kya," the girl said with a dazzling smile. "I'm Sylvester's foster sister. What might your name be?"

Karria thought that Kya was the prettiest girl she'd ever seen. She had long honey-colored hair, a sparkling smile, and the most beautiful hazel eyes. Her ears were long and pointed, and her brows were slightly slanted like the other elves. Her face was slim, her skin pale and flawless and her frame slender. Karria had thought the elves she'd seen were pretty, but none of them could even come close to her!

"My name is Karria," she said, holding out a hand for the other girl to shake.

She had to admit that she was more than a bit jealous of the elf. Back home, she'd been the envy of Woods Clearing. There had

175

already been suitors lining up for when she came of age, but this girl was something else entirely.

She chastised herself then, remembering what her brother had told her so long ago.

Who was she to judge someone based purely on their looks? This girl introduced herself and had been quite friendly with her. There was no need for jealousy. Besides, she wasn't looking for suitors right now. She was trying to get into the magic school.

Instead of focusing on her looks, she decided to ask about something else that had stood out to her.

"You said you were Sylvester's foster sister?"

"Yes," Kya replied, flashing that dazzling smile again.

"Sylvester and I aren't really the king and queen's children," she explained. "There is a law in the Goldenleaf Forest that the rulers must care for the orphans of their subjects, should they have no family of their own."

"Wow," Karria said, astonished at the care the rulers gave their subjects.

"Yes, it's quite generous of them," Kya said, still smiling. "Sylvester and I are currently the only orphaned children around without some sort of extended family. The king and queen aren't required to treat us as family, but they insist on showing us both all the care they would, had they been our birth parents."

Karria smiled when she heard that. They sounded so kind and generous. Maybe she would be able to stay here. Maybe the king and queen would take her in as well. Although she wasn't an elf, she had saved Sylvester's life and even now, he must be telling them what she'd done for him.

That thought made her relax a bit.

"I am curious how you to came to meet Sylvester," Kya said. "Would you like to tell me what you've been through? I can feel quite a bit from you right now, and I've gotten a few snatches of memory, but I can't get a clear picture."

Karria blanched a bit at that.

"How do you know what I'm feeling?" She was on her guard now.

Kya just laughed again.

"It's my magic," she explained. "I have what's known as Connection magic. Basically, I can understand people better." She leaned forward in a conspiratorial whisper.

"It's not a very powerful magic, but I can sometimes see into people's minds," she said with a devilish grin. "You wouldn't believe the things some people are thinking about!"

Karria stared at the girl for a long moment as Kya's grin grew ever wider.

"Really? What kinds of things?" she asked, more than a little curious.

Kya leaned in just a bit closer, her voice lowering to a whisper. Karria's face went red as Kya spoke, and when she moved back, she stared at the girl in astonishment.

"There's no way that happened!" she hissed, but Kya, despite the way she was flushing as well, merely grinned back.

"Oh, it did. I can tell you more if you'd like…"

"No! That's fine," Karria was quick to say, eliciting a chuckle from the elf girl.

When she'd first seen her, she'd thought the girl was a proper princess, but after what she'd just said, she could see that she was anything but.

Karria decided right then and there that she liked this girl and proceeded to tell her entire story. How her family had been killed, and she captured by slavers. How she'd met Sylvester and escaped with him. How she'd been forced to kill the tracker. Karria faltered at this part of the story but forced herself to continue on. She finished recounting her tale, with their meeting Silver and her discovery of magic on the way here.

Kya listened in rapt attention as she spoke, her earlier smile fading. By the time she was finished, she looked about ready to start crying. She moved forward, wrapping Karria in a tight hug.

"Oh, you poor thing," she said, squeezing her a bit harder. "To lose so much at once and have your life change so drastically. It must have been terrible!"

Karria was a bit surprised that someone she'd just met was so caring but hugged her back all the same. She could feel a soothing sensation coming off the girl and had to wonder if she was using her magic on her.

"And about that man you killed," Kya said quietly.

Karria stiffened up at this. That man's death had been plaguing her for weeks. Some nights she would close her eyes and see that man's dying face staring back at her.

"It wasn't your fault," she whispered soothingly. "I feel the same pain and anguish you do for what you had to do. But you have to know that it wasn't your fault. You can let go."

Despite herself, Karria suddenly felt as though a massive weight had lifted off her shoulders. All the guilt she'd been feeling just melted away as though it had never been. By now, she had no doubts as to whether Kya was using magic on her or not. But she was too relieved to care. She sat back from Kya, tears budding in the corners of her eyes and at a loss for words.

"Thank you," she whispered.

Kya just smiled and hugged her again.

"Since you're obviously going to be staying with us, let's be friends."

Karria laughed at this, sniffing and wiping at her eyes.

"Let's," she said, in total agreement.

25

The king and queen finished their talk and came to sit down across her and Kya a few minutes later, with Sylvester taking a seat between them.

"First, let us introduce ourselves," the queen said. "I am Blyss, queen of the elves."

"And I am Alvine, king of the elves."

"First of all," Blyss said. "We would like to thank you for accompanying our son on his journey back home."

"Sylvester told us of what happened to him," Alvine continued. "We know how much you might feel you owe him, but don't fret, Sylvester was glad to do all those things for you."

Karria's brows furrowed when he said that, confused.

"I'm sorry, but I don't understand what you mean by that. Why would I feel like I owe him anything?"

Blyss' eyebrows drew together, and her mouth hardened into a flat line.

"I would think that you would be just a little grateful to him after he saved you from those slavers!" she said, outraged.

"Or," Alvine interjected, also clearly annoyed. "For having to kill that tracker after you botched up a plan and were too scared to act."

"Or when he saved you from those Gila lizards out on the Flatlands!" Blyss continued, "I should think you would be on your knees, thanking him!"

To say she was shocked would have been the understatement of the century. Karria gaped, first at the king and queen, and then at Sylvester, who seemed unable to meet her gaze and instead looked out over her head.

"I did all those things!" she finally burst out, feeling shock turn to anger. "All those things he claims to have done for me! I did them all for him!"

She was on her feet now, pointing accusingly at him.

"This little coward wouldn't have survived a day without me! He was too scared to kill that man, and I saved his life!"

"Young lady!" Blyss exclaimed, also getting to her feet. "I know that you've had a traumatic few weeks but going so far as to claim credit for someone else's deeds!" She shook her head. "Truly shameful behavior!"

Karria blanched a little at the queen's icy glare, but she wasn't about to back down, not when she knew she was in the right.

"Well it seems, Your *Majesty*," she said, lacing the word with as much sarcasm as she could. "That your son also forgot to mention that another man was along for a good part of this journey. I am sure that if we can track him down, he will tell you what a lying snake your son is!"

She saw Sylvester flinch at this and felt a small amount of satisfaction at seeing him squirm.

"I see no man here!" Alvine bellowed, now standing up as well, his face livid with rage.

"All I see is a sad little human girl trying to take credit for my son's heroic deeds! If a man did travel with you, where is he now?"

Karria took a step back at this and began stuttering.

"I... I don't know where he is!" she shouted. She could feel a headache coming on. "Silver just left us at the edge of the forest and told us that he had to leave!"

Karria stopped her tirade as the king and queen had gone absolutely still, their faces taking on an ashen appearance. Alvine and Blyss looked at each other for a few moments, fear clearly written on their faces.

"Did you say a man named Silver brought you here?" Alvine asked quietly.

Karria was confused as to why it would matter who Silver was, but she nodded. She was having a hard time keeping her rage in check.

"Did this man have wild red hair, purple eyes, and orange-colored skin?" he asked again.

Karria nodded again, her eyes fixed on Sylvester and imagining all the different ways she'd like to throttle the lying bastard. And why the hell did it matter what Silver looked like?

Alvine and Blyss both looked at Sylvester now, who appeared to be trying to hide a look of discomfort. It seemed that he'd clearly not wanted Silver's name to be mentioned, though she couldn't be sure as to why.

"You didn't mention meeting a man named Silver," Blyss said in a quiet voice. "Tell me, Sylvester," the queen sounded quite angry now, "Why would you not mention meeting this man, and what else have you not told us?"

"We didn't!" he said quickly. "I don't know what she's talking about! She's just grasping at straws and trying to take credit for all I've done for her."

He looked her in the eye then and plastered a look of disgust onto his face.

"I should never have saved your life, you disgusting human. I should have let the slavers keep you!"

Karria was stunned! Why was he acting this way, and where was this all coming from? It was as if the last two months they'd spent together meant nothing to him. Why had he bothered bringing her with if he'd just planned to lie about her?

She could feel her anger begin to boil over now, and her headache intensified to an almost blinding degree. She knew what it was this time and didn't try to hold back the torrent building up inside.

"You filthy lying bastard!" she roared, allowing her magic burst free.

There was a boom of displaced air as her power exploded out of her. There was an audible crack as the fine table snapped down the center, and Sylvester was sent flying back into the opposite wall. He slammed into it with a bone snapping crunch and fell in a limp heap on the ground.

She heard the sound of steel scraping against leather as the guards drew their weapons and advanced on her. Her head throbbed in agony as her magic flowed through her, and she screamed in pain and rage, allowing her magic to explode outward and sending the guards flying in all directions.

Karria glared down at the king and queen, who were now looking at her in fear.

How dare they doubt her! How dare that bastard lie about her and to her face, no less! She felt rage like she'd never felt before and thought about all kinds of punishments to unleash on these horrible people. She could tear the entire palace down around them. She had the strength for that. She knew that would show these people what she was made of!

Just as she was preparing to unleash a devastating attack, she felt a hand on her shoulder. She looked back in confusion to see Kya standing there, a look of concentration on her face.

She was about to brush her off when she felt a calm, soothing presence begin rolling over her in waves. She could feel her anger slowly start to ebb away, the rage leaving her, and the tension in her muscles slackening. She took a deep, shuddering breath, slowly sinking to her knees.

What had she done? Had she really lost control like that? Why had Sylvester betrayed her? And in such a horrible way!

These questions and more whirled through her mind and finally, she just couldn't take it anymore. She began to cry, burying her face in Kya's shoulder as wracking sobs overtook her body. Kya, for her part, just sat there with her, patting her back and whispering soothingly into her ear.

"There, there. Calm down. Everything will be fine."

After what felt like an eternity, Karria began to calm somewhat. Sylvester had been rushed out to see a healer, but the king and queen were still there. Blyss bent down next to her and laid a hand on her shoulder, though it didn't escape her notice that the room was now lined with grim-faced soldiers.

"We're sorry we didn't believe you," she said, looking into her eyes. "It's clear that Sylvester was lying to us now, though we couldn't figure out as to why he was doing so just yet. Kya says that she has the real story and we will get to the bottom of this."

Alvine bent down as well, though his face looked less apologetic.

"It was very foolish of him to lie about Silver as well. If he was the one who sent you, then he did so for a good reason. One of which is immediately obvious."

Karria looked up then, her eyes red and puffy.

"What's wrong with me?" she asked in a frightened voice.

"There's nothing wrong with you, my dear," Blyss said quickly.

"You just have very powerful magic and must learn to control it. Even among the elves, who are gifted with a higher affinity than most races, it is very rare to have any at all these days. Only one in every twenty or so were born with the ability to use magic over the last few centuries, and most are very weak or completely useless, never even reaching Tier 3.

"Though I have to admit that I haven't seen magic that powerful from a Tier 1 Mage in my entire life. In fact, the last person documented with your sort of power lived well over a thousand years ago," she finished.

"Kya will show you to a room where you can get some sleep," Alvine said, motioning the guards to stand back, now that she'd calmed down somewhat. "You must be exhausted. We will speak with you more tomorrow. We apologize once again."

Karria nodded as Kya helped her to her feet and led her out of the throne room.

She kept a steadying hand on her shoulder as she led her to one of the rooms off the main corridor. The room had a large bed in the center with fine drapes hanging off the posts. There was a large desk in one corner and a wardrobe with a mirror on the other side of the room. A pitcher of water and a small bowl of fruit sat on the table, as well as a small vase of flowers. She could also see a small door leading off the room and assumed it to be some sort of washroom.

"Get some rest. I'll be right next door if you need me," Kya said with a gentle smile.

"And don't you worry about Sylvester." Her face morphed into one of anger here. "I'll get to the bottom of this, I always do."

"Thank you," Karria said, wiping her eyes with corner of one sleeve.

Kya hugged her tightly, then she left the room, closing the door gently behind her.

Karria shuffled over to the large bed and fell into it face first. The sheets were cool against her face, and the bed was soft beneath her. She curled up in a ball and closed her eyes. She began to sob again softly, but no tears came this time.

It appeared she wasn't even going to be allowed the comfort of tears. She was far away from home with no family to speak of, all alone in a strange city, and the one person she believed she could count on had betrayed her in the worst way possible.

Then she thought of Kya, and what she'd said right before leaving her. The girl was so empathetic to her plight, more so than any normal person should have been. Perhaps it was just a side effect of her magic, but she found that she was quickly warming up to her. Maybe she wasn't so alone after all.

26

Karria awoke the next morning to a light rapping on her door. Getting groggily out of bed, she shuffled towards it, yawning expansively as she rubbed her eyes. She opened the door to see Kya, holding a small tray in one hand and a bundle of clothes draped over her arm.

"May I come in?" she asked with a bright smile.

Karria just grumbled a little but moved out of the doorway to let her enter. Her head was pounding, and she knew she must be suffering the aftereffects of using too much magic.

Kya set the tray down on the desk then moved over to her bed. She began straightening the covers and then laid the clothes out neatly, smoothing out any creases.

"I don't know how these will fit you," she said as Karria walked over. "We didn't have any extra clothes on hand, but you look to be around my size, so I've brought you some of mine. It may be a bit…um, roomy in the chest area, but you should be able use them until we can get the tailors to fit you for your own."

Karria just nodded, too tired to be insulted at Kya's remark, and went over to the food tray. She had no idea how this girl could be so chipper this early in the morning.

Lifting a small cup full of – what she assumed to be – tea, she took a sip. She almost gagged as the familiar flavor of medicine entered her mouth.

Kya laughed at her expression and held out a cup of fruit juice. She quickly downed the rest of the medicine, shuddering at the taste. Then she took the proffered cup with a nod of thanks and had soon washed the nasty taste out of her mouth.

"I figured you wouldn't be feeling too well after using that amount of magic yesterday. So, I stopped by the healer's this morning to fetch it for you."

Despite how gross the medicine had tasted, Karria had to admit that she was feeling quite a bit better.

She forced a smile onto her face. "Thank you."

"Oh, it was no bother at all," she replied with a bright smile.

Karria noticed then, that despite the early hour, Kya looked as perfect as she had the day before. A bright yellow dress clung to her body, the skirt ending just below her knees. A pair of tight-fitting pants covered her legs. Her hair hung loose down her back, and a small purple flower was tucked behind one ear.

Then Karria looked down at herself. She was still wearing the same clothes she'd had on yesterday. There were grass stains down the front, patches of discoloration and small tears from the weeks of travel. And she didn't even want to *know* what her hair looked like.

Kya seemed to know exactly what she was thinking and gave her a knowing smile.

"I'll leave you to eat and clean up. Just come knock on my door when you're done."

She left then, closing the door gently behind her.

Karria could hear her giggling to herself through the door and blushed, remembering that Kya could sense emotions. She sighed to herself — Nothing she could do to hide them now.

Sitting down, she helped herself to the food Kya had brought her. There were eggs, strips of beef, and a small loaf of bread. There was also the pitcher of juice she'd brought along and a small flaky pastry with apples baked into it.

She enjoyed herself immensely, realizing that this was the first good meal she'd eaten in months. Much to her surprise, she finished everything on her plate and was still a bit hungry afterward. Shaking her head, she stood and stripped out of her dirty and travel-worn clothes.

Heading into the small washroom, she could see a tub with two small spouts. Upon further inspection, she found that one of them gave off hot water, just like the one back home. Unlike the one back home, the second spout let out a strange goopy liquid that smelled like flowers and bubbled when it hit the water.

Karria laughed, delighted, and was soon sitting in a full tub of warm water with bubbles thickly coating the surface. She looked around for a moment before finding a bar of soap and proceeded to scrub herself vigorously. When she tired of soaking in the tub, she left the washroom, still drying her hair with an extremely soft towel. She then went over to her bed and riffled through the clothes Kya had left for her. She found a long-toothed comb along with the clothes and proceeded to work all the knots and tangles out of her hair. Finally, after an hour of work, she was done.

She examined herself in the mirror attached to the wardrobe and smiled. She wore a green dress with the skirt stopping just below her knees, and the same tight-fitting pants that Kya had worn underneath. She figured that this must be the elven style, as she'd seen most of the female elves in the city dressed similarly.

Karria found that she preferred this to the long skirts she was used to, even though she knew her mother would most likely disapprove. It was fairly obvious that the dress had been made with the busty elf in mind, but she thought she'd done a good job disguising it by pulling the back of the dress into a bow, gathering up the loose fabric.

She had combed her hair and braided two strands on either side, then tied them behind her hair in place of a band. She turned once, satisfied that she looked presentable and headed out of her room. She knocked on Kya's door and waited until she was invited in.

Upon entering the room, she could see it was similar to hers, but there were a few personal touches that Karria's didn't have. There was a painting of Kya with the king and queen on one wall and a woven tapestry with a colorful bird in flight on another. A few other personal effects dotted the room here and there.

Kya was sitting at her desk, reading a book, but stood up when she walked in.

"I see the clothes fit," she said with a grin.

"Yes, they fit quite well, thank you," Karria said, returning the smile, noting that she didn't mention the obvious for which she was glad.

The two of them sat by Kya's desk and began talking. Kya asked how she'd slept the previous night and if she found the room satisfactory. Karria told her that everything was amazing, and how nice it felt to be able to take a real bath and dress in clean clothes again.

Finally, with the small talk out of the way, Kya began explaining what she would be doing moving forward.

"I've already spoken with Sylvester and gotten the truth out of him," she began.

Karria stiffened at the mention of Sylvester, but Kya just continued talking.

"In case you were wondering, he has two broken ribs, a broken arm, and three broken toes. He has also bruised the bones in his right leg and left knee."

Karria was shocked at the extent of the damage but was also oddly satisfied with her work.

"In light of what you did to him, I don't think any further punishment will be needed to be doled out, do you?" Kya asked, a slanted eyebrow raised, and a small smirk on her face.

"No," Karria said, a smile twisting her lips as well. "I think he's suffered enough for now."

"Good, I thought so as well," Kya continued with a small laugh. "I've already spoken with the king and queen and told them the full story. Unfortunately, I couldn't find out why he lied about what happened."

Karria just shrugged at that. It didn't matter to her why he'd done it. He had, and she wasn't about to forgive him for it, no matter the reason.

"The king and queen will be meeting with you later today to discuss where you will be living while attending the magic school." Kya paused here, a pensive look on her face.

"You do want to go to the magic school, don't you?" She bit her lip nervously.

"Of course I want to go!" Karria burst out and saw the nervous look replaced by a smile. "I don't have any money, though…"

"Don't worry about that," Kya said brightly. "The royal family has money put away for children with magic who can't afford schooling."

Karria was surprised to hear this.

"But I'm not an elf," she protested.

"Even if he's an ungrateful lying snake, you did save Sylvester's life," Kya said. "And the king and queen think it's worth paying for your schooling for that."

They were silent for a few minutes as Karria allowed it all to sink in.

She would be going to the magic school, after all! And better yet, the king and queen were going to pay for it. After a few more moments for silence, Karria spoke up again. She was curious as to what she would do until the meeting later that day.

"So, what should I do now?" Karria asked. "You said the meeting wasn't until later, and I assume that you have school soon?"

Kya shook her head, her long honey-blonde hair swaying with the motion.

"School doesn't start again for another few days, due to the celebration of the spring moon."

"Spring moon?" Karria asked in confusion. "The winter moon was still in the sky last I checked, and should still be there for another two months at least."

Kya laughed upon hearing that, her brilliant smile seeming to light up the room.

"The celebration of the spring moon is observed halfway through the winter. Don't ask me why," she said quickly. "Nobody knows what we celebrate it in the middle of the winter. It's a tradition, so no one really bothers asking."

Karria nodded at that.

"So, what do you normally do when you're not in school? Do you have many friends to visit with?"

A pained expression crossed Kya's face here, and she looked down with saddened eyes.

"I don't have any friends," she said quietly. "I'm sure you've noticed by now, that I am unusually pretty. I'm not trying to be vain or anything. I just know that it's true. All the elven males are trying to court me already, even though I'm still a year away from adulthood. And because of that, all of the girls hate and shun me for it."

Karria was a little taken aback at seeing tears streaking down the elven girl's face. She was even more surprised to learn that Kya was only a few months older than she was.

"Because of my status as the king and queen's ward, the other girls cannot harm me physically, but they find other ways to make me miserable." She was crying hard now, and tears streamed freely down her face.

"They play mean tricks on me, shun me, and keep me from making any friends. The moment anyone new comes to school, they make sure to let them know that being friends with me would not be in their best interest, and they all listen. The boys don't want to be friends with me, either. Sure, every once in while one of them will speak to me, but they all want the same thing. And as soon as I turn them away, they become just as nasty as the others."

"Why not speak to the king or queen about this?" Karria asked, outraged that such a kind person could be so cruelly treated just because of her looks.

She also remembered her own thoughts about the girl and inwardly cringed at them. Kya was so nice and sweet, and she had been thinking petty thoughts about her.

"I will not trouble them with such minor problems as people being mean to me," she said, dabbing at her eyes with a handkerchief. "I also won't hold it against you if you don't want to be friends. It's hard enough starting somewhere new, and I don't want to make it harder than it has to be."

Karria moved forward then and wrapped the elf girl up in a hug, much as she had done for her the previous day.

"I don't care what those other girls say. I will be your friend, no matter what. You've been kind to me since the moment I arrived, and I cannot think of a better person to be my new friend."

Kya froze for a moment. She could feel the truth with her magic, and the sincerity of Karria's words washed over her in a wave of comfort. She pulled back from the hug, wiping her eyes and sniffing loudly.

"You really mean it, don't you?" she said with a watery smile.

"Yes, I do!" Karria said, her back straight. "And anyone who tries to mess with you will have me to deal with!"

Kya actually laughed at this.

"If Sylvester is anything to go by, then no one will be bothering me for much longer."

The two of them laughed together at this and then lapsed into pleasant conversation. Karria asked about what life was like in the royal manor, and Kya asked what it was like living as a human in the Endless Wood.

They soon found they had many things in common, such as a love for the outdoors, a passion for all things sweet, as well as an interest in the latest fashion. They also had a shared tragedy, a loss of family. Kya said that her parents had been killed on the border of the Flatlands by a gang of slavers. A neighbor had been watching her at the time, and she was soon sent off to live here.

They spoke for long hours, stopping only when a servant knocked on the door with lunch. Karria found Kya to be great company and was glad to have made a friend like her on her first day here.

The sun was beginning to set when she left Kya's room and headed towards the throne room. She walked down the long corridor, looking at the colorful tapestries on the walls, and was soon standing before the large doors again. Stopping before the guards, she waited for one of them to announce her, before walking in to see the king and queen.

27

Karria entered the large throne room and looked around. The king and queen sat at a table along with a third elf that Karria had not seen before. The table looked whole and undamaged, so they'd either fixed or replaced it since Karria's outburst the previous day. A servant walked up to her then and escorted her to the table where she was seated next to the stranger, an elf who appeared in his early forties. He wore a long brown robe and a knotted rope was tied around his waist. A small medallion in the shape of a Goldenleaf tree leaf hung around his neck.

"Karria, welcome," Blyss said with a smile. "May I introduce Vartan, headmaster at the Goldenleaf School of Magic?"

Karria inclined her head to the man.

"It is a pleasure to meet you, sir."

Vartan looked to Blyss with a smile.

"You were right, Your Majesty. She is quite a polite young lady."

Karria blushed a little at the compliment but was then distracted by a number of servants who chose that moment to enter, all bearing covered dishes. A steaming plate of roast duck and stringy vegetables was set in front of her. Her mouth began watering at the smell.

Alvine chuckled at the look she was giving her food.

"Let us eat first. Then we will talk," he said.

And with that, everyone dug in.

Karria could not remember a time when she'd tasted better duck. The skin was crunchy, and the meat was tender and moist. She was surprised when she once again polished off everything on her plate. Vartan looked over at her empty plate with a raised eyebrow.

"Tell me something, Karria. Are you still hungry?" he asked.

Karria, much to her embarrassment, nodded her head, and Vartan's eyes grew just a bit wider.

"Let me explain my odd question," he said, setting his fork down. "The more magic one has, the more energy their body will consume. Thus, strong Mages, even the lower Tier ones, will have to eat a lot more than the average person."

"Well, that would explain why I've been eating so much lately," she said with an embarrassed laugh. "I thought something might be wrong with me."

"Not at all," Vartan answered. "We have many types of Mages at our school, so this is something that I'm used to seeing. However, even my most powerful students would be satisfied after finishing nearly four pounds of roast duck and a pound of vegetables."

He stroked his chin thoughtfully before turning to the king and queen.

"I'm sorry for taking over this meeting, Your Majesties, but this is all quite fascinating," he said, bowing his head.

Alvine just waved his apology away.

"We were aware that the girl had powerful magic and that is why we asked for you specifically. Do you think she would benefit from general schooling, or should she be in private lessons?"

"Well, from a practical standpoint, she is a few years behind others her age," Vartan began. "However, due to the power she displayed, and the nature of her magic…" He trailed off here, thinking again.

"I would say she needed a private tutor, but she would still benefit from going to class as well," he finished.

"What would you recommend?" Blyss asked, cutting into the conversation.

Vartan thought for a second and then looked at Karria.

"Tell me, girl, which would you prefer? You will need a tutor either way, but going to regular class would still be beneficial, though not completely necessary to your overall education."

Karria didn't even have to think about this question.

"I would like to join a regular class," she said confidently. "But I would ask that you put me in the same class as Kya."

Vartan looked at her in puzzlement.

"Why would you ask that?"

"She is the only friend I currently have, and I believe it will be easier for me to adapt if I had someone I knew there with me."

Vartan thought for a moment before slowly nodding.

"Yes, you are quite right. It is beneficial to learning, as well as mental wellbeing, to have a familiar face in a strange place. I will allow you and Kya in the same class."

Karria smiled and thanked him.

"Now, as for the matter of where you will be staying?" Vartan asked. "The school has dormitories, and we have a few open beds available…"

Blyss cut him off here.

"She will be staying with us," she said in a no-nonsense tone. "This girl has no family, and we owe her a debt for bringing Sylvester back safely. It is, therefore, our duty to provide for her."

The headmaster nodded as if he'd been expecting this.

"Now, for the last matter before I go. I would like to perform a magical aptitude test. It will tell me what you will be capable of given time and training. It will also give your teachers and tutor a good idea of where to best focus on developing your talents."

Karria looked to the king and queen, but Blyss just waved her on.

"Have a good night, dear, and do come see us in the morning. We would love to speak with you over breakfast about your results from tonight."

"I will. Thank you, Your Majesty," Karria said.

She stood and followed the headmaster, bowing to Alvine and Blyss before exiting the room.

"Where are we going?" she asked as they headed out into the main corridor.

"I had a room prepared in advance. We normally do this kind of testing in the school, but we wish to be discreet. After all, this will be the first time a human will be joining us in recent history. As far as I know, the last human to join our school was here over four hundred years ago."

Karria marveled at the opportunity she was being given. To be the first human student in over four hundred years was quite an honor.

They walked further down the hall and soon emerged out into the open entryway. Here Vartan turned and headed down one of the side corridors. He turned a few times, leading her deeper into the castle, before coming to a flight of stairs descending down to a lower floor.

Karria followed a bit nervously as they went deeper underground. Finally, they arrived at the only iron door she'd seen in the castle so far. All the doors she'd seen so far had been made out of wood.

Vartan knocked twice, the sound echoing off the walls. The door opened with a groan, and an elderly elf woman stood before them. She did not look happy to be there and gave Karria a once over before closing the door behind them.

"Karria, this is Professor Palmine," the headmaster said. "I thought you might need a tutor after speaking with The King and Queen earlier today, so I asked her to meet us here to evaluate your magic aptitude."

"It is a pleasure to meet you, ma'am," Karria said with a bow.

Palmine just grunted in way of response.

"Well, are we gonna get started or what?" she asked brusquely. "I don't feel like standing around all night."

"Of course. We will begin momentarily. Karria, would you come over here and place your hand on this orb?" Vartan asked, indicating a large, clear glass sphere mounted on an odd-looking pedestal.

She walked over and placed her hand on it. It was warm to the touch and seemed to be humming slightly.

"Now, I want you to close your eyes and follow my instructions." Vartan continued.

Karria did so, and he began to speak.

"Now, close your eyes and concentrate inward," he began in a slow, soothing voice.

"I want you to look through your body for your Origin. The Origin in every Mage's body is the place where their magic is first formed. It will appear as a Core or sphere of light. Every Mage's Origin is located in a different spot, so don't be alarmed if it turns up somewhere odd."

Karria did as she was told, looking inward and focusing. After a few minutes, she could begin to feel a light thrumming coming from the back of her skull. When she concentrated harder, a dimly glowing sphere came into a blurry kind of focus.

She tried to tighten her focus and was rewarded when the image began to slowly sharpen in her mind's eye. Soon a pulsing Core came into focus. It was bright, and all colors of the rainbow swirled through it. The core was small, and tiny beams of lights seemed to be shooting from it to various parts of her body. She tried to follow a few, but they were too quick, and she soon lost track of them.

"I can see it," she said, as if in a trance. "There is a glowing sphere in the back of my skull. Small streaks of light seem to be coming off it, but they are moving too quickly for me to follow."

"Good," Vartan continued in that same calm voice.

Karria's eyes were closed, so she could not see the look that passed between him and Palmine.

"Now, I want you to concentrate on your Origin, and imagine trying to guide some of those streaks of light towards your hands."

Karria focused a bit harder, her brow creasing in concentration as she tried to will the streaks passing from her Origin to shoot to her hands, instead of random directions. Nothing happened at first, but slowly, she noticed the small beams of light were moving in the general direction of her hands.

"I think it's working, but I'm not sure," she said in an uncertain voice.

"There is no need to fret," Vartan kept the same tone of voice, once again shooting Palmine a look.

Palmine, for her part, was now watching Karria very carefully.

"Now I want you to imagine all those small beams collecting in your hands. When you think you might have done this, try and imagine all that light pouring out of you and into the ball beneath your hands."

Karria nodded and began to concentrate again. She felt a light tingling in her hands already and imagined that all the beams firing from her Origin were collecting in her palms. Her hands tingled even more now, and she felt a light pounding begin behind her eyes.

She grimaced a little in discomfort but pushed through the pain and imagined that all the collected energy in her hands was now flowing into the glass sphere. She felt something then, an odd tugging sensation along with an intensifying of her headache. Finally, it became too much for her and her concentration slipped.

She turned away from the ball, holding her head and opening her eyes.

"I'm sorry, Headmaster. My head is hurting too much for me to concentrate. I guess I've failed the test then?"

Much to her surprise, the headmaster didn't immediately answer. It was then that she noticed the odd lighting in the room and turned back to the glass sphere.

A rainbow of colors, the same as her Origin, swirled around inside the glass sphere, making light dance on the walls and ceiling. Karria stared in open amazement as the light seemed to form into different shapes until it became too dazzling for her eyes, and she was forced to turn away.

Vartan was smiling broadly, and Palmine had a thoughtful look on her face, as well as one of grudging respect.

"What does this mean?" Karria asked. Her head still hurt, but she was too curious to care.

"Well, let me explain how the test works, then you will understand what you've just accomplished," the headmaster began in an excited voice.

"Normally, when we ask a student to search for their Origin, they have no success whatsoever. It normally takes around six months for most to be able to find it with regularity. Of the rare few who manage it on their first try, only a small handful can successfully identify their Origin's pattern of behavior," he continued. "You, for example, have beams of light firing off at random. Others may have it conduct through their bones or their muscles.

"Of the rare few who can identify their Origin's pattern on the first attempt, none have been able to get their magic to bend to their will. So, you can imagine how rare it is to not only do all of that but also externalize it on your first attempt! In other words, even though you're only at Tier 1 in your magical abilities, you are at least advanced enough already to keep up with the third-year students at this school!" he said with excitement.

Karria was more than a little shocked at this overload of information, but there were still a few things that she didn't understand.

"What does the glass sphere do exactly? And why does my head hurt so much whenever I use my magic?"

"The glass ball is a method we use to identify three key things: Potential, magic type, and ability. Most students only find their magic type in their third year, when they can successfully externalize it into the sphere. You already knew you magic type when you came in, and while rare, it is not unheard of.

"Your friend Kya is an example of this. She knew almost immediately of her Connection magic, as some have an innate sense of self. The color in the sphere will tell us your type of magic. Most Mages only have one solid color, or in rare cases two or three. The rainbow pattern you see confirms your Mythic magic type."

Karria nodded her head again, understanding a little better now, but the headmaster was still not done.

"Now, normally, the glass sphere would only fill partway and give off a dull light. I have only once seen it filled more than halfway or seen a glow that could give more light than a torch. Yours, however, filled the sphere completely and lit this entire room in brilliant color. This tells us that you have more magic potential than anyone I've yet to meet, and the glow tells us of its intensity, which is quite high, I might add."

Karria had begun to smile here. She'd had no idea she was this powerful or that she had this rare of a talent. She opened her mouth to speak, but Palmine cut her off.

"Don't go getting ahead of yourself, girl!" She snapped. "Just because you have the potential to be great, doesn't mean you are now!"

Vartan nodded at this, and she continued.

"The mere fact that you feel pain at the slightest use of your magic means that you have much to learn," her voice softened a bit, and she continued. "In time, you will learn control, and the pain will go away, for the most part."

Her voice hardened again, and she met Karria's eyes with a steely gaze.

"But let me give you a warning. Do not, under any circumstances, use more magic than you are capable of. The moment you feel your head hurt, cut it off immediately! Lest you end up a drooling, mindless husk of your former self. I have not lost a student yet, and I don't plan on losing one now!"

With that, she left the room, grumbling about being too old for this kind of work.

Vartan watched her go with a bemused smile on his face.

"Well, Karria, it has been quite the exciting night," he said, pulling a small vial of green liquid from his pocket. "Drink this to help with the magic fatigue. It tastes foul, but your headache will soon be gone."

Karria nodded her thanks and downed the liquid with a shudder.

"That's a good girl," he said, patting her on the back. "School will resume in two days' time. Kya will show you around to your classes, so you don't get lost. Now I recommend a good night's sleep to get rid of any residual ill effects of overusing magic. I wish you a good night, my dear."

"Goodnight," she answered, and with that, she headed out of the room.

As she walked back to her room, her mind began to work quickly. She had a lot of information to process and not a lot of time in which to do it.

Maybe Kya could help her out?

With that in mind, she headed to her friend's room. Despite the headache, she couldn't afford to go to sleep just yet. She had a lot to talk about.

28

Arbor peered down the long tunnel, seeing a light up ahead that had nothing to do with the glow stones on the walls. He could also feel the temperature beginning to drop and wrapped the heavy cloak tighter around himself.

He, Grak, and Hord were on horseback and were finally nearing the end of a week-long journey out of the mountain. Even though he could feel the air becoming colder, Arbor was glad to be out of the mountain. It had felt oppressive and dark inside, despite all the glow stones, and he missed the fresh air and open skies.

"Looks like the end of the tunnel up ahead," he called back to the others.

They rode on for another minute before emerging out into bright sunshine. Arbor looked around in astonishment. The entire world was white!

He'd never actually seen snow before, but he had heard rumors about it.

They were quite high up the mountain and looking into the distance, he could see the noticeable change from the snowy mountains to the arid Flatlands. Arbor still had a hard time believing that just moving a few feet in one direction could cause such a drastic change in temperature. The Flatlands truly were unique.

Hord came up beside him, his eyes searching the terrain before them.

"I think it would be best to dismount here and go on foot until we reach more level ground. Otherwise, the horses may slip, and that wouldn't be good for our health."

Arbor didn't know anything about this region, so he deferred to Hord's judgment.

The three of them dismounted and were soon trudging through a foot of fine powder. The going was tough. It was even tougher for Arbor as he'd decided to try a new training method to strengthen his body's resistance to his magic. Now he was constantly keeping a steady flow of magic pumping through his body in ever-increasing amounts, resulting in constantly sore muscles and sensitive skin. He also found that he became hungry more quickly, and it took a lot more food and water to satisfy his appetite.

They continued hiking through the snow all day and partway into the night before Arbor called a halt. They had reached relatively flat ground at this point, and the snow was mostly gone from the area. It had only taken a day to reach the tunnel entrance from the border of the Flatlands when he'd come here with Grak. This time, it had taken them all day and part of the night just to reach the bottom of the mountain. Going down the steep and icy slopes with the horses had been tricky, and they'd had a few near disasters when one of their horses lost their footing.

"We should be able to ride in the morning," Hord said as he pulled an odd-looking metal cylinder from one of his packs.

He placed it on the ground and fiddled with it for a moment before standing back with a satisfied nod. It then began to glow a dull orange, and the area around them became noticeably warmer.

"Oh, wow! This is amazing, Hord!" Grak said as she moved closer to the heating cylinder.

She had been handling the cold worst of the three, and Arbor could tell she was more worn out than she was letting on.

"Why don't you sit down and rest, Grak?" Arbor offered as he fetched the last of their raw meat from his pack. "Hord and I will get supper ready."

She smiled gratefully at him and settled with her back to a rock. Her skin had begun to take on a blueish tinge while they were traveling, and Arbor had begun to worry about the gremlin woman. Now he could see her usual red coloring coming back as she thawed by the fire. He found it odd that an ice elemental Mage would deal so badly with the cold.

Hord took out a large frying pan, and Arbor handed over the large slab of meat. He had taken over as cook, much to everyone's relief. Arbor's cooking wasn't the greatest, and Grak had no idea how to cook at all.

He walked to the glowing cylinder and placed the pan on top. Then, greasing the pan with some oil, he placed the meat to sizzle and pop over the heat source. He sprinkled some herbs onto it and flipped it a few times before placing it on a stone plate. Arbor had taken out some bread and dried fruit, and the three of them enjoyed the hot food as it warmed their bellies.

After everyone was finished eating, Arbor said he'd take the first watch. No one argued with him, and he soon heard the deep rumbling snores of the dwarf and the light breathing of the gremlin woman. He looked out over the wide-open space, interspersed with rocky outcroppings. His stomach began growling, and he sighed.

He was still quite hungry, but he wouldn't go eating extra when their rations were limited. His mind soon began to wander.

He wondered where his sister might be now. Had she already been sold? What if they reached Fivora, only to discover she'd been sold to someone in a distant land? Or worse- that she was dead.

Arbor didn't want to contemplate that line of thought any further, so he instead turned his thoughts to his magic.

He'd definitely begun to notice some changes over the last few weeks. His body, for one. He'd never been overweight, but he had always had a small layer of fat covering his frame. Now, he seemed to have a lot more muscle and his clothes had started becoming tighter in the shoulders and chest. He figured that the constant magic use must be altering his body somehow. Or maybe this was how his body conditioned itself to be able to handle more magic.

When he'd mentioned these things to Grak, she said, blushing furiously, that she'd definitely noticed some differences as well. She told him jokingly that if his shirts got any tighter, he'd be tearing through them whenever he moved.

It may have been a joke, but he had to agree with her.

Another thing his magic had done, aside from making him more muscular, was make him stronger and faster. Even when he wasn't actively channeling his magic, he'd noticed that all physical activity was somehow easier. He could carry greater loads than before, his reflexes were better, and even his sight and hearing were sharper. He was also much better with his weapon than he had any right to be. Nothing had ever felt more natural to him, but he'd only started learning to use it two months ago.

How could it be that he was only at Tier 2? Then again, he'd yet to come across any other Mages, so for all he knew, this was normal.

His mind wandered back to his sister then. He could hardly bear the thought of her locked up in some dungeon, waiting to be sold like some kind of animal. He felt his blood begin to boil at that and had to actively work to calm himself down.

It would do him no good to get worked up about it now.

Taking a deep breath, he concentrated on trying to soothe his anger. He counted to one hundred, taking deep breaths, filling his chest with air and feeling the material of his shirt straining every time he did so.

Grak was definitely right. He did need new clothes.

Hord took over the watch at some point, and Arbor was finally able to roll up in his bedroll. It didn't take long for him to fall asleep. The day had been a long one and he was quite tired.

They set out early the next morning. Arbor couldn't maintain the flow of magic while sleeping, so he felt well-rested as they set out. The air was bitingly cold, but Hord said that a good few hours riding would see them out of the Jagged Peaks and into the much warmer Flatlands.

Arbor noticed that his new magical training seemed to be working. As they rode, he could feel that the five main streams seemed to be expanding, albeit at a slow rate, and more smaller streams seemed to be diverging further and further each day. He couldn't help but wonder what would happen when the magic permeated his entire body.

Would that trigger his breakthrough to Tier 3? Or, would it just stop expanding at some point? He mentally shrugged at this line of questioning. Only time would tell.

They stopped around midday to break for lunch. It wasn't nearly as appetizing as last night's dinner had been, but he wasn't about to complain. Food was food, after all, and he would take all he could get.

They rode on until the sun was beginning to set, and the blue winter moon began its ascent. Arbor could already see the Flatlands up ahead and figured it would be better to camp somewhere warm for the night.

After a few more minutes of riding, the temperature noticeably jumped by a good degree. After five more minutes, they stopped and dismounted. Arbor and Hord stripped down to their underclothes, as the rapid change in temperature had caused them to break out in a heavy sweat.

Grak, after eyeing Arbor up and down for a few seconds, went behind the horses for a little privacy to change hers.

It only took a few minutes for them to dry, and they all put on new sets of lighter clothes more suited to the Flatlands. They had all decided to store their armor as they weren't expecting any kind of trouble, and it was an extra layer that none of them needed. They ate in silence, watching the sky above and just enjoying the warm breeze that wafted across the open plains.

Arbor took out the map, and the three of them leaned over it.

"Here is where we are right now," Hord said, pointing to the border of the mountains. "And here is where we're headed."

He traced a crooked line down to the marked location of the rebel base. The mark was right near a large blue patch which had been marked as the Great Salt Lake.

"So how far is it to the rebel camp from here?" Arbor asked.

"I'd say about a week by horseback, maybe ten days if we're really unlucky," he said with a shrug.

Arbor nodded and rolled up the map, stowing it in one of the saddlebags.

"Maybe we can speed up the journey if you buff up the horses with magic again?" Grak asked, hopefully. But Arbor shook his head.

"I've tried, but so far I haven't been able to do it again. The last time was just an accident."

Grak began to sigh, but after seeing his dejected face, gave him a reassuring smile instead.

"I guess it's not really that important. Besides, I'm sure you'll figure it out soon enough."

She then wished them both a good night, telling them to wake her for her turn on watch.

They continued on for the next few days in similar fashion, stopping each night to camp on the open plains. It all looked the same to Arbor, but Grak and Hord both could pick out the landmarks shown on the map.

It was the nearing the end of the eighth day of their journey. Arbor was extremely sore as he'd pushed his magic until his body had begun steaming as they rode. He found that the steam didn't actually hurt him. Quite the opposite, actually. When he used more magic than he could handle, his body temperature would rapidly increase. His body would then begin shedding steam in an attempt to get rid of all the excess heat. It was really quite fascinating to watch.

He winced as he dismounted and hobbled over to a small rise in the ground to sit down.

"You really shouldn't push yourself so hard," Grak said, giving him a stern look. "You could really hurt yourself, or worse."

"Ah, leave him alone, lass," Hord called out as he pulled the heating cylinder out to start dinner. "He'll have to learn to control his magic, and practice is the best way to do it."

Grak opened her mouth to give an angry retort, when Arbor interjected.

"There's no need to worry about me," he said in a soothing tone. "I'll be a little sore for the night, but I should be fine, come morning."

She gave him one more sideways glance that said she clearly didn't believe him, but all the same, went off to tend the horses after a few moments.

"We should arrive at the rebel base sometime in the morning," Hord said, walking over to him and laying a plate at his feet. "We're actually only around twenty miles or so from the base."

"Then why don't we just continue on tonight?" Arbor asked.

He was eager to arrive at the rebel base and was even more eager to raid the slave city.

Hord gave him one of those looks, as if he questioned his sanity.

"No matter if they are allies or not, they are still a rebel force. So, coming up to them in the dead of night would probably not be the smartest thing to do."

Grak made a very unladylike snort at this remark as she tried to cover a laugh. Arbor looked at her with a raised eyebrow. She tried to hold it in for a few more moments, but the look on his face was apparently too much for her.

Her laughter echoed out across the Flatlands and she was soon hunched over, wheezing for air. It didn't take long for Hord to join as well, and Arbor just folded his arms, glowering at them. This just seemed to make them laugh even harder, and that annoyed him even more.

It took a few minutes, but the two finally calmed down, small chuckles still escaping as they both caught their breath. Arbor stood then, holding back a wince of pain as his sore muscles twinged.

"Just for that, you two will be keeping watch tonight," he said sullenly.

Then he walked over to his bedroll and wrapped himself up in his blankets. He could still hear quiet laughter as he closed his eyes, and grumbled to himself about his so-called friends, but the long day's ride, coupled with his sore muscles, soon had him sound asleep.

His peaceful slumber was disrupted just a few hours later by an urgent shaking on his shoulders.

"What is it?" he asked, rubbing sleep from his eyes.

Grak was standing over him, and she looked worried. He could also see Hord getting into his armor and he looked at Grak, all thoughts of sleep now forgotten.

"I'm not sure what it is," she said, looking out onto the Flatlands, where a cloud of dust was rising in the distance. "But something is coming this way, and it's moving fast."

29

Arbor stood with Grak and Hord as they watched the approaching dust cloud growing larger. He was clad in the breastplate that Hord had made for him, as well as the leather bracers and greaves that the king had supplied. Grak stood in her leather armor, holding her rapier at her side and Hord was in a full set of plate mail, his hammer in hand.

Arbor concentrated inward and after a moment of effort, his vision sharpened. The night around him lit up, the light of the moon now more than enough for his enhanced vision. He looked at the approaching dust cloud, and the approaching enemies came into view.

"There are nine of them," he said, squinting a little. "They're some kind of scaly creatures with spines running down their backs."

"Gila lizards," Hord said with a sound of disgust. "Nasty little bastards. They're the only creatures that live on the Flatlands. They can survive by drinking salt-water and eating anything that moves."

Here he paused with a grimace. "Including others of their kind."

Arbor drew his glaive, the green and brown metal glittering in the moonlight. He pumped himself full of magic, in preparation for the fight ahead. He remembered his breastplate's ability to take the full brunt of his magic for a short while. Something like that may very well be the difference between life and death in this battle.

"Anything else we should know about them?" Grak asked.

"Watch out for their teeth. They carry a very corrosive acid that will melt skin and even bone if it gets in too deep."

Grak shuddered at this but took a deep breath and began to carefully allow a small amount of her own magic to flow into her hands.

Arbor was amazed at how quickly she'd adapted to having magic, and how quickly she'd begun to utilize it with her sword. Frost soon coated the blade, coming off in small wisps as the air cooled slightly around them. The icy blue light reflected off the gremlin's red skin and made her dark blue hair seem to shine in the pale moonlight.

Aaron Oster

"Here they come," Arbor said, letting his vision fade back to normal.

He took up a fighting stance and took a few practice swings. He was ready.

Then the lizards were upon them — muddy brown things with long pointed teeth and claws. The first one rushed Arbor, its mouth opening wide to take a chunk out of his leg. Arbor took a deep breath, then dodged nimbly to the side, his glaive whistling through the air to slice into its side.

The creature screeched in pain as green blood bubbled out through the open wound. It turned to its side, tail lashing out at his feet, but he danced back quickly. Then, increasing the flow of magic to his legs, he shot forward in a blur of motion and used the momentum to bury the two-foot blade through its skull. It fell dead at his feet, and he ripped the weapon free, quickly rolling to the side, as his magic warned him of an incoming attack.

Two lizards crashed into each other in the exact spot he'd been standing only a second ago. He ran forward, his magic assisting his speed, and he focused on pouring more magic into his arms. Leaping forward, he covered the twenty-foot gap with one step. He roared his defiance and sunk his blade through one lizard's head and partway through the one next to it.

Ripping the blade free, he spun his glaive in a half-circle, caving in its skull with the spiked end. This glaive might have been light as air, but it definitely didn't lack power.

He looked over to the others then. One lizard was standing very stiffly, and Arbor could see that frost coated its scaly hide. He also saw two more lying on their sides, with their heads bashed in, and Grak was just finishing another off.

Arbor turned quickly as his magic warned him of another attack. There were only two lizards left now, and they were both converging on him, teeth bared and hissing. He took a step forward to take them both on, but Hord shot past him with a roar. Not to be outdone, Arbor rushed forward as well, his own shout echoing across the Flatlands.

It didn't take long for the two of them to finish the last of the lizards off, and they were soon cleaning their blades and examining the creature's corpses.

"Do you think we can eat them?" Arbor asked as his stomach rumbled loudly.

He was quite hungry before the fight, but now he was practically starving.

"I wouldn't recommend it," Hord said. "Their meat is rancid and can make you violently ill."

"I'll avoid eating any, then," Arbor said, taking an exaggerated step back from one.

Hord was right. The wind picked up, and Arbor could tell that the corpses were already beginning to stink terribly.

"We need to go now!" Hord said, running over to collect his things. "Other lizards will smell this and come running."

Arbor and Grak moved to follow his example and soon had their horses packed and ready to go. The moon was still high overhead, and he estimated that there were still four hours until sunrise. He turned to look at Grak. She looked worn out, but otherwise unharmed.

"Alright, let's head for the rebel camp. We'll deal with any problems that arise once we get there," Arbor said, and the other two nodded.

He turned his horse and was soon galloping away from the pile of dead lizards. They hadn't been riding five minutes when Grak called out a warning.

"There's another pack of them behind us!"

Turning in his saddle, he saw six more Gila lizards catching up to them at an alarming rate.

How were they so much faster than the horses?

"I think it's best we dismount," he said, pulling his horse to a stop. "We wouldn't want the horses to get injured."

They quickly dismounted and once again drew their weapons.

The fight was short and brutal, but they killed all the Gila lizards and were soon riding at a breakneck pace once again. They'd only ridden another few miles when Hord called out that he'd spotted another pack.

What was going on? Why were there suddenly so many of the creatures? He hadn't seen a single one in all the time they'd been traveling.

"Why are there suddenly so many of them?" Arbor yelled to Hord. "And how do they keep finding us?"

"They're attracted by smell!" the dwarf yelled back. "We just killed a whole lot of them. Even though we were careful, some of their blood must have gotten onto us. They'll be coming from miles around for us now."

They were forced once again to dismount, this time to fight eight more. They managed to kill them all, but Arbor was beginning to feel the pain of overusing his magic. They rode on in silence, pushing their horses as fast as they could go, all the while hoping not to encounter more of the creatures.

They were only two miles from the camp and Arbor could now see the small outcropping of rock that marked the rebel camp boundary.

"We're almost there," he called out, looking back at the other two.

His heart nearly stopped when he saw what was coming up behind them. He'd been keeping his vision enhanced since they'd run into the second pack, so he could clearly make out what was coming for them. Twenty-two ravenous monsters were coming up quickly from the rear.

He heard Grak shout a warning and looked to his right. Another pack of fourteen was coming from that direction. Hord came up beside him as he slowed the horse's frantic pace a little. Hord's mouth was set in a thin line and he looked grim.

"What should we do?" Arbor asked as Grak came up along his other side. "I don't think we can take that many."

"Neither do I," Hord agreed. "I say we just ride like hell and hope we make it."

Arbor didn't have a better plan, and Grak didn't seem to have anything to add.

"I guess we're going with your plan then," Arbor said, then kicked his horse in the ribs and shouted.

His horse took off, Hord and Grak close behind him as they ran for their lives. The outcropping of rock was coming up fast now. Just a few more seconds and, there! Just as that thought crossed his mind, they flew past the outcropping and into the rebel's area of control.

He pulled his horse to a stop and the other two came up beside him, their horse's sides heaving. He looked around, trying to find an obvious entrance, but nothing stood out to him.

"Where is the entrance?" Arbor asked, panicking a little now.

He looked back. They'd managed to put a little distance between themselves and the lizards, but they were coming up fast. He estimated five minutes before they would be on top of them.

They quickly dismounted as they began to search for an entrance. Arbor could see the Great Salt Lake off to their left and hurried that way. The air smelled strange here, and Arbor guessed it had something to do with the water. He cast about frantically, as he knew their time was limited.

He looked over his shoulder. The lizards were much closer now, and judging by their numbers, a few more packs had joined the other two. He ran back over to Grak and Hord, who were now frozen in terror, staring at the oncoming horde of monsters.

"I can't find an entrance anywhere!" he yelled as he ran up alongside them.

He counted more than fifty of the ugly brutes approaching and knew they were probably going to die. He thought of his family, of his sister, of the promise he had made. He could not afford to die here! He had too many people counting on him.

"You two get behind me!" Arbor called out. When they didn't move fast enough, he grabbed them both and yanked them back.

"I'm going to try something. If it works, we might still get out of this in one piece."

Hord looked skeptical, but Grak gave him a nod of encouragement, doing as he said.

He drew his glaive, then took a deep breath and tapped into his armor's enchantment. He'd found that there was a specific way to activate it. He didn't know exactly how much time he would have, so he needed to be quick. Once the enchantment timer ran out, he wouldn't be able to use it for another twelve hours.

The lizards were only about a mile out at this point, their hissing and screeching audible at this distance and getting louder.

He took another deep breath to calm his racing heart and concentrated. The Core at his center thrummed, and the streams coming off him were flooded with magic, pumping power through his body. He really had to give it to Hord's workmanship. He didn't feel even a twinge of discomfort.

He concentrated all of his magic into his legs and arms. He could feel the power building, and his body actually began vibrating with the amount of energy running through it. There was a limit, though, imposed by him still being at Tier 2, and before long, he felt himself come up against it as he couldn't draw out anymore. By that point, both Grak and Hord had run back a good few hundred feet, so he didn't need to worry about them getting in the way.

Holding his glaive tightly, he slowed his perception down. He would be moving very quickly, so he needed to be able to see what he was doing.

The mass of lizards were only a hundred yards away by now. Arbor widened his stance. Filling his lungs, he let loose a cry of defiance. Then he threw himself at the oncoming horde.

To anyone watching, it would seem like an explosion hit the pack of lizards, sending their body parts scattering in all directions. They would be shocked to learn that this was the work of just one man.

Arbor sprang forward, his slowed perception allowing his mind to keep up with his massively charged body. Holding the glaive out in front of him, he hit the oncoming creatures with grim determination. His glaive whirled into motion as he hacked and slashed his way through the horde of monsters.

He spun his glaive and swung hard, cleaving three lizards in half with a single blow. Leaping forward fifty feet, he impaled another, and ripping the blade free, he cut the heads off two more. Ducking the slashing claws of a lizard, he impaled the spiked end into its eye. Then he kicked another, cracking its skull and sending it flying.

He went on a literal rampage, hacking and slashing his way through the monsters before they could so much as react. By the time he reached the other side of the pack and turned to face them once more, he could see that he'd already killed more than half.

He grinned a bloody grin, his armor coated in rancid green blood and viscera. Less than half were left. With his armor taking all the strain, he should easily be able to handle this many.

That was, of course, where things went horribly wrong.

Arbor screamed in pain as the enchantment wore off. His muscles suddenly spasmed, then began tearing themselves apart at a prodigious rate. Steam began pouring off him in waves as his skin blistered, and his body tried to vent the excess heat. He gritted his teeth as his vision began to blur, and he stumbled as another muscle in his leg tore.

There were at least twenty of the lizards left, but his body would only hold out for a few more seconds. He pushed through the pain and concentrated all the magic he could into his arms.

This was it. He only had enough strength left for one more attack. He would just have to pour as much power as he could into his arms and hope he could cut through enough of the lizards to give Grak and Hord a chance.

The lizards moved in on him as one, sensing he was almost finished and eager to claim their meal. He poured more magic into his arms, the blue Core at his center somehow continually supplying more for him to use. He gritted his teeth one last time as the lizards came into striking range.

Then he felt it.

Something was different than it had been just moments before. His magic was different somehow. He was momentarily filled with doubt as the lizards opened their gaping maws, now only a few feet from his face.

Could he really do it? Was he strong enough? Another voice inside him screamed at his hesitation. There was no time to think! He needed to act now, or he would die.

His doubt overcome, he pulled his blade back and took a massive swing, roaring in pain as he felt his right arm snap like a twig, the strain on his body too great. He forced the movement through, cutting into the first of the lizards. Then unexpectedly, he felt the magic he'd poured into his arms leave his body and flow into his blade.

The magic left the glaive with a resounding boom, and a pure white flash of power lit up the night sky. Arbor swayed in place for a moment, the glaive dropping from his nerveless fingers. He tried to take a step forward but fell to the ground, his bloody and aching legs no longer able to support his weight.

As he hit the ground, his concentration finally slipped, forcing him to release his magic. The fire in his body abated slightly as he did so, but not by much. His eyes began closing, and he quickly forced them back open and blinked a few times trying to clear the spots from his vision.

He ached all over. His arm was on fire, and the rest of his body felt as though he'd been run over by a bunch of horses. He could vaguely see someone running over to him now, but his vision was too fuzzy to make out who it was. He tried to rise, but an excruciating pain shot through his body, and he mercifully blacked out.

30

Karria looked up at the large walls looming before her. She and Kya were nearing the school grounds for the first day back after the holiday, and she was more than a little nervous. The wall was made of solid stone and stood roughly twenty feet tall. She could see an open gate where a few other students were entering and fell a thrill of fear and excitement.

She looked over at Kya and saw the other girl looked just as nervous.

"I'm sure we'll be fine," Karria said, forcing a smile onto her face and giving Kya's hand a reassuring squeeze.

"Yeah, it'll be fine," Kya said as she stepped towards the gate.

She sounded as though she were trying to convince herself as much as her, but Karria couldn't fault her for that. After all, she had just as much reason to be nervous as she did.

They approached the entrance to the grounds, and an older elf holding a sheaf of papers stopped them there.

"Names?" she asked curtly, giving them a once over.

If she was surprised to see a human standing there, she didn't show it. They gave their names, and after a few seconds of rifling through the stack of papers, she let them pass.

They walked through the gate and emerged onto the main path. Karria gawked, open-mouthed, at the massive grounds sprawled out in front of her. The grounds spread as far as she could see in all directions, with the exception being the wall stretching out to either side of them. When she looked to her left, she could see a bunch of trees with the expected golden leaves, and to her right, the grounds were open grassland. Looking down the main path ahead, she could see it leading to an open square with five buildings surrounding it. There were many smaller paths branching off the main one, some leading into the trees, while others wound through the open grounds.

"We're here a little early," Kya said, snapping her out of her gawking. "I figured I'd show you my favorite spot before more of the students arrive."

Karria looked around as they began walking down the path, taking everything in. Now that they were closer, she could see that the open courtyard in the center of the buildings had a bunch of tables and benches around the perimeter. A large fountain stood in the center of the courtyard, where two elves stood proudly, both holding a book and leaning in as if to read. Unlike the grassy area they were in, the courtyard was made entirely of cobblestone.

Instead of heading to one of the buildings as Karria had been expecting, Kya led her down a smaller side path and into the copse of trees. Karria could hear birds chirping overhead as they walked and could soon hear the sound of running water.

After a few more minutes, they emerged out of the trees and into a small clearing. A large pond sat in the center with water fountaining up from its center, creating a pleasant splashing sound. Ducks paddled around on the pond's surface, and Karria could see small flashes of silver as fish flitted about under the surface.

She marveled at the peace and serenity she felt standing there. Closing her eyes, she could imagine that she was back home and Arbor was working only a few feet away.

"Come on, we're almost there," Kya called out, grabbing her hand and leading her to a shaded area right near the pond.

There was a small table perched right at the water's edge, and the two of them sat.

"This place is beautiful," Karria said, once they'd settled into their seats.

"This is the only place in the entire school I can come to escape all the teasing and bullying," Kya said, looking out over the pond with a sad smile on her face.

Karria felt a little awkward to be intruding on Kya's secret hiding place. She squirmed a little in her seat until Kya seemed to snap out of her melancholy.

She looked over at her with an embarrassed smile. "Sorry about that, I didn't mean to become all gloomy. It's just a little hard being back here after a holiday."

"Don't worry about it!" Karria was quick to reassure her. "I'm your friend, remember? You don't have to explain yourself to me."

Kya gave her a grateful look, and Karria cast about for something to take her friend's mind off her gloomy thoughts.

"What can you tell me about the school?"

She immediately regretted asking that question as Kya's face fell once again. She was about to tell her that she could forget about it, when Kya began speaking.

"As you saw, when you came into the grounds, there are five buildings in total. Each building, moving from left to right, are for the different age groups. The first building on the left is for thirteen and fourteen-year-olds', or the first and second years. We'll be in the second from the left, in the third- and fourth-years' building."

Karria frowned at that.

"I'm not going to be fifteen for another two months, though. Isn't that going to be a problem?"

Kya laughed here, her previous sour mood finally lifting.

"No, not at all! If you will be turning that age at any point during the school year, you will be in that age group. I, for example, only turned fifteen two months ago, but school began four months ago."

Karria thought about it for a minute and then nodded her understanding. Then she began to worry again.

"How will I know what to do? I'm starting so late in the year."

"There's no need to worry. We always begin something new after a holiday, and if you have any questions, don't be embarrassed to ask. Remember, this is a school, and questions are rarely discouraged."

Karria smiled at that, feeling a little better now about keeping up with her class. Kya continued her explanation about the school.

"There are currently four different classes in our building — two for our year, and two for the year above us. There are four professors in total, and they rotate between classrooms for a total of four, hour and a half long lessons per day. That's a total of six hours of class time."

"We have classes for six hours in a row?" Karria blanched at that.

There was no way she could sit still for that long.

"Don't worry about that," Kya said with a giggle. "We get breaks to stretch our legs and eat lunch. There is a twenty-minute break between classes, and we get an hour for lunch after the second class."

Karria thought about that. So, if they started at the eighth hour every morning, that would mean that they wouldn't leave until the sixteenth hour. When she mentioned this, Kya nodded.

"Yes, it does seem like an awfully long time to spend here each day, but the time goes by quickly. We don't have school every day. We have the seventh and first day of every week off, and we also get to leave early on the sixth."

"So, we only have four full days, and what, one half day?" Karria asked.

"Exactly! Now, the four classes are as follows. We have magic control as our first class, next is magic theory, followed by magic history. After magic history, the last class is divided. There are a few of us that can already use our magic, so for us, it's practical magic use. For the ones who can't yet use their magic, it's more magic control."

"I'm really confused right now," Karria said with a small laugh. "I didn't understand a thing you just said."

"Magic control," Kya began with a roll of her eyes. "Is where we learn to feel the flow of our magic from our origins and learn to direct it at will. It's basically a lecture followed by a whole lot of silence and groans of frustration."

Here she lowered her voice a little, a mischievous smile spreading across her face.

"I open my eyes every so often to peek, and it looks like the lot of them are constipated, it's all I can do not to burst out laughing!"

Kya giggled here, and Karria joined in, imagining an entire classroom of people with their faces scrunched up as though needing to use the bathroom.

"Magic theory," Kya continued, still giggling a little. "Is where we learn of the different applications of magic and how they can help in our daily lives, as well as what types of magic there may be, that we have yet to discover. Magic history is pretty self-explanatory. We learn the history behind magic, where it came from, and great mages of the past.

"The last class is the most fun. Here we get to actually use our magic. There are only three students in this class out of the twenty-six of our year. The two classes are combined for this one.

One teacher takes the smaller class and teaches practical magic use, while the other watches the rest sit with scrunched up faces."

Kya began laughing again, and Karria joined in. The two of them were nearly falling from their seats in hysterics as they pictured the scene once more.

"Wow, that *is* a lot to take in!" Karria said once she'd calmed down sufficiently enough to speak.

"I know that you will be having a private tutor, and I'm guessing that she'll be taking you during the last class. You're really lucky, by the way," Kya said, with a wistful sigh.

"I overheard the king and queen discussing that Professor Palmine hasn't taught anyone personally in over twenty years!"

"Who is she exactly?" Karria asked, curious about the cranky elf woman.

"She teaches one class in the school, the oldest advance class."

"What's an advanced class?"

"After you leave the third- and fourth-year building, the classes are re-done. Those who have stronger magic – Tier 3 and above – and can actually use it are placed into the advanced class. Those that have less useful magic or those that still cannot externalize it are sent to the other. This class usually leaves after they finish their sixth year.

"After the sixth year, the classes are once again split, this time into three classes: Battle Mages, healing Mages, and skill or trade Mages. Once they reach the tenth and final year of schooling, the brightest of the three classes get one lesson a day with Professor Palmine. So, you can now see why you're so lucky."

Karria just nodded dumbly.

She would be getting private lessons from someone who only accepted the most exceptional students after they'd trained an entire nine years.

"I see what you mean by that," Karria said.

She opened her mouth to ask another question, but just then, a loud bell began tolling.

Kya stood with a sigh.

"That means that classes will begin soon. Let's just hope we don't run into Eletha," she said as she smoothed her skirt.

"Who's that?" Karria asked as she stood as well, mimicking Kya's movements.

She really was enjoying the shorter skirt and leggings, as they were much easier to keep neat.

"Oh, I'm sure you'll find out soon enough," Kya said with a grimace and led her to the path towards the main grounds.

Karria took one more look around the peaceful clearing before following her.

She really hoped Arbor was still alive. This was the sort of place where he'd spend hours of his day. Looking out over the water, she could almost picture him there, crouching over the water and running his fingers through it.

She shook off her wandering thoughts and ran to catch up with Kya, wiping a tear from the corner of her eye as she did so.

31

Karria followed Kya closely as they exited the trees and headed onto the main path. There were a lot more students now, all heading towards the central square. She and Kya were soon surrounded by elves of all ages, ranging from their preteens to their early twenties.

She immediately noticed all the stares she was getting and did her best to pretend not to notice. They entered the main square, and she turned towards the second building to the left, but Kya placed an arm on her shoulder to stop her.

"What's going on?"

Instead of answering, Kya pointed to an empty space ahead of them that all the students seemed to be avoiding. As she watched, the cobblestones in the empty space began shifting and rising off the ground, stacking one on top of the other until they had formed a stage.

Karria stared in open amazement as Vartan, the headmaster of the school, walked onto the raised stage. As if there were an unspoken signal, the students around her moved forward, Karria being swept along with them, and they were soon all standing before the impromptu stage.

"The headmaster always gives a speech before the start of a new term," Kya whispered to her, as the students began to quiet down.

Vartan cleared his throat a few times, before beginning to speak.

"Welcome back, students!"

His voice boomed out across the open area, making Karria jump. She was surprised at the volume but figured it must be some sort of magic.

"It is good to see you all back, refreshed, and ready for study. I hope you all had a good break. I know I did," he said jokingly.

All the students laughed at his joke, and Vartan waited for the laughter to die down. His tone shifted and took on a more serious note now.

"At this great school, we strive to help those with magic talent to hone their skills, so they may help our great nation to reach even greater heights. These are, of course, troubled times. There are wars being fought to the north, slavers attacking our outer settlements and rebellions rising up against the king of Laedrin.

"It may not be for some time yet, but we may one day face a war of our own. To that end, it has been decided that we will no longer turn away those of other races seeking magical knowledge and guidance."

He paused here and looked around at all the faces staring back at him.

"You may have noticed that there is a human girl among you."

Here, low murmuring broke out among the students, and those near Karria looked at her with new interest.

Karria felt herself begin to turn red from all the scrutinizing gazes. Her heart started beating faster and a cold sweat broke out on her brow. She'd never been very good in front of crowds. It was then that Kya's magic washed over her, the soothing sensation calming her nerves.

Vartan waited for the murmuring to die down before continuing.

"Karria has been taken in by the king and queen themselves and will be the first non-elven student to attend our school in recent history. I ask that you treat her with the same kindness and respect you show your fellow elves. Now, head off to class and remember the motto of our great school."

Here he paused as if expecting something and as one, the students all answered.

"Strive for greatness, not perfection!"

Vartan smiled brightly at them, and the stone stage began to descend back into the ground.

"Come on. Let's get inside before they all try and mob us," Karria heard Kya whisper in her ear.

She felt the elf girl grab her hand and pull her towards the second building from the left. The noise dropped by a noticeable degree once the doors closed behind them, and Karria looked around in interest. They were in a large entryway. Ahead of them, a staircase led up to the second floor. She could see two hallways, one to either side and Kya pulled her down the left one.

"This side is for the third years," she explained. "The staircase leads up to the dining room, where lunch is served at the twelfth hour. It's only served in the last twenty minutes of our lunch hour, so make sure not to miss it."

She passed one door and stopped in front of the second one.

"Well, this is it," she said with a nervous laugh. Then she pushed the door open.

Karria looked around the neat room. There were ten small tables and chairs as well as a large desk at the front of the room. The wall behind the desk was painted black, and she wondered what that was there for. A large window took up a good part of the wall, and she could see a wide-open area behind the building. The back of the room was lined with bookshelves, all crammed full of books. No one was there yet, and Kya moved quickly to one of the small tables near the window.

"Come, sit here," Kya indicated the seat next to hers. "Seats are fixed normally, but since they move students around every semester, we get to choose new ones at the start of a term."

Karria sat down next to her and noticed that the small table had an open shelf right in the front.

"What is this open space for?" she asked, sticking her arm into it.

Kya giggled a little at that.

"That's where we keep our books."

"But I don't have any books," Karria said, looking suddenly fearful.

Would she be the only one without any books?

"Don't worry," Kya was quick to reassure her. "The professors will hand out books at the beginning of class. Those are the ones we'll be using this semester."

The door opened then and three elf boys walked in, all chatting. They looked over at Karria with curiosity, then noticed Kya. They all gave her wide grins – their eyes clearly roaming over her body – but none of them so much as waved, instead moving towards the front and taking seats there.

Four elf girls came in next, all chatting animatedly. They all stopped when they saw Kya and began speaking in hushed whispers. One even sneered at her and then said something which made the other girls laugh.

Karria looked over at the elf girl. She was becoming annoyed that no one had bothered to come over and introduce themselves. She was even more annoyed that the other girls had been so rude to her friend, but Kya just shook her head.

"It's not worth fighting over. You'll just make them angry," she whispered.

The door opened before she could reply, and one more elf walked in. Karria had to physically restrain herself as Sylvester shot her a dirty look, then walked over to join the other elf boys. He was completely healed and she guessed that magic had something to do with that.

A real pity, as she would have liked to see him in bandages at least once.

"Why's he in our class?" Karria whispered.

The girl looked just as surprised as she was and shrugged.

"I don't know. He wasn't in my class last term."

"Didn't you say there were twenty-six students in the third year?" Karria asked. "Why are so few in this class?"

"Oh, that part is easy," Kya answered. "Although it's not official, one class is for the more advanced students or those with better grades. Sylvester always had poor grades, but he did manage to use his magic when he was with you. He must have figured it out at some point after he left. That explains why they decided to move him here."

Karria just glowered.

The first day of school and the lying bastard was already ruining it. She felt Kya's hand on her arm.

"Don't let it bother you. He may sneer or make comments behind your back, but he won't do anything to hurt you."

"How can you be sure?"

"Because the king and queen have taken you in. He can't do anything to you without me making sure they'll know," Kya said with a sly smile. "Besides, from what I can tell, he should be more afraid of what you'll do to him if he tries. And if he isn't, I know more than a few secrets that'll get him to stay away."

Karria was about to answer when the group of girls that had entered earlier approached them. The one who had made the earlier comment to her friends, completely ignored Kya, instead, sitting down on her desk, as if she wasn't even there, and faced Karria.

"I heard we had a human in our school," the girl said. "I just didn't think we'd be lucky enough to have you in our class."

Karria already disliked the girl. She was pale and slim, like the other elves. She had brown hair, brown eyes, and a small sardonic grin on her face and looked at Karria as if she were some sort of animal or toy that had caught her interest.

"My name is Nina, what's yours?" she asked, examining her fingernails.

"My name is Karria," she answered with clenched teeth.

This girl didn't even have the decency to look at her. What a bitch!

"It's only polite to look at someone when you're speaking to them," Karria said as she tried to contain her growing anger. "I would also appreciate it if you would get off my friend's desk. I don't think that's a very decent way to treat someone."

She heard a gasp of shock from the other girls around her, and Nina's face became markedly less friendly.

"Let me explain something, human girl," she said, getting off of Kya's desk and leaning over her. "You may not know this since you're new, but my older sister Eletha runs this school."

"Really?" Karria said with a raised eyebrow. "I was under the impression that the headmaster, Vartan, ran the school."

Nina's face twisted into an expression of anger as one of the other girls giggled at Karria's comment.

"My sister is in the sixth year and a powerful Tier 4 Mage. She will be in the battle magic class next year, and she made a very strict rule. She said that Little Miss Perfect over there is not to be spoken to."

Her voice took on a menacing tone.

"People who break my sister's rules often find that accidents can happen around them, and I would just hate for something bad to happen to you."

"I'm touched by how concerned you are for my safety, but I think I can handle myself," Karria said, waving her false concerns away. "I'll be friends with whomever I please, and no one will stop me."

She paused here, giving Nina a once over.

"Unlike some people, I have no need to hide behind others for protection."

She said this with as much contempt as she could muster and heard Kya snicker a little as Nina's face went beet red. She'd opened her mouth to retort when the door opened, and a young-looking elf came into the room.

"Find your seats, and settle down," he said distractedly as he headed to his desk.

Nina shot her one more glare, promising that this was not over, before heading to her desk with the other girls.

She felt Kya squeeze her hand and looked over to see the pretty elf girl smiling from ear to ear. Karria smiled back, feeling a little better about the whole thing. Just seeing how happy she'd made her friend was worth the trouble she knew would be coming.

32

The first and second classes of the day went by quickly, and Karria soon found herself walking up the stairs to the dining room together with Kya. As they entered, sound washed over them, and Karria looked around, curious what it would be like to eat with so many other students.

There was a table along the back wall, and an elf stood behind it. There were trays of chicken, meat, and vegetables sitting on the table and she could see students standing in line holding large wooden plates.

She followed Kya through the nearly packed room and took a plate from a pile near the back wall.

"Wow, I didn't expect there to be so many people up here, seeing as our year only has twenty-six students," Karria said as the two of them got in line.

"Most are from the fourth year," Kya explained as the line moved forward. "They have over fifty students in their year."

"Why do they have so many more than ours?"

"No idea. Some years the classes can be small, like ours, and others they can be large. The largest class right now is the first-year class, with eighty students."

Karria couldn't help but notice how much the serving woman was piling onto some of the plates. She shared her observation with Kya, who nodded.

"I'm sure you've noticed that your appetite has gone up significantly in the last few weeks. Mages tend to need more food than the average person, and the school makes sure that we have enough to eat to sustain our magic."

The line moved forward once again.

"In fact, she knows exactly how much to put on each student's plate," Kya remarked, eyeing the serving woman.

"That's pretty impressive," Karria said, looking at the woman with newfound respect.

"Yes, she can sense how much magic a person has. It's quite a rare talent."

"And yet the school has me serving meals instead of teaching a class," the woman said good-naturedly as Kya walked in front of her.

She piled two pieces for chicken, a strip of beef and a large helping of vegetables onto her plate. She also placed a small cup filled with fruit and handed her a large mug filled with an amber-colored liquid. Kya smiled and thanked the woman, then turned to Karria.

"I'll go sit down there," Kya said, pointing to a mostly empty table. "Come join me once you've gotten your food."

Balancing her large plate with her mug, she walked towards the table.

Karria walked up to the woman who smiled at her.

"Ah, it's the famous human girl the headmaster spoke of earlier. It's nice to meet you!" she said with a warm smile.

"It's nice to meet you as well, ma'am," Karria said, attempting to curtsy politely.

It was made a bit difficult by the large plate she was holding and looked a lot less graceful than she would have liked. The woman just laughed at that.

"None of that ma'am business. Call me Ash." She scrunched up her brow for a moment and then her eyebrows shot up in surprise.

"Is something the matter ma'... I mean, Ash?" Karria asked, wondering if she'd somehow offended the woman.

Ash seemed to shake herself a bit before answering.

"No, not at all, dear. I was just a bit surprised at the amount of magic you have. It's going to take quite a bit to fill you up," she said and began piling food onto her plate.

She piled four pieces of chicken, three pieces of beef and at least two pounds of stringy vegetables. She put a cup of fruit on as well and handed her a mug of the same amber liquid she'd given Kya. She paused for a moment and then placed another piece of chicken on her plate.

"I think that should be enough," she said with a bright smile. "But if you're still hungry when you're finished, please feel free to come back for more."

Karria thanked the woman and, feeling a little embarrassed at all the looks she was receiving, made her way over to Kya. Setting

228

the heavy plate and mug down, she took a seat near the elf girl who eyed her plate with a look of bemusement.

"I see that we've been under-feeding you at the palace," she said with a wry smile.

Karria just smiled cheekily at her and began devouring her meal at a speed that shocked even her. She hadn't realized how hungry she'd been and had soon polished off her entire plate.

"What's in the mug?" she asked Kya, who was looking at her with a newfound respect after the amount she'd just eaten.

"Oh, it's a fruit juice made from apples grown here on the school grounds," Kya explained.

"What's an apple?" Karria asked.

Back in the Endless Wood, they'd had all kinds of fruit, but this one was new to her.

"Just drink it, I promise it's good," she said with a grin.

Karria shrugged and picking up the mug, took a long sip. It was delicious! Sweet and tangy at the same time, the cool fruit juice seemed to wake her up and re-energize her all at once.

Kya just laughed at her expression.

"See, what did I tell you? It's very good. We normally only get water with our meals, but I'm guessing this is a sort of welcome back treat."

Karria quickly finished the contents of her mug and sat back with a sigh. It felt a bit odd to be full. It had been so long since she'd felt this way that she'd almost forgotten the feeling.

"You were right about Ash. She knew exactly how much to give me," Karria said with a lazy smile.

Kya had opened her mouth to answer when a grimace twisted her face.

Karria looked over her shoulder, wondering what had ruined her friend's mood. Nina and a group of girls were coming over, and she felt her mood sour as well.

"Well, it looks like the sow has finally finished her feeding frenzy," Nina said with a nasty grin.

The girls behind her began to laugh, and Karria felt her face color slightly. She took a deep breath and responded in as calm a tone as she could muster.

"I couldn't help but notice how empty your own plate was, Nina," she said, looking the girl in the eye. "Guess some people can have all the energy they need from just a few bites."

Now it was Nina's turn to blush, and she made a visible effort to contain her anger. Kya was watching with an interested look on her face and snorted a laugh at the implied insult.

"What are you laughing at, Princess?" Nina yelled, whirling on her.

Karria wasn't backing down, so she figured Kya would be an easier target.

Kya instantly paled and looked down.

"I...I wasn't laughing at anything," she said in a quiet voice.

"It's just as I thought," Karria said, giving the girl an icy stare. "You can't make me tremble in fear, so you pick on those you can. You act all tough, but deep down, you're just a scared little girl who's so insecure about herself that she feels the need to bring others down to her level."

She stood then and faced the girl, staring her down until the elf looked away.

"Come on! We're leaving!" Nina snapped to the other girls.

She shot Karria one last glare before whirling around and stalking off, her back rigid.

"You didn't have to do that, you know," Kya said quietly.

Karria could see tears budding at the corners of her eyes, and it only made her angrier.

"I did have to do it," she said, sitting down next to her friend and handing her a kerchief.

Kya nodded gratefully and began dabbing at her eyes.

"When I was younger, maybe ten of eleven, a group of girls in our town were being very mean to me. They wouldn't let me play with them and would throw sticks at me whenever I tried."

"That's horrible!" Kya said, folding the kerchief and handing it back.

A wry smile crossed Karria's face.

"It was, until one day when my big brother saw what they were doing to me. I'm still not sure what he said to them, but from then on, they were nicer to me. When I asked my brother how he'd managed to get them to stop, he just smiled at me. He got down on one knee and told me to always stand up for myself, and should a friend ever be in need, to always stand up for them as well."

A tear streaked down her face when she finished the story, and she quickly wiped it away.

"Your brother sounds like a truly amazing man," Kya said, and Karria was surprised to hear a wistful tone on her voice.

"He is," she said quietly. "I just wish I knew if he is alive or not."

The two of them sat in silence for a few more moments, before a loud bell chimed, announcing the end of lunch. They stood, brushing off their skirts, and headed down the stairs.

"You know this isn't over, right? Nina won't let you get away with what you said to her," Kya said as they approached their classroom.

"I'm sure it won't be, at least not before I meet this Eletha you've told me so much about," she replied, pushing the door open.

They entered the classroom. Everyone was already sitting, and the history professor gave them both a glance as they settled into their seats.

As he began his lecture, she couldn't help but wonder where her brother was now. What he might be doing, or if he was looking for her. Or if he was even still alive. She knew he was most likely dead but just couldn't force herself to accept it just yet.

33

History class had just come to an end when a young girl came into the classroom. She looked around for a few minutes before spotting Karria.

"Professor Palmine said to meet her behind the fifth building in twenty minutes," she said shyly.

Karria smiled and thanked the girl, who quickly scurried away.

She turned to Kya, who was putting her books away and tidying her desk.

"Looks like you were right. Professor Palmine is giving me lessons behind the fifth building."

Kya looked at her in surprise.

"Wow, you're getting to train in the tenth-year training grounds. I'm kind of jealous." She flashed her a smile and stood from her desk.

"My next class will be behind our building. They do it outdoors because they don't want us to destroy anything by accident."

"That makes sense," Karria said, thinking back to the crater she'd left when she'd attacked the lizards.

Kya headed out of the classroom, and Karria followed. They were on break for the next twenty minutes and it would be nice to get some air. Exiting the building, she looked around for a few moments before spotting the building where her next lesson would be.

"Care to walk me over there?" Karria asked. "I wouldn't want to get lost."

"Sure, I don't mind," Kya said with a mischievous smile. "Besides, when will I ever have another excuse to go see the tenth-year training grounds?"

She sounded really excited, and Karria wondered if a training area should really elicit such a response. Her doubts were soon alleviated as the two walked into a massive open space behind the fifth building. The area was walled off, and she had had to give her name to a guard blocking the entrance, just to be allowed in. Looking around at the area, she could see why.

Two students stood on opposite ends of a roped off area. One of them was covered in burns, while the other looked as though he had a few broken bones. As Karria watched, the girl covered in burns lunged forward, a stone spike flying from her hand, as the man across from her launched a fireball.

She raised her hand and a stone plate formed from thin air, blocking the incoming ball of fire. The man, temporarily blinded by his own attack, didn't see the stone spike until it was too late. It took him in the chest with a dull crunch and the man went down without a sound.

"Stop!" a familiar-sounding voice called out.

The girl stopped and immediately stood at attention.

"What did I tell you about using the same move too many times?" Palmine admonished the elf, who was now lying on his back as a pool of blood spread around him.

She waved her hand once, and a pulse of energy washed out from her hand. As though they'd never been there in the first place, all the injuries on both the students vanished instantly.

"That was well done," she said to the girl, patting her arm. "But you would do well not be injured so severely just to secure a victory."

They both thanked her and headed into the building, the elf girl flashing them a smile as she passed.

Karria stood there, dumbfounded as the two elves left the training area. She hoped that she wouldn't be asked to do that. It looked terrifying!

Kya, on the other hand, was practically bouncing up and down in excitement.

"That was incredible!" she half-whispered, half-screeched. "I've never seen fighting like that before. They must be training to be battle Mages!"

Karria thought the display had been quite impressive as well. However, she did not share her friend's enthusiasm.

"Ah, you're here early, Karria. Good. I can't abide those who are late." Palmine had come up to them while they were speaking. "What are you doing here, Kya? Doesn't your next class start any minute?"

Kya jumped at the sound of her name and looked a little embarrassed.

"Sorry, Professor. I was just showing Karria the way here."

"Yes," Palmine said in a dry tone. "And I suppose it had nothing to do with wanting to watch the tenth-years while they worked."

"Oh, nothing like that at all, Professor!" Kya was quick to assure her.

Palmine gave her a look that suggested she better be on her way, and she took the hint.

"Bye, Karria. I'll see you after class," Kya said over her shoulder as she sprinted off toward the exit.

Palmine watched her go for a moment, then turned to Karria.

"Well, I suppose we should get started then. Follow me."

With that, she headed to a grassy area with a few cushions strewn around.

With a sigh of relief, Karria followed and breathed a silent prayer of thanks to the Almighty for sparing her from the ring.

Palmine sat down on one of the cushions with a grunt and motioned Karria to sit across her.

Karria sat down, finding that they were quite comfortable. She wondered what this area was doing in a training ground that only the tenth years could use. She didn't have to wonder for long, as Palmine began to speak.

"Our lessons will be divided into three parts every day. The first half hour, you will be meditating here and attempting to gain conscious control of your magic. The second half hour, we will be focusing on building your body's resistance to handling your magic, and the third half hour, we will be attempting to externalize your magic."

Palmine shifted a little in her seat.

"Any questions?" she asked.

Karria opened her mouth, as she had several to ask, but was cut off immediately.

"No questions? Good, then let us begin."

Karria snapped her mouth shut, a little annoyed at the old woman. If she hadn't intended on answering any questions, why bother asking in the first place?

"Now, close your eyes and reach for your Origin," Palmine said, pulling an hourglass from a small case at her side.

Still annoyed, Karria closed her eyes and reached out to the area in the back of her skull. It came into focus easier this time, and she could see the small streaks of light shooting off in all directions.

"Once you have found your Origin, I want you to concentrate on making all the beams of light flow towards your hands. Once you have accomplished this, let me know."

Karria took a deep breath and began to concentrate.

She'd managed it on her first try last time, so this shouldn't be too difficult.

Bringing her Origin into sharper focus, she began to will the light to change direction and to flow directly towards her hands. At first, nothing happened. Then, ever so slowly, the beams of light began shooting in the desired direction. A little while longer, and they were all moving towards her hands, and she could feel a slight tingling beginning there.

"I've done it!" she said, opening her eyes and smiling brightly.

Palmine lay the small hourglass on its side and noted the time. She then picked up a piece of paper and wrote something down before looking up at her.

"That took you sixteen minutes and forty seconds," she said, not smiling back. "If this were a battle and you needed to use your magic, you would be long dead!"

The smile slipped from Karria's face as Palmine spoke, and she glowered a little at the older woman.

"You will keep repeating this exercise until you can move power from your Origin to your hands in under five seconds. Now, close your eyes and try again!"

Karria closed her eyes, but had a hard time concentrating.

How was she supposed to cut her time down by that much? Was this woman crazy? If it had taken her nearly seventeen minutes to do it the first time, how was she expected to do it in under five seconds?

Taking a deep breath, she tried to clear her mind and once again reached for her Origin. She concentrated again, trying to will the beams of light to her hands. They moved again, changing direction ever so slowly. Finally, they were all moving in one direction and she opened her eyes. Palmine set the hourglass on its side again and noted the time before writing it down.

"Sixteen minutes and thirty-eight seconds," she said dryly and Karria grimaced.

All that work and she'd only cut down her time by two seconds?!

"Well, our time is up for today on this lesson," Palmine said, getting to her feet. "Follow me."

She led a very annoyed Karria over to an area with long boards that had leather straps on them. She looked at them a bit nervously, as Palmine began fiddling with the straps on one, muttering to herself.

"Um, Professor," Karria said nervously. "What are these for?"

Palmine fiddled with the straps for a few more seconds before turning around.

"We are going to train your mind to handle more magic than it's used to. The straps are there to hold you in place, lest you lose control and hurt yourself or others around you. This is the path to unlocking more of your power and moving to the next Tier."

"I've been meaning to ask about that, Professor," Karria said as she walked over. "What exactly is a Tier? I've heard it mentioned several times now."

Palmine stepped back and motioned Karria towards the table. She lay down then felt the leather restraints tighten around her arms, legs, torso, chest, and head.

"A Tier simply refers to the amount of magic one can draw from the Origins at any given time. It doesn't actually measure a Mage's level of power, but those of a higher Tier are usually stronger than those of a lower one."

"Is there any way to measure if a Mage is more powerful than you? If Tiers won't tell me if I'm outmatched, is there something that will?"

"Yes. There are several levels of power that are generally used when referring to a Mage. These are measured by their potential power output, meaning how much potential damage they can cause. From the weakest to strongest they are Non-combat, Enhanced, Over-enhanced, Destructor, Wrecker, Shatterer, and Calamity.

"Now, obviously, a Tier 10 Enhanced Mage will likely win against even a Wrecker class Mage, if they're only at Tier 1. But anything above that and you can just forget it. The Mages in the Shatterer class have enough power to destroy entire nations, and Calamity Mages, the entire world if they so choose."

"Wow!" Karria exclaimed, having had no idea that Mages of such power could even exist.

"So, what class am I?" she asked, trying to be as nonchalant as she could.

Palmine just shook her head, tightening the last of the straps.

"I don't know yet, as your class of magic isn't well known. Only time will tell."

Once Palmine finished tightening all the straps, she stood back and tested them a few times by tugging on a few. Satisfied, she now began the next lesson.

"I want you to close your eyes and find your Origin again. This time, instead of controlling the flow of your magic, I want you to try and increase its output. Try to make the beams of light come out faster and with greater speed. I want you to do this until you start to feel discomfort. Once you do, hold the flow of power there."

Karria was a bit annoyed at the change of subject and made a note to ask Kya more about it later. Once again, she closed her eyes and felt for her Origin. She felt it pulsing lightly and beams of light would emerge with each pulse, firing off faster than she could follow. Taking a breath, she attempted to force the beams out faster. Unlike with the control exercise, the speed and intensity immediately increased, as if the magic wanted to run wild.

A light pounding started in her head as she did this, and she attempted to try and keep the flow of power steady. She took deep, shaky breaths and gritted her teeth, but she found herself constantly trying to slow the flow of power down. After a few more moments, she was forced to stop and release her magic completely. Her head was pounding, and she winced as the bright sunlight nearly blinded her once she opened her eyes.

Palmine was sitting over her and once again tipped an hourglass on its side.

"Three minutes and eleven seconds," she said, making another note on her paper, then looked up with a small smile.

"Not bad at all for a first attempt." She waved her hand and Karria felt blessed relief as a cool sensation washed her pain away.

"We will be doing this exercise every day until you can handle that level of power for ten minutes. Once you can hold it steady for that amount of time, we will increase the power output again. This should help push you to the next Tier so you can draw out more of your power."

She then held up a small rectangular device with a small needle in the center and fifty small notches around the outside.

"This will help me measure your magical output so we can keep it steady each day." She then pointed to the second notch on the device.

"This is where you should be able to hold your power without discomfort." She pointed to the fifth notch. "This is where your head will feel like it's splitting open from the strain." She pointed to the eighth notch, "And this is where you fry your brain and end up a drooling vegetable."

Karria shuddered at that, or she imagined she did. The straps held her too tightly to do anything other than breathe, but the thought was discomforting all the same.

"Right now, we will attempt to hold steady at the third notch. Now try again."

They continued that exercise for the next twenty-five minutes, with Karria being able to hold steady at three minutes and forty-six seconds. Palmine let her off the table. She seemed genuinely pleased that she'd managed to increase her time by more than thirty seconds in one lesson.

The exercise had been exhausting and even with the healing, Karria was ready for it to end. All she wanted to do was get into her bed and sleep for the next day.

"Now, for the last exercise of the day." Palmine had led them to a range, with targets set at intervals of ten feet. "You will be attempting to externalize your magic and fire it at the targets. Mythical magic, from what little we know, should have a variety of ranged attacks. So, you will attempt a small blast to knock the closest target down. This part of the day brings the previous two exercises together. You must gather the magic in your hands, then increase the power until you have enough to knock the target over. Use too much magic, and you'll destroy them. Use too little, and the targets won't budge."

Karria nodded, resigned to another grueling lesson where she would inevitably fail for some reason. Concentrating once again, she felt for her Origin and attempted to change the direction of the beams towards her hands. After a few moments of effort, they began to flow where directed. Next, she increased the output of power, being careful not to let too much through. The tingling feeling soon came to her hands and with an effort of will, she released the pent-up energy.

Five targets lined up before her exploded in a shower of splinters, the shockwave so intense that it forced her to stumble back. She looked over at Palmine who was once again taking notes, with that stupid hourglass tipped on its side.

"Twenty-one minutes and thirty-eight seconds, and five targets completely destroyed."

She pulled a splinter of wood from her hair.

"I don't think we'll be making another attempt today, as I have now figured out what area to focus on."

"You have?" Karria asked in confusion.

Wasn't she already teaching her?

"From the three lessons I gave you, I can see that you have a massive amount of power, but very little control. So, from now on, we will be focusing on bringing that power under control."

She made one more note on her paper and then rolled it up.

"You are dismissed. I expect you back here every day at the same time."

With that, the older woman walked off, once again muttering to herself.

Karria walked tiredly toward the exit. Kya wouldn't be done for another five minutes. She sat down on one of the benches in the plaza to wait for her. She was utterly drained, and this had only been the first day!

She groaned quietly to herself as she contemplated the entire week ahead.

34

Arbor came to slowly, his eyes cracking open. He blinked a few times to clear his vision. He was lying in a bed and staring up at an unfamiliar ceiling. His body felt stiff, and he noticed an odd pressure around his arm and both his legs.

Moving the covers off himself, he could see that he was in his underclothes and that both his legs were heavily bandaged. His right arm was splinted and tied to his chest, presumably to stop him moving it in his sleep. He felt a moment of panic when he noticed that his pendant and Karria's necklace were missing from around his neck but breathed a sigh of relief when he saw them both, as well as his money pouch, on a small table near his bed.

He looked around the small room. Aside from the bed and small nightstand, it was quite bare. There was a waterskin and some fruit on the stand near his bed. Sitting up, he used his left hand to slide the pendant and necklace back over his head and tucked them under his shirt. He would have to find a better spot for his money.

Picking up the waterskin, he pulled the stopper with his teeth and took a long slow sip. It felt amazing, as though he hadn't had a drink in days! His stomach rumbled then, and he realized how hungry he was. Picking up a piece of the fruit, he popped it into his mouth. Chewing slowly, he tried to figure out where he was.

He must be in the rebel base. Where else would he be? But how had he gotten there? And more importantly, how was he still alive? The last thing he remembered was fighting the Gila lizards, and then nothing.

The door to his room opened, and Grak came in, carrying a tray with bread and meat. She looked haggard, as though she hadn't slept in days.

"Grak?" Arbor asked, "You look terrible! What happened?"

The tray dropped to the ground with a loud clatter as Grak looked up at the sound of his voice.

"Arbor?" she asked, as if not quite believing he was awake.

Her bottom lip quivered a bit, and he wondered what could have happened to make her act this way. She took a few hesitant steps forward, then broke into a run and tackled him in an embrace.

Arbor winced as Grak landed on him, feeling his tender muscles twinge.

"Ow! Not so tight!" he groaned as she squeezed him.

"I'm sorry! Did I hurt you?" she asked, quickly getting off him.

She started examining him, poking at his arm, his ribs, and his legs.

"Yes, it actually did hurt," he said as she looked him over.

She looked up from his legs then, and he could see a tear sliding down her cheek. She shook herself and quickly wiped it away.

"I'm sorry if I hurt you," she said as she sat back on the bed. "I was just so relieved to see you awake that I couldn't help myself."

He could see tears threatening to come again, so he was quick to reassure her that he was okay. This seemed to calm her a bit, and she even attempted a smile.

Grak took a deep breath and composed herself, then went to pick up the platter she'd dropped upon entering. Most of the meat had miraculously stayed on the plate, and so had the bread. She carried these over to him and sat down on the edge of the bed, an embarrassed smile coming to her lips.

"I'm sorry I acted that way," she began, dabbing at her eyes with her sleeve.

Arbor remained quiet and let her speak.

"You've been unconscious for over two weeks. I was so worried that you'd never wake up again. When I heard your voice, I was so relieved. Hence, the reaction."

Arbor was shocked, and he felt his heart skip a beat. He'd been unconscious for two weeks?! It was a wonder he hadn't starved to death, or that he'd woken up at all!

"Would you mind telling me what happened?" he asked in a gentle voice. "The last thing I remember is a horde of Gila lizards coming at us."

Grak nodded slowly and set the platter down in front of him.

"I want you to eat first. Then I'll tell you what happened."

Arbor was very curious, but he was also famished. It was a little difficult, eating with his left hand, but he managed to wolf everything down in a matter of minutes. He looked over at Grak once he was done, noting that she looked a lot calmer now. Clearing her throat a few times, she began recounting what had happened.

"The massive horde of Gila lizards were fast approaching, and we couldn't find the entrance to the rebel base. I watched as they drew nearer, their numbers too overwhelming for any chance of victory. I was sure we would die, but then you stepped forward to fight them all alone."

She paused here as her eyes began to water again.

"You managed to stop them all somehow. I've never seen anything like it! You moved so quickly that I couldn't follow you with my eyes. All I could see is where you'd been, the area marked by dead monsters and severed limbs. I did see you when you stopped, though. You were glowing with a brilliant light. You shone so brightly that the entire area was lit up and I could barely look at you."

She paused again, folding her hands in her lap.

"You then swung your weapon, and all the light seemed to concentrate there, before flowing out in a massive explosion. When the light faded, all of the Gila lizards were lying on the ground. Most were missing great chunks from their bodies. Some were even split right down the middle. One or two were still alive, but their legs had been blown off, and they weren't much of a threat. The ground itself was split open as well, nearly twenty feet long and several feet across."

She shifted a bit on the bed to find a more comfortable position and continued.

"I ran over as soon as I saw you collapse. You looked awful."

She stopped once again, her voice sounding a bit choked.

"You were covered in burns, your arm was broken, and your legs were a mass of cuts and bruises. I was more worried and afraid than I'd ever been. You looked so horrible that I was sure you were dead!"

She took a deep breath, calming herself once again.

"I felt your neck and listened by your chest and heard a heartbeat, so I used my magic to try and cool your body. It worked to a degree, as your breathing seemed to ease a bit. Then the rock that marked the rebel's territory slid to the side, and a small troop rode out on horseback. After I fetched the letter from Akkard, they brought us inside. They had a healer look at you immediately.

Unfortunately, their only magical healer wasn't here at the time, so he patched you up as best as he could. I made sure to keep watch over you and Hord managed to get out of bed to visit a few times."

"Wait, what happened to Hord?" Arbor asked worriedly.

"Oh, he did something stupid. He thought it would be funny to kick one of the legless lizards, but the thing caught his leg in its mouth. By the time he'd managed to kill it, his leg was covered in acid burns from the monster's teeth."

She giggled at that.

"I know it's not funny that he got hurt, but you should have heard him. He cursed and yelled and carried on like a child when he found out he'd be off his feet for a month. The healer said he'd make a full recovery, but he's been confined to bed for most of the day."

Grak lapsed into silence here as Arbor took everything in.

He wasn't sure what he'd done to himself by using all that magic, but one thing was very clear. There was a very real possibility of death if he pushed himself too far without the proper training. He resolved himself right then and there to go to the Goldenleaf Forest once he'd rescued Karria, just as Silver had told him.

As he stared at the red-skinned woman, he found – oddly enough – that he no longer wished to die as he once had.

Whether it came from his near-death experience or that Grak had seemed so relieved to see him alive, he wasn't sure. He still felt the pain of losing his parents and Florren, but it was muted somehow as if the pain was a distant one.

He looked at Grak and for what felt like the first time in months, he felt a smile attempting to creep onto his face. His lips twitched a few times, before settling back into its customary straight line.

It appeared that he still couldn't bring himself to do it. Arbor mentally shrugged at that. All things come with time.

The slight movement wasn't lost on Grak and her face split into a smile that seemed to light up her entire face. *It wasn't much,* she thought, *but it's a start.*

"So, what will we be doing now?" Arbor asked. "Have you spoken with anyone about the attack on Fivora?"

Grak nodded, her bright smile slipping here for some reason.

"I spoke with one of the Co-founders last week. She said that most of the rebels have moved into the Endless Wood a day's ride from here. That is why their magical healer wasn't here to patch you up."

"Why the Endless Wood?" Arbor asked.

"The Endless Wood is the only way to reach Fivora undetected," Grak explained.

Arbor was about to ask another question when Grak clamped a hand over his mouth.

"No more questions. I want you to rest. Once Co-founder Ramona finds out you're awake, she'll want to meet you right away. Until then, you will lay here and recover."

She stood then, brushing the front of her pants and stretched mightily.

"There's someone standing outside your door if you need anything," she said, straightening and covering a yawn. "If you need anything, don't hesitate to call for me."

Arbor nodded. Then she did something unexpected. Leaning down, she kissed him lightly on the cheek. Her lips were soft and warm, and Arbor found that despite her being of a different race, he quite enjoyed it, though it made him feel guilty as he was reminded of his dead fiancé. Grak pulled back then, her cheeks burned a dark red, and she couldn't seem to meet his eyes. She didn't apologize, however.

"I'm glad to see you awake. It hasn't been the same here without you."

Arbor pushed down the roil of conflicting emotions threatening to break loose. He could think about them another time.

"I have to say that it's good to be alive," he said after a few seconds.

Grak nodded, quickly backing towards the door. Her back bumped into it, and she finally met his eyes. They were shining with unrepressed emotion, enough to make Arbor feel distinctly uncomfortable. She then broke eye contact and waved one more time before leaving, closing the door gently behind her.

As soon as she was gone, he lay back in bed and closed his eyes. Grak was beautiful, in a strange alien sort of way. He knew that she wanted their friendship to be more, and if he had to admit it to himself, he was beginning to feel much the same. However,

Florren's face would pop into his mind whenever he'd think about it. It was confusing and painful at the same time, as he was torn on what to do. Eventually, he decided that it wouldn't do him any good to think about it now.

It was troubling that he'd been out so long and that he'd apparently been hurt so badly. He tried to move his arm again, but it was tied to firmly to his side. He knew he should examine himself with his magic to see how bad it was, but he just couldn't bring himself to do it. Instead, he just contented himself with sleep.

A knock at the door woke him, and Grak entered the room, carrying another tray.

"Rise and shine," she said with a smile, placing the tray of eggs and sausage in front of him. There was also a large loaf of bread and a pitcher of water.

She helped him sit up and wash the sleep from his face with some of the water. Feeling refreshed, he picked up the fork and awkwardly started to eat.

Grak watched with some amusement as the right-handed Arbor attempted to eat with his left.

"Here, let me help," she said, attempting to take the fork from him.

"I'm fine!" he said, getting annoyed. "Just let me eat."

She was being too pushy, and he still didn't know how to feel about the kiss she'd given him earlier.

Despite his plea, Grak wasn't about to give up.

"Come on. I don't mind. Just give me the fork and let me feed you." She tried grabbing the fork again.

"I said I was fine!" he shouted, starting to become angry.

"And I said that it wasn't a big deal! Now stop being so stubborn and let me help!" she shouted back, lunging for the fork.

Her hand caught the bottom of the food tray and sent it flying everywhere. Eggs, sausage and an entire pitcher of water soaked into his blanket and shirt.

"Now look what you've done!" Arbor shouted, his face going red in anger.

"Arbor, I'm sorry!" Grak said, pulling out a handkerchief and trying to clean up the mess.

"Stop! Just stop!" he yelled, and she finally did.

She looked upset and hurt, and Arbor knew that he was probably overreacting. He was lashing out, instead of dealing with his emotions, but right now, he was just too mad to care.

"Just leave me alone! I'll clean it up myself."

She sat back, her back stiff as a board. Her bottom lip was quivering slightly as she tried to hold back tears.

"If that's really what you want, I'll go."

Arbor knew he should stop her, but he was too angry now to do so. Seeing that he wasn't going to answer, she spun on her heel and rushed out of the room.

Arbor was sure he heard a sob before the door closed. Looking down at himself, he sighed. He knew that he'd overreacted. Grak was only trying to help.

With a grunt, he rolled out of the bed and got shakily to his feet. They were both heavily bandaged, and he only had one arm to work with. He was soaked through and so were the blankets.

This was going to be unpleasant.

35

Arbor was sitting up in bed and reading a book when there was a knock at the door, and Hord hobbled in. His right leg was bandaged, and he had a crutch under one arm. He bumped the door closed with the crutch and then sat heavily on the corner of the bed. He then gave Arbor a questioning look.

"So, can you tell me what's got the gremlin lass so upset? She's locked herself up in her room and seeing as you're the last person she spoke with, I thought you might be able to enlighten me."

Arbor snapped his book shut and scowled at the dwarf.

"It's nice to see you too, Hord," he said in a flat voice. "I hear that a half-dead lizard took a chunk out of your leg."

Hord just gave him a smarmy grin.

"I know what you're trying to do, lad, and it's not going to work. Now tell me what happened."

Arbor sighed resignedly and told Hord the story. Now that he said it out loud, he could see how bad it actually sounded. He'd basically gotten upset over nothing.

As expected, Hord was shaking his head by the time Arbor finished his story. He backed further onto the bed until his back was against the wall and sighed in relief as his injured leg straightened out in front of him.

"Let me ask you something, and be perfectly honest with me," Hord said, turning his head to look at him.

"I suppose I can answer honestly," Arbor grumbled.

"Were you dropped on your head as a baby?"

Arbor sat up a little straighter, his mouth turning down in a frown.

"What exactly do you mean by that?"

"Exactly what I asked," the dwarf exclaimed, throwing his hands up as if begging for divine intervention.

"Here you have a lovely young lady who was just trying to be nice, and what do you do? Blow your top like a spoiled child!"

"I know I overreacted, but you don't have to insult me as well!" Arbor said, his voice now rising as well.

"It seems as though I do!" Hord yelled back. "You're eighteen years old! A full-grown man, by anyone's reckoning, and apparently can't keep a cool head around one of the only people who genuinely cares about you!"

Arbor just folded his left arm under the sling and glowered. He knew he was in the wrong. He'd even admitted as much to himself. He just wasn't about to admit it to Hord, though.

"Do you have any idea what she's done for you, how much she cares about you?" the dwarf asked in a lower tone. "She made an oath to protect you. Did you know that?"

Arbor was surprised to hear this.

"What do you mean, protect me? And how do you suddenly know so much about her?" he asked suspiciously.

For all he knew, the dwarf was making this all up to make him feel even guiltier.

"Did you forget that you've been unconscious for the last two weeks?" he asked with a raised eyebrow. "In all that time, she hardly ate or slept. She was constantly by your side, tending to you. So, I asked her one day why she was so insistent on doing it herself when there was a healer that could do it for her. Do you know what she told me?"

Arbor was dumbfounded by this revelation. Had she really spent the entire time taking care of him?

"She told me that she once asked you what you would do once you got your revenge. You told her that you would be able to die in peace. Now, first off, let me just say that that is a terrible idea. I mean, what kind of idiot thinks they can just up and die when there are still people counting on them?"

Arbor's expression tightened for a moment, but he didn't say anything.

"That's beside the point, however," Hord said, and his expression turned grim. "Because of that stupidity you spouted that night, she made a promise. That no matter what it took, she would protect you, even with her own life, if need be. She would pull you from despair and save you the same way you did her. Her vow was only reaffirmed when you awakened her magic, and then again when you saved her hand after the fight with the Roc-Jaguar."

Hord's expression grew even more serious here, and his voice took on a softer tone.

"She cried for days thinking you would never recover, all the while blaming herself for being too weak to protect you."

Arbor sat back, now completely at a loss for words. Had she really done all of that for him? A sick feeling began in his stomach and had soon spread throughout his entire body.

"I can see it's sinking in now," Hord said, standing up stiffly and picking up his crutch. "I'll leave you to your thoughts. Someone will be by with a meal in an hour or two. I hope for her sake that you apologize to Grak the next time you see her."

He limped towards the door, but Arbor stopped him.

"How is it you know so much about women?" Arbor asked.

The dwarf flashed him a wide grin.

"There's a lot you don't know about me. I've had to learn these lessons first-hand when I said the wrong thing to my wife."

"Wait, you have a wife?" Arbor exclaimed.

Hord just winked cheekily and, with a chuckle, closed the door behind him.

Arbor closed his eyes with a sigh. Of course the smug bastard would have a wife and not tell him about it. It was just like the dwarf to do so. The question remained as to where she'd been when he'd disappeared, or why she hadn't been there when he'd left. But he supposed that was a question for another time.

He really did owe Grak a massive apology. No, she deserved a lot more than just an apology. He began to think of what he could to make up with the gremlin woman, but no ideas came to him. With a grunt of frustration, he gave up on that line of thought for now.

There were other things he still had to figure out. For example, he'd been putting off examining himself to see the extent of his injuries.

No time like the present, he thought and concentrated inward, toward the Core of his magic.

There were some immediate changes that jumped out at him the moment he closed his eyes. The first thing he noticed was the Core's massive increase in size. Originally, it had been a small sphere in his center, with five streams running off it. It was now at least five times as large and thrummed with suppressed energy. There were also so many smaller streams breaking off the five main ones at this point, that he could no longer keep track of them.

Another major change was the new color that seemed to light his body from within. His magic had always appeared blue in color, with the space in between being black. Now, however, the black space was completely white and shone with a brilliance he'd never seen before. He was sure this white light was magic, as he could feel the power of it immediately. How he hadn't sensed it until now was mind-boggling, as this power was far greater than his Perception magic.

Another thing he noticed was that the white magic wasn't coming from the blue Core at his center, so there had to be another source. Scouring his body, he soon found a white sphere, located in his chest. This was obvious, by the familiar black space immediately surrounding it, and making it stand out like a beacon.

Did he have two sources of magic now? He wondered what the white magic could do. It was obviously the source of the light that had somehow killed all the lizards, but how did it work?

He concentrated on the white Core in his chest to try and figure it out. He felt power emanating from the Core, but it wasn't the same sort of power that his Perception magic gave him. The blue Core at his center gave him power over his body. He could strengthen himself, sense the movements of others, and slow down his perception. It would even heal him once he stopped actively using it, and it strengthened his body every time it did so.

This magic, however, gave him a completely different feeling. It felt as if it were going outward instead of inward and seemed to want to be released, unlike his Perception magic. The energy in that Core only wanted to be contained, to power his body and make him stronger, and faster. It hadn't been easy to heal Grak with his magic, and it had been very taxing to do so.

He took a deep breath and allowed the new magic to begin leaking from his arm. It seemed almost eager to escape and began flowing out quickly. Opening his eyes, he saw himself glowing brightly, wisps of the white light seeming to flow off him and giving him an otherworldly appearance. With the light cloaking him, he could sense the world around him through his skin. He could feel the entire complex, the ground trembling slightly where footsteps fell, the air swishing as people moved about, even the subtle vibrations of shifting ground above him.

Tightening his concentration, he found that he could feel every muscle and fiber in his body, down to the tendons and nerves. To his surprise, he found himself completely whole and undamaged under all of his bandages. His muscles and bones were unblemished, and his cuts and bruises were all gone!

He ripped the splint from his arm and flexed his fingers, then rotated his arm and threw a few punches, noting that there wasn't even a hint of discomfort.

His fist flashed through the air and with the light still coating his arm, the movements seemed to cause an odd sort of distortion. He held his arm up and stared at it for a few moments, a faint memory sparking at the edge of his consciousness.

Something had happened right before his last attack on the Gila lizards, but what was it? It was right on the edge of his thoughts, but he couldn't quite reach it.

Arbor almost shouted in frustration as the memory slipped away and slammed his still glowing fist into the wall. As it turned out, that was a very big mistake. There was a loud boom, and he nearly fell out of bed in surprise as flecks of stone sprayed the right side of his body and the room filled with a choking dusty smoke.

Coughing, Arbor could see that a small crater now stood in the wall, a line of cracks spreading outward in a spider web pattern from where his arm had impacted.

He gaped at the massive cracks he'd left in the solid stone and immediately tried to contain the destructive power, except it didn't go out. He could feel the magic fighting him, and the white Core in his chest flared with power. It didn't want to be contained. It wanted to be released.

Arbor gritted his teeth, fighting the magic with everything he had as it fought against his control. Finally, with a monumental effort of will, he managed to force the magic back in. Surprisingly enough, it stopped fighting him the moment it was contained, and the white Core in his chest calmed.

Arbor sat still for a moment, panting heavily from the effort it took to contain this magic. This magic was powerful, but it seemed that his control over it was almost non-existent.

He took one more look at the crater in the wall. At least he now understood what had happened to the lizards. If he could do that to solid stone, he didn't think that flesh and blood creatures would hold up much better.

Leaning down, he ripped the bandages off his legs and slowly got up off the bed. His balance was a little off and he swayed slightly before he caught himself.

He walked around the small room a few times, and felt his strength returning. After a few more minutes of walking, he sat back down and began to ponder what this could all mean.

He'd destroyed his body, to a point where he should have died. But now here he was, just two weeks later, completely healed. Not just that, he now had a new type of magic and was quite sure that his body was stronger as well. Just what kind of freak was he?

Against his better judgment, he allowed a small amount of the white magic to collect in his palm. He stared at it for a few moments, before attempting to make it go out. This time, there wasn't too much resistance, and it went out after a few seconds.

This new magic was clearly extremely powerful and very dangerous. He'd passed out and was unconscious for two weeks after using it last time, but he couldn't be sure if that wasn't just the fatigue and pain from using his Perception magic.

Yet another thing he need to worry about.

He thought Silver said that everyone could only have one type of magic. The crazy hermit must not have known what he was talking about, as he clearly had more than one. That just confirmed that he needed to go to the Goldenleaf Forest even more than he had previously.

There was a knock on his door, and he moved to answer it. He stopped, realizing he was dressed in just his underwear and it wouldn't be proper to greet anyone in this state.

"Just a moment," he said, slightly panicked.

He scrambled around the room for a few moments, trying to find some clothes. Finally, he had to give up, just grabbing the blanket and wrapping it around his shoulders.

This will just have to do, he thought as he opened the door.

A woman stood there, and Arbor took a step back at the unexpected guest. She was the most striking woman he'd ever seen. Long silver hair, streaked with purple, flowed halfway down her back and the tips of slightly tapered ears poked from the fine strands. She had tan skin and her brows were slanted like Grak's, but were a lot less exaggerated. She had golden eyes that seemed to glow in the dim lighting of the outside corridor.

A tight-fitting sleeveless leather vest covered her upper body. And though the collar came up to her neck, it was so tight as to leave little of her figure to the imagination. Her legs were likewise clad in a pair of form-fitting leather pants, and the scabbard of a sword was slung across one hip.

One thing stood out to Arbor. Aside from her looks, he could somehow feel power radiating off her. Palpable and heavy, it hung in the air before him.

She gave a polite cough and Arbor flushed as he realized he'd been staring. The woman smiled then, a small movement of her lips that seemed to light up the entire corridor.

"I am Ramona, one of the Co-founders and leader of the third regiment of the Defiants. May I come in?"

36

The first week of school went by in a flash for Karria, and aside from a few more glares from Nina, there was no further trouble from the girl. Sylvester seemed to be avoiding her as best he could but took the chance to shoot her dirty glances every time they did come into contact. She ignored these looks, along with any others thrown her way. She wouldn't give any of them the satisfaction of reacting to their jibes or barbed comments.

The weekend couldn't have come fast enough, and she was now sitting with Kya in her room. The tailors had made her some new clothes, and Kya had insisted she try them all on so she could see how they looked on her. Karria had never done anything like this before, but she found that she was enjoying the experience.

Kya would clap and make *oohs* and *ah's* every time she came out in a new dress. By the time she came out in her last one, a dark green with a floral pattern on the skirt, the two of them had devolved into fits of giggling laughter.

She flopped down on her bed near Kya, the two still laughing hysterically, for no reason whatsoever. She tried to calm down by taking a few deep breaths, but then started laughing again, and Kya, who had just started calming down as well, joined in. Soon the two of them were clutching their sides and trying desperately to stop, as tears of mirth streamed down their faces. At last, they both managed to calm down, and they sat in silence for a few moments, each catching their breath.

Karria turned to her friend then.

She'd seemed a bit reserved when they'd first met. Now, however, she seemed to be opening up more and more each day. She could only assume that her situation at school was the cause of this, and she was glad she'd decided to stick with the elf girl.

"So, what do you do during your days off?" Karria asked.

"Oh, well, I normally just stay in my room," Kya said, looking a bit embarrassed. "I'll read a book or write in my journal. Sometimes I have meals with the King and Queen when they're not too busy..." She trailed off here and shrugged.

"Well, we will not be staying inside the entire weekend!" Karria declared, bouncing to her feet. "Come on. There have to be tons of things to do around the city."

Kya looked at her with a pensive expression.

"Well, there are a few things to do, but I've never really done anything. Sylvester would take me out from time to time, but since he's returned, he's hardly spoken a word to me."

"Don't worry about him. He's probably still sore that I threw him across a room," exclaimed Karria, a wide smile spreading over her face.

"Yeah, you're probably right," Kya said, perking up a bit. She thought for a moment, "There is actually one thing I've really wanted to do for a while now." She paused, biting her bottom lip.

"Come on, let me hear!" Karria said, excitement creeping into her voice.

"Well…" Kya began uncertainly. "There's a sweet shop in the city that gives classes on how to make all sorts of things. They have one every weekend. Would you maybe be interested in going?"

Karria was practically bouncing from foot to foot at this point. "Of course I'd be interested in going!" she exclaimed.

They'd never had anything like this back in the Endless Wood. A class on how to make candy?! She could hardly contain her excitement.

"So, when do they start?"

Kya smiled, her pretty face lighting up at Karria's enthusiasm.

"We'll need to sign up by the shop in advance," she said, getting up off Karria's bed and sliding her shoes on. "If we hurry, we can make it in time. The first class of the course starts sometime tomorrow."

Karria quickly slid into her shoes as well, and the two headed out into the hallway, chatting excitedly about what kind of sweets they'd be making.

They were nearly to the exit when a voice called out.

"Where are the two of you off to, if I might ask?"

Turning, Karria saw Alvine coming out of one of the side corridors flanked by two guards. She and Kya dipped into curtsies, and Kya beamed up at the king.

"We are going to sign up for classes at Srila Sweets," she said brightly.

"Are you now? It's good to see you going out." The king beamed back at her. "Do you have coin for the classes?" he asked, reaching into the pocket of his long robes.

"Yes, the queen makes sure I have money whenever I need it," Kya said.

"Very well then, don't let me keep you young ladies from your activities. Enjoy your day." The king smiled at them once more, before turning and heading down the main corridor, his guards following silently behind.

They watched the king's retreat back for a few moments, then headed quickly out of the large double doors. They walked through the colorful garden, both commenting on their favorite flowers and which they would most like to see planted next.

The two gate guards let them through, and they were soon making their way into the busy city. Karria looked around in wonder.

The sounds and colors, as well as all the people, didn't cease to amaze her. She didn't think she would ever tire of hearing friendly merchants calling out to try their wares. Or the children that ran laughing through the streets. There had been something that had been bothering her a little, so she chose now to ask her friend.

"Why don't you have guards accompanying you when you go out?" she asked.

Her friend just laughed at that.

"I'm not a princess, only a ward. The king and queen care for me as I were their own, but I will not become queen when they die."

They walked on in silence for a few more minutes, weaving through the busy streets until Kya stopped them outside a small shop with a sign over the door. It read 'Srila Sweets' in bright letters, and the most delicious smells were coming from inside.

Walking into the store, Karria looked around in excitement. She was quite interested to see what a sweets shop would look like, as they didn't have one back in Woods Clearing. The walls were hung with bright decorations, and small paper bags stood on a shelf against one wall. She was a bit disappointed at the empty store, until they approached the counter. She could see a large variety of sweets, cakes, and other delicious looking treats resting there. There was only one of each type of product, which she found to be odd.

An elf dressed in a colorful apron came out of a back room and gave the two of them a friendly smile.

"How can I help you young ladies today?"

"We would like to sign up for the sweets making class," Kya said shyly.

The elf smiled even wider at that.

"Well, you're in luck! There are just two spots left," he said, pulling a piece of paper and some charcoal out from under the counter. "May I have your names, please?"

They gave their names, and the elf wrote them down, scribbling on a sheaf of paper with a charcoal pencil.

"Now, we have one class for two silver each, or ten classes for one gold. The classes include all of the ingredients you'll be using, a book where you can record any recipes, and you'll be able to take home anything you've made at the end of the class."

Kya thought for a moment, then took a small coin pouch from her waist. She fished out two gleaming golden coins, with a crown stamped on one side and a man's profile on the other and placed them on the counter.

The elf smiled, taking the two coins and placing them in a small box behind the counter.

"The first class will be tomorrow afternoon at the fourteenth hour. Is there anything else I can help you with?"

"Can we please have two ounces of chocolate?" Kya asked, pulling a silver coin from her pouch.

"Of course," the elf said, taking the coin and heading into the back room.

He re-emerged a moment later, holding a cloth napkin containing two dark brown squares. He placed them each into a small paper bag and handed them over, as well as five copper coins, which Kya placed in her pouch.

"Will that be all?"

"Yes, thank you," Kya said, taking the bags.

They left the store and Kya handed one of the bags over.

"Here, enjoy. They have the absolute best chocolate in the city."

Karria thanked her, and the two of them nibbled slowly on the small squares as they walked.

"Why did they only have one of each sweet on the counter?" Karria asked.

"The ones on the counter are only for display. They make them fresh every day, but it would be a waste to keep changing the display, so they only do it every few weeks," she answered, taking another small bite from her chocolate square.

"That makes sense," Karria replied, taking another bite of hers as well.

Kya was right about the chocolate. It was even better than the one that nice elf had given her when they'd come into the city for the first time. Her mood soured a bit as she thought of Sylvester, as he had been with her when she'd gotten the chocolate. The only thing really bothering her was why he'd said those horrible things to her. She'd thought they were friends, especially after all they'd been through.

As they left the city, the sky overhead began to grow darker. And though she wasn't sure why, Karria felt a small shiver run down her spine. Something wasn't right.

She looked around nervously but didn't see anything out of the ordinary. Instead of this making her relax, it only served to make her more nervous. They walked for a few more minutes, the houses around them growing more lavish and expensive looking. Her shoulders had just begun to relax, thinking she must have been imagining things, when she got that odd feeling again.

This time when she looked back, her heart skipped a beat as she saw a group of girls coming from behind them. Nina was out in front, and walking next to her was a girl that looked remarkably similar to her, only a bit older.

"Damn," Karria cursed under her breath, gritting her teeth in anticipation of the upcoming confrontation.

She nudged Kya in the side and pointed back.

Turning to look, Kya's face went pale as she saw who was approaching.

"Eletha," she muttered, confirming her suspicions.

It looked as though the trouble she'd been expecting had finally found her.

37

"Well, look at what we've caught," Nina said, as the group quickly moved to surround the two of them. "The Princess and the Sow, out for a stroll," she said, getting laughs from the other girls.

Karria scowled and took a step forward.

"I can't help but notice that you always need a large group behind you whenever confronting someone. You afraid to do anything yourself, or are you that much of a coward that you need ten to one odds?"

Eletha stepped forward then, holding up a hand to stop Nina's angry retort, a look of derision on her face.

"So, you're the one who's been breaking all of my rules. I don't appreciate it when people don't do as they're told."

Karria felt a tugging on her sleeve then.

"Come on, Karria. We should leave while we can," Kya whispered urgently.

Despite the urgency in her friend's voice, Karria was not about to back down.

"Oh?" she asked, stepping forward as well. "I wasn't aware that I've broken any rules."

"Is that so?" Eletha asked, her teeth clenching in anger. "There's a rule in our school that no one talks to or befriends the little bitch hiding behind you. I'm sure my sister made you aware of that rule, and yet you are clearly in violation of that rule right now!"

"Since when do you run the school?" Karria demanded, her voice becoming heated. "And even if you're delusional enough to think you do, it's kind of hypocritical to come after me for talking to someone *outside* of school. Or are you so brain damaged that you think you run the entire city as well?"

Eletha's went a deep shade of crimson, reminiscent of an angry beet, and took a threatening step forward.

"I think someone needs a lesson taught to them about questioning her betters!"

Karria did not flinch, meeting the older girl's gaze with a defiant one of her own.

"I don't see any of my betters around, just an angry, jealous dog who can't stand the fact that she's not the hottest girl in school."

Eletha lunged forward then, a scream of rage escaping her throat. Karria was prepared for this and was about to step back when two of the girls moved from behind her. They grabbed her arms, wrenching them behind he back and holding her in place. She heard a scream and turned to see Kya being held by two other girls in a similar fashion.

Eletha smiled then, a cold bone-chilling smile that had no warmth whatsoever.

"I think that people who break the rules need to be punished, don't you?" she asked, taking a step forward and cupping Karria's chin between her fingers.

She knew she was in a bad position, but she couldn't resist one last jab at the girl. Leaning forward until just Eletha could hear her she whispered, "At least my fiancé didn't leave me because and I quote 'had the face of a bulldog and the temperament of an angry hog.'"

Karria had recently found out the real reason Eletha hated Kya so much. She'd pestered her friend for days, saying that her looks weren't a good enough reason for the way she was treated. Finally, Kya had relented and told her the real reason.

Apparently, Eletha's long-time boyfriend and fiancé had propositioned for Kya's hand in marriage once she came of age. Kya had, of course, turned him down, but Eletha had found out. When she asked him what had happened, demanding answers, he told her that he'd never loved her and left. He'd also called her a bunch of unflattering names involving dogs for some reason.

Eletha, of course, blamed Kya for what had happened, and from then on, she had made sure to torment her at every opportunity. Very few people knew this story and Eletha had apparently threatened to kill Kya if she told anyone.

Eletha went pale for a moment, shock written across her face. Then a look of rage contorted her features, her face going from white to red in a matter of seconds.

"I'm going to enjoy this, you bitch!" she screamed and drew her fist back.

Karria's head was rocked to the side with the force of the blow, and her cheek exploded with pain. Worse, a massive shock went through her entire body as the blow connected and Karria screamed in pain. Her eyes flicked up as Eletha's fist drew back again, and saw something sparking across it, right before it connected with her face again. Her body locked up as a shock ran through it again, lighting her very nerves on fire.

She tried desperately to reach for her magic, but another blow connected with the side of her skull. With a cry of pain, her concentration was shattered as lightning coursed through her body. Her entire face ached and her nerves were ablaze with pain, but the cruel girl wasn't done yet. She felt two hands press together on the side of her head and suddenly it felt like her brain was on fire. She screamed and writhed, smoke wafting off her head as Eletha began running an electrical current through her skull.

Karria was sure now that she was dying. Her head was on fire. She'd never felt pain like this in her life.

"Got nothing to say now? Huh, bitch?" Eletha asked, laughing as she shocked Karria's brain over and over.

"Stop it! You'll kill her!"

Kya's voice sounded from beside her. This was followed by a loud smack and a cry of pain.

"Shut up, you damn spoiled Princess! You'll get your turn soon enough!"

Karria vaguely heard Nina screaming from behind her.

"Now, here's a lesson for you, you human swine! When I make rules, I expect them to be followed."

With that, Karria felt a massive pressure in her head as Eletha jolted her brain yet again. She screamed one more time, tasting blood in her mouth. Then everything went black.

Karria swam in an endless sea of black. Someone was shaking her shoulder, but why were they bothering her? Couldn't they see she was sleeping?

She tried to push the hand away, but they were insistent.

"Leave me alone," she said weakly, trying to shove the hand away, but found that she couldn't move her arms.

Why couldn't she move?

The shaking started again, more insistent and frantic.

"Karria! Wake up!"

Someone was calling her name. It would be rude of her not to answer. Karria's eyes cracked open, and she winced at the bright light beating down from overhead. She was lying on her back and staring up at the sky.

"Oh, you're awake! Thank the Almighty!"

She felt someone's arm wrap around her and groaned in pain.

"What happened?" she asked, her voice rasping out.

The last thing she remembered was Eletha laughing as she did something to her.

"Eletha kept using her magic on you until you passed out. I was sure she would keep on going until she killed you, but the other girls pulled her off. They left soon after."

Karria sat up slowly. Her head swam and throbbed as she did so. Something wasn't right. She couldn't keep any coherent thought for long and the world seemed to swim around her.

She looked at Kya. She had a bruise under her left eye and her skirt was torn on one side. Tears stained her cheeks, and Karria could only imagine what they'd done to her.

She was about to get up when a sharp pain shot through her head. She leaned over with a groan, clutching it tightly, and gritted her teeth. It felt as though someone was shoving hot needles into her skull.

Kya placed a worried hand on hers and her eyes widened.

"Karria, Karria! Look at me!"

She sounded panicked, Karria wasn't sure why though. She looked at her again, her vision becoming fuzzy.

"What's wrong?" she tried to ask, but it just came out as an unrecognizable slur.

She tried to speak again, but pain wracked her entire body this time, and she fell to the ground and began shaking violently. A hard slap across her face brought her back to consciousness as her vision began to go dark once again. She looked up in shock to see Kya bring her hand back to slap her again.

What the hell was she doing?

Another slap from Kya woke her up completely.

"Why are you hitting me?" she tried to ask, but once again, all that came out was a bunch of slurred words.

Tears were streaming down Kya's face as she brought her hand back to slap her a third time when a voice that she vaguely recognized called out.

"What do you think you're doing, girl?"

Karria heard Kya gasp and say something in a panicked tone. She couldn't hear what she was saying clearly, though. Blackness began creeping around the edges of her vision, and a warmth seemed to surround her. Her eyes began to close, and she felt oddly peaceful as they did so.

Her peace was shattered when, what felt like an icy wave, washed over her entire body. She jerked awake instantly, gasping as the cold permeated every inch of her body. Just as quickly as it had come, it was gone, leaving her clear-headed and devoid of any pain.

She blinked a few times, looking up. Professor Palmine was kneeling over her, a look of concentration on her face. Kya was standing behind her, clutching her hands to her chest and looking terrified.

"What happened?" Karria asked.

Why was she lying on the ground? Why was Professor Palmine here? And why was Kya crying?

"You nearly died," Palmine said plainly. "If I'd been another minute, you would no longer be among the living."

"What?" Karria exclaimed. "Dead? How?!"

"Calm down, girl. You're likely to give yourself a heart attack," the professor grumbled.

"I thought you were going to die!" Kya shouldered her way past the older woman and wrapped Kya in a bone-crushing hug.

"I was so worried! I felt that your thoughts were all funny with my magic, and then you were having trouble speaking. I had to keep hitting you, so you'd stay awake! I'm sorry! It's all my fault! If it wasn't for me, this wouldn't have happened!"

Karria rubbed her friend's back awkwardly as she bawled her eyes out into her shoulder.

"I will need an explanation of what happened here," Palmine said, standing up with a groan. "For now, go home. I expect that the king and queen will want to hear of this as well."

Karria nodded as her teacher rose and headed down the street, muttering something about children not knowing how to behave. She held Kya for a few more minutes until she'd calmed down enough to talk again. She stood and helped her friend to her feet.

It was good to see that Professor Palmine had seen fit to heal her as well. Karria smiled, pulling a kerchief from her pocket and dabbed at her friend's eyes.

"There's no need to cry anymore," she said soothingly. "I am quite alright, thanks to Professor Palmine, and it's not your fault at all for what happened. That girl wouldn't have been content to leave you alone, even if I hadn't been here." A frown creased her face here.

That psycho had nearly killed her, and for what? Talking to Kya? Saying a few words, she didn't want to hear? This girl was clearly far more dangerous than a mere bully if she were willing to go so far. Someone like that had to be dealt with.

"This girl is clearly a danger. Not just to you and me, but to everyone around. We will be speaking to the king and queen, and you will tell them what she's been doing to you, as well as what happened today."

Kya nodded, her lower lip quivering a little as tears threatened to start falling again.

"None of that!" Karria said, "You don't have to cry anymore. I'm alive, you're alive, and we'll get them back for what happened here today!"

Kya nodded again, forcing a smile onto her face.

"It's about time we get rid of her."

Karria smiled back and together they headed back towards the palace.

38

Suffice it to say that that night was a busy one. The guards at the gate – upon seeing the state they were in – had immediately escorted the two of them to the king and queen.

After hearing what had happened, and what had been going on at the school, Blyss immediately called for the headmaster and sent guards out to arrest Eletha.

Vartan had come in just a few minutes ago, and now the five of them were sitting around the table in the throne room. Kya was sitting between the king and queen, with Vartan and Karria sitting across them.

The headmaster was outraged at what had been going on behind his back and had immediately sent a messenger with a letter of expulsion for Nina. Unfortunately, it appeared that Eletha had gotten a warning and had managed to escape before the guards had shown up.

"We have our military scouring the city as we speak," Blyss said with barely contained rage.

"To think," Vartan said, anger in his voice as well. "That all of this was going on without my knowledge. I will step down as headmaster immediately for this affront, Your Highness. I am not worthy of the position."

"I don't think that will be necessary, Headmaster," Alvine said. "After all, everyone was keeping it a secret, so if anyone is to blame for this atrocity, it is us."

Karria was about to object, when she was cut off by Blyss.

"You are absolutely correct, my husband. As Kya's surrogate parents, we should have noticed that something was wrong. We were too busy with our own affairs to give her our full attention. Rest assured, we will be rectifying our mistake."

She hugged Kya tightly to her side, kissing the top of her head.

"Mother, please don't do that in front of everyone," Kya said, as she flushed red with embarrassment.

Karria had noticed that she'd been calling the king and queen 'mother' and 'father' since she'd come in. Kya had immediately burst into tears once more, once she'd seen them, and Karria was surprised at the amount of affection the king and queen showed her.

"I will do whatever I please!" the queen said, kissing her on the cheek and hugging her even tighter.

There was a knock on the door, and an elf dressed in armor with two stripes on his shoulder came in a saluted.

"Reporting in, Your Majesties," the elf said with a bow.

"What have you found, Captain?" Alvine asked, leaning forward in his chair a bit.

"We have been unable to find the runaway in the city. We must, therefore, surmise that she has escaped into the forest."

"I want that sister of hers brought in for questioning," Alvine said. "Perhaps she will know where that devil of a girl has run off to."

"And be careful when you do find her," Vartan put in. "She's been classified as a Destructor class Mage and is currently at Tier 4. She's extremely dangerous, especially if she's gone rogue."

The guard nodded to the headmaster, then to the king.

"We'll keep that in mind and keep you updated regularly."

The elf captain then bowed at the waist and left the room.

Vartan stood up then, shaking his head in disbelief.

"I will go back to the school now. I will need to speak with the professors to make sure something like this will never happen again. If you will excuse me. Your Majesties," he bowed to each of them, then swept from the room.

Blyss and Alvine now looked at Karria. She squirmed a bit in her seat under those gazes.

"It would appear that we once again owe you a debt for saving one of our children," Blyss said in a tone that Karria could not quite place.

"No, I was glad to help. After all, Kya is a wonderful friend and I wouldn't see any harm come to her."

"All the same," the king said. "Without your intervention and aid, our daughter may very well have been killed. If not today, then maybe in a month or a year. You were right that that girl would not have been content just leaving her alone. Not to mention that you were nearly killed yourself, just for standing up for her."

He sighed here, leaning back a bit in the chair and looking suddenly very tired.

"So long as you stay with us, we will make sure to care for you. If you are ever in need of anything, just name it, and it will be yours."

Karria was flattered by the king's gratitude and stood to bow to them.

"If it's quite alright with you, Your Majesties, the only reward I want is to continue to attend the magic school with Kya."

Alvine and Blyss smiled at that, and she saw Kya's lip trembling again.

"If you will excuse me. I am very tired and would really like to get some rest."

"Of course, dear," Blyss said. "Have a good night."

Karria waved once to Kya before heading out of the throne room, heading down the hall and into her room where she flopped back onto her bed with a sigh.

She was exhausted. Physically, she felt fine. She had Palmine to thank for that. It was the mental strain of the day that was just too much for her. She just wanted to lay there and fall asleep, but she knew she should change out of her dirty clothes at the very least.

With a groan, she forced herself to get up and change into a nightgown. Picking up her torn dress, she examined it in dismay.

It had been her favorite one, and she'd only gotten to wear it once. It was only then that it really began to sink in. She'd nearly died today and all because she couldn't use her magic at will. Worse, her friend could have been killed, and it would have been her fault.

She felt tears of frustration and shame begin to fall. Her self-loathing was interrupted a moment later by a knock at her door. Quickly wiping her eyes, she walked over to open it. Kya was standing there, dressed for bed as well, and holding a pillow under one arm.

"Would you mind if I sleep with you tonight?" she asked in a quiet voice. "I don't think I'll be able to sleep alone."

Karria nodded, moving aside to let her friend in. She was secretly glad that Kya had come, as the thought of sleeping alone that night terrified her.

The two of them slid into Karria's bed. It was quite large and there was plenty of room. Karria leaned over and turned down the lamp, leaving only a sliver of moonlight peeking in through the curtains.

"There are guards posted through the hallway," she heard Kya say. "Mother and father insisted on it."

"I've noticed you've started calling them that since you first saw them earlier," Karria commented.

She felt Kya shifting around a bit next to her, before she heard a reply.

"I used to call them that all the time when I was younger. I'm not sure why I stopped, but at some point, I just did."

There was a pause here and Karria thought that she was finished talking, but after another few moments, she continued.

"Today, after seeing what that horrible girl did to you, I realized something. I realized who really matters most to me in this world. I may have lost my birth parents, but the king and queen raised me as if I were their daughter. It would be disrespectful of me to call them anything but mother and father."

Karria nodded, though she wasn't sure if Kya would be able to see her in the dark. She was happy for her friend. Sure, she could feel jealous that Kya still had a family and she didn't, but she wasn't that kind of person.

Then a thought occurred to her, something she should have thought of the moment Alvine offered her anything she could ask for. She opened her mouth, licking her lips nervously then asking, "Do you think the king and queen could find out if my brother is alive?"

"If you ask them, I have no doubt that they will," Kya answered. "He must really be special, for you to still have so much hope for him."

Karria heard that same odd tone of longing in her friend's voice. She'd heard it the last she'd spoken of Arbor and wondered what it could mean.

Shaking her head, she rolled over and closed her eyes.

Tomorrow would be a new day she could think about it then.

"Goodnight, Karria," she heard Kya's gentle voice say through the darkness.

"Goodnight, Kya," she whispered back.

She pulled the blanket up to her chin and promptly fell asleep.

39

"Of course, come right in, um…" Arbor said, unsure of the proper form of address.

The striking woman smiled a knowing smile, then stepped past him into the empty room.

"When we are in public, the correct term of address is Co-founder or General," she said, looking around the room for a moment before sitting on the corner of his bed.

She eyed the cracked wall with a raised eyebrow, then gave him an appraising look.

"When we are alone, or in smaller groups, you may call me Ramona. If you are ever unsure, just call me by my title."

Arbor nodded stiffly and just stood there, shuffling his feet and pulling the blanket tighter around himself.

"Well, don't just stand there. Sit," she said, motioning to a spot next to her on the bed.

Arbor felt a bit uncomfortable at the thought of sitting down next to a woman he'd only just met, especially one that was so brazen as to dress the way she did.

There was also the way she was looking at him, seeming to see right through him and to his very soul. It was unnerving. He shivered a bit, then settled on leaning against the opposite wall.

"I'm fine here, thanks."

Ramona just shrugged.

"Suit yourself."

She stared at him for a few more minutes in silence, her fingers steepled under her chin. Arbor had begun shuffling uncomfortably under that stare before she began speaking again.

"I can't help but notice that all your wounds seem to be gone," she said, giving him a questioning glance.

"It's my magic," Arbor answered quickly, glad that the tense silence had finally been broken. "It takes a heavy toll on my body if I use too much. Once I stop using it, though, my injuries will usually be healed." He shifted slightly to find a more comfortable position against the wall and continued speaking.

"What I'm not sure about is how far I can push myself before my ability to heal will cease to function."

Ramona had a thoughtful look on her face as he finished his explanation.

"That is indeed interesting," she said, seeming to pin him in place with that piercing gaze. "Your magic is unlike anything I've heard of before. Nor have I heard of someone with that much power, at least not at your current Tier…" She trailed off here, and he shifted again.

Noticing his discomfort, she shook her head and patted the bed once again.

"That wall doesn't look very comfortable. Stop being an idiot and just sit down."

Arbor thought about refusing for a second, then just shrugged. If she didn't mind, why should he? It was his bed, after all.

Walking over to the bed, he sat on the opposite end and leaned against the headboard, a small sigh of relief escaping his lips.

"I don't mean to be rude or anything," Arbor began. "But I've never seen anyone quite like you before. You are quite striking, your eyes, your hair, even your ears."

There was a time when he would never have been quite so bold with a woman, especially one this pretty. However, he'd recently discovered that asking direct questions and not dancing around the subject was the best way to get answers.

"There's also some kind of…" he paused here, trying to find the correct words. "Presence flowing from you. I can feel it even now."

Ramona started a bit at this last comment and looked around furtively as if someone might be listening in. She stood then and quickly opened the door, looking both ways before closing it and coming back inside.

Arbor wondered if he'd somehow insulted her, but when she sat back down and began speaking, his worries were alleviated.

"To answer your first question, I am a human. However, my grandfather was an elf and as you can see, I have inherited some of their traits, though no one could mistake me for a full-blooded elf."

So, it was possible for the other races to have children with one another, Arbor noted. So Grak's interest in him wasn't completely unfounded. Arbor's line of thinking was interrupted, though, as she continued.

"As for your second question... I will only answer if you tell me how you knew."

"How I knew what?" he asked, his eyebrows coming together in confusion.

"How can you sense this power radiating off me, as you so put it." She looked at him intently, waiting for his reply.

Arbor could see that this was some kind of test. She was sizing him up and seeing whether he was trustworthy or not.

"Well, to tell you the truth, I'm not entirely sure," he said, scratching his chin.

How had he felt that power? It might have something to do with his new magic. His thoughts trailed off here as the answer seemed to smack him right in the face.

"It's magic! That's what I'm feeling from you, isn't it?" he asked in triumph.

He'd never met another Mage before, well aside from Grak, anyway.

She smiled at him then and nodded.

"I am indeed a Mage. It's one of my most closely guarded secrets, and very few know of its existence."

"How do you manage to keep it a secret?" he asked, curious. "If you're one of the leaders of the rebels, shouldn't your magic be well known?"

"First of all," she said, a small frown creasing her brow. "Don't call us rebels. We are the Defiants, a group of people who believe the king's rule is unjust and wish to see him removed from the throne. Second, the reasons I have been able to keep my secret is that I have been very careful to hide its existence. My magic tends to deal with the mind and therefore, can be hidden."

Arbor raised an eyebrow.

Ramona smiled a bit at that and elaborated.

"I have the ability to cast illusions. In battle, this could give us an advantage. For example, I can make our force seem smaller, or less well equipped than they are, to make our enemies overconfident. The trick to keeping it a secret is to never stretch the bounds too far into the realms of the impossible."

Arbor was intrigued. "What do you mean by that?"

"I can, for example, make them believe there is a massive monster standing right in front of them. The problem with that would be when the monster didn't attack, or if they attacked it, they would discover it to be insubstantial."

This was all quite fascinating. A magic that dealt directly with what people perceived to be real or not. He wondered if the illusions were conjured, or if Ramona's magic dealt directly with people's minds and made them see what she wanted.

"What is your magic called, if I might ask?"

"I'll tell you, but only if you tell me what yours is called, how it works, and what your magic is classified as." Ramona smirked a bit at this.

Arbor found that he was quickly warming to the woman.

She knew what she wanted and wasn't shy about asking. She was just what he'd expect of a military leader. Not that he really knew any military leaders other than her.

He shook his head to clear his wandering thoughts once again. He needed to find out more about her, especially if she was his way to get to Karria.

"Very well, but I expect an answer once I'm finished with my explanation."

Ramona nodded in agreement and he began explaining his magic.

"My magic is called Perception. I can strengthen my body, predict other's movements, and slow the world around me as I fight." He left out quite a bit of the finer details, as he was sure she had.

He liked the woman but wasn't about to reveal all his secrets.

Ramona nodded, though her brows creased.

"You still haven't told me what your magic classification is, but I guess everyone wants to keep theirs a secret. As for my magic, it's called Misdirection, and I've already explained what I can do with it. Surprisingly enough, it's classified as a Non-combat type magic, though I really don't care what they say. What I really want to know is what kind of power you used to kill all those lizards," she said, leaning forward a bit, her piercing gaze back on him.

Arbor still had no idea what she was going on about with magic classifications and figured it was something he'd have to ask about without seeming too suspicious. She was on to him about his new magic, and he had to come up with a reasonable explanation without giving himself away.

"I used my Perception magic. I heightened my strength and speed to the point where the lizards could not react in time. I then proceeded to kill them all, but I greatly damaged my body in the process."

She raised an eyebrow and he found he didn't enjoy the expression nearly as much, now that it was being used on him.

"I've heard reports of a bright light before the lizards died," she said, searching his face for any sign of deception.

"I don't know anything about a bright light that killed those lizards," Arbor said, trying to meet her gaze.

He immediately knew he'd slipped up somehow when a look of triumph spread across her face.

"I never specified that the lizards were killed by this light. I only said that there was a bright light before they died." She smirked in a self-satisfied way.

"Did I say the light killed them?" Arbor asked, panicking a bit. "What I meant to say, was that I never saw any light at all." Even to him, this sounded very bad. He'd never been a very good liar.

"I suppose that crater on your wall just happened to form on its own, as well?"

"I got annoyed and hit it," he said lamely.

She quirked an eyebrow at him once again.

"I suppose that's possible. However, an impact like that would most definitely have done some damage to your hand at the very least. You wouldn't mind if I look at it, or perhaps call the healer?"

He could tell that she was sure he was hiding something by now. It was now just a matter of whether he would fess up or not.

"Very well," Arbor sighed, giving the Co-founder a sour look.

They were both well aware that the healer would find nothing wrong with his hand. Even if he used the excuse that his magic had healed it, this woman seemed like the kind of person who could get people to spill their secrets.

"But before I say anything else, I will have you swear an oath of secrecy. This can be potentially dangerous information, and I'll not have it leaking out. In fact, I'd prefer it if no one knew what we spoke about today at all."

Ramona thought for a moment, then nodded gravely. "You have my word."

Arbor nodded, then brought his arm out from under the blanket.

He really hoped he would be able to control it this time. Taking a deep breath, he allowed the white magic to begin leaking off his skin, feeling the thrumming power from his chest once again.

Ramona's eyes widened as he did this and she stared at him in shocked amazement.

"You have a second Origin?"

40

Arbor sat in silence as Ramona stared at his glowing hand. Then, after a few moments, he contained it with an effort of will, the light winking out. She seemed to come to herself then, and when she looked at him again, it was with an odd expression that Arbor couldn't quite place.

"What did you mean when you said I had a second Origin?"

"Exactly what I asked," Ramona replied. "This is clearly a different kind of magic than the one you described to me. I thought that you were perhaps hiding certain aspects of your power, but this…" She trailed off here, her mind going into overdrive.

"You still haven't explained what you meant, though."

He was growing a bit annoyed that she wasn't giving him a straight answer.

"What part of that didn't you understand? You clearly have a second Origin."

She seemed genuinely confused by his question, and he couldn't understand why.

"What's an Origin?" he asked, seeing her eyebrows raise in disbelief. "And since I'm asking, what did you mean when you asked about my magic classification?"

"Your source of magic," she said slowly, looking at him as though not quite believing he could be this naive.

"Oh!" he said, finally understanding. "So the Core of magic I can feel is called an Origin. Well, that does explain it!" Arbor was more than a little embarrassed by this, and he felt his cheeks color a bit.

"What about the magic classifications?"

"Didn't they teach you that at the Magic Academy?" Ramona asked, seeming surprised.

Here it was Arbor's turn to look confused.

"I never went to magic school. Didn't Grak tell you what we've been through in the last few months?"

Ramona gaped openly at him for moment, then realizing that it was unbecoming of a General to act this way, she snapped her mouth shut.

"I only saw her for a few minutes after the two of you were brought in. There are many things that require my attention, so I haven't heard your story yet. But if what you say is true, and you've never been to a magic school, how is it that you even have the slightest bit of control?"

Arbor shrugged.

"It wasn't easy in the beginning. A few months ago, I wasn't even aware I had any magic at all. I was a carpenter, living in Woods' Clearing. I'd never even held a weapon before then."

"Now I know you must be lying," Ramona said, anger clouding her features. "It takes years of discipline and study to be able to control your magic, let alone control of two types!"

"I'm not lying," Arbor said plainly. "Believe me or not. It was challenging in the beginning, but I soon had the general idea of how to use my Perception magic. As for this white magic…" he said, letting his palm light up once again. "I only noticed it about thirty minutes ago, and I wouldn't say I have control over it."

A mix of emotions flitted across Ramona's face as he spoke, going from shock to outright disbelief and finally settling on anger.

"There's just no way that's possible!" she said, as she sprang to her feet and began pacing agitatedly. "There hasn't been someone with a second Origin born in the last thousand years, and you're telling me that you only noticed it thirty minutes ago?!" She threw her arms in the air and laughed hysterically.

Arbor began to feel a little worried at this and wondered if it would have been better to try lying.

"Ramona," he said, trying to exclude a calm demeanor as he spoke. "Look into my eyes and tell me if you really believe that I'm lying."

She stopped then and sat back down on the bed.

"You had better not be!" she hissed.

Leaning forward, she stared deep into his eyes, searching for the truth in them. He did his best to look as sincere as possible, and finally, after a few minutes of intense scrutiny, she seemed to relax.

"Fine. I believe you," she said in a quiet voice.

She then moved further back onto the bed, placing her back to the wall and pulled her knees up to her chin. She looked at him through the corners of her eyes, her lips twitching to form a small smile as she did so.

"You must be quite the powerful Mage to be able to control your magic so soon after discovering it. Even the few prodigies I've met took years to master their magic fully, yet you've done what even they would call impossible."

Arbor raised an eyebrow at that.

"What do you mean by impossible? I helped Grak awaken her magic, and she used it only minutes later, though it did end up costing her her fingers," he said this last part to himself, and thankfully Ramona didn't hear it.

"Did you say you helped her awaken her magic?"

She was sitting upright again and staring at him in rapt attention.

"Yes," Arbor said with a sigh.

He really needed to keep his big mouth shut.

"We were fighting a Roc-Jaguar that had invaded the Jagged Peaks. When I saw that we couldn't beat it, I had Hord distract the beast and went to awaken her magic to give us a chance at victory. I'd sensed it in her on the way to the dwarf city. She'd been injured fighting a gremlin force sent after us, and while I was healing her, I stumbled across it."

"You failed to mention that you had the ability to heal others," Ramona said, not missing a beat. "You seem to be full of secrets. don't you?"

Arbor cursed silently to himself.

Hadn't he just admonished himself for having a big mouth?

"Anyways," he continued, trying to gloss over his latest slip up. "I found that she had some kind of magic, but it was dormant, so I used my magic to awaken it. After I did that, she saved me from being eaten, by freezing the beast's leg, thereby allowing me to kill it."

A thoughtful look crossed her features at that and she slowly nodded.

"Well, I have seen your armor and weapon, and after what you've told me, I have no trouble believing your story. It's just too outrageous to be made up. What interests me, however, is that the gremlin girl could use her magic right away."

She scooted closer to him then, her body practically touching his. "Can you try it with me?" she asked in an eager voice.

Arbor could feel his cheeks heating at the close proximity, especially seeing as he was dressed in just a pair of underwear. The only thing keeping him covered being the blanket he'd tossed over his shoulders. He may be comfortable speaking his mind, but women could definitely still unnerve him.

"Can I try what?" he asked, clearing his throat nervously.

"Try feeling for my magic with yours. No one's ever done it before," she said, moving just a bit closer and holding out her hand. "There were people who could sense my magic back in school, but I've never heard of someone who could awaken dormant magic in others."

Arbor stared at the proffered hand for a moment, before carefully sliding his arm out through a gap in the blanket and taking it. He still wasn't sure if this was a good idea, but getting on the good side of the person in charge was never a bad thing. Closing his eyes, he concentrated on his center, following the streams of magic to his fingertips.

He found that it no longer took conscious effort to move the magic. All he needed to do was will it, and the magic obeyed. He did have to be careful not to let any of his new magic leak out though. The last thing he needed was to accidentally blow Ramona's arm off.

Unlike his perception magic, this new magic didn't seem to follow a specific path. Except for the small space that outlined his second Origin, and the clear paths of his first Origin, his entire body was permeated by the white magic.

Taking a deep breath to calm his nerves, he allowed his Perception magic flow into her. It was even harder than the last time, since he had to force his Perception magic out, and keep the new magic contained all at once. He was basically forcing two types of magic to do the exact opposite of their apparent nature.

He heard the expected gasp once his magic finally entered her body, and he felt it immediately. An electric sort of energy was coming from the base of her neck. He saw small purple balls of light drifting throughout her body. The purple balls were interspersed with sliver colored ones every once in a while, and he wondered at the two different colors.

Did she have a second Origin as well?

Then he saw it. Her Origin was completely different than his or Grak's. Unlike theirs, Ramona's was a mix of the two colors he'd seen moving through her, with the majority being purple, and just around ten percent being silver. He made his magic flow upward until it was right in front of her origin. He could feel the power coming off it and got the sense that she could do much more than cast illusions.

"Your magic is different than the ones I've previously seen," Arbor said, keeping his eyes closed. "Your Origin has two colors, and I find that very interesting."

He felt her hand tighten a bit as he spoke.

"Most only have one color, as you said, but there are a few that have two, and some even have three. My teachers at the academy believed that it had something to do with my elven heritage."

Arbor nodded. It made sense, though the news that some people had more than one color, but only had one Origin confused him somewhat.

"Why don't you have two separate Origins like I do?" he asked, his eyes still closed.

He needed to decide whether to strengthen her or not. He knew instinctively that he could, and unlike with the horses, this would be permanent.

"Most people who have more than one color to their magic will have more innate talent than those who don't. There are many theories as to why some have more than one color in a single Origin, while there are a rare few who have single colors but have more than one. The one that most agree on is that those with a second Origin will be able to use more than one type of magic. While those with different colors in their Origins will have one type of magic be dominant over the rest. There are a rare few cases when the different colors complement one another, and an entirely new type of magic is created."

Arbor could feel the truth through their connection. He could also see that while he could strengthen her magic, he could not separate the two colors. He made up his mind then and taking a deep breath, he moved his magic up to her Origin.

The moment their two magics touched, he felt her go stiff as a board. Memories and sensations flooded him, and his concentration nearly slipped. He breathed deeply again and began pouring his magic into her origin, feeling his magic mixing with hers.

He could feel it working, as Ramona's Origin reacted to his magic, beginning to glow brightly and grow in size. He had to keep concentrating as the flood of memories grew stronger and began battering at his consciousness.

Ramona as a young girl being made fun of for her parentage. Ramona in school, projecting her first illusion and feeling pride at her accomplishment. Ramona coming home one day to find that her father had been killed by the king's soldiers. He could feel her sorrow and anguish as she realized what had happened. The anger and hatred she felt towards the king...

He abruptly pulled back as the memories became too painful, retracting his magic back into himself and breathing hard as sweat beaded his brow. Opening his eyes, he saw her trembling slightly as she hugged herself.

"Ramona?" he asked in a quiet voice.

She opened her eyes and looked at him then. There was so much sadness behind those eyes, but there was anger as well- a deep burning well of rage that burned just as hotly as his did. Taking a deep, shuddering breath, she composed herself and stood from the bed.

"I can feel what you did to me."

Her voice sounded shaky, and not at all like the person he'd been talking to just a few minutes ago.

"I thank you for what you've done," her voice steadier now. "I asked you to do this, so I have only myself to blame. However, I will ask that you keep this a secret, just as you have asked me to keep yours."

Arbor nodded. He understood her better than he even understood himself at the moment. More than that, he understood the rage and pain she'd felt at losing her father. Then a frightening thought occurred to him.

"Were you able to see my thoughts too?" he asked uncertainly.

Ramona looked at him for a moment before nodding, a look of sorrow coming back to her face.

"I have felt loss before, but you are in so much pain." She shuddered a little at that. "I am angry as well, but even I couldn't bear so much suffering. It would drive me mad."

Arbor just sat there in silence, not sure of what to say. It appeared that there was yet another part of his magic that he didn't understand. And why hadn't the same thing happened when he'd awakened Grak's magic?

Ramona cleared her throat and finally met his eyes.

"I understand what your goals are now. We both want to take the slave city. I, to weaken the king and add to our army, and you to free your sister. I will have your weapons and armor returned to you. Come see me tomorrow after you are well-rested, and we will discuss this further. Do you agree to this, Arbor?"

Arbor looked up at her, fire in his eyes.

He was nearing his goals now. He was closer than ever, and this woman would give him the chance to do so. Even better than that, he now likely knew her better than anyone else, and he trusted her motivations.

"I agree. So long as our goals align, I will stay with the Defiants."

Ramona relaxed here and gave him a sad smile. She surprised him then by walking over and wrapping her arms around him.

All these touchy people were really beginning to annoy him.

"We are one and the same, Arbor," she said quietly into his ear. "But do not let your anger and rage rule you, lest it destroy you someday."

She released him then and walked to the door. She looked back at him one more time as she pulled it open, her golden eyes full of sorrow. Then she left, closing the door gently behind her, leaving Arbor to sit there and ponder his future.

41

A few weeks had passed since the incident with Eletha, and things were finally beginning to settle down a bit. The headmaster had made a speech in front of the entire school the day after the attack. He'd made it clear that if anyone was caught harming another student, they would be immediately expelled. If that student was over the age of sixteen, they would be arrested and jailed for their crime.

He also made it clear that the kind of bullying that Eletha had been doing would not be tolerated, and if any students were caught, they would be facing a two-week suspension. If there were more than three such suspensions, the student would then be expelled.

Suffice it to say, the other students were shocked at how serious the normally easygoing headmaster had been and realized that more than a few students were no longer among them.

Karria had found out that aside from Nina, seven others had been expelled for the part they played in her torture, and two others had been suspended. Of the seven expelled, three had been arrested and were now sitting in prison.

Eletha was still missing, and any questioning of Nina hadn't led anywhere. Unfortunately, Nina was still too young to go to prison, but Karria had found out she was being punished in a different way. She would be forced to do menial labor for the next year, then would be conscripted into the military.

Kya was still a bit worried that they hadn't found Eletha yet, but Karria did her best to reassure her. For the first two weeks after the attack, they had even been escorted by guards everywhere they went, but Kya soon convinced the king and queen that it was necessary. School had also gotten much better once their tormentors were gone. Their other classmates now actually talked to them and treated them with respect.

Kya was quick to forgive and accepted their apologies with grace. Karria wasn't so forgiving. These same people had tormented her friend for over two years, and now they suddenly wanted to be friends?

One thing she did notice was that Sylvester's attitude towards her had changed. When he saw her, he would wave or even give her a smile. She turned her nose up at him, too. She knew she was probably being bratty, but he wasn't going to get off that easily, especially after what he'd done to her.

Another good thing happened to her the morning after the attack. She'd gone to see Blyss and Alvine, and they'd agreed to help look for her brother. They said they would let her know as soon as they had any news. She'd been ecstatic and had thanked them profusely. That bit of news had kept her excited all that week and into the next.

It soon wore off when no news was forthcoming, and right now, she was far from ecstatic. She let out an explosive breath as she opened her eyes and allowed her magic to slip from her grasp.

That damned hourglass was on its side again, and Professor Palmine was marking down her time.

"Fifteen minutes and thirty-eight seconds," she said in a flat tone. "That's a whole second faster than yesterday, and two seconds slower than the day before that!"

Karria scowled at the woman.

It wasn't her fault that she wasn't getting any better with her control. She'd been trying her best, but no matter how hard she pushed, her magic was always slow to respond. It made her wonder how she'd been able to use it twice before without conscious effort when she could barely get it budge now.

"At this rate, I'll be long dead by the time you can direct the flow of your magic fast enough to use it," Palmine grumbled, as she scratched her chin.

"Well, it's not my fault!" Karria exclaimed, frustration clearly tinging her voice. "I keep trying, but it's as if my magic were moving through quicksand! It doesn't want to follow my direction all!"

Palmine looked up sharply as she said this, and her eyes widened a bit.

"Say that again."

"Say what again?" Karria asked in annoyance.

"The last thing you said, about your magic's direction," she said impatiently. "And be quick about it, girl!"

"It's as if it doesn't want to follow my direction at all?" Karria repeated, her brows knitting together in confusion.

"Of course!" Palmine exclaimed and stood from her cushion to begin pacing. "Your magic comes from your Origin in beams of light, and they shoot in random directions. Trying to force magic out of its usual path is difficult! Why didn't I think of that?"

"Um, professor?" Karria asked. "Would you mind explaining what you're going on about?"

Palmine stopped her pacing and looked down at her student, before composing herself and sitting back down.

"I believe that we've been going about this all wrong," she said, breathing out a heavy sigh. "I suppose it's partly my fault for not considering that your Origin may act a little differently than normal. Let me ask you a question. Have you been able to follow any of the light beams coming from your Origin?"

Karria shook her head.

"All I've been doing is trying to make them move towards my hands. They move too quickly for me to follow."

Palmine nodded as if expecting this answer.

"I want you to try a new exercise for me."

She leaned forward and took up her charcoal and paper again.

"Close your eyes, and this time, I want you to try and slow the beams of light. It is the opposite of our next exercise, but I don't think it should be too much trouble."

Karria looked uncertain but did as she was instructed. Closing her eyes, she soon found her Origin. The rainbow-colored sphere was pulsing in the same way it always did, with random light beams shooting off faster than she could follow. Concentrating hard on her magic, she willed the beams of light to slow down. To her utter amazement, it immediately responded, her Origin's pulsing slowing to a point where she could now follow the light beams.

"I did it!" she exclaimed, opening her eyes.

She saw Palmine tip the hourglass on its side and make a note.

"Forty-eight seconds," she said, smiling for the first time all week. "Now, this time, when you slow the light beams down, I want you to follow the paths of ten separate ones and tell me where each one goes."

Karria nodded and closed her eyes again. She was ecstatic! This was the first time she'd managed to do anything so quickly.

Finding her Origin more, she slowed the light beams down and followed them as instructed. The first one made a winding journey through her spine and ended up by her foot. She thought it would stop there but was shocked to find it make its way back up, until it joined her Origin again.

This revelation stunned her, and she was quick to follow a few more. They each took a different path, but all ended up rejoining her Origin in the end. It was as if her Origin was constantly cycling magic through her, before returning it and repeating the process. She opened her eyes and shared her revelation with Palmine.

Her teacher looked excited and self-satisfied in a way Karria could very well understand.

"I think I've figured out your magic's flow," she said, putting her charcoal down and giving Karria her full attention.

"I believe that your magic follows through your nervous system, traveling through your nerves on fixed paths. The light may seem to be random, but I think that if you look closely, you will find that every beam has a fixed loop. Try doing it like this- close your eyes and find the loops passing closest to your hands, then try and keep the magic there when it reaches that point."

Karria nodded and once again, closed her eyes. It took her no time at all to slow the magic down, and she searched carefully until she found two loops that passed through her wrists. As soon as light reached the space, she concentrated on making them stop. Surprisingly enough, it worked! The lights stopped there, but that wasn't the end of it. Soon another beam of light came down the same track and was stopped behind the first one.

She immediately allowed her magic to speed back up, and in a matter of seconds, she could feel the power building. Opening her eyes, she released the flow of magic, and beamed at her teacher.

"I did it!" she cried out in exaltation.

Palmine made another note and looked up at her with a smile.

"One minute and two seconds. Try it again."

Closing her eyes, she did it again. She knew where to look now, and it was much easier to let the magic collect this time. She opened her eyes again, and Palmine turned the hourglass on its side again.

"Thirty-two seconds. Again!" she snapped.

Karria wasn't sure why the professor was insisting she keep doing it, but she did as she was told.

After ten more minutes, she'd further shortened her time by over half. She could now direct her magic to her wrists in eleven seconds. When she asked Palmine why she had her repeat the exercise so many times, she explained.

"I don't want you to forget that feeling. To make sure the lesson sinks in, we will keep repeating it until you can bring your speed down to five seconds or less. Then, when you can do it one hundred times in a row, we will move on to the next lesson."

"A hundred times in a row!" Karria exclaimed. "I don't think it's possible for me to do it any faster."

That last time was about the fastest she thought she could manage at the moment.

Professor Palmine just shook her head.

"You must train yourself to be able to follow your magic at a faster rate. The less you have to slow down the flow, the faster your magic will collect in any one given area. This part, however, will be all up to you. You must practice daily, even when you are not at school."

Karria nodded.

The old woman may be harsh, but she was undoubtedly the best teacher at this school. She would never have thought it possible to slow the flow of her magic. True, it had taken weeks for her to figure it out, but when she did, Palmine had taken her time down from nearly sixteen minutes to eleven seconds in about ten minutes of work!

Karria walked home that evening with Kya. She was in a considerably better mood than she'd been that morning.

"You seem happy," her friend observed.

"Yeah," Karria replied with a smile. "My lesson with Professor Palmine went quite well today."

"Really?" Kya asked with interest.

She'd been listening to the endless complaining from her friend about the impossibility of her lessons over the last few weeks.

Karria went on to explain what had had happened. During target practice, she'd managed to destroy all the targets, and in record time! Her aim was still dreadful though, and Palmine had made sure she'd known it.

"I'm really glad to hear," Kya said, as the two entered the palace.

They began to walk to their rooms, now chatting about their latest class at the sweets shop. Last week they'd learned to make taffy, a chewy sweet that could have all sorts of flavors. The upcoming lesson was what they were looking forward to most, as they were going to learn how to make chocolate. Karria could hardly wait or this one and neither could Kya.

They were about to enter Kya's room when a guard rushed over to them.

"The king and queen would like to see you, miss," he said to Karria.

She looked curiously at Kya, but her friend merely shrugged and motioned her to go.

"They want you, Lady Kya, as well," the guard said with a slight bow.

"Lead the way, then," she said, the two girls following the guard to the throne room.

Entering the large circular room, Karria was surprised to see the king and queen by the table, instead of on their thrones. Even more surprising was that Sylvester was there. He looked scared and squirmed in his chair uncomfortably as the queen glared at him.

The two of them approached and bowed to Blyss and Alvine, before taking two chairs across from them.

"What's going on here?" Karria asked, looking from the queen's angry face to Sylvester, who wouldn't meet her gaze.

"It would appear," the king began, grabbing Karria's attention. "That your brother is indeed alive."

Karria sat back in stunned amazement. She could feel tears trying to work themselves from her eyes, and her heart skipped a beat.

"How do you know this?" she asked, her voice quivering with emotion as she fought to contain herself. Her heart was pounding, and she could scarcely breathe.

Here Blyss spoke up, taking her glare from Sylvester and looking at her.

"Apparently," she began, making a visible effort to contain her anger. "Sylvester has known for months but didn't think it was important enough to share until now!"

42

Karria sat in stunned silence for a few moments, staring wide-eyed at the king and queen. She looked at Sylvester then and felt hot anger begin to boil inside her.

"Look at me, Sylvester," she said in a dangerously calm voice.

Sylvester wouldn't meet her gaze. She was about to start yelling when she felt a hand on top of hers, and a calming sensation washed over her. Looking over, she gave her friend a grateful smile.

It wouldn't do to lose her head over this.

Kya looked at Sylvester then, concentrating hard. She sat back after a moment, a grim look on her face.

"It's true, I can feel it," she said in a flat tone. She turned to the king and queen. "I'm guessing that you wanted me here, to confirm he was telling the truth?"

"Yes," Alvine answered with a sigh.

He was afraid of this and looked nervously to Karria. He clearly remembered what had happened the last time Sylvester had pulled a stunt like this, and how it had ended.

He was mildly surprised at the calm expression on her face. Glancing down, he could see Kya's hand resting on hers. He was glad he'd asked her to come. Her magic was likely the only thing keeping Karria from throwing Sylvester through another wall.

"How long has he known?" she asked, not even bothering to look at Sylvester now.

"He found out more than two weeks before you arrived here," she said quietly. "Apparently someone named Silver told him to keep it to himself."

Karria felt her anger returning then and felt Kya's hand tighten as she attempted to keep her calm. What possible reason could Silver have to keep it a secret? How had he even known that Arbor was alive?

As if reading her mind, and Karria thought she may very well be doing exactly that, Kya answered her unasked question.

"Your brother spent a month with Silver before you met him. He'd actually only left a week before the two of you met."

"He was only a week away?!" Karria asked, her anger boiling over.

Even Kya's magic wasn't enough to calm her now.

"I thought my brother was dead!" she screamed as she shot to her feet, the chair clattering to the floor behind her.

"How dare you keep that from me?! He was only a week away! We could have gone after him! I'd probably be with him right now, if it weren't for you!"

Sylvester cowered against his chair as Karria's voice grew louder and louder. Guards had rushed in at the screaming, but Blyss waived them back, looking worried.

"Karria, we can understand how upset you are," she began in a soothing voice. "It is true that he kept this from you, but it was Silver who asked him to do so. It would have been folly for him to go against his will. Even now, he took a risk by telling us."

She didn't care about whose fault it was. She had thought that Sylvester had been her friend, even if just for a little bit. Now she could see that he'd been lying to her from the start!

Kya's magic washed over her again in deep soothing waves, and Karria tried to calm herself, clenching and unclenching her fists as she battled with her emotions.

Nothing would be gained from yelling at the hapless elf or throwing him through another wall.

She stooped and righted her chair. Sitting down again, she felt Kya's hand back on hers. The calming presence of her magic washed over her again, and she felt herself relax a bit more.

Her brother was alive! That's what really mattered. Now all she needed to know was his location.

"Do you know where he is?" she asked Alvine.

"Unfortunately, we do not know his location at the moment," the king said, with an annoyed look at Sylvester. "All we could gather was that Silver seemed to hint that he would be coming here sometime to train his magic. That is all we have to go on at the moment."

"Well then, tell me," Karria said, her fist clenching at her side and her eyes narrowing a bit. "Who is Silver, really? Why do you seem so afraid of him? The man I knew was kind and gentle. He looked out for me and helped me find my way here."

The king and queen exchanged a nervous glance, then Blyss spoke up.

"It is not our place to divulge his secrets, nor could we even if we wanted to. Let us just say this. It would be unwise for any of us to disobey him."

Karria could see that the queen was not going to budge on this.

She had to wonder what kind of man could frighten the king and queen of the elves so much that they wouldn't even speak of him. Just what kind of person had she traveled with and why had Silver not told her that her brother was alive?

Another shocking revelation hit her then, as the words Alvine said only a few moments ago sunk in. Silver had hinted that Arbor had magic, just like her!

This was all too much for her. She had to be alone right now. Taking a deep breath, she stood from her seat.

"If you will excuse me, Your Majesties. I have a lot to think about."

With that, she spun and walked quickly from the room, ignoring them as they called after her. Her mind was in turmoil, and she decided to go on a walk through the garden to clear her head.

Walking quickly outside, she noticed that the sun was already beginning to set. She had at least another hour before the moon rose, so she set off walking through the garden. She walked down the main path and soon turned into a side path. She walked between the rows of colorful flowers, the setting sun reflecting beautifully off them. Thoughts swirled through her mind, each vying for her attention, but there was just too much to process.

Coming to a halt, she took a seat on a small bench near a water fountain and breathed in deeply. The pleasant scent of flowers entered her nose and she breathed in again, feeling her tension ease a bit.

She sat there for the next hour, thoughts of Arbor, Sylvester, and Silver swirling through her mind. One thought stood out from the rest, and it was something that seemed to lift a huge weight off her heart. She wasn't alone. Her brother was alive and would be coming here one day soon.

She kept repeating that to herself, the thought calming her, and making her feel more at peace than she'd felt in a very long time.

It was nearly dark out by the time she headed back inside the palace. Walking down the hallway, she knocked on Kya's door.

She needed someone to talk to, and Kya would always listen. She waited a few moments then knocked again.

That was odd. Why wasn't she answering?

She knocked a third time.

Kya always answered her door. Even if she was in the middle of a bath or already in bed, she'd still come to see who it was.

She stood there for a few more minutes before finally giving up and shrugging to herself. It was possible that she was asleep, or maybe she was still with the king and queen.

Going back into her room, she closed the door and got into her nightgown. It had been a long day, and she was looking forward to a good night of sleep. She was getting ready to turn down the lamp, when a knock came at her door.

Must be Kya, she thought as she slid out of bed and went to answer.

She was surprised, however, to see Sylvester standing there instead, a worried look on his face.

Karria glowered at him.

"What do you want?"

She had no patience for him right now, especially since she'd found out he'd been keeping such a big secret.

"Have you seen Kya?"

"No. Last I saw her was right before leaving the throne room," Karria said curtly.

Sylvester's face grew pale at this. "Are you sure you haven't seen her?"

"Why would I have seen her?" she asked, now growing a little worried herself.

"Because she went after you just a few minutes after you left!" Sylvester said, now beginning to panic.

"Then why are you so worried?" Karria asked, growing annoyed.

Sure, she hadn't seen her friend, but she was probably just sleeping. Sylvester handed her a piece of paper in answer. He was pale and his hands were shaking.

Karria took the paper and opened it, deciding to amuse the elf, if only to get rid of him faster. As she read the note through, she felt a cold horror wash over her.

To the Human Sow:

I have the little Princess. Meet me a day's march to the east through the forest. Come alone. If I hear any soldiers, I'll slit her pretty little throat.

~Eletha.

"Where did you get this?" Karria asked, looking up at her former friend.

"Nina handed it to me. I'd gone out of the palace grounds for a walk when she approached me with this note. She said to make sure you got it."

He looked as though he was going to be sick.

"Why didn't you tell anyone about this?!" Karria demanded. "We need to go to the king and queen right away!"

She quickly slid on a pair of slippers and tried to head out of the room, but found Sylvester blocking her way.

"You can't tell anyone!" he said, panic in his voice. "You read the note. If soldiers come, she'll kill Kya before they can save her!"

Karria had half a mind to put Sylvester through the opposite wall, but what he said did make sense to her.

If they went to the king and queen, they would undoubtedly send soldiers after them. Kya might very well end up dead if that happened, and Karria would rather die before allowing any harm to befall her friend.

Calming her racing heart, she stared Sylvester in the eye.

"It looks like the two of us will have to go after her alone."

Sylvester swallowed hard but nodded.

"Meet me at the entrance in fifteen minutes. Make sure to wear sturdy clothes and bring plenty of water."

Sylvester nodded again and rushed off down the hall to do as she said.

Closing the door quickly, Karria stripped out of her nightgown and put on the sturdy dress she'd had made for her lessons with Palmine.

She'd found out rather quickly that regular fabric didn't hold up too well when she was throwing magic around. She'd had a sturdy dress made of hard leather to avoid any wardrobe malfunctions. She slid the dress over her head and pulled a pair of tight-fitting pants on underneath.

The dress wasn't pretty, but it would be perfect for running through the forest. Next, she opened her desk drawer and pulled out the sheathed dagger Silver had given her before he left. Pulling the dagger out quickly, she made sure the red blade was sharp, before sliding it back in.

Belting it to her waist, she pulled on a pair of leather boots, lacing them up as quickly as she could. She looked around the room one last time once she'd finished, to make sure she hadn't forgotten anything, then rushed into the hallway and headed to the entrance.

Sylvester was already waiting. He was holding two large waterskins, a small bag of dried meat, and a long dagger at his waist.

"How will we get past the gate guards?" he asked, as they opened the main door and began jogging down the path.

The spring moon was now high in the sky, its brilliant green light shining off the flowers around them.

"Don't you worry about that," Karria said. She turned quickly onto a side path and headed to the wall.

In truth, it wasn't much of a wall, more like a tall stone fence. The problem was the tall metal spikes protruding from the top. She looked around a few times to make sure no one was watching then turned to Sylvester.

"Use your magic to pry those bars apart," she whispered.

Sylvester just shook his head at her.

"Did you really think it would be that easy? The metal is immune to magic. It's made of the same material the slavers used to restrain me."

Karria cursed under her breath at their bad luck. She would have to revise her plan on the fly and hope it worked.

They headed back to the main path and approached the gate. She could see two guards standing there and felt her heart speed up as the approached.

"Who goes there?" one of the guards called out, holding up a torch.

"It is Karria and Sylvester," she called out, coming out into the torchlight.

The guard seemed to relax a bit. Then he took in their state of dress, as well as the weapons on their belts.

"I'm not sure where the two of you are going, but I'm afraid I won't be able to let you out."

"Will you really be stopping us from doing an errand for the queen?" Karria asked, quirking a brow. "If you would like, I can go fetch her. What's your name again?"

The guard seemed to blanch a bit at that.

"No, no, that won't be necessary," he said quickly and began unlocking the gate. "I just wonder why you're both carrying weapons."

"I'm sure you remember that a dangerous criminal is still on the loose," Karria answered smoothly as she stepped past the guard. "Don't worry. We will be returning shortly."

"Would you like us to escort you?" the guard asked uncertainly.

"That will not be necessary, but thank you for the offer," Karria said, flashing the guard a brilliant smile.

The guard saluted, and the two of them headed quickly from the gates.

She'd likely bought them some time, but she couldn't be sure how long it would be before the guard reported them. They would just have to hurry and hope they made it through the gates before the king and queen found out.

"Wow! I had no idea you could lie so well!" Sylvester whispered once they were a good distance from the palace.

"I'll take that as a compliment," Karria said, shooting him a glare.

She might need him to help rescue Kya, but he was by no means forgiven.

They walked on in silence for the next few minutes, Karria's mind racing. They would still need to get past the guards at the city gates, and she began to worry that their plan was doomed to failure. She didn't have long to worry, however. As she approached the gates, she could see they were slightly ajar.

That was quite strange. The gates should have been locked at this hour. Another thing she noticed that was out of the ordinary was the complete absence of guards. They slipped out of the open gate, and the mystery of the missing guards was soon made evident.

Two bodies were slumped against the outer wall, and scorch marks marred the gate, the wood blackened and charred, and the smell of smoke lingered in the air. Leaning down, Karria could see that their faces were covered in horrible burns. She stepped back quickly, the sight almost too much for her to handle.

Eletha had clearly been this way.

She saw Sylvester go pale at the sight of the two bodies, but she just ignored him. The path into the forest stretched out in front of her and she set out, walking briskly as Sylvester scrambled to catch up.

Eletha couldn't be more than two hours ahead of them, and Karria's fists clenched as rage boiled up inside her.

If Eletha had so much as scratched her friend, she would make her regret the day she'd been born!

43

Arbor woke up the next morning to a light rapping on his door. Getting out of bed, he opened it and was surprised to see Grak standing there, holding his weapons and armor.

"Good morning. Can I come in?" she asked in a quiet voice.

Arbor stood aside and let her enter, closing the door behind her.

Grak placed his armor on the bed and leaned his sheathed glaive against the wall. She didn't look up at first, fiddling with the straps on his armor, and fixing the sheets on the bed.

"Grak, about what I said yesterday," Arbor began, but she cut him off.

"No, it's my fault," she said quickly. "I know I shouldn't have pushed you so much. I'm sorry."

He put an arm on her shoulder and turned her to face him.

"No, it's not your fault, it's mine. You were only trying to help, and I overreacted in a very bad way. Can you forgive me?"

She was silent for a minute, before her lips curled upward in a small smile.

"Friends fight from time to time; it's only natural. Yes, I forgive you."

He smiled, and the two of them embraced, Grak squeezing him just a little tighter than usual. He could feel her burying her face in his chest and had to suppress the urge to shove her away too quickly. He still wasn't sure how he felt about her, and Florren's death kept popping into his mind every time he tried.

"Hord came to visit yesterday," Arbor said, deciding on a safer topic, once they'd broke apart. "He told me what you did for me while I was unconscious. That you cared for me the entire time, hardly eating or sleeping."

Grak shuffled awkwardly at that, looking down at the ground, her red skin going a deep shade of crimson.

"He also told me that you blamed yourself for what happened to me."

She looked up at him then, and he could see she was trying to hold back tears.

"It was my fault, though! You were so hurt, and I couldn't do anything!" She was crying again, and tears began streaming down her face.

"If only I were stronger, I could have helped you against those monsters. You wouldn't have had to be so badly injured. I could have done something."

Arbor walked forward and wrapped his arms around her once again, allowing his friend to bury her face in his chest and cry.

"It's not your fault," he said as he gently patted her back. "There was nothing you could have done. If it's anyone's fault, it's mine. It was foolish of me to take them on alone, especially with the way I was using my magic. I'm sorry I worried you so."

They stood there for a while, him holding her, as she cried into him. He knew he was to blame for her suffering and knew he had to become stronger, so he would never have to put her through something like this again.

She finally pulled back, wiping her red-rimmed eyes on her sleeve. She seemed a lot calmer now as if a great weight had been lifted from her shoulders. Sniffing a few times, she looked at him.

"I'm sorry for that, and I'm sorry I was too weak to help you fight last time, but I promise you that I will become stronger. The next time we have to fight overwhelming odds, you won't be alone."

She looked determined and Arbor nodded, agreeing with her. That nod was all Grak needed apparently, because a wide smile stretched across her face, and the last traces of sadness and guilt were wiped away.

She motioned to the armor sitting on his bed then.

"The Co-founder told me to bring you this and asked that we meet with her as soon as we can. Are you ready to go now, or do you still need time?"

"Just give me a few minutes to get ready," he said, going over to the corner where they'd left a new set of clothes for him.

His previous set of clothes, and even the leather armor, had been destroyed during his fight with the lizards.

"Of course," Grak said, lingering in the doorway. "I'll just wait in the hall. Come out when you're ready."

Arbor waited until she closed the door, which seemed to take her an inordinate amount of time, before sitting down on the bed with a sigh. He picked Karria's necklace up from where it sat beside his bed and fingered the small lily hanging from the end.

He couldn't forget that Grak wasn't the only person counting on him. He needed to become stronger so he would have a chance when the time came to rescue his sister.

Standing up from his position on the bed, he slipped the necklace and pendant over his neck. He'd finally found a new place to keep his money and strapped that onto his belt, covering it with a leather flap he'd cut out to hide it.

As he was pulling on his shirt, he couldn't help but notice the amount of muscle he'd gained. He didn't seem to have an ounce of fat on him now, and when he tried tightening the breastplate Hord had made for him, he found that he couldn't pull the straps as tightly as before his big battle two weeks ago. Shaking his head in amazement at his magic's ability to keep strengthening him, he grabbed his sheathed weapon and slung it over his shoulder, tightening the strap under his arm until it sat comfortably across his back.

He walked out into the hallway and closed the door behind him. Grak was leaning against the wall and straightened as he came out.

"Which way to the Co-founder?" Arbor asked.

Grak motioned her head to the side and began walking down the corridor. They passed numerous doors, and new corridors constantly branched off, showing more doors and hallways. Arbor found that it was surprisingly light inside for being an underground base. Looking up, he could see tiny cracks crisscrossing the ceiling with sunlight shining through.

They continued walking for another ten minutes, and Arbor started to grasp how big the underground base was.

"This place is huge!" Arbor exclaimed after another five minutes of walking.

"As far as I know, this base extends for twenty miles in all directions," Grak answered, taking a right into a larger corridor.

"Twenty miles?!" Arbor asked, shocked at the scope of the place. "How haven't they been found out yet?"

"They have been, a few times, but they managed to kill off any gremlin patrols that have been sent out here."

They continued walking through the long hallway until another odd thought struck him.

"Why are there no people down here? In a place this big, I would expect thousands to be wandering around."

"I'll leave the explaining to the Co-founder. Once we get there, she'll tell you everything."

Arbor nodded, and the two walked on in silence. After a few more minutes, they finally emerged into a wide-open area that stretched out in front of them for at least a thousand feet. He could see a massive ramp sloping upwards over a hundred feet and ending in a solid wall of stone. He also saw a massive winch and long steel spikes driven into the rock.

That must be how they move it, he realized.

There were two guards standing by the winch, and they both waved to them as they passed.

"That's one of the entrances to the base," Grak explained as they waved back to the guards.

There were several hallways leading from the chamber they were in, and Arbor could hear the faint sounds of horses echoing down from one of them. They entered another hallway and after a few more minutes of walking, stopped before a plain looking door. Sounds of argument could be heard from within. Arbor stopped, not sure whether they should enter or not, but Grak knocked twice before pushed the door open.

They walked into a large room with a high domed ceiling. Banners, depicting the three moons on a field of black hung from the walls, and a large table with an unrolled map spread across it, occupied the center of the room.

Ramona stood by the table. She was dressed in armor and looked as though she'd recently been fighting. Two men and a woman stood near her, and Arbor could now see the source of the argument he'd heard from the hallway. Both men were staring each other down, each trying to get a word in over the other.

Upon closer inspection, Arbor could see that one of the men wasn't human. His features were like Ramona's, only sharper, and a lot more exaggerated.

Ah, this must be an elf, he thought as he approached the table with Grak.

Ramona looked up as the two of them approached and gave Arbor a grateful smile.

"Arbor," she said loudly, making the two men stop their bickering. "I am glad to see that you made it here so quickly."

Arbor bowed slightly at the waist.

"You called for me, Co-founder, and I came."

Ramona smiled even wider at this and greeted Grak as well. He couldn't help noticing that the gremlin woman was a little cold to the Co-founder. Not rude, of course, just answering her questions and bowing the same way he had, but he knew her well enough to tell that she didn't like Ramona.

"Arbor, this is my second in command, Captain Tenor. You will be working under him."

Arbor looked the man up and down. The captain had dark skin, a short black beard and no hair at all. He was tall and broad shouldered and seemed to have an air of confidence about him. Arbor instinctively liked the man and stuck out his hand.

"It's a pleasure to meet you, Captain."

Tenor looked at him for a moment, scrutinizing him before taking his hand as well.

"The pleasure is mine."

He had a deep rich voice that Arbor found both comforting and commanding. This man had most definitely earned his place as Ramona's second in command.

After a moment, the captain let go of his hand, and Ramona continued speaking.

"This woman here is my assistant, Lea." The woman bowed at the waist. "And the surly elf over there is my advisor, Durlan."

Durlan merely scowled at the two of them before storming from the room.

Arbor felt a flash of something as the elf walked past him. A profound feeling of wrongness. It chilled him to the bone but was gone in an instant, leaving him to wonder if he'd imagined it or not.

Ramona watched him go with a sour expression on her face.

"I'm sorry you had to see that," she said, looking at the two of them. "He and Tenor were arguing about what our next move should be. As you can see, we've been fighting. We found a gremlin patrol poking around near the lake this morning. Durlan thinks it was a single patrol and we have nothing to worry about. Captain Tenor, on the other hand, thinks we should postpone our plans of leaving the base, and recall the rest of the Defiant's forces."

She looked troubled as she said this.

"Regardless, it's too risky for us to leave now, and recalling the troops isn't a decision I would make lightly." She trailed off again, and Arbor cleared his throat.

"Pardon me, Co-founder," Arbor began. "But can you please explain why we were summoned here? After all, it doesn't really sound like there's anything we can do."

"Yes, of course," she said, motioning the two of them to join her by the table.

"This is a map of the kingdom of Laedrin," she began. "Here is where we are." She pointed to a spot near the Great Salt Lake. "And here is where we are headed." She traced a line to the Endless Wood. "From here, we will march through the woods until we reach Fivora." She traced a winding path that led past where Arbor's home had been, to a spot some eighty miles to the south.

"Right now, the bulk of our forces are here." She pointed to the spot in the Endless Wood she'd indicated earlier. "They are there awaiting the rest of our forces, who are currently here with us- the other three Co-founders, and even the Commander, are there as well."

"Wait, there are three other Co-founders and a Commander?" Arbor asked in confusion. "I thought there were only two of you."

"It's a common misconception," Ramona said with a smile. "When people hear the word Co-founder, they just assume there are two of us, and we don't say anything to the contrary. It's good to keep our enemies guessing as to our exact numbers."

Arbor pursed his lips as she finished her explanation.

He had just made an assumption based on what he'd heard about the Defiants. This was a valuable lesson about not underestimating anyone, including his allies.

"Our forces are split into four separate units, with a Co-founder commanding each," Ramona continued.

"Each Cofounder has five captains working under them, and each captain has command of over one-thousand soldiers. There are, of course, others under the captains, but I won't get into that right now. As of this moment, only five-thousand fighting men are currently in our base. The other fifteen-thousand are already in the Endless Wood, awaiting our arrival.

"As I previously mentioned, the commander is there as well, and as his title implies, he is the one in charge, the leader of the Defiants."

"So, there are four Cofounders in total and a Commander?" Arbor asked again, trying to clarify.

"Technically, there are five, but Naff was elected by the four of us to be the Commander. There is no one alive more suited to lead us against the king. After all," Ramona said with a smirk. "Who better to defeat an enemy than his own son?"

44

"His son?!" Arbor and Grak exclaimed at the same time.

"But why would the king's son want to kill his own father?" Arbor asked.

"Quite simple, really," Ramona answered. "Years ago, the king had an affair while he was out on a campaign. He left for the capital soon after, but unbeknownst to him, he got the woman pregnant. Years later, once he was grown, Naff went to the capital and presented himself before his father. Instead of the warm welcome he'd been expecting, the king ordered him to be executed."

"He ordered his own son's death?" Arbor was appalled.

What kind of a man would do that to his son?

"Yes, he was dragged off by the guards to be thrown in prison while he awaited his execution. By some lucky coincidence, a certain person happened to be walking by when this happened. He offered to take custody of the boy, claiming to have some questions for him. This man was well known and respected, so the guards didn't think twice about handing him over. Instead of bringing him to the execution block, the man helped him escape the city. He was hung for his crimes, and Naff swore he would see the king dead for it."

"Who was the man that saved him?" Arbor asked.

"He hasn't told anyone," Ramona said with a sigh. "No matter how many times I've asked. You two are a lot alike, you know. You have the same intensity about you." She trailed off here, a slightly wistful look on her face.

Grak cleared her throat noisily.

"Tell us, Cofounder. What would you have us do? You still haven't answered Arbor's question. Why are we here?"

Arbor noticed the frosty tone again. She was practically glaring at the other woman and he had to wonder why she disliked her so much.

"Yes, of course," Ramona answered, coming back to herself. "I will leave Captain Tenor to answer that particular question. Captain, if you will," Ramona said, motioning him to speak.

"Very well, Co-founder." Tenor turned to the two of them. "As a result of the gremlin party we found this morning, the Co-founder has decided to send out a few teams to scout the surrounding area. She believes there may be more of them around and wishes to confirm that the area is clear before moving the rest of our troops to the Endless Wood. It would be unwise for us to move without first confirming that there are no other gremlins about. We have the families of over twenty thousand soldiers living here, and we would not want to leave them unguarded."

That news surprised Arbor. He hadn't been aware that the families of the soldiers were living here as well.

It made sense to him, though. Where else would they live?

His thoughts were interrupted as Tenor continued speaking.

"We will be sending out ten groups, composed of five each, to scout the surrounding area. If anyone spots enemy activity, they are to report back here immediately."

Arbor nodded, but he still had a few questions.

"I understand the need to send out scouts before making a move, but why call me in specifically?" he asked, turning back to Ramona. "You could have just as easily told us when you gathered the rest of the scouting party."

"As Mages, you two are a rare resource," Ramona answered. "Of the five thousand soldiers we have here, only fourteen can use magic."

Arbor's eyebrows shot up in surprise. He glanced over to Grak, who was shocked as well.

"Why so few?" she asked.

"Magic is quite rare in this day and age," Ramona answered. "So rare, in fact, that most Mages have a fairly easy life wherever they go. They are highly sought after and can be quite expensive to hire. You can imagine that not many would be willing to trade a life of luxury for the one we lead."

"It still doesn't answer the question," Grak said, her eyes narrowing in suspicion now. "It's true that Mages are rare, but why call us in here separately? We hardly know one another."

Ramona shared a sideways look with Tenor before he spoke.

"We want the two of you to go out on your own. We don't want you taking a group with you, as we feel it would slow you down."

"So, in other words," Grak said, her tone heated now. "You want us to go out on a potentially deadly mission alone?"

Arbor had to admit that she had a fair point. It was one thing to ask them to go out in a group. It was another to ask them to go out alone.

Ramona sighed audibly, and Lea rushed over with a chair. She sank into it gratefully and looked up at them with a tired expression.

"You may have noticed that you've seen very few people around the base," she paused here, and Arbor nodded.

Aside from Grak and Hord, the only other people he'd seen were Ramona, the woman who brought him food and clothes, and the two guards by the ramp.

"The reason is quite simple. We put you in an entirely different section than the rest of the Defiants. We believe there is a spy in our midst, so we have sworn to secrecy the few who saw you the night you arrived. Until we ferret out the traitor, we want to keep your existence to ourselves."

Arbor thought about this for a moment.

If there were so few Mages here, then keeping the existence of two hidden from the spy could give them a great advantage.

He saw Grak opening her mouth to deliver another angry retort, so he spoke quickly.

"We understand the position you're in. We will scout on our own, but I expect to be compensated for this later," he said, folding his arms over his chest.

Ramona looked at him for a few moments, her golden eyes searching.

"Very well. We'll get you the supplies you need. Be ready to leave within the hour. You are dismissed," she said briskly.

The two of them nodded and headed towards the door. Arbor stopped short, hearing Ramona call out to him.

"Arbor, I would like to speak with you for a moment. Alone," she said, eyeing her assistant and second in command.

He turned around, wondering what she could possibly need that they hadn't already spoken about the day before. Captain Tenor and Lea nodded to Ramona and headed to the door, but Grak didn't budge, eyeing her with distrust.

"Go on. I'll be out in a few moments," Arbor told her.

She gave him a hurt look, but then turned and left the room. Ramona stood as the door closed and approached him.

"Do you trust your gremlin friend?" she asked.

The question completely shocked Arbor, as it had seemingly come out of nowhere.

"With my life. Why would you ask me that?"

"Don't be offended," Ramona said, a soft smile coming to her lips. "Let me ask you a question." She put her back to the table and leaned against it. "How many gremlins do you think are part of the Defiants?"

"I don't know. A thousand, maybe?" he said, with a shrug.

"There are none," she answered. "Of the twenty or so thousand people fighting for the Defiants, there is not a single gremlin among them. There are humans, there are dwarves, even a few elves, but not a single gremlin. Do you know why that is?"

"I don't understand," he said, brows knitting together. "I would think that many of them would come. I've heard stories from Grak about how bad it is for some of them."

"And yet Grak is the first gremlin to not try and kill us on sight." Ramona crossed one long leg over the other and continued. "The reason is quite simple, really. The entire gremlin race has been enslaved by the king. They do what he wants without question and will attack anyone who harms his men on sight. So, the real question is. Why hasn't she tried to kill you?"

This new revelation about the gremlins came as a shock to him. Arbor knew the gremlins worked for the king, and Grak had told him that no one knew why.

"How do you know that this is true?" he asked, more than a little skeptical.

"Naff has friends in high places. It cost many people their lives to discover this particular piece of information, but the source is quite trustworthy."

"I don't know why she didn't attack me," he said. "All I know is that I trust her with my life. She is a very dear friend, and one of the few people I still care about in this world."

He lapsed into silence here as he thought of something.

"Do you have any idea how the king has enslaved all the gremlins? If you can somehow break his hold over them, they would undoubtedly join our side. A blow like that would also severely weaken him at the same time."

Ramona shook her head sadly here.

"Unfortunately, we don't know how the king has enslaved them. That's why I asked you, as your friend seems to be the exception to this rule."

She pushed up off the table and approached him then, her voice lowering until he could barely make out what she said.

"The gremlin's enslavement isn't the only strange thing happening."

She was so close now that Arbor began to feel uncomfortable. He tried to take a step back, but her arm shot out, wrapping around his wrist and stopping him from doing so.

"Don't you wonder why all the races in Laedrin speak the same language? Why we all use the king's coin instead of our own? Why the elves and dwarves think they have their own kingdoms, but are still part of Laedrin? Or why the king hasn't crushed both the dwarves and elves already? It's not like he doesn't have the numbers to do so."

Her tone took on a more serious note here.

"There are not many who would even think to ask these questions, let alone try and find the answers."

Arbor was becoming a bit worried now as well.

Why hadn't he considered any of these questions? The dwarves and elves had their own cities, and the king seemed content just to leave them. Sure, he'd stage an attack on the dwarves every few years, but he'd never committed a large force. The elves seemed to be untouched as far as he knew.

"I can see that the message sinking in," Ramona said, taking another step forward, her voice so low now that Arbor had to strain to make out what she was saying.

"There is a secret we must uncover. The answer may just tell us the real truth of what happened to the salamander race, and what the king had to do with their downfall."

She stepped back, looking around furtively as if someone may have heard what she just said.

"That's impossible!" Arbor finally burst out, sure that she was messing with him now. "What could the king possibly have to do with the fall of a race that died out thousands of years ago?"

He was cut off from his outburst, as Ramona's hand clamped over his mouth. She looked both angry and terrified at the same time.

"This is not something to be discussed out loud!" she hissed, then seeming to calm herself a bit, she removed her hand.

"I'm sorry. I overreacted. Please be careful of who you say this to. These are dangerous questions to be asking, and many have already died for asking them carelessly."

Arbor nodded, a bit shaken by the whole experience.

"Why trust me, though?"

"Did you already forget? I know you, Arbor. I've seen inside your mind and know you are a trustworthy person. I just ask that you be careful when pursuing these answers. I've grown quite fond of you in the short time we've known one another, and I would not have you die needlessly."

She winked at him then, taking a step back and leaving Arbor to wonder just what she meant by that. The woman was an enigma.

Arbor nodded his understanding, bowing at the waist and returning the compliment.

"I must admit I've grown fond of you as well, Co-founder Ramona. If I find the answers to any of these questions, I will make sure you're the first to know."

"Thank you," she said, giving him a genuine smile this time.

"If you don't mind, could you explain what you meant when you spoke about magic classifications the other day?"

Ramona's eyebrows went up.

"I'd forgotten that you haven't actually had anyone explain this to you. I can tell you what I know."

She leaned back against her desk, crossing her legs into a more comfortable position before continuing.

"As you know, a Mage's power is restricted when it's first awakened. As they train, they can unlock more and more of their latent power in stages. We refer to these stages as Tiers. The amount any Mage has is predetermined from the time they awaken their magic, and when they hit their limit, they won't be able to draw out any more power.

"You seem to have been able to change that. When you worked on my Origin earlier, I felt a distinct increase in my strength, as well as the amount of magic I could use at once. I can also feel that I can continue advancing, unlocking even higher Tiers of magic.

"We're getting off topic. While we measure the amount of power a Mage can use by Tiers, the actual power a Mage can use, meaning the potential destructive force, is measured on a different scale called a classification. In order, from the weakest to strongest, they are Non-combat, Enhanced, Over-enhanced, Destructor, Wrecker, Shatterer, and Calamity.

"These classifications do not measure how much power a Mage has at his beck and call, but how much potential damage he can dish out. That is why, for example, a Tier 8 Enhanced Mage would be able to defeat at Tier 3 Over-enhanced. While the Over-enhanced has a more powerful ability, the amount of power they have to draw on would be less than the Enhanced."

"Wait, so if you're classified as an Over-enhanced, does that mean that it's possible for you to reach a higher Tier than someone at the Enhanced to Non-combat levels?" Arbor asked, trying to wrap his head around all the information.

"No," Ramona said, shaking her head. "Tiers and classifications are two entirely different things. You could, for example, have a Destructor, who could never reach past Tier 1, with a magic ability that would allow him to crumble stone into dust on a mass scale. He would obviously be a huge threat to cities, but with such limited use of his magic, he wouldn't be able to do much.

"But you have to remember one thing. All this goes out the window when dealing with the last two. Shatterer and Calamity Mages are no joke, and unless you're on the same scale as them, you won't stand a chance."

"You mention all these different classifications, but I'm having a hard time understanding their scale of power. Can you explain it to me?"

Ramona nodded.

"Non-combat Mages are considered the weakest on a purely destructive-based system. They can do about as much damage as an average person, so they don't pose much threat. Enhanced are those slightly stronger than the average, for example, enhanced strength, speed, reflexes or the like. Over-enhanced are for those who can control some aspects of nature and have the ability to fight at ten-to-one odds with average people and come out on top. This is the category most Mages fall into.

"Destructor Mages have a wider range of attacks and abilities but have the capacity to destroy a group of one-hundred ordinary people without much effort. Wrecker Mages can level small towns and take on an army of one thousand and still come out on top. Shatterer Mages can destroy entire cities, and some were known to level kingdoms. And Calamity Mages have the power to destroy entire continents.

"This is all assuming that they have the power reserves to do so. As I said, the strength of one's ability is greatly dependent on the individual. And the Tiers vary greatly from classifications. While I did say that a higher Tier Mage of a lower class is likely to win, remember that those of a lower class have more power to unleash with each successive Tier."

Arbor rubbed at his temples, feeling a headache coming on.

"It seems like there's a lot of contradictory information. It's all very confusing."

Ramona laughed at that but didn't deny it.

"Yes, it's quite confusing. To make it easier, I'll explain it in simple terms. Every classification is stronger than the last by a factor of five, and each breakthrough is more potent as well, unlocking roughly twice as much power as the class beneath with each successive Tier. This applies to all, except for the Non-combat, Shatterer, and Calamity Mages. Non-combats have their own measuring system, which I won't get into right now. But Shatterer Mages are ten times as strong as Wreckers, and their Tiers are three times more potent. And Calamity Mages' are ten times stronger than Shatteres, and their Tiers are five times as potent."

Arbor was still confused but nodded all the same. He was sure he could work it out if given enough time.

"Could you guess what my classification would be?" he asked, stroking his chin.

Ramona shrugged.

"I can honestly say that I have no idea. Before I knew you had a second Origin, I would have guessed a weak Destructor, but now, who can say for sure? You could be on par with a Calamity Mage, for all I know. Only time will tell."

Arbor nodded, deciding to keep a closer watch on his second Origin. He couldn't even tell what Tier it was, which was very strange. He'd checked his Perception Core and found that he was on the cusp of Tier 3, so he knew that he hadn't lost the ability to check. It only gave him more questions without answers, which aggravated him.

Deciding that it was best put off for another time, he decided to drop the subject and ask Ramona a different question, one more pertinent to his current situation.

"Would you mind if I visit Hord before I leave on my mission? He's probably going stir crazy, lying in bed all day."

"Yes, I would imagine he is," Ramona said with a chuckle. "Dwarves aren't known for their patience. You may visit your friend but be sure to meet Captain Tenor by the ramp in the main chamber in half an hour."

Arbor nodded, bowing one more time before he left the room. There was a lot he had to think about.

45

Arbor walked out into the open hallway deep in thought, only for them to be interrupted by Grak.

"What did she want to see you alone for?"

Arbor jumped a little, caught off-guard by the loud voice.

Grak was standing a little way down the hall. Her arms were folded over her chest, and she didn't look happy at all.

"Oh, nothing too important," he said quickly, remembering Ramona's warning about not telling anyone.

"Nothing important, you say?" She stalked over to him and glared, eyes flashing.

Arbor took an involuntary step back.

"Grak? Why do you seem so upset?" he asked nervously.

"Upset? Why would you think I'm upset?" she shouted, stepping even closer now.

Arbor tried to take another step back, but found he couldn't, as his back was to the wall.

"For someone who isn't upset, you sound quite put out," he said carefully.

"You think I'm upset? Why would I be upset that Co-founder Ramona wanted to see you alone for a private meeting? Why would I be upset that you don't want to tell me what the two of you talked about?"

Arbor swallowed nervously. He didn't care what she said. She was definitely upset. He couldn't fathom why she hated Ramona so much, or why their private meeting had made her so angry, but he needed to placate her.

"We just spoke about you. The Co-founder told me to watch out for you since you're the only gremlin we have here."

It was a white lie, but it was better than telling her the truth. Grak's anger seemed to abate somewhat, but she still looked suspicious.

"Is that all you talked about?"

"I also asked if we could visit Hord before we leave, and she agreed to let us," he said, hoping the change of subject would get her to drop it.

She stared at him for another minute, before a smile spread across her face.

"Well, we'd better get going then," she said in a cheery voice before turning and heading back to the main hall.

Arbor just stood there for a moment, stunned. Then he hurried to catch up with her. *Women!* He thought with an inward sigh. What was wrong with them? One moment they were yelling, and the next, smiling as though nothing had happened!

They walked on in silence for the next few minutes, until they reached the main hall. Here Arbor saw two horses being prepared, along with supplies for their trip. Only two people were working here - the guards from earlier - and they both waved again before returning to their work.

"Looks like Ramona wasn't exaggerating," Arbor said, as they crossed the main hall and into a smaller corridor.

Grak's head whipped around at this, the scowl back on her face. "So, she's *Ramona* now? What happened to *Co-founder*?"

Arbor started.

"Oh, she just told me to call her that when we're alone."

He immediately knew he'd said the wrong thing when Grak's eyes narrowed, and her scowl deepened.

"What do you mean, when you're alone?" she asked in a dangerous voice. "Is there something you're not telling me?"

Arbor stopped himself from saying the first thing that came to his mind. He didn't know why, but he had the feeling that telling her Ramona had visited him privately the day before, would not be a good idea.

"Oh, she just said something about titles being annoying when we're in small groups, that's all." He tried to look as sincere as he could.

She stared at him for another few seconds, and then the smile was back.

"Okay," she said, and turned down a side passage towards Hord's room.

Arbor raged inwardly at his inability to figure his companion out, as they continued walking, finally stopping outside a wooden door. Grak knocked on once, and when Hord answered, the two of them entered.

Hord was lying in bed, propped up by cushions and reading a book. He closed it as soon as he saw them, and a smile spread across his face.

"About damn time you came for a visit!" he said in a booming voice. "Another day alone in this place, and I'd have started losing my sanity!"

Grak laughed and went over to hug the disgruntled dwarf. Arbor couldn't help but notice the affection she had for him and wondered when that had happened. He remembered that Hord did say that the two of them spent time together when he was unconscious.

It was good to see his two friends getting along so well and he walked over to shake the dwarf's hand, though he couldn't help but feel a small pang of jealousy. That, in turn, revived his confused feelings for his gremlin companion and he was quick to squash them, forcing a smile onto his face.

"We can't stay for long," Arbor said, pulling up a chair. "We have a scouting mission, and we have to meet Captain Tenor in the main hall in a few minutes."

"A mission, you say. I hope you were planning on taking me along with you!" Hord said as he tried to get out of bed.

Grak pushed him back down with a firm hand.

"You will not get up until you are better," she said in a voice that would brook no argument. "I wouldn't want to have to tell your wife that you got yourself killed because you went into battle with an injury."

Hord seemed to blanch at this and quickly stopped fighting her.

"You're probably right, lass." He leaned back against the pillow, and Arbor again had to wonder exactly how much he'd missed in those two weeks.

The three of them talked for a few minutes about their upcoming mission, and what they would do if they ran into any trouble. But finally, it was time for them to go, and they rose regretfully to leave.

"Grak," Arbor said cautiously, wondering if she'd explode again. "If you don't mind, can I speak to Hord for a moment, alone?" He cringed inwardly, expecting her to start yelling again.

"Sure, but don't be too long."

She gave Hord one last smile before leaving the room. Once the door closed, Arbor heaved a sigh of relief.

The dwarf cocked an eyebrow at him.

"What's got you so twisted up in knots?"

"The last time we spoke, you said you knew women, right?" Arbor asked, hopeful.

"As well as any man really could," Hord answered carefully. "What's on your mind?"

Arbor quickly explained what had just happened between him and Grak, how she seemed to hate Ramona and got angry at any mention of her name. By the time he was finished with his story, Hord had a knowing smile on his face.

"It was smart of you not to mention your previous meeting with the Co-founder. At least you've got a bit of sense in that thick head of yours. Now, I can't tell you everything. Otherwise, you'll never figure it out for yourself. I will give you one piece of advice. Don't mention Co-founder Ramona around the gremlin lass."

Arbor was even more confused now.

"Why not? Why does Grak hate her so much?"

Hord just shook his head and laughed.

"That part, I'll leave you to figure out on your own. Now off with you. You have a mission, and I need my beauty sleep."

Arbor gave the dwarf a sour look.

"Thanks for nothing," he grumbled as he stood to leave.

He exited the room to see Grak leaning against the wall, a small smile curling her lips.

"You ready?" she asked, seeming not at all upset at having to wait.

Arbor just nodded curtly and turned to walk down the corridor.

He didn't know how, but he was sure that Grak had overheard some of his conversation, and that the dwarf had known about it.

He silently fumed as they made their way to the main hall.

46

Arbor was riding out on the Flatlands. The sun was shining high overhead and beat down on him, feeling like a physical weight. He and Grak had already made a wide circle around the Great Salt Lake, but there was nothing in sight. At first, they'd been very careful, moving slowly and trying to make as little noise as possible, but they were soon riding at full speed, dust billowing up behind them.

According to Captain Tenor, the gremlin patrol had come from the north. They'd been ordered to make a wide circle around the lake before heading in that direction. Arbor didn't understand why they had to circle the lake first, but they were orders, and he intended to follow them. If nothing was found, their orders were to head north and ride for two days. If they still found nothing by then, they were to return and make their report.

He pulled his horse to a stop and waited for Grak to catch up to him.

She seemed to be in an oddly good mood over the last day, but he couldn't fathom why. It was scorching hot and dry out here on the open Flatlands, with no breaks in the scenery in sight. If anything, she should have been grumpy and annoyed.

"Nothing in sight near the lake," she said as she pulled her horse to a stop as well. "I guess that means we head north?"

Arbor nodded as he squinted out over the plains. The wind was blowing, and large clouds of dust were being driven along the ground, making it hard to see for more than a mile in any direction. He didn't like that, but there was nothing he could do about the wind.

He clicked his tongue and his horse began moving again, picking up the pace until they were moving at an easy lope.

They went on like this for the next few hours, until the sun soon grew low on the horizon, and the spring moon rose. Arbor finally called a halt when he saw a good spot to make camp for the night, and the two of them dismounted.

"Do you think we'll find anything out here?" Grak asked.

They were both rubbing down their horses from the long day's journey. It was a lot cooler at night, and the horses could become sick if they weren't properly taken care of.

"I couldn't say," Arbor said, as he poured water into a leather folding bucket and held for his horse to drink.

The water sloshed around noisily as the horse drank its fill, and Arbor slowly patted its neck. They'd ridden hard that day, and the horses deserved a good rest.

Grak finished up as well, and the two of them sat down tiredly. They'd agreed that lighting a fire would be too dangerous, as it could be seen for miles on the open Flatlands.

Arbor chewed on the hard beef jerky sourly – he didn't think he'd ever get used to trail rations. He looked over at his friend and was a little annoyed to see her smiling as she ate.

"Why are you in such a good mood?" Arbor grumbled. "The food can't be that good."

Grak laughed a little at this.

"Nope, the beef jerky tastes like crap."

"Then why are you so happy?"

"This just brings back memories of the last time the two of us were out here alone," she said with a happy sigh, sounding almost wistful.

"The last time we were alone on the Flatlands, we were running for our lives," Arbor said with a raised eyebrow. "Or have you already forgotten?"

"Oh, I haven't forgotten." She leaned back against a large rock and looked up at the sky. "But it's nice to be out here again, just the two of us."

Arbor was silent at this, staring out into the distance and listening to the sounds of the night. The last time things had been simpler. Now he had so many things to worry about, that it almost gave him a headache just thinking about it.

"It's beautiful out tonight," she said in a quiet voice. "Really makes you think, doesn't it?"

Arbor looked back at Grak, who was lying on her back and looking up at the full green moon overhead. Her dark blue hair was splayed out behind her head and back, the tips of her pointed ears poking out. He noticed that her eyes seemed to shine in the moonlight and found his eyes drawn down to her full red lips.

"Yes, it is beautiful out here," he said, clearing his throat nervously and looking up at the sky as well.

"It's so bright as well," she continued. "As though another moon were lighting the sky."

It is a very bright night, he thought as his eyes were inexorably drawn back to his companion. He froze then, suddenly very alert. Something that Grak said suddenly clicked in his mind and activated his danger sense.

It shouldn't be nearly this bright out.

He stood slowly and began scanning the surrounding area, taking extra care not to miss a single detail. Grak, sensing something was wrong, stared silently up at him, a questioning look on her face.

Arbor kept on looking. Still not spotting anything out of the ordinary, he channeled magic into his eyes, greatly enhancing his vision.

There!

Some twenty miles to the north, he could see a bright flickering light. He let his magic go and dropped back down.

"There's a fire to the north. A large one," he said grimly.

"What should we do?" Grak asked. "Should we go back and report?"

"No, we have to see it for ourselves." He began lacing up his boots.

The horses would be too loud so he would have to go by foot.

"How will we approach without being seen?" Grak asked, strapping on her rapier and tightening her breastplate.

"*We* will not be going," Arbor said, slinging his glaive over his shoulder and tightening the sheath. "I can approach the camp quietly on my own, and I'll be able to move faster by myself."

Grak looked indignant at the suggestion.

"You will not be leaving me here alone!" She folded her arms.

"Using magic, I can reach the camp in just under an hour. If you come, we'll need to take the horses. Then we'll have to find a safe spot for them at least five miles from the camp and approach by foot. A trip like that would take us at least three times as long."

Grak gave him a sideways smile.

"I guess you'll have to carry me then."

Arbor blanched at the suggestion.

"I'm not a horse!" he spluttered, though that wasn't the only reason he didn't want to physically carry the gremlin woman.

Grak narrowed her eyes at him.

"You'll carry me, or we'll take the horses. Either way, I'm coming with you."

Arbor gritted his teeth in frustration at her stubbornness.

"Fine! But you'll need to remove your armor," he growled, removing his glaive and belting on his knife instead. It would be impossible to carry both her and his weapon.

"Get on," he said, crouching down with his back to her.

He heard her armor hitting the ground, and her arms soon wrapped around his neck. Sliding his hands under her knees, he straightened with a small grunt, feeling the softness of her body as she pressed against him.

"Are you sure you removed all your armor?" he asked, then felt her cuff his ear.

"I'll pretend I didn't hear that. Now come on, we should really get going," she said, resting her head against his shoulder.

Arbor just scowled, shoving down the troubling mixed emotions once again and tried to concentrate on anything *other* than the woman currently snuggling into his back.

He took a deep breath to calm his nerves, then concentrated on his center, speeding up the flow of magic from his first Origin. He was nearing the 3rd Tier at this point, so the amount of magic he began pumping through his body wasn't enough to cause any strain, though it was enough to significantly increase his speed and perception.

"Better hold on tight," he said once he was ready.

Grak pulled tighter to him, and he could now feel her heart pounding as she squeezed him, even through his breastplate. It seemed that she was just as nervous as he was.

Taking one more deep breath, he took off running. He heard a squeak next to his right ear and Grak tightened her arms around him even more. He felt some small satisfaction at that.

That'll teach her to treat me like a horse, he thought in grim satisfaction.

He picked up the pace as he didn't feel any strain at the current speed, his legs pumping mightily as he ran. He wasn't sure how fast he was going, but he was pretty sure that even a horse

Aaron Oster

would have trouble keeping up with him now. The wind whistled around them, and he heard Grak laughing wildly, he understood the feeling all too well.

It was exhilarating! He felt as though he were flying.

He ran on like that for the next half hour, and soon the light started becoming brighter. Just how big was this fire?

Another few minutes of running soon answered his question. Massive bonfires towered twenty feet into the night sky, and Arbor could now see tiny dots spread out for miles in either direction. The small dots soon resolved themselves into tents before long, and Arbor's steps faltered at the massive camp sprawling ahead of them.

"What's wrong?" He heard Grak's voice from his ear.

Remembering that she couldn't see the camp yet, he slowed down to a light run.

"There's a massive camp up ahead."

He felt her stiffen as he said this, and she shifted around so she could look over his shoulder.

"I only see light," she said. "I can't see any campsite."

Arbor nodded – he'd been enhancing his vision so as not to trip in the dark.

It was important to enhance his vision when moving at the speeds he'd been going. He remembered well the first time he'd tried running like this. He'd tripped within the first minute and scraped himself up pretty badly.

He shook his head to clear his wandering thoughts.

"I'm going to keep running. The moment you see the camp, let me know, and I'll slow down."

"I can't see anything while you're running," Grak said, shifting around again. "You're going to have to carry me in your arms if you want me to see."

Arbor snorted. Fat chance of that happening.

"Guess I'll have to stop every few minutes and let you have a look then."

He could feel her slump against his back in disappointment and could imagine her pouting behind him. That thought made him lose focus for a second, and his magic slipped, forcing him to stop.

"Why'd you stop?" he heard her ask.

He could hear it in her voice. She was pouting! Here he was, carrying her like some sort of pack animal, as they ran across the

320

open plains on a scouting mission, and she was pouting because he refused to carry her like a princess!

He didn't know why, but he found the entire situation hilarious. He could feel something bubbling up inside him then, something from the deepest part of his being, and just had to let it out. His laughter boomed out over the open plains, and he dropped Grak as he doubled over in a fit of giggles.

He turned around after he realized what he'd done, and she glared up at him, rubbing her behind and wincing. The sight only made him laugh harder, and he doubled over once again as tears of mirth streamed from his eyes.

Grak scowled at him for another minute, before she, too, began to laugh. They went on laughing for some time, not caring whether they were heard or not.

It felt good to smile and laugh. Arbor had almost forgotten the feeling.

He sat down next to her as his mirth finally subsided.

"If all it took for you to smile was dropping me on my ass, you should have done it ages ago!" Grak said, practically beaming at him.

She'd done it! She'd finally gotten him to smile! Even better, she'd gotten him to laugh! She thought about the promise she'd made and felt an enormous amount of pride.

The first part of her oath had been fulfilled. She was sure he no longer wished to die, and the thought made her happier than she'd been in weeks. Now all she had to do was help him rescue his sister and she will have kept her promise.

Arbor finally stood back up and brushed the dust off his pants. He held his hand out to her and she accepted it. She smiled at him then, wondering if he was finally going to kiss her, like she'd been wanting and hinting at for months.

"Thank you," he whispered, his eyes shining in the light of the distant fires.

"So, will you carry me in your arms now?" she asked, her red lips quirking up in a smirk.

"Not a chance," he replied, squashing her hopes that the moment might turn romantic.

He turned around then, and she grudgingly climbed onto his back again, resigning herself to have to wait just a bit longer. She'd accomplished something tonight. Now all she needed to do was help him realize that he cared about her in the same way she did him.

Arbor took off at a dead run once she was secure, the ground flying by beneath him as he did. A smile worked itself onto his face as he ran, and he reveled in the sensation.

It felt good to smile!

They were soon forced to slow down, as Grak said she could spot the camp now. She hopped down from his back and squinted out at the massive camp sprawled out before them.

"Do you think it's a gremlin force?" she asked.

Arbor sharpened his sight again and soon enough he could see thousands of red figures moving throughout the camp.

"Looks like it."

"I have an idea," Grak suddenly said, a thoughtful look crossing her face.

"Let's hear it then," he said, already knowing where she was going with this.

"You say it's an all gremlin camp. I know you probably won't like it, but I think I can sneak into the camp and gather information on the enemy force."

Arbor had opened his mouth to immediately object, but then stopped himself. Grak was right. She was the only person in the entire Defiants force who could safely infiltrate a gremlin camp. He needed to stop being so overprotective of her.

"It's a good idea. You should go," Arbor said, hating himself, but knowing it had to be done.

A force that large could not be here by coincidence and the Defiants could not be caught off guard.

Grak had opened her mouth, prepared to argue with him, but quickly snapped it shut, surprised he'd agreed so readily.

"I'll be back by daybreak. If I haven't returned by then, go back to the Defiants and tell them what we've found here."

Arbor nodded, and she quickly headed off in the direction of the camp.

He watched her go for a few minutes, then looked around until he found a tiny outcropping of stone. Walking over to it, he settled himself down for the long wait.

47

Karria was exhausted. She'd been walking through the forest all night chasing after Eletha. At first, they'd moved quickly, thinking to catch up to her, but they soon discovered that they were somehow managing to keep ahead of them.

Sylvester had insisted they slow down, saying that they would catch up eventually, seeing as Eletha wanted them to. Now the sun was peeking over the horizon, and she blinked tiredly as they continued following the trail.

"Do you think we'll be seeing them soon?" Sylvester asked from behind her.

She turned to glare at him but didn't respond. He'd tried to talk to her at first, but when she didn't answer, he'd soon stopped. He'd try and strike up a conversation every hour or so, and Karria found it exceedingly annoying.

There wasn't any time for his chattering! Kya was missing, taken by a sadistic psycho who was probably torturing her as they spoke.

She was frustrated and angry, but above all, she was afraid. What if they were too late and Eletha had already killed her?

She shook her head as the thought popped into her mind for the hundredth time since getting the letter.

It would do no good to think like that. Kya was alive. She had to be.

As she walked, she could spot the faint tracks on the path ahead. There were three sets of footprints, or so Sylvester had said. How he knew, she had no idea. Maybe it had something to do with his magic. Either way, she was glad they would only have to face two of them.

"The trees are thinning overhead," Sylvester said, snapping her out of her thoughts. "We must be approaching a clearing."

Karria shook herself a few times, trying to force herself more awake.

She didn't know how, but she was sure that Eletha was waiting for her in that clearing. She looked back at Sylvester and nodded.

They'd come up with a plan on the way there. It was the one time she'd spoken with him all night.

Karria would go into the clearing alone, distracting Eletha and whoever else was with her. While she was doing that, Sylvester would hide himself with his magic and sneak up on them. His job was to recuse Kya, and Karria would take care of Eletha and the other person with her, most likely Nina.

She'd threatened him with severe bodily harm if he froze like last time. He had nearly cost them both their lives, and she'd been forced to step in and save him. She also made sure to tell him that if he hesitated and she had to make a choice between him and Kya, he would have to fend for himself.

Karria continued moving forward and Sylvester slipped quietly off the path. He quickly gathered leaves and bark around himself and was soon lost from view as he blended in with his surroundings. She emerged into the clearing, not sure of what would be there, but expecting the worst.

Eletha was standing in the middle of the clearing, and her sister stood next to her. Nina was holding Kya by her hair and pressing a knife to her throat. Karria felt her blood boil as she saw numerous cuts and bruises marring her friend's face.

She could hardly imagine the kind of pain she'd endured so far, but she would make sure to pay it back ten times before she ended these psychos and put them in the ground.

"So, you got my letter, Sow," Eletha sneered as Karria came out of the forest. "I'm glad to see you've come alone as instructed."

"Where's the little elf prince I gave the letter to?" Nina asked as she pulled hard on Kya's hair, eliciting a moan of pain from the girl.

"He's not here," Karria said in a flat voice. "I've come alone, just like you told me to. Now I would appreciate it if you let my friend go."

Nina and Eletha looked at each other for a second before they both burst out in fits of hysterical laughter.

"That's rich, you filthy human," Eletha said, wiping the mirth from her eyes. "Let me make one thing perfectly clear."

Her eyes narrowed and a scowl spread across her face. "No one will be leaving here alive. Neither you nor the princess."

Karria took a step forward, but Nina quickly pulled Kya's hair back and pressed the knife harder to her throat. A small line of blood trickled from where the knife cut into her skin, and Karria stopped in her tracks.

"That's a smart girl," Eletha said, walking forward. "Now you are going to stand there and do nothing, while I cook you from the inside out."

She walked up to Karria and grabbed her by the throat.

"Make one move to resist, and Nina will cut her throat."

Karria swallowed hard, feeling the pressure around her neck tighten. She looked over Eletha's shoulder at Kya. She was barely conscious. The only reason she was still standing was Nina's hand in her hair, and the knife at her throat. She glared at her hated enemy, a look of pure malice that conveyed her utter disgust of the girl standing before her.

"Do your worst, bitch!" Karria growled.

She needed to buy Sylvester enough time to save her friend, and then she would have her revenge. Until then, she would be forced to endure.

A cruel sneer crossed Eletha's face as she drew her fist back. Karria knew what was coming, she gritted her teeth in anticipation, but could not stop herself from crying out in pain, as the fist crashed into her face, sending lightning coursing through her body.

Sylvester could see what was happening. He could see Karria talking to Eletha, and Nina holding his sister hostage. He was afraid. His heart pounded in his chest as he moved carefully through the forest, his magic helping him blend into his surroundings.

He crept up on the clearing, moving very slowly as to not make a sound, seeing Eletha move toward Karria. He stopped right on the fringes of the forest and sat down.

This should be close enough, he thought.

Closing his eyes, he concentrated on the trees around him. There were no vines in the Goldenleaf Forest. However, all trees had roots, and that was what Sylvester was interested in. Concentrating on his Origin, he allowed his magic to flow into the world around him, feeling for the roots running underneath the clearing. There were thousands upon thousands that he could sense, and he couldn't help but smile at his apparent luck.

His eyes snapped open when he heard Karria's first scream. She was being beaten by the larger girl, and he could hear the distinct zap every time her fist struck home.

Karria won't be able to last long like this.

He quickly closed his eyes and concentrated once again. He could feel the roots under Nina's feet, and he began slowly shifting them up towards the surface. It was hard for him to concentrate through Karria's screams of pain and Eletha's cruel laughter. He gritted his teeth, remembering what had happened the last time he'd failed her.

He would not fail her again, not when his sister's life was also at stake.

He gritted his teeth, and with an effort of will, the ground around Nina's feet exploded outward in a shower of dirt and debris. Sylvester clenched his teeth at the expected pain of controlling so many plants at once, but he pushed through, forcing them upward to surround Nina from all sides, cutting off her escape.

Karria had nearly passed out from the pain, when a loud shriek brought her back from the edge of unconsciousness. Looking over Eletha's shoulder, she saw Nina wrapped up in roots and suspended tenderly ten feet in the air. Kya had fallen to the ground and was lying on her side. Karria felt a knot of fear in her stomach as she saw this.

Is she still alive?

She breathed a sigh of relief when she saw her friend's body moving with her slight breathing.

Eletha had spun around at the sound of Nina's scream as well. She was whipping her head back and forth, trying desperately to find the unseen assailant, fearing an attack on her as well. When no attack was forthcoming, she turned her gaze back on Karria, a snarl of rage crossing her face.

"I warned you not to bring anyone! Now I'm going to kill you, and once you're dead, the princess is next!"

She brought her fist back, charging it up with power for a final devastating blow, but Karria no longer had to stand still and take it.

As soon as she'd seen Kya breathing, she'd quickly concentrated on gathering her own magic. She soon felt the familiar

326

tingling in her palms and willed her Origin to pump out her magic faster and in greater amounts than she'd ever used before.

Just as Eletha drew her fist back, Karria finally felt she had enough magic to finish the elf in one blow.

"Not this time, you bitch!" Karria yelled as she slammed both fists into Eletha's ribcage, right beneath her chest.

With a shout, she released all the stored magic in one massive blast. Karria felt a rush of energy leave her body with a loud boom, the shockwave leaving a cone shaped crater in the ground from where she stood, expanding out over twenty feet.

Karria heard the distinct sound of bones snapping as she released her magic and a spray of blood splashed across her left cheek. Eletha screeched in pain as she was thrown back over forty feet by the force of the blow. She hit the edge of the clearing, and her back smashed into the trunk of a tree. There was another sound of snapping bone as Eletha's body bent backward at an unnatural angle, before falling limply to the ground.

It was then that Sylvester rushed out of the woods and ran over to check on Kya.

"She's badly hurt, but she's still breathing," he said as Karria limped over.

It was then that Karria noticed her own pain. Adrenaline had kept her going for the last few minutes, but now that she had a moment to think, the agony began to set in. Her jaw was broken, and so was her nose.

Her whole body felt as though it were on fire and her skin felt raw and tender, as though she'd been badly sunburned. She felt gingerly at her face and winced as her hand came away bloody.

"Let me down! I'll kill you for this!"

Karria looked up to see Nina wrapped from shoulders to knees in tree roots. Sylvester had lowered her to ground level, and she did not look happy. Her face was red with anger and she was flailing her legs as best she could. Karria walked up to the elf girl and stared her in the eye.

Nina just sneered back at her.

"What are you looking at, Sow?" she snarled, then spat in her face.

Karria calmly wiped her face clean, then drew her fist back and smashed it as hard as she could into the elf's nose. She felt it break with a loud and very satisfying snap. Blood poured out of Nina's nose and she screamed in pain, writhing against her bonds in an attempt to clutch her face.

Karria stepped back, shaking her hand and wincing. Though she'd seen men in her old village doing it in the past, no one had told her how much hitting someone in the face would actually hurt.

She looked back at Sylvester, but he was smiling from ear to ear. Nina had deserved that for what she'd done to Kya, and he was glad to see it done.

Karria bent down painfully beside Sylvester and brushed a lock of hair from Kya's face.

"We need to get her back to the city. Help me carry her."

They were getting ready to lift her when a voice called out from behind them. She had not been expecting to hear that voice ever again, and it chilled her to the bone.

"It's not over yet, you human Sow!" Eletha shrieked.

Karria stood and slowly turned around.

Eletha stood at the other end of the clearing. Her left arm was twisted at an odd angle, the right side of her head was matted in blood, and there was a noticeable indent where her chest had once been. Despite this, she was somehow still alive.

48

Karria slowly approached the bleeding and deranged elf girl with slow shuffling steps. Every step pained her, but she forced herself to keep moving until she was standing just ten feet from her enemy.

"How are you still alive?" she asked, then grimaced in discomfort.

Her broken jaw made speaking quite painful. Eletha spat out a wad of blood then bared her teeth in a gruesome approximation of a smile.

"Did you think I'd go down so easily? I've been planning my revenge for weeks, waiting for the perfect opportunity! Do you know how hard it was to evade all those guards who were looking for me? Or how long it took me to get back into the city? You ruined my life that day, so it's only fair you pay for it with yours!"

"I didn't ruin your life!" Karria shouted, ignoring the pain and continuing to speak, anger clouding her voice. "You tried to kill me! And for what reason? Because I talked to someone that you didn't like?!"

She took a step forward, feeling her magic collecting in her hands again.

"No!" Eletha shrieked, madness now clouding her features. "You broke the rules and had to be punished! I was stopped before I could finish it last time, but no one is here to stop me now!"

Sylvester rushed towards them then, roots already coming up from the ground, but Karria waved him back.

"Don't worry about me! You need to protect Kya. Make sure nothing happens to her!"

He faltered, looking between his sister and his friend. He gnashed his teeth in frustration, but Karria was right.

"You better not lose!" he yelled, running back to Kya.

"Kill the bitch, Eletha! Make her bleed!" Nina shrieked from her bound position on the ground. "And when you're done, let me kill this one here for what he did to me!"

She opened her mouth to speak again, but a bunch of roots quickly flowed over it, effectively gagging her.

"Don't worry, sister. I'll be done with her soon. Then we can take our time killing the other two," Eletha said, as she rushed forward.

Karria, who'd been distracted by Nina's rambling, quickly turned her eyes back to Eletha, just in time to catch a punch to the stomach. Karria doubled over, gasping in pain as electricity coursed through her body. Stars danced in her vision as Eletha's fist withdrew and slammed into the side of her face, sending her sprawling.

She lay twitching and writhing on the ground as Eletha walked over to her, a crazed grin plastered across her face.

"I'm going to enjoy killing you. Then that interfering prince is next!"

She brought her foot back and kicked Karria hard.

Karria screamed as she felt a rib crack and was thrown back a couple of feet by the force of the blow. She gasped, trying to get a lungful of air, and struggled to get to her feet, but Eletha just kicked her again, sending her sprawling once more.

"After I kill the prince, I'm going to take my time with that little elf princess."

Eletha was stooping over her now, and Karria could see her charging her power up as she prepared to deliver the finishing blow.

"Maybe I'll cut her pretty little face off!" Eletha cackled madly. "She won't look so pretty without a face!"

As she brought her hand back to deliver the final blow, Karria felt something snap in her.

She wasn't going to let this deranged psycho kill her friends! She'd been too weak to do anything about it last time, but not now! Gritting her teeth against the agonizing pain of her broken and bruised body, she forced herself to move.

She would not die here.

Karria reached down to her belt and clutched the hilt of her dagger, ripping it free from its scabbard. With a scream of rage, she plunged the red blade up to the hilt in Eletha's leg. She felt the dagger scrape against bone and twisted it savagely before ripping it free.

Eletha screamed in pain as the dagger tore her leg open, blood pumping from the wound and soaking into the ground.

What the hell just happened? The moment that dagger had touched Eletha, her magic had vanished! She couldn't remember the last time she'd been unable to sense her magic. The emptiness, the complete lack of her power. It was more terrifying than the thought of death!

Karria rose slowly to her feet, the dagger clutched in her shaky hand. Eletha stumbled back as she approached, finally falling down backward, groaning in pain. Karria kept on moving closer, rage clouding her features.

Eletha tried to scramble back, but Karria stomped down viciously on her injured leg and reveled at the scream of pain it tore from her throat.

She would kill this monster for what she'd done to her, and she'd even enjoy it!

She stomped down on the leg again, and blood began pumping from the open wound even faster.

"How's it feel, bitch, being on the receiving end, for once?" Karria yelled.

She bent down and grabbed the elf by her hair, pulling her head back to expose her throat.

"Fitting that you should die in this way! This was how you planned to kill Kya, wasn't it?"

Eletha just whimpered as the sharp blade pressed against her throat.

The empty feeling was back again. She couldn't feel her magic!

Karria felt a hand on her shoulder then. She turned to see Sylvester standing there, a look of concern on his face.

"Don't do this. I know what she's done to you, but she's already dying! There's no need to be so cruel."

Karria just shoved him away and turned back to the downed elf. She took the dagger and raised to her throat again, but felt Sylvester pull her back. He grabbed the sides of her face, and she winced as he aggravated her broken jaw.

"Look at me! You are a kind and gentle person. I know you've been forced to kill before, but if you go through with this, you'll regret it for the rest of your life!"

Karria looked from Sylvester's pleading face to Eletha, sobbing pitifully on the ground beneath her, and recoiled in horror as it finally sank in. What had she been doing? Was she really the type of person who could torture someone and enjoy it?

She stumbled back from Eletha and dropped the dagger with a sound of disgust. She looked at her hands. They were shaking and covered in Eletha's blood. She quickly put them to her sides, clenching them into fists to stop the tremors now wracking her body.

She turned away from the sobbing girl and looked to her friends instead. Kya was still lying on the ground, unconscious, but Sylvester looked relieved and even gave her a small smile. She was better than Eletha. She would not stoop to her level.

"You are a cruel and hateful person," Karria said in a low voice, so only Eletha could hear. "You will die soon, and when you do, you will die alone. Hated by everyone and remembered by no one."

She began walking away from the girl who had nearly killed her twice, feeling oddly at peace. She had fought hard and persevered. Most importantly, she'd saved her friend.

She smiled at Sylvester, who was still watching her as she walked towards him. He started to smile back, but then a look of horror crossed his face, and he opened his mouth to try and shout a warning. Karria began to turn around, a sinking feeling already in her stomach, but then felt a blinding pain overtake her. Looking down, she saw the handle of her dagger protruding from her side, the roaring tiger's head staring back at her. She turned, trying to figure out what had just happened.

Eletha stood behind her, a grin of triumph on her bloody face.

"Looks like you're the one who will die here, Sow," she whispered in glee.

Then she twisted the dagger, just as Karria had done only moments before, then ripped it free.

Karria felt herself falling then, her vision fading as she did so. She hit the ground with a thud and lay there, unmoving.

49

Arbor was really starting to worry. It was nearly midday, and Grak still hadn't shown up yet.

He'd begun looking out for her once the sun rose as she'd instructed, but she was still nowhere to be seen. He got up and began to pace, all kinds of worrying thoughts flashing through his mind.

What if she'd been found out? If they caught a spy, they would likely torture her.

He quailed at the thought of Grak being strung up and beaten for information. Arbor stopped his pacing and looked up at the sky again.

If she wasn't back by midday, he would go get her himself, even if he had to fight off an entire army of gremlins.

Luckily for him, he spotted Grak's familiar form approaching from the direction of the camp only a half hour later. Quickly enhancing his vision, he could see that she looked tired and drawn. It must be bad if she looked so grim.

He looked around to see if there were any other gremlins in sight. It wouldn't do to give their position away if they were being watched. Not spotting anything, he reached for his first Origin and quickly pumped magic into his legs. Breaking out into a run, he was soon covering the distance between them with shocking speed. He saw Grak's eyes widen a bit as she saw him approaching, but she calmed down once she could make out who it was.

It took him another few minutes of hard running before he finally reached her. The distance on the open Flatlands was quite deceiving. He stopped in front of her, a cloud of dust swirling around him and making her cough.

"What did you find out?" he asked, not wasting any time on pleasantries.

"There are way more of them than we first thought," she said as she slumped to the ground. "We need to get back and report right away. They know where the base is, and they're planning an attack as we speak."

Arbor felt his blood run cold at that statement.

"How many are there?" he asked in a quiet voice.

They had originally estimated somewhere around six thousand.

"Over ten thousand," Grak answered, in a grim tone. "But that's not even the worst part." She looked up at him now, a look of fear flashing in her eyes. "One of the four gremlin generals is leading the army."

"Who are the gremlin generals?" Arbor asked.

He knew Grak wasn't easily frightened, so they must be truly dangerous for her to look so scared now.

Grak just shook her head, instead of answering.

"Not now. It will take too long to explain, and I only want to have to do it once."

Arbor nodded and bent down to scoop her up. She yelped as he did so, wrapping her arms around his neck. She gave him a slightly indignant look and swatted his breastplate.

"Warn me the next time you're going to do that!"

Arbor smiled cheekily at her.

"Don't worry yourself, princess, I don't plan on doing this again. I just figured I owed you for sneaking into that enemy camp all on your own. You could probably use a rest, as you won't be able to when we reach the horses."

Grak opened her mouth to reply but quickly shut it as Arbor began to run. Despite her exhaustion, she enjoyed the rush of wind on her face, as well as the feeling of being cradled in Arbor's strong arms. If she wasn't so tired, she might have attempted to use the situation to her advantage, but as it was, she could already feel her eyes closing. She hadn't gotten any sleep the previous evening, so being able to rest now was nice.

It took just under an hour for Arbor to reach their horses, and he was becoming quite sore by the time he did. He had to rouse Grak, as she'd fallen asleep on their way back. He hated to do so, as she'd looked so peaceful slumbering away in his arms, but he had no choice. They had an important mission to complete.

She was a little groggy at first but soon became more alert as they packed up their campsite and saddled their mounts. Soon they were riding as hard as they could back to the Defiants' base. They rode through the afternoon and well into the night, only taking short breaks to feed and water the horses. By the time they spotted the familiar outcropping of rock, Arbor was completely exhausted and having a very hard time keeping his eyes open.

He dismounted clumsily, his legs wobbly from being in the saddle so long, and stumbled tiredly over to the outcropping. His hands scrabbled over the surface of the rock until he found the hidden lever. He pulled down until he heard a distinct click, then he shuffled back to his horse and mounted up once more.

The two of them watched as one of the large boulders slowly moved to the side, revealing a long sloping ramp heading into the ground. They rode forward, the sound of their horse's hooves soon echoing off the walls of the underground chamber.

There were two guards waiting at the bottom of the ramp, and when they could make out who the riders were, one of them nodded to the other, then quickly ran across the open hall and into one of the side corridors. The other guard pulled a lever set into the wall, and the winch began turning in the opposite direction, closing the entrance once again.

The two of them dismounted tiredly and the guard took the reins. He could see that they'd been riding hard and looked worried.

The second guard came running out of the side passage and stopped in front of them, breathless.

"Co-founder Ramona is waiting for you in the war chamber," he panted.

Arbor thanked the man and was about to walk off when a thought occurred to him.

"Would you do me a favor and fetch my friend Hord? He's a dwarf with a short red beard and a splinted leg. You should find him in one of the rooms down that corridor," he said, motioning toward the opposite direction the guard had just come from.

The man didn't look too happy at being ordered around, but nodded all the same, and took off in the indicated direction.

He peered down at Grak through bleary eyes. She looked to be asleep on her feet and Arbor had to call her name a few times before she answered.

"What?!" she yelled, giving him a sour look.

He understood the feeling, but this was no time to be falling asleep. Grak needed to be awake for this meeting. She had all the important information. He reached out a hand and grabbed hers.

It would only be temporary, but it would serve its purpose all the same.

"What are you...?" Grak began to ask, just before a flood of energy entered her body.

She'd been on the verge of falling asleep, but now she felt as though she could run ten miles with ease.

"What did you do?" she asked, looking at him with a raised eyebrow. "If you can erase tiredness, why didn't you do so earlier?"

"I didn't erase your tiredness," Arbor said, covering a yawn. "I only revitalized you for a short while."

He concentrated for a moment, then pumped his magic up to his brain and felt his fatigue melt away as well.

"It'll wear off in about an hour, and then you'll feel all the fatigue come back in a rush, only about twice as bad as before. Now come on, we don't have a lot of time."

Grak looked like she wanted to ask more questions but nodded in agreement. The information they had was more important than satisfying her curiosity, but she would find out more once there was time to talk.

They walked quickly down the corridor and were soon standing outside the room in which they'd previously met Ramona. Arbor only had to knock once before the door was thrown open. Ramona stood there, dressed in a tunic and trousers. She looked as though she'd just been roused from sleep but ushered them quickly inside.

Arbor and Grak entered the room, and Ramona closed the door behind them. Looking around the room, Arbor could see that there were now half a dozen chairs by the large table, as well as a pitcher of water and some fruit.

The two of them walked over and sank down into the chairs. Arbor had to admit to himself that it felt nice to sit on something that wasn't constantly moving under him. He also silently thanked Ramona as he and Grak quickly devoured the fruit and drained the entire pitcher of water.

Ramona gave them a few minutes to eat, then approached the table and sat down across the two of them.

Grak couldn't help but notice that despite only just having woken up, the Co-founder still looked as perfect as ever. She scowled as the woman took a seat near Arbor, then quickly composed herself.

It wouldn't do to show the woman how much she disliked her. Besides, Arbor hadn't shown any clear interest in her, so maybe she wouldn't have to worry about competing with her.

Arbor opened his mouth to begin their report, but Ramona spoke before he could.

"I'm glad to see that the two of you made it back alive."

She spoke in a soft voice and Grak couldn't help noticing that she only looked at Arbor when she spoke. She gritted her teeth and had to make a concerted effort to stop a barbed comment from leaving her lips.

It was infuriating, the way she always looked at Arbor and completely ignored her presence. Truth be told, the way she constantly looked at Arbor annoyed her far more than her being ignored. Maybe she did have something to worry about, after all.

"What do you mean by that?" Arbor asked, anger clouding his features. "Were you expecting us to die out there?"

"No, not at all!" Ramona was quick to reassure him. "None of the other scouting parties reported back when they were supposed to. We began to worry, so we sent men out after them."

She stopped here, her expression growing grim.

"All the search party found of the scouts were their heads. They were neatly piled up just a mile from our base."

Arbor recoiled in horror and opened his mouth to ask a question, but Grak cut him off this time. She wasn't about to be ignored by this self-important princess.

"We know who did it."

Ramona turned to look at her for the first time, an eyebrow quirking upward in an unasked question.

"There's an army of over ten thousand gremlins less than a day's march from here," Grak said, having to suppress a smile at the look of shock that spread across Ramona's face.

Let Little Miss Perfect chew on that!

50

Arbor rubbed his temples in an attempt to alleviate a slowly worsening headache. As soon as Grak had mentioned a force of over ten thousand gremlins, Ramona had immediately stopped her from speaking any further. She'd stood and rushed out to one of the guards in the main hall and asked him to gather her captains for a council of war.

It was now an hour later, and the magic keeping him awake had worn off. He dared not do it again, as it could be quite damaging to his brain if he overused it. Strangely enough, Grak was still doing fine, if not a little annoyed at being forced to wait. The last captain had just walked in, a male dwarf by the name of Liron, flanked by three of his lieutenants.

Ramona stood by the table, now dressed in armor, with a sword belted at her waist. Arbor had to admit that she looked every bit the commander of a force of over five thousand warriors. The captains all took their seats, with the exception of Tenor who went to stand beside the co-founder.

"I'm sure you're all wondering why I've gathered you here in the dead of night," Ramona began. "We have just received a report that over ten thousand gremlins are marching on us as we speak."

She was forced to stop as everyone started talking all at once, with every captain and lieutenant trying to voice their opinions. Ramona just stayed silent and waited for everyone to calm down before continuing to speak.

"All our other scouts were killed, as you well know. But these two," she waved back at Arbor and Grak. "Managed to infiltrate the gremlin camp and receive vital information about their forces."

There was a hushed silence as all eyes in the room settled on them.

Arbor sat up a little straighter under all those scrutinizing gazes and stared back in turn, a calm expression painted on his face.

"How do we know we can trust them?"

This came from Durlan.

Arbor found that he didn't like the elf very much. He looked at the both of them as though they were worse than dirt.

Some of the captains started nodding their agreement.

"After all, should we put all our trust in a gremlin and some farm boy we've never met?"

"I saw them!" Grak said, shooting indignantly to her feet. "I went into their camp! They will be here in less than a day's time."

"I'm sure they will be," Durlan waved his hand dismissively before turning to Ramona.

"Please tell me that you didn't wake us all in middle of the night on the word of this gremlin simpleton," he drawled.

"Now listen here you, pompous piece of crap!" Grak said, her face darkening as she became angrier. "General Sor'shin is at the head of that army and they outnumber you more than two to one. If you want to wait until they kick down your doors and butcher you while you sleep, then by all means. Go ahead!"

The entire room had gone silent at her outburst, and Grak huffed in annoyance before sitting back down. The room promptly erupted into chaos and everyone started talking once again, each trying to voice their opinions. This time, Ramona was not content to let them quiet down on their own. She pulled a small mallet and sheet of metal from under the table, then began banging the two together, creating a horrible racket. It served its purpose, and everybody soon quieted down.

"If what Grak says is true, and I don't doubt that it is," Ramona said, shooting Durlan a glare, as he opened his mouth to object. "Then we are in serious trouble. Not only are we outnumbered two to one, but the Bloodbather himself is leading the charge."

"Bloodbather?" Arbor asked Grak quietly.

"General Sor'shin is also known as the Bloodbather. He got that name after donning rocky plate armor and killing so many men that he'd appeared to have bathed in blood."

"He has magic?"

"He's one of the most powerful Mages in Laedrin. He wouldn't be one of the generals if he wasn't. From reports, he's assumed to be a Wrecker class Mage and at the 14th Tier, no less!"

"If we are boring you with our war council, you are more than welcome to leave."

Arbor looked up to see Durlan once again sneering at them. He turned to Ramona and could see that she was clearly becoming annoyed with the elf as well.

"If you interrupt me one more time, *Advisor* Durlan, I will have you escorted from this room," Ramona said, in as calm a voice as she could muster.

Durlan blanched at this but shut his mouth, glaring daggers at the two of them.

Arbor had to wonder why the elf seemed to hate them so much. After all, there were three other elves in the room, and none of them seemed to mind them.

"As I was saying," Ramona continued. "We will have to shore up our defenses and try to slow them down on their approach."

She gestured to the map spread out in front of them.

"Captain Tenor has suggested we erect our three walls around the entrance they will most likely target. Hopefully, this will slow them down somewhat and give us time to prepare. After they have broken through the last wall, we will ride out with our cavalry and attempt to interrupt their lines."

She motioned to two spots on the map.

"Captain Liron and Captain Tenor will take their forces and exit from these two points. While our cavalry is engaging the enemy from the front, you two will flank them from the sides. With that, we will hopefully be able to break their lines and drive them back."

The two captains nodded their agreement and she continued.

"Once they begin their retreat, we'll have our archers fire on them. This will hopefully cut down their numbers even more. I know it's not very honorable, but this is war and we must win at all costs or die trying."

She looked at all the captains and lieutenants standing around the room. They all looked somber at the thought of battle ahead, especially when they were outnumbered so badly.

"This attack will by no means win us the war," Ramona continued. "But it will win us the day and hopefully whittle down their numbers enough so we can fight on more even terms."

The door slammed open then, and Hord hobbled in. He looked to be in a foul mood and began talking as soon as the door closed behind him.

"That's a load of horse shit and you know it Co-founder!" he said as he approached the table.

"As we currently stand, we have no chance of victory. We're too badly outnumbered and they've caught us off guard. You'll last maybe two days before you're all killed."

One of the captains opened her mouth to utter an angry retort, but Hord just cut her off.

"Oh, I'm sure you'll all die bravely enough, but you'll be dead all the same. Now I have a plan. There is still a way we can…"

He was cut off mid-sentence.

"Who do you think you are to come barging in here as if you could tell us what to do?"

Arbor turned to look and uttered a sound of disgust.

Of course, it was Durlan who spoke.

The pompous elf was standing there with a look of outrage plastered on his face as he stared down at the dwarf.

Hord bared his teeth in a grim approximation of a smile.

"I," he said, taking a step forward and puffing out his chest. "Am Prince Hordvig of the Jagged Peaks, brother of King Akkard of the Jagged Peaks!"

The entire room was stunned into silence by his proclamation.

Arbor leaned over to Grak and whispered.

"Do you think he actually has a plan?"

Grak nodded, a pleased smirk plastered on her face.

"I'm sure he does, but just look at Durlan's face! He looks like he's about to have a heart attack."

Arbor had to agree with her assessment and could feel a smile creeping onto his own lips as well.

"And who might you be?" Hord asked the advisor with mock interest.

Durlan's face had gone a beet red in color and he began spluttering as he tried to save face.

"Lies! All lies! There is no way you're telling the truth!"

He whirled to the rest of the captains.

"This dwarf comes hobbling in here, making all kinds of wild accusations and we are just expected to believe him?"

It was then that Arbor felt it. The profound wrongness he'd felt from the elf the last time they'd met, and this time, he knew he wasn't imagining it.

Arbor noticed then that Ramona was subtly trying to get his attention. He rose and walked over to the Co-founder as the elf ranted to the other captains. Oddly enough, they all seemed to be listening to him and nodding along in agreement.

"What is wrong with him?" Arbor hissed at her. "I thought you said he was your advisor. I didn't realize you took such an impulsive and quite obviously unhinged man's advice."

"I don't know what's wrong with him, either!" she hissed back. "That's why I called you over. Durlan has always been challenging to deal with, but he's a sensible man."

"He doesn't look too sensible to me. He looks like a deranged idiot. How is he even winning them over?"

Ramona looked worried and bit her lip as she thought.

"Something seems off about him. Is there any way you can detect if there's any magic at work here?"

Arbor had to think about that for a moment. He was almost sure that something was wrong, but was there any way from him to see it?

"I can try, but if there's any foul play at work here, and I suspect there is, I may have to act right away. Is that alright with you?"

Ramona nodded her agreement, and that was all he needed. Closing his eyes, he felt for his second Origin.

The odd white magic seemed to be able to wipe out vast numbers of enemies at once but could also seemed capable of attuning him to the magic in his surroundings.

It was very difficult for him to control the magic once it left his body, so he needed to be careful with how much he used, lest the magic take over and run wild. He allowed a small amount of the soft white light to begin leaking from his skin as he concentrated on the elf, fighting against it the whole time, as it tried to escape in greater amounts. He began sweating with the effort of holding it back, but after a few seconds, it seemed to settle.

It was then that he could sense that something was definitely wrong with the elf, but his senses weren't fine-tuned enough to pick up more than that. All he got was the same vague sense of wrongness he'd been feeling until now. He growled in frustration before an exciting possibility occurred to him.

What if it was possible to see what was happening? If he could sense things with the magic coating his skin, perhaps he could see things with the magic coating his eyes!

Quickly putting his new theory to the test, he concentrated on pulling the magic back into himself. He was happy that he hadn't let too much out, as he didn't have the time to fight it right now. The other captains were now looking at Hord as though he were an intruder, and one or two were even clutching weapons.

Once the magic was back in his body, he willed it to move up and into his eye sockets. Allowing a minuscule amount to leak out, he felt a momentary flash of pain as his eyes were coated in the soft white light. He blinked a few times and rubbed at them to clear his vision as they began tearing up. But when his eyes came into focus, it was as if they'd been opened for the first time.

Color filled his vision. Color of all shades and hues stood out to him in stark contrast to the dull colors surrounding them. He could see magic!

Turning, he could see the pale blue light surrounding Grak and the purple and silver around Ramona.

He could also see various colors coming off of all the captains' various armor and weapons. Looking down, he could see two distinct colors, overlaid by a mix of browns and greens. Blinking a few times, he concentrated again. Sure enough, his breastplate swirled with the distinct colors of the Roc-Jaguar. Looking back to Grak, he could see her rapier giving off the same colors as his breastplate.

This must be what the Mythicallium looks like to magical sight, he realized.

He was sure that if he unsheathed his glaive right now, he would see the same colors swirling in his vision. He also noticed a small swirl of color from where his pendant hung around his neck. The pedant swirled with all the colors of the rainbow and shone more brilliantly than any of the other magic around him.

Just what kind of magic did the pendant possess to give off so much light?

He felt a nudge in his ribs and looked over to see Ramona giving him a questioning look.

Remembering why he was doing this, he quickly shook away the question of his pendant. There would be more time to examine it later.

He glanced over at Durlan and froze. A sickly green light was twined around the elf's arm. Every time he gestured or spoke, the light would lash out at whomever he was talking to, and the person became instantly more agreeable to what he was saying. Half the people in the room were already completely covered in the sickly green light. There was something else wrong, though.

Durlan's entire body seemed *wrong* somehow, as if someone else were inhabiting it.

His thoughts trailed off at that, as the true horror of what was standing before them struck him. That thing was not an elf, but what could it be? What was that thing?!

Arbor shook his head quickly.

There was no time for questions. He must act now before the creature noticed it had been spotted.

"You're no elf!" Arbor yelled as he reached for his magic.

The entire room turned to look as Arbor launched himself at the elf. He crossed the room in a matter of seconds, but he could already see the creature beginning to react, reaching for something at its belt.

He didn't have time to draw his glaive, so against his better judgment, he allowed the white magic to explode out from his body, the energy whipping off him as it fought to be free. The creature tried to avoid the blow, but Arbor had caught it off guard and was moving way too fast.

The creature shrieked in horror as Arbor drove his glowing fist into its abdomen, the shriek so loud that it momentarily deafened everyone in the room. Then there was a bright flash of light from the point of impact, and a deafening boom shook the entire room as his magic took effect.

A massive hole was blown straight through Durlan's body, painting the opposite wall with his innards as the creature dropped to the ground in a heap.

Arbor stood there for a few moments and stared at his bloody fist, as he battled with all his might to suppress the magic now flowing out of him. He could feel the magic's desire to be free, to run rampant, and destroy everything in its path.

It took a great deal of effort, almost more than he had, but at last, he managed to cut off the flow of magic, but he now faced a new problem. The magic still coating his body didn't want to go back in, and no matter how hard he tried, it wouldn't obey him.

It was then that he saw Durlan stirring out of the corner of his eye. The hole in his stomach began to knit itself shut, and he glared at Arbor with undisguised hatred as he got shakily to his feet.

Arbor didn't hesitate for even a moment. He quickly gathered the excess magic still coating his skin and focused it all on his right arm. Then he brought the arm back, and swung it outward in a wide arc, releasing it at the end of its trajectory.

There was another loud boom as the white magic flew from his arm and hit the creature in the stomach once again. He didn't even have time to utter a sound this time, as the magic cut straight through him. Durlan's body hit the ground with two distinct thumps, and this time, he didn't get up.

51

There was a shocked silence in the room as Durlan's body hit the ground, blood pumping from both halves and pooling on the ground beneath him. There was also a massive crack running across one wall where the magic had impacted after cutting through the creature.

Arbor looked down at his arm in wonder.

There wasn't a mark on him. That didn't make any sense. All magic had a price, especially magic this powerful. He then remembered the struggle he'd had when trying to get the magic under control.

He'd nearly lost it. The magic may be powerful, but using it again so carelessly may cost the lives of everyone around him. He would not use his second Origin in this way again, at least, not until he understood what it was.

Ramona, Grak, and all the other captains had rushed over the moment he'd struck and now surrounded the body. Even as they watched, the corpse slowly morphed into that of a human, but it was a human like Arbor had seen before.

"What is that?" Grak asked in disgust.

Arbor had to agree with her sentiment. Its body was horribly twisted and hunched – he could see that even though it had been split in two. The skin was black and blue, as though its entire body was covered in bruises. The open staring eyes were a dull red with slitted pupils. It had no nose and its teeth all appeared to be sharp as needles.

"An Infiltrator," Ramona said, giving the body a fearful look. "They are a group of individuals with a talent for mimicking other living creatures. The king uses them as spies and assassins when he really wants certain information or a particularly gruesome death for an enemy."

She stepped away from the creature and went back to the table.

Arbor looked at the thing dubiously. It really was a nasty looking thing.

He turned away from the corpse, only to realize that the entire room was staring at him.

"What? Did I do something wrong?" he asked, addressing his question to Ramona, who had just sunk into a chair.

"No, you did nothing wrong, lad," Hord answered as he hobbled over on his crutch. "They're all just staring at you because you just pulled off something that would have taken over fifty men to accomplish, and you did it in a matter of seconds."

He was beaming and clapped Arbor on the back, congratulating him.

"All I did was kill Durlan," Arbor said, feeling a bit embarrassed at the whole thing. "I did it before he could react, so it wasn't much of a fight."

He looked down at the corpse again.

"What exactly is it, though? It looks almost human, but all wrong."

"Infiltrators were once human."

Arbor turned his gaze back to Ramona as she spoke.

"They gave up their humanity, and more, in the search for power. The king granted them powerful magic in exchange for their undying loyalty and obedience. A single Infiltrator could easily kill a force of thirty soldiers and could overpower even the most adept of Mages. Their magic isn't exactly powerful, but it's the power they wield that's truly terrifying. They can nullify most types of magic, and their bodies are enhanced to superhuman levels. That is why they are considered to be so dangerous."

Arbor was shocked, to say the least. That thing lying at his feet could really do all that? He knew something was off when he'd seen it and had acted without thinking, and now he was glad he did. A creature that dangerous could not be allowed to live. The thought that the king could grant others magic was quite frightening as well.

Then another thought struck him, and he felt the icy thrill of fear clutch at his heart.

"Do you think there are more of them here?"

Ramona shook her head.

"There will not be another Infiltrator within a hundred miles. No one knows why, but they can't be any closer than that to another of their kind."

Arbor breathed in a sigh of relief.

The creatures had a limited use as a force if they couldn't be within a hundred miles of one another, but as assassins and spies, they would be perfect.

"I don't know exactly what Durlan was doing, but every time he gestured at someone, it was as if his magic was making them more agreeable to him."

"That's not Durlan." Captain Tenor spoke up as he walked over and stooped to examine the body. "Durlan is long dead. I don't know exactly when he died, but an Infiltrator kills its victims to possess their bodies."

He pulled the cloak from his back and covered the dead Infiltrator, hiding its grotesque form from the rest of them.

"You have done us a great service once again, Arbor," Ramona said, rising from her seat and walking through the still silent crowd. "You have saved a lot of lives here tonight, my own included. The Infiltrator would likely have killed everyone in this room if you had not acted when you did."

She smiled at him, and he could see nods of agreement from the other captains and lieutenants around the room.

"Make any request of me, and if it is within my power, I will grant it for you."

Arbor had to think about that. He looked over to Grak, who looked angry for some reason. He wanted her advice, but she wouldn't meet his gaze. Finally, he had to give up and make his mind up on his own.

What did he really want? He had more money than he knew what to do with. His weapons and armor were better than anything she could offer as well. No. He didn't need anything.

He nodded to himself, sure of his decision.

"All I want is to rescue my sister from the slave city, and to see the man who killed my family dead for what he did."

He said this in as calm a voice as he could manage, but he felt his blood boil at the thought that somewhere out there, Ramson was still alive, likely killing more innocent families and taking their children.

Ramona nodded once solemnly. "Then I have a question for you. Will you fight for us in the upcoming battle?"

Arbor squared his shoulders and looked her in the eye.

"You are my best chance of saving my sister. I will fight for you so long as you keep your promise."

Ramona nodded once again and stuck her hand out, and the two shook on it.

"As touching as this moment is," Hord said, interrupting with his usual lack of tact. "I believe I was in the middle of telling you all how doomed you were before that thing bleeding all over the floor interrupted me."

He looked around the room again, meeting each of the captain's gazes.

"I have a plan, but you will need to hold out for three days."

"I thought you said we wouldn't last two," Ramona said with a raised eyebrow.

"That I did," Hord said with a wide grin. "But if you want to live, you'll have to survive for three."

Ramona shook her head at the dwarf's twisted logic but motioned for him to keep going.

The dwarf nodded graciously and continued.

"As of right now, you don't have the forces needed to win. However, you do have the forces you need just a day's march from here."

A murmur of conversation started throughout the room before they were silenced by a glare from Captain Tenor.

Hord smiled even wider.

"I see that my plan is finally sinking in. I don't know why none of you idiots thought of it until now. And you all call yourselves captains and lieutenants."

He shook his head in mock disappointment, then turned to look at Ramona.

"You can't spare even one man on this upcoming battle. Luckily for you, I am temporarily unable to fight. I will ride to the Endless Wood for reinforcements. All you guys have to do is stay alive until my return. What do you say?"

Ramona looked at the dwarf for a moment, then looked around to her other captains.

"Well, rude as the little man is, he has a point. I agree, what about you?" she asked in a loud, carrying voice.

Her question was answered by a resounding cheer from the captains and lieutenants. Smiling, she looked back at the dwarf.

"It looks as though you've got your answer."

She slipped a ring from the middle finger of her left hand and handed it over to Hord. "Take this ring and present it to Commander Neff. He is the leader of the Defiants. Tell him we need aid urgently and not to let Juwei bog them down in procedure. If I die because of her, tell him that I will personally haunt him from the grave!"

Hord accepted the ring with a chuckle.

"Will do, Co-founder."

Turning to Arbor and Grak, Ramona addressed them directly.

"I'm sure you must be tired from your mission. Go now and rest. We will have someone wake you when the enemy is sighted."

Arbor nodded gratefully, but Grak just turned her back without saying a word, and the two of them followed Hord out into the corridor.

They walked in silence for a few moments before Grak turned at him and burst out, "What was that all about?"

Arbor was taken aback at the sudden outburst and looked to Hord for help.

"I'm not getting involved in this," he said, falling back a few steps.

Arbor looked back at Grak and saw she looked angry.

"Can you tell me what I've done to upset you this time?" he asked carefully.

"You!" she said, jabbing her finger into his breastplate, "Once again rushed headlong into danger without a second thought. You could have gotten yourself killed!"

"I'm sorry," he said, raising his hands in defense. "I didn't know what I was attacking, but I needed to act quickly. Otherwise, it would have caught on."

Her expression softened a bit as he said this.

"I know that you needed to act, I just wish you wouldn't rush headlong into danger like that every time we're faced with a problem."

"It's not like I go looking for danger. It just seems to find me. If it makes you feel any better, though, I'll do my best to avoid it when I can."

He smiled at her, but she just huffed and sped up, walking quickly down the corridor, and was soon lost from view.

"She worries about you. She just doesn't know how to express it that well."

Arbor turned back to see Hord still walking behind him. He'd forgotten the dwarf was even there. That alone highlighted how truly exhausted he really was.

"When do you ride out?" Arbor asked, falling into step beside the dwarf.

"As soon as I make it to the stables," he answered. Then he looked at Arbor with a worried expression. "What kind of magic were you using when you killed that monster?"

"I'm not an idiot!" he said when he saw Arbor's surprised look. "I could clearly see a difference between how you fought when I first met you and how you fought just now. It was the same magic you used on those lizards, wasn't it?"

Arbor's lips compressed into a line, but he nodded all the same.

"I don't know exactly what it is, but I do know one thing. It's extremely powerful, more powerful than you can imagine. I think that I've only just scratched the surface of what this magic can really do.

"It may be very powerful magic, but I don't think it's worth the price I might one day need to pay for using it," he finished in a quiet voice, remembering the struggle he'd had controlling it earlier.

Hord didn't speak for a minute, and the two walked on in silence, finally coming into the main hall.

"I can't tell you what to do about your new magic," he said as they stopped in the middle of the open chamber. "I can say this, however. Whether you like it or not, that power is a part of you now. You can either control it or let it destroy you."

He clapped him on the back one more time, and Arbor watched him heading down the tunnels towards the stable.

He walked tiredly back to his room and closed the door behind him. There was a large tray of beef and bread as well as a change of clothes sitting on the small nightstand. Quickly stripping out of his clothes and armor, he got into the clean clothes and washed his face in a small basin near the nightstand.

He was soon sitting on his bed and wolfing down his meal, the delicious flavors of the seasoned beef and crusty bread lifting his spirits. Up until he'd seen the food, he hadn't realized just how hungry he was, and it didn't take him long to polish off the entire tray.

A short while later, Arbor found himself lying in bed, thinking over what Hord had told him.

When he now thought of using his new magic, he felt fear grip his heart. A fear unlike any he'd felt before. His heart pounded in his chest as he replayed the feeling over and over in his mind.

The glowing magic, the blow he'd struck against the Infiltrator, the gaping hole he'd left in the creature, and finally, the last attack that had split it in half. It wasn't the death of the Infiltrator or the gruesome way he'd killed it that was gnawing at him. It was the unknown that made his heart begin to pound, and a cold sweat break out on his brow.

He didn't know what this magic was or how it worked. He could understand his Perception magic. If he pushed too hard, it would cost him. But at least he knew his limitations, and exactly how it worked. This other magic felt different. There seemed to be endless possibilities, as though it weren't constrained to any single type of magic.

Arbor shuddered and tried to force his mind away from such a dangerous line of thinking.

He couldn't use this magic carelessly, no matter how much power it gave him. Hord was right about one thing, however. He would need to resolve whatever this was or be destroyed by it. He allowed himself to admit, at least internally, that he was afraid, but not of any person or thing. He was afraid of himself, of what might happen if he lost control of the magic. How many people would die as a result if he ever did...

An urgent pounding at the door awoke Arbor from a troubled sleep. Getting quickly out of bed, he went to open the door, rubbing tired eyes and yawning widely. Grak stood there, dressed in her armor with her rapier strapped to her belt.

"Scouts just reported back," she said, throwing a bundle of clothes at him. "Get dressed. The gremlin force will be here in an hour."

She turned her back on him as he stripped down to his underclothes, further highlighting the seriousness of the situation, and put on the shirt and pants she'd brought him. She then helped him tighten his breastplate with the roaring jaguar's head embossed on the front. He tied on a hardened leather skirt, similar to the one Grak wore, and buckled his belt on over them. Lastly, he slid on his bracers and greaves. He'd finally received a pair made of steel and was happy to be going into battle with a little more protection.

He slung his glaive over his shoulder and looked at his companion.

"Let's not keep them waiting, then," he said, and the two of them headed out into the corridor towards the main hall.

52

Sylvester looked on in horror as Karria hit the ground, the deep gash in her side pumping out blood at an alarming rate.

"Kill her! Then cut me free so I can get my turn!" Nina shrieked.

Sylvester looked over to see that only a small portion of her upper body still bound.

He cursed himself quietly for losing his concentration and quickly had the cursing girl bound up again. He took a step toward Nina, but Eletha's voice stopped him in his tracks.

"Take one more step, and I cut her throat."

Sylvester looked to her and saw her kneeling over Karria, with a dagger pressed to her throat. His heart beat ever faster as he watched the pool of blood under her growing with each passing second.

By the way she was bleeding, Karria had two minutes left, at best, before she died.

"That's a good boy," Eletha said as she shifted a bit on Karria's prone form.

He noticed then that she grimaced in pain as she did so, and seeing the injuries covering the girl, he was shocked she was still alive.

"Now, you're going to release my sister, then you're going to let her tie you up. Try anything, and I'll kill the Sow."

She pressed the dagger harder to Karria's throat, causing a small line of blood to appear.

Sylvester didn't know what to do. On the one hand, he had to protect his sister and he knew that if he released Nina, they'd all be killed. Karria would die soon, of that he was certain. The only question remaining was if he and Kya would be joining her.

"Make it snappy. We don't have all day!" Eletha screamed, pressing the knife down a bit harder.

Sylvester didn't move, wracked once again by indecision.

Seeing that Sylvester was not making a move to free her sister, a nasty smile crossed Eletha's face.

"Very well then," she said and raised the dagger high over her head.

"I think you've done quite enough."

Sylvester jumped, and Eletha faltered, stopping the dagger mid-stroke, as a man walked into the clearing.

Sylvester turned slowly, his eyes widening in recognition. He knew this man, knew him for what he really was, and it terrified him. The mere sight of him standing there scared him more than the deranged elf standing over his friend.

"Who the hell are you?!" Eletha demanded, glaring up at the stranger who'd interrupted her, right when she'd been about to get her revenge. "This is none of your business, human. This is the Goldenleaf Forest. Now get lost!"

"I think that it is my business. After all, that dagger is not yours," the man said, approaching Eletha and the prone Karria. "It belongs to the girl you're currently threatening. And seeing as I have a vested interest in seeing her live, I'll have to ask you to get off her. If you don't, I'll have no choice but to remove you."

"Remove me? Do you have any idea who I am, you stupid human?" Eletha shouted, waving the dagger in the air. "I am the strongest battle mage in the Goldenleaf School of Magic! Take one step closer, and I will destroy you!"

Sylvester took an involuntary step back from the two of them and almost tripped over Nina's prone form, hearing a groan escape through her gag. He did not want to get in Silver's way.

"I somehow doubt that you're a battle mage," Silver said, a look for scorn on his face. "In fact, you're barely an Enhanced Mage past the 4th Tier. Where I come from, even a child would chew you up and spit you out like the garbage you are."

He turned to Sylvester then, his eyes narrowing.

"This is the second time you've nearly gotten her killed."

He did not look happy.

The grin that Sylvester was used to seeing on the man was no longer there. Instead, he had an expression of burning anger.

"How is this my fault?" Sylvester asked, indignantly.

Unfortunately for him, his voice cracked as he spoke, greatly diminishing his attempt at being outraged.

"If you hadn't stopped Karria from killing her, this weakling would by lying on the ground instead of her!" His voice grew lower and more dangerous now. "If this happens a third time, no one in the entire world will be able to save you from my wrath, boy! Do you understand?!"

Sylvester took an involuntary step back, and this time, he did trip over Nina, landing hard on his ass. He looked up in fear at the man standing just feet away and nodded quickly.

"I promise it won't happen again!"

Silver nodded then turned back to Eletha, who was staring at him, her mouth open in disbelief.

"What do you mean *almost* killed?" she asked, waving the red dagger in front of his face. "None of you will be making it out of here alive! I'll kill...!"

She was cut off by Nina's muffled shrieks and rolled her eyes.

"I'll kill you, then cut my sister loose so *she* can kill the prince. Then I'm going to cut the lovely Princess' face off. Won't that be nice?" she asked with a deranged smile. "She won't look so pretty anymore, when she doesn't have her face!"

"I'm going to tell you one last time," Silver said, taking a step forward. "Drop the dagger and release the girl."

Eletha just cackled madly and lifter the dagger, then brought it plunging down towards Karria's chest.

"Not a chance in hell!"

The dagger never made contact with Karria, as Eletha was blasted off the girl and flew through the air to land ten feet away. A shriek of pain was forced from her throat as her already mutilated body hit the ground with a thud.

Silver was at Karria's side in a flash and quickly placed his hand over the still bleeding wound. Sylvester could see that Karria had gone a deathly pale. He wasn't sure what Silver could do for her, but he really hoped that he would be able to save her.

There was a flash of light and the smell of burning flesh where Silver had placed his hand. When he removed it, the wound was sealed shut, and a large burn mark surrounded the area.

"Sylvester," Silver snapped. "Get over here and look after her. I've closed the wound as best I can, but I'll need to be able to fight without any distractions."

Sylvester nodded and quickly rushed over, reaching for his Origin. Using the roots under the ground, he moved her gently over to Kya, then stood protectively in front of them.

Silver nodded his thanks and turned back to Eletha, just in time to catch a bolt of lightning to the chest. There was a huge explosion and Silver was completely engulfed in smoke.

"What did I tell you about interfering, human?"

Eletha was somehow back on her feet, completely shocking Sylvester.

Silver was most certainly dead after that! He knew he was about to die but had to marvel at the insane girl's tenacity. She had a stab wound in her leg, a shattered rib cage, a broken arm and a nasty gash on her scalp, yet she was still standing.

"Damn it all. I really liked that shirt," Silver's voice drifted out of the smoke cloud as if taking a bolt of lightning to the chest was no bother at all.

The smoke soon cleared, and Sylvester could see that somehow he was completely unharmed. His shirt hung in tatters and he was looking down at it forlornly.

"I've noticed you have a bad habit of attacking people when their backs are turned," he said dryly.

"How are you not dead?" Eletha was staring in shock at the man. "No human could survive that!"

"Oh, that's pretty simple," Silver said, taking his shirt the rest of the way off and dropping it to the ground. "You keep calling me human. Why would you assume that I am human?"

Sylvester could hear his voice deepening as he spoke, and felt his heart skip a beat. He wouldn't really do it here, would he?

Silver looked back at him then and smiled. It wasn't his usual kind and friendly smile, though. It was a predatory smile, full of hunger and the promise of death.

"The elf behind me knows what I am," Silver said as he turned back to Eletha, who had now gone a sickly pale as she watched Silver's transformation.

He was growing taller as he spoke, and his shoulders were noticeably broadening. His pants began to strain and finally tore at the seams, muscular legs showing underneath. His skin was darkening as well and was soon black as pitch. His skin seemed to crack in certain places, leaving glowing, violet lines all over his body, tracing strange patterns on his skin.

The sky darkened overhead, and a wind began to blow, sending leaves fluttering in all directions. The transformation finally came to an end, the entire thing taking place in seconds, but seeming to take an eternity. Silver now stood nearly eight feet tall and towered over the elf girl. His glowing purple eyes were glaring down at her.

A white aura surrounded him, wisping off his skin, and the air crackled with unspent power.

Sylvester was not one of the rare few who could sense magic, but even he could feel the immense power radiating off the man.

No, not a man, he thought to himself, with a shiver of fear. *A monster!*

Eletha took one step back, then another and another, finally feeling her bad leg buckle under her and she went sprawling backward on the ground. A look of pure terror crossed her face, and she knew true fear for the first time in her life.

She'd never been this afraid before, not when she'd nearly killed Karria and had to run for her life. Not when she'd broken into the city to take the princess. Not even when she'd killed those guards at the gate that had nearly caught her.

Now, looking at this man, she could feel her heart seizing up and her breath catch in her throat as she desperately tried to escape from this monster.

"That's impossible, all the Salamanders are dead!" she screamed, trying desperately to cobble together some magic as a defense.

She never got the chance. A loud, piercing scream rent the early morning air, as she was engulfed in a brilliant white light and her entire body was torn apart. When the light faded, not a shred of evidence was left to suggest that Eletha had been lying there just a moment before. In her place was a massive crater with jagged cracks running in all directions from the center. Nothing else remained.

Silver then turned back toward Sylvester, his glowing eyes on the still bound Nina and he slowly approached. The vines melted off the elf girl who was now frozen in fear, looking up at the approaching nightmare.

"Leave her alone!" Sylvester said, stepping directly into Silver's oncoming path and spreading his arms out wide.

"What do you think you're doing, boy?" Silver boomed, the very air trembling as he spoke.

"She didn't actually hurt anyone. She only did as she was told," Sylvester said.

His heart was nearly coming out of his mouth, and he didn't know whether he'd lost his mind standing up to a salamander, but he knew in his heart that it was the right thing to do.

"Did nothing?! She held a knife to your sister's throat while Karria was being tortured! If she had her way, she'd be killing you right now. So why do you protect her?"

He took another step forward, the ground shattering under his foot and jagged cracks spreading from the impact.

"That may be true, but I won't judge her for what she would have done. Sure, she may have held a knife to my sister's throat, but she didn't kill her. She may have even killed me, but she didn't! I believe in giving people second chances, don't you?"

He really hoped his argument would make him back down. If Silver decided to kill Nina, there would be nothing he could do to stop him.

Silver paused and seemed to think for a moment. Then he exhaled mightily, the white aura leaving his body as he began to shrink. His skin tone changed to the usual light orange color, and the glowing purple lines vanished as well.

"You have a soft heart, boy. It will get you killed one day," he said, bending to fetch his ruined shirt and putting it back on.

Before he managed to close it, Sylvester could almost swear he saw a scar on the man's chest. A deep, jagged line running over his left pectoral muscle. It was silvery white, as though the wound had healed a very long time ago. He had to wonder who could leave a mark on a monster like that.

"You really should be getting home," Silver said, walking back to the four of them.

Sylvester looked down then in concern. Kya was still unconscious and Karria was very pale, her breath coming in shallow gasps. Nina shivered on the ground, weeping in terror and relief at having narrowly avoided death.

"There's no way I can get them all home in time," Sylvester said worriedly.

Karria definitely wouldn't make in time.

"Luckily for you, I can get you home without too much trouble."

Silver then looked Sylvester in the eye, and his voice took on a more menacing air.

"And don't forget my warning, Sylvester. Should harm befall her again because of your actions, I will be coming for you."

Karria's red dagger was placed in his hand, then suddenly his surroundings vanished. A moment later, he found himself in the center of the throne room, back in the palace. He looked around in confusion. Karria, Kya, and Nina were all lying on the ground next to him.

The forest was gone, and so was Silver. Looking up, he saw Blyss and Alvine staring at him with disbelieving expressions, as guards rushed over to them.

He felt a smile creep onto his lips before he collapsed on the ground, unconscious.

53

Arbor looked out over the open plains at the approaching army. He was standing next to Grak, on top of the outermost wall that had been erected almost overnight. There were three such walls, each made of hardwood and around twenty feet tall.

When he'd asked how they'd managed to erect the walls so quickly, one of the dwarves next to him had explained that they'd already been built in advance for just such a situation.

They'd been constructed beforehand and then brought out by teams of horses in sections. They were designed in such a way that the sections could be clipped together, and then long boards were slotted across the inside to reinforce the structure. Hard spikes had then been driven into the ground to hold it all up.

The results were three walls, each over five miles long, and arching inward in a semi-circle. The walls were set up at one-mile increments to give them room to fight and to set traps when they broke through. The gremlins could try and circumvent the walls, but the archers would greatly reduce their numbers if they attempted to do so much as near the wall.

They could retreat and come around in a wide circle, but that would take time. Ramona was hoping they would try and circle around in a wide arc. This way, she could avoid losing any fighters, while buying time for Hord to return with the main force.

Arbor didn't think they would be so lucky. From the way he was described to him, General Sor'shin wasn't the type to take the long way, just to spare the lives of some of his gremlins. He would most likely just push until he broke through.

There had been a change in plans, and now they were going to try and hold the walls for as long as possible, instead of using them as breaks. Even now, there were people working on the innermost wall, building it further around, in an attempt to make a full circle.

The gremlin army came to a halt just out of bowshot, and a rider came forward, carrying a white flag. As he approached, Arbor noticed Ramona coming up onto the wall, flanked on both sides by her personal guard. She was dressed for battle, wearing gleaming plate armor from head to toe. Her head was bare, leaving her silver and violet-streaked hair to blow in the early-morning breeze. Arbor could see a steel helm resting under the crook of her arm.

All the soldiers stopped what they were doing to salute as she passed. Arbor stood at attention and began to salute as well, but she waved him off, leaning against the wall and watching the approaching rider.

"Have you ever been in a battle like this before?"

"I've only fought in small skirmishes before this," he admitted.

"Are you afraid?" She looked at him out of the corner of her eye.

"Yes," he answered honestly.

He was afraid, more afraid than he cared to admit. His fists were clenched at his sides to stop them from shaking and his heart was thudding so hard, he was sure the whole world could hear it.

Ramona turned and flashed him a grim smile.

"Good. You'd be a fool not to be."

Arbor was relieved to hear that. He'd been afraid to answer honestly, as he didn't want to be seen as a coward.

"Do you think we can win?" Ramona asked in a quiet voice.

He raised an eyebrow at the Co-founder.

"Why ask me? I don't know anything about battle, and I'm your newest recruit."

Ramona chuckled lightly at that and looked out onto the plains again. The rider was nearly at the wall now.

"You may not believe it, but I think you are far more important than you give yourself credit for. You have a big part to play in overthrowing the king, and it's not just me who believes it."

Arbor's eyebrows went up in surprise.

"What are you talking about? Barely anyone here knows me. How could anyone believe that a carpenter's son from the middle of nowhere could be important?"

Grak spoke up for the first time since Ramona had approached.

"She's right, you know. Look around you. People can feel you're special. Look how they've cleared space for you. They speak to you with respect and deference, despite never having met you before."

She smiled then, the corners of her lips turning up.

"You are special. The only one who doesn't see it is you."

Arbor just shook his head at the two of them.

"I have no idea what you're talking about."

He wanted to deny what they were saying, but even he was having a hard time convincing himself that they were lying. He'd noticed the stares he'd been getting. The awed expressions on the faces of strangers as they watched him pass.

"I think someone may have spread a rumor that you singlehandedly killed an Infiltrator," Ramona said in a casual tone, but Arbor could see the corners of her mouth twitching as she tried to suppress a smile.

"I thought you were trying to keep my magic a secret."

"I was, but you killed the spy," Ramona waved her hand dismissively. "Besides, your magic would be on display in the upcoming battle anyway, and it will boost the troops' morale to see such a great warrior fighting with them."

Arbor shook his head in amazement. Leave it to her to find an advantage in any situation. It was really quite crafty.

The rider stopped in front of the wall and pulled his horse to a halt.

"Hear me, you rebel scum!" His voice boomed out over the Flatlands as he spoke. "I come to speak to you in the name of the great General Sor'shin! Surrender now, and you will be sold as slaves, but stay and fight, and we will kill you all!"

"Shoot him," Ramona said calmly.

The rider had opened his mouth to speak again when there was a twanging of bowstrings, and the rider was subsequently turned into a pincushion.

The Defiants on the wall cheered as the rider fell to the ground, his black blood staining the parched ground beneath him.

"Was that really necessary?" Arbor asked as he heard horns being blown from across the field.

"It will send a strong message. Also, I didn't much like the terms the little bastard offered us. I don't much fancy being a slave, do you?" she asked rhetorically.

Arbor simply shook his head, watching as the sea of red began moving forward, drums pounding and horns blowing.

"Can you see what magic they've got on them?" Ramona whispered to him.

This part of his magic was one that they were trying to keep secret. The ability to sense magic was an extremely rare one and could come in handy when fighting enemy Mages.

Arbor took a deep breath and allowed his second Origin to power his vision. The approaching army had a few spots of color, but a lot less than he'd been expecting.

"It looks like there are around a hundred or so Mages, and another few hundred with magic weapons or armor."

Ramona nodded as though she'd been expecting this.

"Like I said before, magic is a rare thing in this land. It doesn't matter for which side you fight. A rare resource will still be rare."

One of the captains approached Ramona then. She was an elf, the leader of the archer contingent under her command. She saluted, then spoke.

"Shall I have my lieutenants give the signal?"

"On your command, Captain." Ramona nodded and turned to head down the wall. She looked back before leaving.

"Take care of yourself, Arbor. You are very important to me, and I'd rather not see you die in this battle."

Then she left, her contingent of guards marching after her.

Arbor had to wonder about her last statement. Didn't she mean he was important to the Defiants?

He shrugged and chalked it up to her being under stress. Turning to look at Grak, he could see her visibly fuming, which was quite impressive given her complexion.

He placed a hand on her shoulder, and she looked up at him, as though surprised he was still there.

"Why do you seem so upset?"

She opened her mouth to reply, when a loud order went down the line.

"Archers ready!" A loud voice called out, and Grak turned to look out at the gremlin army. They were now almost within bowshot, and they heard a loud creaking, as hundreds of bows were drawn back at once.

"Fire!"

There was a collective sound of twanging bowstrings as the archers fired.

Arbor followed the storm shafts as they arched through the air and came down on the enemy force. He could hear screams of pain as they found their marks and saw the front-line stumble.

"Fire!"

Arbor had been watching the approaching army and hadn't noticed the archers preparing another volley. He watched the arrows fly again and plunge into the approaching line of gremlins.

"Doesn't he care about his forces at all?" he asked Grak as a third volley was loosed at the enemy.

"Not in the slightest," Grak answered back. She looked grim as hundreds of gremlins fell with each volley.

"Maybe we'll be able to cut them down before they even reach the wall."

Arbor was becoming hopeful as another volley brought down more of the enemy force.

"I wouldn't count on it," Grak said, then threw herself to the ground with a loud curse.

Arbor didn't have long to wonder why, as the archer near him went down with a shout of pain. Looking down, he could see crossbow bolt protruding from his chest.

Arbor quickly dropped below the lip of the makeshift wall and peered over. The front line of gremlins was nearly at the wall now, and he could see the crossbow-wielding gremlins reloading for another volley.

The archers had time for one more volley of arrows before the gremlins crashed into the wall.

Arbor could feel the wooden floor reverberate as they did so. He saw the archers quickly sliding down ladders on the other side and running to their horses. They would now go to the second wall and wait for the approaching force again.

He heard the rattle of wood and saw the tops of ladders hitting the wall.

"Looks like it's our turn," he said, flashing Grak a grim smile.

"Looks that way," she said, returning the grin.

Then the first gremlin reached the top of the wall. His face had barely cleared the lip when Arbor's glaive took his head from his shoulders.

Raising his weapon above his head, he roared his defiance. It was now their job to cover the archers' retreat. They were to hold the wall until they were all safely to the second position. More gremlins swarmed over the wall, and the battle now began in earnest.

Arbor hacked his way through the first few gremlins to come up the ladders, but they were soon on the wall, more and more swarming over the lip by the second. He blocked a sword thrust to his leg and took the gremlin's arm off, before kicking him off the wall.

He danced back, narrowly avoiding a spear, then sheared the top off the weapon when it was thrust at him again. The gremlin tried to take a step back, but Arbor's glaive sliced through his chainmail, nearly cutting him in two.

He was amazed at the weapon's sharpness. Hord had not been lying when he'd said it could cut through almost anything. He blocked another sword thrust with the haft of his weapon, then cut the offending sword in two. The gremlin stared in shock at his stump of a sword. Then Arbor brought the spiked end of his weapon across his face, cracking his jaw and sending him flying off the wall.

He was being careful to limit the amount of magic he was using at any given time.

Sure, he didn't need to use too much to beat these soldiers, but this was a battle, and he had to pace himself. Otherwise, his body might give out at the wrong moment, and a mistake like that could cost him his life.

He cut through three more gremlins before he heard the horn sound. The archers were at the second wall. He heard the call then spreading down the wall.

"Retreat to the secondary position!"

Arbor looked to his left and saw Grak running over. She was breathing hard, her breastplate covered in blood and gore. Looking down at himself, he could see he didn't look too much better. His once gleaming brown and green breastplate was now covered in blood and grime, and the smell was almost enough to make him gag.

He pushed down the reflex and examined their surroundings. The wall was clear in their section, but he could see bodies littering the wall in both directions. Looking down, he could see a force approaching, all riding massive hairy beasts that walked on their knuckles and hind legs. They were humanoid in appearance, and he heard Grak cursing silently next to him.

"What are those things?" he asked in concern.

"War apes," she said, turning her back on the oncoming force and running for a ladder. "Come on; they'll be over the wall in a matter of seconds once they reach it."

Arbor took one last look out at the approaching apes. They did look quite imposing. He hurried to follow Grak, sliding quickly down the ladder and sheathing his weapon as he did so.

He had to wonder why he hadn't come across any other Mages yet, but shrugged, figuring that he'd run into them eventually.

The area between the first and second walls were littered with pitfalls and traps, all set up by the brilliant dwarf engineers, and they had to be careful, dodging around them as they ran.

He could see other soldiers running around him, all heading for the second wall. He was shocked that so few were left. There had been over five hundred holding the wall, but he now counted fewer than fifty running alongside them. Looking back to the wall, he saw the first apes coming over. It didn't take them long, just a few seconds, as Grak had predicted.

Once they landed on the other side, they were quick to break the support beams, and soon the wall was broken wide open, and a teeming horde of gremlins poured in through the breach.

They reached the second wall a minute later and quickly climbed the ladders. Once they reached the top, the ladders were quickly hoisted up. Grak leaned against the wall next to him, panting and out of breath.

Arbor was a lot better off, due to his magic, and now stared in horror as a massive section of the first wall came crashing down, gremlins spilling over it in a wave.

He took a deep breath, clearing his mind and allowing just a bit more magic to flow to his arms and legs, as the call for the archers rang out once again. They were supposed to hold out for three days, but he wasn't even sure they would see the next sunrise.

54

Arbor stumbled back, narrowly avoiding an ax strike to the face, then stepping forward, skewered the offending gremlin through the eye. They were fighting on the ground between the second and third wall, trying to hold back a horde of gremlins to give the archers time to retreat.

The sun was already beginning to set, yet there was no sign of the battle winding down. Arbor stepped back and let another person take his place on the front line. Grak handed him a waterskin, and he nodded his thanks, taking a long draft before handing it back.

"How much longer to we have to hold here?" Arbor asked, wiping the blade of his glaive with a rag.

He was getting pretty tired at this point. Magic or not, he'd been fighting for hours now, first on the wall, and now here.

"Another hour or so until dark," Grak said with a grimace.

She'd been wounded in the fight and had a cloth bandage wrapped around her left arm.

Arbor had been injured as well, and while the breastplate he wore didn't have so much as a scratch on it, the armor he wore on his arms and legs weren't as fortunate. He'd lost a bracer on one arm, and a nasty bruise spread across it from where he'd blocked a hammer strike poorly. He also had a shallow gash on the back of his leg. He'd gotten that one when a gremlin had snuck up behind him and tried to slice his leg off. Luckily for him, his magic had warned him in time, and he'd stepped forward right as the gremlin swung, only receiving a shallow cut.

He looked out at the battle raging before them. Five hundred or so men and dwarves stood in a line, trying to hold back the gremlin forces.

"Do you think we'll be able to hold out?" Grak asked, rubbing at her arm.

"I don't know," Arbor said in reply and prepared to go back into the fray. "All I know is that we need to survive for another two days, so that's what I plan on doing."

"Arbor, don't go back yet. We need you."

Arbor turned his head to see Captain Tenor marching over with five other men and women.

"What is it, Captain?" Arbor asked, coming to attention, noting that the man definitely looked worse for wear.

His head was tightly wrapped in bandages, and his arm was in a sling.

Tenor motioned him to relax, then began speaking.

"If we want to have any chance at holding the third wall for another day, we'll need to get rid of those apes."

Arbor had to admit that the captain was probably right. The war apes were a real problem. They'd taken down two of the walls already and now only one stood in their way. The archers had managed to bring a few down, but the enemy still had about twenty of the beasts left. And for every one that they'd managed to kill, it had cost them nearly forty men in the process.

"What do you propose we do about it?" Arbor asked.

"We have put together a small force of elite soldiers." He motioned to the five warriors behind him. "They will attempt to break through enemy lines and take out the beasts."

Arbor was getting the idea but was still confused as to why the captain was talking to him.

"What would you like me to do?"

Tenor sighed heavily here and looked him in the eye.

"I need you to clear a path for them. Get these soldiers through the lines, and they will do the rest. I know it's a lot to ask, but there is no way we will survive if those apes are not dead by nightfall."

Grak came over and placed a hand on his arm.

"He's not going," she said vehemently. "It's a suicide mission, and you know it! He'll never make it back if he goes out there."

Arbor gently took her hand off his.

"I have to," he said solemnly. "Otherwise, we won't survive the night."

"I'll clear a path for them, Captain," Arbor said, straightening and looking the five men over. "How much time will they need to kill the apes?"

"No more than a few minutes."

"Very well, then. Let's get going." Arbor took a step forward but was stopped by Grak's arm once again.

"If you die out there, I'll kill you," she said, clearly not happy about his decision.

Arbor smiled at that.

"Then I'd better stay alive."

With that said, he moved towards the front line, the five soldiers following closely behind.

"Stay close to my back," Arbor called as they ran forward. "Move too far, and you'll be cut off!"

He heard the affirmative from the five following him and reached for his magic. This was going to hurt!

Arbor quickly pumped magic through his body, greatly increasing his strength and speed. Then he heightened his perception to give him a better chance of detecting danger.

In one on one combat, it was easy to feel and predict an opponent's movements. However, in a battle this large, it was almost impossible. Taking one more deep breath, he roared his order.

"Charge!"

Arbor ran forward, careful not to outpace the people behind him. He saw the line coming up, and then he was in the middle of it. He swung his glaive in wide sweeping arcs, sending gremlins flying through the air with his enhanced strength. He now moved too fast for the gremlins to react, as he hacked and slashed his way through their ranks.

Every time a new enemy stepped in front of him, they'd either be cut in half by the blade or have their bones broken by the spike. This burst of power wasn't without consequence, though. Arbor could feel his muscles becoming sore at an alarming rate, steam was pouring off his skin, and there were still quite a few enemies between them and their targets.

He cut another five gremlins in two with a wide sweep of his glaive, momentarily clearing a small space. Another one ran forward, and he was forced to block a blow, then sheared the gremlin's sword in two and took the upper part of his body off as well.

He could feel his muscles beginning to tear, *just a few more feet...* With one last shout of effort, he slashed his way clean through the line. The moment he was through, he released his magic, feeling the strain lessen and his muscles relax. Looking back, he saw that only four out of the five had made it.

He turned just in time to see the apes and their riders approaching. The other gremlins had quickly backed away at the sight of the approaching beasts, giving them room to fight.

"How much time will we need?" Arbor shouted at the leader of the group, a young-looking elf, holding a very long spear.

"There are twenty of them and four of us. We'll need at least five minutes, maybe more if one of us is killed."

Arbor nodded as the four soldiers ran at the apes. He looked behind him, to the carnage he'd left in his wake. At least thirty gremlins had been killed as he fought through the line.

Now all he had to do was keep them from attacking the others until the apes were dead. The gremlins were standing back, clearly afraid to get in range of his deadly weapon. That was fine with him. He needed a break after that extreme use of his magic.

One gremlin stepped forward then, breaking through the gathering crowd and Arbor immediately noticed that he didn't look like the rest. He was over five and a half feet, tall for a gremlin, and dressed in full plate armor instead of chain mail or leather. He drew a massive, double handed ax and leaned it against his shoulder with casual ease.

"General Sor'shin, I presume?" Arbor said, taking up a fighting stance.

He was very sore at the moment and hoped to end this quickly. If he could kill the general, the enemy force would break, and they would be victorious.

"You presume wrong, human!"

The voice coming from behind the visor was gruff.

"The General doesn't have time to waste on the likes of you, so he's sent me here to kill you instead."

Arbor widened his stance a bit as the gremlin took his ax in a double handed grip and took a shuffling step forward. The other gremlins quickly moved to surround the two of them, and Arbor heard a roar of pain, seeing the first war ape go down out of the corner of his eye.

He just had to buy them a few minutes. He quickly reached for his second Origin and examined the gremlin for magic. Nothing. The gremlin didn't have a speck of magic on him.

Arbor smiled to himself, then leaped forward and swung his glaive down hard, enhancing his strength as he did, so he could cut the gremlin in two.

His blade hit the armor, but instead of cutting through as he'd been expecting, the blade screeched to the side in a shower of sparks and sunk into the ground. Arbor was shocked that his blow had been deflected and was nearly killed by a return blow from the gremlin.

He stumbled back, off balance, and a gremlin tried to skewer him from behind with a spear. Luckily for Arbor, his breastplate was made of Mythicallium, and the spear point was halted in its tracks. He felt the wind knocked out of him and knew that he'd just received a nasty bruise. The armor might protect him from being killed, but it would do nothing to stop the force of a blow from impacting his body.

The attack forced him forward, and he ducked just in time to avoid losing his head as the armored gremlin swept his ax in a wide arc. He pulled the glaive toward him and enhancing his strength again, spun in a half circle, cutting down two gremlins that had thought to sneak up on him from behind, and breaking a third's arm, sending him stumbling away.

Arbor released his magic and took stock of the situation. He was surrounded on all sides by enemies, and his blade had been turned aside for some reason. He had to find out why.

"How did your armor stop my blade?" he called to the approaching gremlin.

He heard a barking laugh from inside the helmet as he ran forward and took a massive overhead swing with his ax. Arbor easily sidestepped but was then forced to roll to the side as another gremlin tried to stab him in the back.

"You thought your magic weapon could damage my armor?" the gremlin shouted as he moved forward again. "My armor is made of pure Reflum!"

Arbor had been paying attention to what the gremlin was saying and caught a slash on his arm for letting his concentration slip. He winced and was forced to dodge the ax again but couldn't move too far as another gremlin tried to skewer him with a spear.

This was becoming extremely frustrating. He couldn't fight the gremlin champion while having to fend off attacks on all sides! An idea came to him then, one that he hoped would work. He wasn't normally one to taunt an enemy, but in this situation, it would be justified.

"Aren't you a brave warrior, attacking me while your men do all the hard work?"

He was forced to dodge another ax stroke, but this time struck the side of the warrior's helm in a return blow. His blade was once again blocked by the armor, but the force of the blow, enhanced by Arbor's magic, still forced him to stumble back.

"I see you for what you really are," Arbor taunted as he dodged another spear thrust, killing the gremlin who'd attacked him. "You're a coward who can't fight for himself."

He then held his arms out to the side, leaving himself completely open to attack, and trying to be as insulting as he could.

"Anyone who attacks the human will lose their head!" the gremlin champion roared. "I don't need their help. No magic can harm me while I wear this armor, human. Reflum is completely immune to magic!"

He laughed, then ran forward and swung his ax again. Arbor was forced to duck, but this time when he came up, no attacks came from the rear. The gremlin stumbled a bit at his missed swing and turned to reorient himself.

The ax was a mighty weapon, but it was slow. He could keep dodging, but that wouldn't solve the issue. The problem facing Arbor now was how to kill the gremlin if his armor was impervious to magic. The answer came to him as the gremlin raised the ax overhead.

Of course! There were areas that armor could not cover. Otherwise, it would be impossible to move! All he had to do was bait the gremlin into overextending himself.

Arbor stood straight as the armored gremlin turned once again to face him and held his arms out to the side once again.

"On second thought, maybe you should have your warriors help you. Otherwise, you'll never hit me with that lump of metal you call a weapon!"

The results were even better than expected. The gremlin roared in rage and charged forward, heedless of any danger. Arbor waited for the last possible moment, then dodged to the side, bringing the spiked end of his glaive crashing into the back of his helmet. The gremlin stumbled forward, the momentum of his charge and Arbor's attack, leaving him completely off balance.

Arbor didn't waste a second and drove the tip of his blade through the gap between the gremlin's helmet and into the back of his neck. There was, of course, chain mail in the way, most likely made out of Reflum as well, but the plate only held up to his blows because they could stop the enchantment on the blade. Mail was a lot easier to cut through, especially with his enhanced strength.

The now headless gremlin fell to the ground, blood pooling under his corpse, his helmeted head rolling to a stop at Arbor's foot. He looked around at the other gremlins in the circle, placing his foot on the head of their champion.

"Who's next?" he asked mockingly.

They were hesitating, but he knew they wouldn't be for long. He had to break free of the circle, otherwise, they would overwhelm him.

He could see the last few apes fighting over to his right, so he ran in that direction. He brought his glaive back and swung as hard as he could, pumping magic to his arms. He gritted his teeth as muscles began to tear anew, but fought on, finally breaking out of the circle.

He pumped magic to his legs, moving quickly towards the last three apes. There was only one person left who was fighting them now. The corpses of the other warriors lay broken and twisted amidst the war apes they'd killed. Even as he approached, the elf drove his spear through one of their eyes, killing it on the spot. He tried to pull back but was too slow. Another ape crushed him under a gigantic fist, his spear staying stuck in the dead ape, as his lifeless body hit the ground.

That was it. There were two apes left and no one to kill them — no one but him.

Arbor gritted his teeth again and sped forward, resolved to see this through to the end. His body couldn't handle the amount of magic he needed right now, so he tapped into his only available resource, his breastplate. He felt the strain leave his body instantly, as the enchantment took hold.

He had two minutes, so he'd better make them count.

He leaped into the air and buried the blade of his weapon in one ape's forehead. Ripping it free, he turned, only to be slammed backward by a crushing blow. He hit the ground hard and rolled to try and lessen the impact. His left arm felt numb and looking down, he could see his shoulder protruding oddly. He wondered why there was no pain.

Probably the adrenaline, he reasoned.

Looking up he could see the ape running at him, its teeth bared in a snarl. It would be a lot more difficult to fight using only one hand, but he had no choice. This monster had to die.

He poured magic into his legs, his form blurring slightly as he moved.

"Die, you hairy bastard!" he roared, barely dodging a swipe from its hand. He danced forward and slashed his blade across the ape's throat. He had to jump back quickly to avoid being showered by the monster's blood. The ape clutched at its throat for a moment, before it finally fell with a loud thump.

Arbor stood still for a minute as the battle raged all around him, trying to catch his breath as the fear and violence of the last few seconds threatened to overwhelm him.

He couldn't stay here. He had to get back. Looking over his shoulder, he could see at least a thousand gremlins between him and the Defiants' front line. He couldn't fight his way through on his own. He was too tired and only had one working arm. He saw a gremlin with a sword and shield charging at him. A crazy idea came to him as he saw the shield.

This would hurt, but then again, dying would probably hurt a lot more.

He slid his weapon into the sheath on his back, then neatly sidestepped the swing, bringing his knee up and into the gremlin's groin. The gremlin, predictably, dropped to ground, howling in pain and clutching at his crotch.

"Thanks for that," Arbor said, wrenching the shield from the gremlin's arm.

Clutching it tightly in front of him, he began to run at the line of gremlins. He pumped magic into his legs as he did, feeding them more and more power.

It was then that the enchantment wore off, and he began feeling the strain of his magic once more. He could see steam rising off him in waves and felt the muscles in his legs begin to tear. He ran on still, pouring on speed as he approached the gremlin force. A few of them turned to face him as he came nearer, brandishing swords and spears.

Taking a deep breath, he said a quick prayer to the Almighty. Then, gathering his feet under him, he leaped as high as he could. The forward momentum of his run, and his magically assisted leap carried him a good fifteen feet into the air.

Arbor felt his stomach drop out from under him as he sailed over the ranks of gremlins, their red faces gaping up at him as he flew past them. He could feel himself slowing down and knew his flight was nearly at an end.

He was almost to the other side. *Just a bit further!*

Quickly placing the shield beneath his feet, he landed hard on the heads of a bunch of gremlins, driving them to the ground. Using the shield as a springboard, he launched himself forward the rest of the way, landing on the ground and rolling to avoid breaking anything.

He sat up, groaning in pain. His legs throbbed and he was sure he'd done some serious damage to them.

Luckily for him, the gremlins he'd landed on with the shield had taken the brunt of the force instead of him. Getting shakily to his feet, he looked down the wall until he spotted a ladder. Walking over, he slowly climbed to the top, dragging himself up with only the strength of his arm. He stopped for a moment when he was about halfway up, looking over his shoulder at the field, now covered in blood and corpses. It was not a pretty sight.

Coming over the top of the wall, he collapsed, leaning tiredly against the battlements. It was nearly dark now, and horns finally sounded from the enemy force, calling a halt to the day's fighting.

Arbor looked up and saw Grak and Captain Tenor approaching with one of the healers. He leaned his head back and stared up at the night sky. A long sigh escaped his lips. He was bruised, battered, and was pretty sure his shoulder was dislocated, but they'd survived the first day.

55

Arbor was sitting by a small table that had been set up in the main hall. Ramona, Captain Tenor, and Captain Leron sat at the table as well. A somber silence seemed to hang over them as they sat, waiting for the last person to arrive. Captain Ashryn came down the ramp and sat down next to them with a sigh.

Arbor looked around sadly. Aside from the captains sitting at the table, and the four lieutenants standing behind them, none of the others were still alive. One of the captains and eight of the lieutenants had been killed.

As soon as the enemy force had called a halt to the day's fighting, Ramona had called a council of war. Arbor had been summoned as well, much to his surprise. He'd asked Grak to come with, but she'd refused, saying she was too tired.

He didn't blame her, as he could barely keep his eyes open. *Thank God they were able to patch me up and reset my shoulder,* Arbor thought, wincing at the memory.

It had been thoroughly unpleasant to have his shoulder wrenched back into its socket. His muscles were very sore as well, but thankfully they seemed to be healing, judging by the unbearable itching sensation coming from all over his body.

An attendant came running over to the table and began placing plates of steaming chicken and bread in front of everyone. A full four chickens were set in front of Arbor, and his eyebrows went up as a loaf of bread and a waterskin were placed there as well. He looked around to see what the captains thought of that, but none of them were even looking at him, too absorbed in eating their own meals.

"It's not a mistake."

He looked up to see Ramona had a full two chickens on her own plate.

"There was a lot of fighting today. I'm sure you've noticed your appetite has been on the rise since first discovering your magic. It can be especially taxing after a battle, where you've most likely used it non-stop all day."

Arbor nodded uncertainly but dug in all the same. He was quite hungry and hadn't eaten since that morning. As the first bite hit his tongue, he realized that he wasn't just hungry, he was famished! He quickly tore into the chicken, using big chunks of bread to wipe up the gravy that had been poured on top. He was so absorbed in his meal that it almost came as a surprise to him when Ramona started speaking.

"Captain Tenor, what are our casualty reports?"

Arbor looked up and was about to put his fork down, when Ramona just waved him to continue. He nodded gratefully and went back to demolishing his second chicken.

"We've lost over two thousand already, and a further twelve hundred are too injured to fight."

Ramona winced at that. "How many are still fit to fight?"

Tenor looked down at a sheet of paper in front of him.

"We still have a thousand cavalrymen, as they were not part of today's fighting."

"Well, that's good news, at least. They could be the difference between victory and defeat," Ramona said, folding her arms before her.

"We have four hundred and sixteen archers out of the original one thousand and eighty-two," Tenor continued.

Ramona winced once again, and Arbor inwardly cringed as well.

Their archers had been very effective today, and to have lost so many would put them at a severe disadvantage for the next day's fighting.

"We also have three hundred and eight swordsmen and one hundred and forty-seven spearmen,"

He put the sheet of paper down with a grimace.

Ramona was silent for a few moments, one hand resting on her chin as she did the math.

"That would leave us just shy of nineteen hundred troops. How many did they lose?"

"We estimate somewhere around four thousand."

Arbor balked at that number. He'd really been hoping that they would have managed to do more damage than that.

"That leaves them with somewhere around six thousand," Ramona looked grim. "They outnumber us even more now than they did when they first arrived. How many Mages do we have left?"

Tenor picked his paper up again and looked at it for a minute before answering. "Including Arbor and Grak, we have eight left."

"Eight out of sixteen." Ramona sighed and rubbed at her temples. "Is there any good news?"

Captain Tenor had to smile here. "The war apes were completely wiped out, so we should be able to hold the last wall for some time. The engineers also finished constructing the rest of the wall, so we are protected on all sides for the time being."

"Well, at least something good came of today's battle. Tell me, Arbor, did you run into any Mages today?"

Arbor put his fork down and finished chewing as he thought over the day's battle.

"I didn't run into a single magic user today, which I find quite strange. I did run into a gremlin wearing a full set plate armor that seemed to be resistant to magic. I think he called it Reflum. I'm not completely sure what that is, though."

Ramona looked surprised to hear that.

"A full set of plate made of Reflum. Are you sure?"

Arbor nodded, not really understanding the significance.

"Reflum is one of the rarest metals in Laedrin," Ramona exclaimed. "Though not many know of its existence, it is the only metal that is completely resistant to magic. It can even stop a Mage from accessing their power if they are bound with it."

"If this metal is as rare as you say, why would they waste a full set of plate armor on a random gremlin? Wouldn't it make sense to give it to a powerful Mage?" Tenor asked.

Captain Leron spoke up here.

"Weren't you listening to what the Co-founder was saying?" he asked with a chuckle. "The whole point of using Reflum is to counteract Mages. If a Mage wore the armor, they wouldn't be able to use their magic."

Tenor looked a little sheepish at having not understood the dwarf.

"My apologies, Co-founder, it has been a long day, and I am not quite myself."

Ramona just sighed and stood from the table.

"I don't think any of us are quite ourselves. We will convene for now. The battle will most likely resume in the morning. Get some rest. We have a long day ahead of us tomorrow."

The captains all rose and saluted before leaving. Arbor rose as well, for once feeling quite full after finishing everything on his plate. He was surprised at having eaten so much, but figured he probably needed the extra energy.

He was heading to the corridor that led to his room when Ramona caught up with him.

"Would you mind if I escorted you to your room?" She looked troubled.

Arbor nodded, wondering what the woman could want, but too tired to ask. He headed into the corridor, Ramona falling into step next to him. They walked in silence for a few moments before she began speaking.

"I'm worried that we haven't run into any Mages yet. It makes me think that they're planning something."

"It's been bothering me, as well," Arbor admitted, glad he wasn't the only one.

"Another thing that's bothering me is that the general hasn't been spotted yet either," Ramona said, her brow furrowing.

"Why would that trouble you? Don't generals normally lead from behind?"

"Normally, yes, but Sor'shin is famous for plunging into battle headfirst without any regard for his troops. They also seem a lot more organized than usual, which leads me to believe that someone else is pulling the strings here."

That was a thoroughly troubling thought. If Sor'shin wasn't leading the enemy force, then who was?

"That's not what I wanted to talk about, though," Ramona said. "I want you to fight with me tomorrow."

Arbor looked over at her with a raised eyebrow.

"I have a good reason. No need to give me that look," she said, a smirk creeping to her lips. "Though I would very much enjoy your company, I have something else in mind. I want you to help me hunt down all the enemy Mages. If we can eliminate them, we may be able to gain some sort of advantage."

"That makes sense," Arbor said, though he was a bit apprehensive. Grak would not be happy if he went off alone with the Co-founder.

"If we remove their Mages, we won't have to worry that they're plotting something. It also gives us the advantage of having magic while they don't," Ramona said, seeing that he wasn't entirely convinced.

She went silent then as they walked, allowing him time to think, for which he was grateful. On the one hand, they could deal a crippling blow to the enemy. On the other, they were taking a huge risk going off alone. But when they stopped outside his door, Arbor had already made up his mind.

"I'll come with you tomorrow to hunt them down," he said, against his better judgment.

Ramona smiled at him and clapped him on the shoulder, giving him a wink.

"I know what you did today, and I know what it could have cost you. Just know that your actions may very well be the difference between victory and defeat. Hopefully, you can pull off another miracle tomorrow."

She turned then and left, heading back down the corridor.

Arbor watched her go for a few seconds before entering his room. He was glad to see a bowl of steaming water and some soap, as well as a fresh change of clothes. He groaned in relief as the steaming water washed over his tired and aching body, the heat seeming to leach into his very bones and relax his still tense body.

Once he was clean, he collapsed into bed, exhausted, and was asleep in seconds.

56

Karria came to slowly. Sunlight streamed in through an open window, and she could hear the sound of birds chirping outside. She blinked a few times, trying to piece together where she was.

"Oh, good, you're awake."

Karria turned her head to the side.

"Professor Palmine, what are you doing here?" she asked, her foggy mind not quite comprehending what was going on.

"Making sure you stay alive," the gruff elf woman said, bustling around the room.

Making sure I stay alive? What was she talking about?

Then it suddenly came back to her in a rush, and she sat bolt upright in bed.

"Kya! Professor, we have to go help her, she's in danger! Eletha has her, and she's going to kill her…" She trailed off here as Palmine raised an eyebrow at her.

"Do calm down, girl. Everyone is safe and well."

Karria blinked.

"What?"

"I said everyone is fine! What part of that didn't you understand!" Palmine exclaimed, throwing her hands over her head in frustration.

"Fool girl, running off with that boy and trying to rescue her all on your own! You could have been killed!"

Karria was a bit taken aback at the woman's outburst. She had no idea how she'd gotten back. The last thing she remembered was turning her back to Eletha, and then a sharp pain in her side.

She froze, then quickly pulled up the nightgown to inspect the area.

"I'm sorry." Palmine's voice was quieter now, a note of sadness in her voice.

"By the time you got back, it was too late. There was nothing I could do."

Karria looked down in horror at the long, jagged scar on her side. The skin was puckered and pink and slightly raised. She slowly traced the scar, feeling the odd bump left by it. She stopped then and let her nightgown fall back down, then looked up at her teacher.

"Can you tell me what happened?" she asked in a quiet voice. "I don't even know how I got here."

"I will leave the telling of that story to someone else. Now that you're awake, the queen and king will be wanting to see you."

Karria nodded and moved to get out of bed.

"You will stay in bed until I say otherwise!" she snapped, and Karria froze. "They will come see you here. I'll go send for them now. They've been anxiously waiting for you to wake up." Karria nodded as Palmine shuffled out of the room.

She leaned back against the bed frame and looked around for the first time. Noticing a small tray near her bed, she leaned down and picked it up. There was a small bowl of fruit and a cup of water. She ate slowly, enjoying the sweet taste and sipping her water slowly, wondering how long she'd been here.

It must have been a few days, at the very least, seeing as she felt so rested.

She was setting her tray down on the table when there was a knock on the door, and the king and queen walked in.

"No need to get up, my dear," Alvine said, as Karria moved to stand.

Palmine entered behind them and closed the door, moving into the corner and sitting on a rocking chair.

Blyss and Alvine sat down on two plush chairs near her bed, the both of them looking oddly at her, as if not knowing how to begin.

"How is Kya?" Karria asked, no longer able to contain herself.

"She is alive and recovering," Blyss said in a soft voice, shifting a bit in her seat.

"When can I see her?" Karria asked with a smile.

Her friend was okay!

"You'll be able to see her in a few days," Blyss answered again.

She looked somber and not at all happy. The smile dropped from Karria's face then. She wouldn't be looking so depressed if Kya was really alright.

"What's wrong?"

Alvine took a deep breath before giving his answer.

"The kidnapping and subsequent torture took a great toll on her, I'm afraid."

Now that she looked closer, Karria could see that they both looked haggard as if they hadn't slept in days.

"What do you mean by 'great toll'?" she asked, fear now creeping into her voice.

"The entire affair was a shock to the poor girl," Blyss said.

Her voice cracked as she spoke, a soft sob escaping her throat.

"All she does is stare out into space all day. She doesn't say a word, doesn't talk to anyone, just sits there with a blank expression on her face," Alvine finished, placing a hand on his wife's, trying to comfort her.

"How long has she been like this?" Karria asked, feeling hollow inside at the news.

"She's been like this ever since she woke up a week ago," Blyss said though her tears.

A week ago! That would mean that she'd been sleeping for at least an entire week. Karria was stunned at how long she'd been out, but her worry for her friend was overpowering her shock at the moment.

"Isn't there anything the professor can do for her?" she asked, looking to Palmine, who was rocking gently in the corner.

"Injuries of the body are a lot easier to heal than injuries of the mind," Palmine said with a sigh. "That poor girl has suffered a great deal. More than any one person should have to deal with in a lifetime."

"So Eletha got what she wanted in the end, after all. She won," Karria said, a bitter tone entering her voice.

There was a silence after that, with Blyss still sobbing quietly next to her. Karria decided to break the tension. She needed answers, and there was no one better to give them to her than the king and queen.

"How are we still alive, and how did we get here?"

"Silver was responsible for that," Alvine said, Blyss now being too far gone to speak.

"Silver?" Karria asked in surprise. "Is he here? How did he manage to win against Eletha?"

Alvine just shook his head.

"Silver is of the salamander race. I would not presume to know his power or his secrets. I only know what Sylvester told me. When you turned your back on her, Eletha stabbed you with a dagger. The blade nicked one of your kidneys, and you were bleeding out at an alarming rate, when Silver came to your rescue. He closed up your wound, killed Eletha, and got the rest of you back safely to us."

The news shocked Karria, more than anything she'd heard so far. She was glad to hear of Eletha's death and had to wonder how he'd managed it. It appeared that she once again owed the strange man her life. More than that was the fact that he was from the nearly extinct salamander race. She had suspected he knew a lot more than he let on, back when he'd escorted her and Sylvester, and resolved herself to finding out what he knew about her and her brother the next time she saw him.

"How is Sylvester holding up?" Karria asked, slumping down into her pillows.

This was all too much to take in.

"He's doing as well as can be expected," Alvine answered. "He was completely unhurt in the rescue. The only one apparently."

"What happened to Nina?" Karria asked, not having heard her mentioned.

"Silver was going to kill her, but for some reason, my son saw fit to intervene and saved her life."

Karria had to smile at that. Sylvester may be a lying coward at times, but he had a truly gentle heart. He had begged for mercy when Karria was about to kill Eletha and had apparently saved Nina's life.

"What will you do with her?" she asked in a soft voice.

"At first, we wanted to execute her. After all, she was the one who held a knife to my daughter's throat while you were being tortured," Alvine began in a tired sounding voice.

"However, after Sylvester begged for her life, we threw her in prison for the time being. She may only be fifteen, but she deserves a far worse punishment for what she did."

They sat in silence for the next few moments as everyone was lost in their own thoughts.

"So, what will happen to me now?" Karria asked.

"You will continue on as you were, if you'd like," Alvine said, handing his wife a kerchief. "Even though it was an extremely foolish thing to do, you have once again saved our daughter's life. You will always have a home here, no matter what may happen."

Karria felt grateful to the two of them and thanked the king and queen for their generosity.

"There is no need for thanks, child," Blyss said, standing and walking to sit on the bed. "Without you, our daughter would be dead right now."

"A whole lot of good I did, if what you say about her is true," Karria said, the bitter tone creeping back into her voice.

"Do not blame yourself, my dear," Blyss said, wrapping her in a warm embrace. "She may not be whole, but she is alive. We have that to be grateful for at least." She pulled back and kissed her on the forehead.

"We will come visit again tomorrow."

She and Alvine rose from their seated positions and came to stand beside her.

"Rest up, my dear," the king said. "We will speak more on our next visit."

With that, the king and queen left the room, closing the door gently behind them. Palmine rose then and headed to the door as well.

"I have a few others to attend to right now, but I'll be back soon. Sylvester would like to come see you a bit later in the day. Is that alright with you?"

When Karria nodded, Palmine grunted once, then shuffled out of the room.

Only when the door closed did she allow her mask to drop. She let out a soft sob and felt hot tears spilling down her cheeks. She had saved her friend's life, but she hadn't been fast enough. Her heart may be beating, but she wasn't truly alive.

Sylvester came to visit her later that day, and he told her the rest of the story, including Silver's terrifying transformation, and how he'd completely obliterated Eletha. This part of the story gave her a sort of savage joy.

That psycho deserved what she got. She only wished she'd been conscious to see it.

When she asked about Kya, he just shook his head sadly.

"She doesn't even respond to her own name when you call her, and only eats when the food is placed directly in her mouth."

The news saddened Karria even farther, but she would have to see for herself.

Palmine kept her in bed for a few more days. The king and queen visited every day, making sure that she was being well cared for, and that her recovery was going smoothly.

She noticed that they always steered clear of their daughter whenever she brought her up, and this worried her more than anything.

On the day she was finally allowed to leave, she made sure that her first stop was Kya's room. She knocked gently on the door, but when there was no reply, she opened it and walked in.

Kya was sitting by the window, a vacant expression on her beautiful face as she stared out into empty space. Karria approached her slowly and knelt down in front of her.

"How are you feeling?" she asked in a gentle tone.

Kya did not budge, staring out the window with the same vacant expression.

"Kya, I know you're in there. You have to wake up!" Karria said, shaking the girl's hands.

She could feel tears brimming in her eyes now, but the elf girl didn't stir one bit. Karria grabbed her face and turned her to look into her eyes.

"Look at me, Kya! You have to snap out of it!" she screamed, as hot tears fell from her eyes.

She looked into Kya's eyes, but they just stared blankly back at her, and Karria let her go with another sob. That may have been Kya's body, but her friend was gone, and she didn't know if she would ever be back.

57

Arbor stood on top of the wall and watched the sunrise. He could already see the gremlin camp stirring and watched as it slowly came to life. Hundreds of Gila lizards swarmed the open area where the fighting had been taking place, the smell of blood having attracted them during the night. He hoped that the monsters would deter the gremlins from advancing, but he wasn't about to count on it.

Grak climbed up the ladder behind him, yawning widely, and came up next to him.

"Get any sleep last night?" Arbor asked.

"Not nearly enough," she grumbled, covering another yawn behind her arm and rubbing at her eyes. "Those lizards really are a nasty bunch of bastards."

She wrinkled her nose as they watched two lizards fighting over a gremlin corpse.

"Do you think they'll stay once the gremlins begin their advance?" Arbor asked.

"Not likely."

Arbor turned at the sound of the voice and saluted as Ramona came walking down the wall, flanked by Captain Tenor, who still had his arm in a sling.

"How can you be sure?" Grak asked, her tone frosty as she watched the Co-founder approaching.

Arbor still didn't understand what she had against Ramona. Hord seemed to know the answer, but the stubborn dwarf had refused to tell him when he'd asked.

Ramona seemed not to notice the icy reception and motioned out over the battlefield.

"Notice how not a single lizard has even approached the camp."

Arbor did notice that, now that she mentioned it. They were all staying well clear of the gremlin force, instead helping themselves to the abundance of already dead bodies.

"They're not stupid creatures. They'll kill when they have to, but a battlefield is full of easy pickings. Why would they risk death, when all they have to do is wait for night to get an easy meal?"

Arbor nodded at that. It did make sense to him.

If faced with a similar situation, any wild beast, especially an opportunistic one, would take the easy, risk-free choice.

"When do you think they'll attack?" he asked, now noticing activity in the enemy camp as the sleeping gremlins were roused from their slumber.

"I'd say we have about an hour before the first attack begins," Captain Tenor spoke up for the first time, peering out at the enemy camp.

"The enemy may not attack for another hour," Ramona said. "However, we have a mission to complete, and I'd like to catch them off guard."

Arbor turned to her, clearly confused.

Ramona laughed lightly at his expression and motioned him to follow her. Grak was about to follow as well, but Ramona stopped her.

"I have a special assignment for you, Grak. Captain Tenor will fill you in."

Grak looked to Arbor, who just shrugged.

"Be careful out there," she said, eyeing Ramona with distrust.

"You be careful, as well," he called.

He'd half turned to follow Ramona, when Grak practically crashed into him. He was momentarily surprised when she wrapped her arms around him, squeezing him tight and burying her face in his chest. Her dark blue hair tickled his chin, and her scent filled his senses.

"I mean it," she whispered. "You'd better come back to me alive. Understand?"

Arbor nodded solemnly, wrapping her in an embrace as well. The two of them stood there for a few long seconds, before they were interrupted by Ramona.

"Come on, you two lovebirds. We've got a mission to complete, so either make out or get a move on."

Grak pushed back from him so fast he had to wonder if she had somehow acquired Perception magic, her already red complexion turning a deep shade of crimson.

"Mind your own damn business!" she screamed, hiding her face behind her hands.

Before Arbor could say anything, she'd bolted from the wall, her hair fluttering in the wind as she was lost from sight.

"What was that all about?" he asked, turning to Ramona with a raised eyebrow.

He was feeling annoyed, with both himself and the Co-founder. He was annoyed with her for ruining the moment, and with himself, out of guilt for his dead fiancé. If he admitted it to himself, he really was hoping that the moment would become something more.

Ramona shrugged, unapologetic.

"There's no time for theatrics. Now, are you coming or not?"

Arbor just rolled his eyes and followed her as they walked down the wall a small way, until they were out of the way of prying ears. Ramona stopped then and looked down the wall in both directions. There was a guard standing some way down, but not close enough to overhear them.

"Before I explain what we will be doing, I need you to confirm something for me," she said.

"And what might that be?"

"I want you to look out over the gremlin camp and tell me where all the Mages are."

Arbor shrugged, and after a moment of concentration, the world lit up in the brilliant colors of magic vision. He looked at the gremlin force, not spotting anything at first. He looked farther down the line, and finally spotted a clump of colorful specs near the back of the camp.

"There's a large concentration of magic near the back of the force," he finally said.

Ramona smiled in triumph, as if expecting this answer.

"Most Mages are, by nature, cowardly and spoiled," she explained to his unasked question. "They're used to people bowing and scraping to them because of their talents, so you can imagine that they'd demand the best tents at the rear of the camp, where they're the least likely be attacked."

Arbor nodded again. He'd heard from her before how Mages were treated in Laedrin, and it came as no surprise to him.

"Once the fighting begins, they will most likely just stay in their tents. I thought that it was odd that you hadn't encountered any Mages yesterday and was afraid that they'd been planning some sort of attack in the night. However, it appears that they're all just cowards that won't do anything until they're forced to," she continued. "Either that or they've got something else planned that requires them to stay out of the fighting for now.

"Either way, we're going to make sure that they don't get the chance to carry out that plan. We're going to take a wide arc around and come from behind. Once the battle starts, we will sneak into their tents and kill them all."

Arbor wasn't so sure about this plan and voiced his doubts.

"How many soldiers do you think we can sneak past without their noticing us?"

"That's the best part," Ramona said with a wicked smile. "It'll be just you and me."

"Isn't it too risky for the general to leave on such a mission with just one other person? Who will be in command while you are away? What will happen to the Defiants if we fail and get killed?"

There were so many things wrong with this plan that he couldn't even begin to count them. Like how two people could wipe out over a hundred, without getting caught. Or how they'd even manage to get into a gremlin camp unnoticed.

Ramona waved off his concerns.

"Captain Tenor is perfectly capable of commanding the Defiants in my absence. Yes, it's a risk for me to go out alone with you, but if no risks are taken, then the battle is already lost."

"Why don't you at least take a few more guards with you? Why only me?" Arbor asked. "Surely there are better candidates for this mission."

Ramona shook her head.

"I can cast illusions and make us appear to fit in with the gremlin force. Since our first meeting in your room, I have been able to make my illusions far more convincing. I can make us look, sound, smell, and even feel like gremlins. The problem is that I can't cover more than two people at once for the time being. I'm sure that with practice I'll be able to do more, but for now, that's all I can manage."

Arbor opened his mouth to ask another question, but she held up her hand to forestall him.

"As to why I'm taking you with me, well, that's pretty simple," she smiled here, her teeth flashing white in the sunrise, and her golden eyes sparkling with mischief.

"You're the only person I know who can get us out of there alive once we're done."

58

Arbor ran over the open Flatlands, a small plume of dust kicking up in his wake. Ramona's arms were wrapped around his shoulders, and his hands were under her knees, supporting her weight. They'd already made a wide circle around the gremlin camp and were now approaching it from the rear.

When Ramona had told him that he would be their mode of transportation, he'd been quite annoyed with her. He'd been holding his tongue so far, but he was far from happy. At least she wore armor, so he didn't have to feel her soft curves pressing into him as he ran. That would just have been too much.

Finally, his annoyance bubbled over, and he just couldn't hold it back anymore.

"I'm not a horse, you know," he grumbled as the ground blurred by under his feet.

"What was that?" Ramona asked. "The wind is very loud. You'll have to speak up."

"I said, I'm not a horse!" he yelled, feeling her shift a bit in his grip.

"Why would you think you're a horse?"

"It seems that all women I know think I am! First Grak, and now you. Is that all I'm good for, transporting people on my back because I'm strong and can run quickly? Sounds an awful lot like a horse to me."

He shifted his grip as they continued running. His arms were beginning to cramp, despite increasing his strength. Ramona was a lot heavier than Grak had been. He'd almost said so when she'd climbed on his back at the beginning of their mission but quickly thought better of it. He may be dense, but even he wasn't stupid enough to comment on her weight. *Besides,* he thought to himself, *Grak wasn't wearing armor at the time, and Ramona is taller.*

"I'm sorry you feel that way.

Arbor was snapped back to the moment as Ramona finally answered.

"Just know that I don't view you that way. The reason I chose you is because you give us the greatest chance of succeeding in this mission. There is no other Mage or soldier under my command that can do what you do. I would have brought horses, but they're too loud and also tire more quickly than you do, from what Grak told me."

Arbor thought she was laying the praise on a little thick, but despite himself, he felt better about being used as a glorified beast of burden.

"She also told me that you can outstrip a horse if you really wanted to."

That part was true. Arbor had tested it out himself on the way back from the gremlin camp. He'd wanted to see what the extent of his speed was, and found that as of right now, he could outstrip a horse at a distance of over three miles. The problem with that was he was soon too tired to continue, and his muscles started shrieking in protest. He hoped his body would continue building itself to support heavier use of his magic. He could only imagine being able to run faster than the wind or being able to lift a boulder weighing several thousand pounds.

Something Ramona had said struck him as quite odd then.

"When did you have all this time to speak with Grak?"

Ramona laughed lightly at this.

"The night you came back with your report."

"When did you have time for that?" Arbor asked.

There hadn't been any time for details and after they were finished with the meeting, they'd all gone to bed.

"I went to visit her in her room after I was finished with my captains. Oddly enough, she was still awake when I knocked on her door, and she was kind enough to offer a detailed report on your scouting mission."

Arbor was about to ask another question when his sharpened eyes picked out the telltale signs of the camp.

"I can see the tents," he said, beginning to slow down.

His legs were a bit sore, but not nearly as badly as he'd been expecting.

"Alright, I'm going to drop the illusion over us now, so try not to stumble when I do. After all," she said with a light chuckle. "Gremlins tend to be on the short side."

Arbor nodded, bracing himself as the strangest sensation washed over him. It felt like his entire body was being coated in a gooey liquid. Looking down at himself, he almost did stumble. His legs were moving way faster than they should, and not at all in time with his actual steps.

"This is very weird," Arbor called back, but was once again surprised.

His voice was completely different, higher pitched, and a little whiny sounding.

"Yes, it is weird, isn't it?"

Arbor did actually stumble this time, and just managed to catch himself before he sent the two of them tumbling.

Ramona sounded exactly like Grak!

He heard laughter then and felt Ramona shaking with mirth. It was so strange to hear Grak's laugh, knowing that it was someone else. Ramona might be one of the Co-founders of the Defiants, but she had a twisted sense of humor.

"That wasn't funny, you know!" he shouted.

When he heard her laughing even harder, he decided to get revenge. He sped up suddenly, digging his heels into the ground and leaning forward. He heard her laughter abruptly cut off with a shriek which caused him to smile.

He hadn't taken Ramona as the shrieking type.

The gremlin camp was fast approaching now, and Arbor could make out the individual tents at the back of the camp. At the speed he was currently going, he could cover a mile in just over a minute. He knew this to be true, as though his perception magic were speaking to him.

"Arbor, you need to slow down, we're moving too fast!" Ramona yelled as the camp seemed to speed towards them at an alarming rate.

Arbor wanted to keep it up for a little longer, but he could already feel the twinges in his muscles that told him he was overdoing it and would soon be paying a hefty price for his little joke. He slowed to a more manageable speed and felt the strain on his muscles lessen considerably.

A few minutes later, he slowed to a walk, and Ramona hopped off his back. Arbor sighed in relief and leaned back, hearing a series of pops and cracks. He turned to look at Ramona then. She did look exactly like Grak. She also had a very familiar expression on her face, and it made Arbor take a small step back.

"Am I really that heavy?" Ramona asked.

It was extremely disconcerting, watching Ramona giving her the same look Grak did when she was annoyed.

"No, not at all!" he was quick to reassure her, waving his hands in front of his face.

He was once again shocked when he saw red hands, tipped with small black claws, waving before his eyes. This was way too strange for him.

"Good," Ramona answered, in the same satisfied way Grak did when she'd gotten her way.

Arbor found that this amused him very much and had to make a supreme effort of will not to laugh.

"What's the plan?" he asked, looking at the cluster of tents a few hundred feet away.

"We walk into the camp, then we go from tent to tent, and kill all the Mages."

Arbor raised an eyebrow at her.

"That simple?"

Ramona smiled then, in a very un-Grak like way.

"I never said it would be easy."

Arbor just sighed in resignation. Here he was, caving into another woman's crazy plan. He had to wonder if disguising herself as Grak had made Ramona pick up some of her traits.

They walked quickly into the camp, Arbor using his magic to find the tents of the Mages and heading quickly in their direction. The camp was oddly silent, with only the occasional gremlin walking by. He was even more impressed with Ramona's magic, when not a single gremlin stopped them for questioning. Soon they were standing outside the first mage's tent.

"You ready?" Ramona whispered.

Arbor nodded, and they rushed in, ready for a fight.

They had both left their main weapons back at the base, as they would be too large and cumbersome, especially on an assassination mission. They came into the darkened tent, both carrying daggers at the ready.

Nothing happened.

They stood there for a moment, looking around the interior. It was large for a tent. There was a table laden with food in one corner, and a large plush rug was spread across the parched ground.

Arbor heard a loud snore then and spun quickly, his dagger raised for a strike. A fat gremlin lay amidst a pile of blankets, fast asleep. Arbor wrinkled his nose as he approached. The gremlin stunk of wine and spoiled food. He looked to Ramona. As she approached silently, she shook her head in disgust, then plunged the dagger into the gremlin's eye, twisting it savagely for extra effect. He died instantly, his body going slack and the snoring coming to an immediate stop.

Arbor flinched a bit at this. He was all for killing an enemy of the battlefield, but he had no stomach for killing unarmed sleeping gremlins, even if they were enemies.

He followed Ramona out of the tent, his mind troubled.

"I know what you're going to say," she said, heading to the next tent in the row. "I don't enjoy doing this either, but this is war." Her voice hardened. "We must do what is necessary to win, even if it's not honorable."

Arbor didn't answer. He knew she was right but killing sleeping and defenseless enemies just didn't sit right with him.

The next few tents were just like the first. They moved quickly, going through another seven tents in rapid succession. As it turned out, some of the tents had several occupants. It looked like the gremlin mages had been throwing parties last night and had invited their friends over.

It was quite a stroke of luck on their part, as the other seven tents had contained a total of forty-three gremlin Mages. After they left the eighth tent, Ramona began moving faster, looking around furtively as though afraid they'd be caught.

"What's wrong?" Arbor asked, stopping right outside the next tent.

"The longer we take, the greater the chance we'll be discovered," she said, throwing back the tent flap. "Better get this over with quickly."

Arbor was about to follow when he heard a voice from inside the tent.

"Who are you, and what do you think you're doing?"

He froze, quickly feeling for his second Origin and using it for his magical sight. His heart skipped a beat as he counted, a mounting terror building within him.

There were over twenty gremlins in the tent, and they were all awake!

59

"Well, explain yourself," the same voice said again from inside the tent.

Arbor's first instinct was to go charging in, but he quickly squashed that thought.

Ramona was disguised as a gremlin. She might be able to talk her way out of this, but if he charged in and started killing them, they would have no chance.

He quietly backed away from the tent entrance and walked around to the back. As far as he could see, most of the gremlins were on one side of the tent, with only one being at the rear.

"Oh, I was sent to see if the esteemed Mages needed anything," he heard Ramona answer.

"Everyone knows not to disturb us during breakfast!" another voice answered. She sounded suspicious, and Arbor didn't think she'd be able to fool them for long, illusion or not.

He quickly plunged the dagger into the side of the tent and cut downward, doing his utmost not to make any noise. Thankfully, the blade was sharp and slid through the fabric without a sound.

"Is that right? Well, the cook told me to check up on you."

Arbor slipped quietly into the tent and crouched behind a small table. All the gremlins were facing away from him, and none saw him as he entered. They were all seated around a large table laden with food. One gremlin was standing, a serving spoon in hand.

"You said the cook sent you?"

The question came from the gremlin who was standing, and Ramona nodded.

Arbor realized her mistake too late. When he'd scanned the tent from the outside, he could only count sources of magic and had assumed that all the occupants were Mages. Now that he looked at the standing gremlin, he couldn't see even a speck of magic on him.

"I'm the cook," the gremlin with the serving spoon said, stepping forward, his eyes narrowing in suspicion as he reached for a knife at his waist. "Who are y…"

Ramona didn't wait for the cook to finish his sentence. She leaped forward in a blur of motion and slashed the dagger across his throat. The gremlin went down with a gurgle, blood spurting from his open throat.

The other gremlins were still in shock as she ran towards them. She stabbed one in the side of the neck and another in the eye before they could even react. She was on top of third, cutting his throat when she was forced to dodge out of the way to avoid a small ball of iron that shot towards her head.

She rolled to the side and came up in a crouch, just in time for a gremlin to grab her by the arm. Not wasting any time, she plunged the dagger into the hand, and when the gremlin let go with a screech of pain, spun and cut his throat. She turned then, her back to the tent wall and saw the rest on the gremlin Mages standing in a semi-circle around her, their hands outstretched as they prepared their magic.

They looked angry and were sneering as they prepared to kill the insolent traitor. There was one thing they didn't see, and Ramona had to suppress a grin. Another gremlin was slowly approaching from behind the group, a dagger clutched tightly in his hand.

Arbor could see that this was going bad, quickly. Five of the gremlins were dead, but sixteen Mages had now surrounded Ramona, and he could see their magic becoming active through his magic sight. They were all at the 4th Tier, and two were at the 5th, but not a single one was stronger than that. His sight wasn't yet good enough to tell their classifications, so he just had to hope that none of them were above the Enhanced class. He quickly let the magic in his eyes fade. It would be too distracting to fight with it on.

Clutching his dagger tightly, he slowly approached the group from behind. He saw that Ramona had spotted him. They made eye contact, and she nodded almost imperceptibly. Then, a gigantic beast stood inside the circle, and all the gremlins took an involuntary step back, with screams of terror.

Arbor had to suppress a grin at the Co-founder's imagination. A gigantic hairy war ape with large curling ram's horns stood in the tent, baring its fangs at the Mages.

He didn't waste any time. Concentrating on his Perception Core, he flooded the streams throughout his body with magic. He pumped as much as he could into his arms and legs without overdoing it. He also sharpened his vision and slowed his perception. Sweat beaded his brow and steam began to rise off him in waves.

Using this much magic, and concentrating it in so many points at once, was extremely taxing. He was right on the edge of the 3rd Tier, but not quite there yet. He wouldn't be able to hold it for long, but if he worked fast enough, he wouldn't have to.

He shot forward, the world seeming to move very slowly around him. He plunged his dagger into the back of a gremlin's head, his increased strength easily cracking the skull. He turned the dagger to the side, cutting clean through another's spine at the base of her neck. He ducked a slashing sword strike and cut the gremlin's arm to the bone, then, stepping forward, crushed his face with a palm strike, killing him instantly.

He danced through them, cutting, stabbing and slashing. He used his fists, elbows, and knees almost as much as the dagger, trying to do as much damage as he could in the time he had. When he pumped his strength up this much, he could kill just as easily barehanded. He didn't know how to fight very well, and just added that to the growing list of things he needed to learn.

Even with his enhanced reflexes and perception, he couldn't avoid blows altogether, not in such a confined space. An iron ball slammed painfully into his side, and if not for his armor, would have gone clean through him. As it was, he heard the distinct snap of breaking bone as one of his ribs cracked from the force of the blow.

He dodged to the side and caved in the gremlin's chest, sending him sprawling and coughing up blood. He narrowly avoided losing an arm, as a green lance of energy flew at him. His reflexes saved the arm, but he felt a searing heat burn across the skin, leaving an angry red welt in its wake.

He ran forward and nearly cut the gremlin's head off, the blade not being quite long enough to finish the job. Blood and gore showered the walls and ground, staining the once opulent tent and furniture. He stabbed another gremlin, but this time, the dagger blade snapped as it struck bone, the steel unable to handle his increased strength any longer. He cursed as his concentration slipped and the magic flowing through him slowed.

He stumbled back, his arms shaking as he tried to catch his breath. He looked up to see that there were still three of them left, and they were all looking at him. That was a big mistake on their part, as they seemed to have forgotten the enemy at their back. Three quick dagger strikes later, and the last of them lay on the ground, bleeding out.

He sat heavily on the ground, wincing at his injuries, but Ramona wouldn't let him sit for long.

"Come on, we need to go now!" she said, grabbing his arm and trying to pull him to his feet. "The noise from our battle has surely attracted attention by now, and reinforcements will be here any second!"

Arbor rose shakily to his feet. He felt so tired. His body was aching all over, and his side was screaming in pain.

His stomach growled loudly, and he looked towards the table laden with food. Most had landed on the floor or was inedible due to the fighting, but he could see that some meat still looked good.

"Just need a minute to catch my breath," he said, stumbling towards the table. "I used too much magic at once and now my body is punishing me for it." He groaned, grabbing a piece of steaming beef and shoved it into his mouth, chewing quickly.

Ramona stared at him in disbelief.

"What the hell are you doing?! This isn't the time to be stuffing your face. We need to go!"

Arbor grabbed a jug and took a deep draft, almost choking on the foul taste.

It was wine. He hated wine.

He drank the entire pitcher anyways, and a warm feeling soon filled his body, seeming to wash away his pain.

"I'm too tired to carry you right now. We'll never make it," he said, stuffing another piece of meat down his throat. "Besides, don't we still have more Mages to kill?"

Ramona glared at him but took a deep breath and seemed to calm down somewhat.

"We can't kill the others now. There's no way they're still asleep after that," she sighed and sat down next to him. "We'll just have to settle for the ones we've already killed. We did get more than half of them."

Arbor nodded as he ate. He could feel an odd sensation taking hold as he continued to eat. He felt his strength returning as his hunger was satiated. His stomach stopped growling and he sighed in relief as his magic began healing his body.

"You almost done?" Ramona asked with a raised eyebrow.

"Just another minute," he said through a mouthful of meat. He was biting into another piece when the sound of loud voices could be heard approaching the tent.

"Damn it all! I told you so! We need to go! Now!" Ramona said, getting to her feet and grabbing Arbor by the arm.

"Just one more piece!" Arbor groaned as Ramona yanked him away from the table and towards the hole he'd cut in the tent wall.

"You can eat all you want when we get back to camp, you insatiable glutton!" She hissed, dragging him through the opening and out into open air.

She stopped short when she saw who stood there, apparently waiting for her. Over fifty gremlins blocked their path, and at their head stood a gremlin nearly six feet tall.

Arbor stumbled out after her, still clutching a strip of meat, and froze as well. He'd never seen a gremlin that tall before or that muscular. The gremlin was dressed in gleaming plate mail painted a deep red.

"Why, if it isn't the Co-founder herself." The gremlin's voice rasped, as though nails were a usual part of his daily diet.

"General Sor'shin," Ramona replied, nodding at him. "Didn't expect you to show your ugly face."

Arbor was shocked to hear Ramona's voice instead of Grak's. He'd been so distracted by the gremlins in front of them that he hadn't noticed her illusion slip. Looking quickly down at himself, he was surprised to see that his disguise was still intact.

Why would she keep me hidden while revealing herself? he wondered.

"I would ask how you'd gotten into my camp, but I can see that we have a traitor in our midst," he said, turning to look at Arbor. "Tell me, traitor, for what possible reason would you betray our glorious king?"

He waited for a moment, but when Arbor couldn't formulate an answer, the general just shrugged.

"I suppose it doesn't really matter. You're both going to die here, anyway."

As soon as he said this, the gremlins behind him leveled their spears at them and began advancing. Arbor looked at Ramona. She had a grim expression on her face and had taken up a fighting stance.

He knew there was no way they could win. Their only hope for survival was escape. He popped the last piece of meat into his mouth before drawing his dagger.

No sense in it going to waste, he thought as his plan solidified in his mind.

He brought the dagger across in a slashing movement. The advancing gremlins froze in confusion, as Ramona's breastplate hit the ground, leaving her in a clinging cloth undershirt.

"Arbor! What are you…?" she exclaimed, but he ducked down, quickly cutting the straps of her greaves. Then he brought it up and cut the straps holding her steel studded skirt in place. She stood there in shock, all her armor on the ground and staring at him in disbelief.

"Looks like you decided to make it easier for us," Generals Sor'shin said with a grin. "Maybe we'll let you live, after all."

Ramona looked at him, betrayal and hurt written on her face, as Sor'shin motioned his men forward.

Arbor wasn't about to wait. He grabbed Ramona by the arm and threw her over one shoulder, then spun and ran back into the tent. He heard shouting from behind him as he came out the front, and took off running, dodging around tent and gremlin alike, as he ran for the open Flatlands.

He burst from the line of tents a few moments later and pumped more magic to his legs, the wind whistling past his ear as he ran. He heard Ramona's protesting voice, but he didn't dare slow down to hear what she was saying. He could hear horns blowing behind him and knew that they would be gathering their horses to follow them.

He took a deep breath and clenched his teeth, pouring on even more speed. He ran like that for the next few minutes before the pain in his legs forced him to stop. Wincing, he put Ramona down, panting for breath.

His magic might make it easy to run, but even he had his limits. For now, anyway…

"What the hell was all that about?" Ramona screamed, glaring down at him. "Why did you cut off my armor?"

Arbor took a few more deep breaths, trying to calm his racing heart, before straightening.

"Come on, Ramona. You're smart. I'm sure you can figure it out."

He normally wouldn't be this disrespectful to her, but he was in quite a bit of pain and knew that before the day was done, he'd be in quite a bit more.

Ramona took a moment to calm herself and thought.

"The added weight of the armor would have slowed you down," she said with a grimace. "What I don't understand is why you didn't warn me about it first. I thought you'd betrayed me."

"When would I have had time to tell you about a plan I came up with on the spot?" Arbor asked, with a raised eyebrow. "Would that be before or after we were dead?"

The last of Ramona's ire leaked away, and she blushed, her cheeks turning red with embarrassment.

"I guess I wasn't thinking very clearly. I thought that since I'd left your disguise intact, you would betray me and get away free." She stopped here and laughed. "It really does sound pretty dumb when I say it out loud."

Arbor smiled at that, his anger leaking away as well.

"It was a bad situation, and you thought we were about to die. I can hardly blame you for that. But I do have to know, why did you let your disguise slip?"

"Did you already forget?" she asked with a smile. "I was disguised as Grak. If we ever need her to infiltrate an enemy camp again, it wouldn't do to have her be recognized."

He nodded once, then looked out towards the gremlin camp. He could now see a faint plume of dust rising off in the distance. He turned his back on her and bent slightly.

"We should get moving. I can already see them pursuing us."

She quickly clambered onto his back, and he winced as he stood.

"Are you alright?" She sounded worried.

"That gremlin with the iron ball definitely broke a rib, maybe two," he said as he adjusted his grip and felt her tighten her arms around his neck.

"Well, at least you'll get the chance to feel me up, since my armor is gone," Ramona said, trying to lighten the mood.

Though it was true that Arbor could now clearly feel her thighs through the thin material of her underclothes, he was in too much pain to care. Seeing that he wasn't answering, Ramona decided to change the topic back to the problem at hand.

"Will you be able to outrun them?"

Arbor winced again as he started walking, concentrating his magic into his arms and legs. He still couldn't break into the 3rd Tier, something which he was sure would make this entire situation much easier. At the 3rd Tier, he'd have access to more power, and therefore, be able to use more without risking his body.

"I'll have to," he said through clenched teeth, and took off running towards their base.

60

Karria was sitting in Kya's room. She'd been coming here every day since she'd been released from the sick bay. It had been two weeks since then, and she still showed no signs of improvement. Karria would sit and talk to her friend for hours, telling her about her day at school and what she wanted to learn to make at the sweet shop when Kya got better.

She would sit and read to her, sometimes falling asleep near her bed. Blyss would visit every day as well, and the two would sit talking quietly near her bed. Kya just lay there with a vacant expression, never responding to anything.

Every day Karria would hope that her friend would snap out of whatever stupor she was in, and each day she was disappointed. Sylvester visited every other day as well, and the two of them spoke of their adventures together. She forgave him for lying, though he still wouldn't tell her why he'd done it.

A knock came at the door and Reah walked in. She was an elderly elf who was responsible for taking care of Kya's basic needs, like feeding and bathing her.

"How long have you been sitting here today, child?" the elderly woman asked, closing the door behind her.

Karria just smiled sadly at her and rose from Kya's bedside.

"Don't you worry about me, Reah," she said, heading to the door. "Kya is my friend and I want to be here when she finally snaps out of this."

She stopped by the door and watched as Reah helped Kya out of bed, the girl shuffling mindlessly along behind her. She turned to leave but was stopped by Reah's voice.

"Don't let your life pass you by. Your friend may be stuck here, but you are not. She might wake up one day, and when she does, she'll want to hear about all she's missed."

Karria turned back to see a sad expression on the elderly woman's face.

"Live for her, as well as yourself." She turned then and helped Kya shuffle towards the washroom.

Karria lay awake that night, her mind replaying what Reah had said.

She was right. Her friend would wake up one day, or so she prayed, but when she woke up, what would she tell her? Would she say that she sat by her side day and night, or that she'd lived her life for the both of them?

She knew her friend well enough that she was sure Kya would want her to live her life to the fullest. Sighing, she rolled to her side.

Then there was her brother. She knew he was alive, but didn't know where. She was sure Arbor would know exactly what to say to make her feel better. He always had.

Her mind soon wandered back to memories of their childhood together and a smile slowly came to her face. She soon drifted off amid memories of summers gone by.

"Four minutes and eighteen seconds."

Karria exhaled as she was forced to release her magic. She was strapped to the table and was sweating profusely.

"You're getting better at increasing your power," Palmine said, releasing the straps holding her down.

Karria got shakily to her feet and wiped her brow. She was now working on holding her power steady at the fifth notch for ten minutes. It was becoming easier to increase her power output, but holding it steady was still just as difficult. It was actually more difficult at Tier 2 than it had been in the beginning, back when she'd still been at Tier 1.

Palmine had explained to her that the more power she pumped out, the harder it would be to control.

"We're working at an accelerated pace, due to your talent," she'd said. "Normally, we would give students a few months before jumping up to using more power. The slower method allows for greater control when increasing power. However, it is still the slower method. In time you will gain greater control, but for now, ten minutes is what I want before we move up."

Karria reached down and picked up a waterskin. Moving a sweaty strand of hair away from her face, she took a deep draft.

It's nice outside today, she thought.

A soft breeze tickled her cheek, and the leaves on the Goldenleaf trees rustled in the wind. The seasons in the Goldenleaf Forest were nothing like in the Endless Wood. Back home, all the leaves would have fallen, leaving the trees bare and dead once the winter moon was in the sky.

Here, the weather was always pleasant, and the leaves never fell, making it feel like an endless summer. Flowers did seem to be blooming more than usual, now that spring was here, and she appreciated the change.

She closed her eyes and imagined what her home looked like now. New buds would be on all the trees and flowers would be blooming in the garden outside their house. They would see mother does with their baby fawns nuzzling against them. She always loved watching the small speckled babies wobbling after their mothers. She also loved to climb trees and watch the birds in their nests. Her mother had always scolded her for that, and a smile came to her face at the thought.

"You done daydreaming yet?"

Karria was snapped out of her daydream and smiled sheepishly at her teacher.

"Sorry, Professor. I was just thinking about home."

Palmine's usual gruff features softened a bit at this.

"It can be hard adjusting to a new life, even after all this time."

She was silent for another moment, then turned her back on Karria and started walking. Karria followed her, but was surprised when they didn't head for the target range.

"Professor, where are we going?" Karria asked as she headed towards the roped off ring that she'd watched the two tenth year students fighting in.

Palmine didn't answer, and Karria just shrugged internally. If the professor didn't want to answer, she wouldn't.

They walked for a few more minutes, passing the roped off area and finally coming to a small lake. Karria gaped in amazement. She hadn't even known this was here.

Palmine turned around then and gave Karria a smile.

"I know your birthday is coming up this week, so I've decided to teach you something new."

409

Karria was once again shocked. She'd completely forgotten about her birthday! She would be turning fifteen in just three days. Had she really been here for over two months already?

Amid all the excitement, Kya's kidnapping, and her lessons, it had completely slipped her mind.

"Yes, I figured you'd forgotten in light of recent events, but the school keeps records of such things. I do hope you'll celebrate, even if you don't feel like it," she said, looking out over the calm water.

"That's not what we're here for. We are going to see if you can do anything else with your magic- aside from blasting things, I mean."

Karria had to admit she was intrigued.

She'd been wondering what else her magic could do but hadn't been able to figure anything out.

"Mythical magic is very unusual, in that there aren't many recorded cases of it, and those that were, never really explained what the magic could actually do. There were a few things written down, and we're going to try one of them today."

Karria could feel her excitement rising as Palmine sat down and motioned her to do so as well. She sat and crossed her legs, smoothing the leather skirt out in front of her.

"You are going to try and project your energy outward and create something."

"What do you mean by that, Professor?"

"You would understand if you let me finish," she snapped, and Karria had the good grace to looked embarrassed.

"You will let the magic collect in your hands as usual, but when the time comes to release it, I want you to try and contain it outside your body. The goal will be to have you eventually create a creature made of magic. From what I've read, they can fight for you, carry messages, or even be used as a mount. For now, you will try to form the magic into a ball and move it around over the lake."

"Why over the lake?"

"So that when it blows up, you don't leave a crater in my training grounds!" Palmine snapped. "Now close your eyes and concentrate!"

Karria did so, grumbling quietly to herself, and concentrated on the small beams of light flowing from her origin. She'd gotten much better at this and within a few seconds, had the necessary power collected in her hands. She tried to push the power out and hold it back at the same time. There was a loud boom and she opened her eyes to see a five-foot wave flowing across the lake.

"Guess that didn't go so well," she said, looking at her teacher.

"I didn't expect you to get it on your first attempt. Try again."

Karria closed her eyes and felt the power gather once more. When she released it, the same boom came, and she opened her eyes to see another wave flowing across the lake.

"Again," came her teacher's voice and once again she closed her eyes and repeated the process.

The expected boom came, and as before, a wave raced across the lake.

"Again."

Karria sighed as she resigned herself to yet another grueling lesson.

61

Karria was walking down the corridor towards her room.

She was exhausted, if not physically, then mentally. She'd been trying for the last few days to externalize her magic and contain it in a ball, but so far had been unable to see even a drop of progress. Every time she let the magic collect in her palms and pushed outward, she would lose her hold over it immediately and send a blast of energy out onto the lake.

She sighed in frustration. It was a seemingly impossible task, but one that her teacher insisted she repeat every day until she managed to do it.

She stopped outside Kya's room and knocked once before entering.

Blyss was sitting at her daughter's bedside and reading a book. She closed it when Karria came in, placing a folded piece of paper between the pages to hold her place.

"I was hoping I'd see you today, my dear," she said, smiling at Karria.

Karria dipped into a clumsy curtsy.

"I must apologize, Your Highness. Professor Palmine has done quite a thorough job of exhausting me."

"That's quite alright. Come and sit down with me." She patted the seat next to her, and Karria walked over to sit down.

"How is she?" Karria asked, looking at her friend.

She looked pale and thin, her lifeless eyes staring out into nothingness. The only sign that she was still alive was the steady rising and falling of her chest.

Blyss looked at her daughter, sadly.

"She isn't any worse than yesterday."

"That's good to hear," Karria said, taking Kya's hand in hers.

It was cold and clammy to the touch, as though she really were dead. Karria squeezed the hand, hoping to get some kind of reaction, but nothing happened.

Blyss watched her for a moment. The poor girl had been through quite an ordeal herself. She was tortured and nearly dead, yet here she was, too worried about her daughter to even think about her own troubles.

"I have a gift for you," Blyss said, and Karria turned to look at the queen.

"A gift?"

"It is your birthday today, isn't it?" Blyss asked with a faint chuckle.

"I suppose it is," she said, turning back to her friend.

It might be her birthday, but she didn't much feel like celebrating today.

"Here," Blyss handed her a small and polished wooden box. "I had this specially made for you."

Karria didn't feel like taking it, but the queen was offering her a gift. It would be rude to refuse.

"Thank you, Your Majesty," she said, taking the proffered box.

There was a small clasp holding the lid shut. When she popped the clasp, the lid opened with a faint click to reveal a golden hairpin in the shape of a lily. It was beautifully wrought, and the detail was exquisite, and he felt herself tearing up a bit as she looked at the gift.

"How did you know?" she asked quietly, fingering the hairpin.

It was her mother's favorite flower.

Memories of her mother tending the garden in the spring and summer came rushing back to her.

Her warm smile, the way she hummed when she would pick them to set on the dinner table. She had always said that if she had another daughter, she would name her Lily. But she'd grown older without having any more children. On her last birthday, her mother had given her a silver chain with a small lily hanging from the end. She remembered how excited she'd been to have such a fine piece of jewelry and had thanked her mother profusely.

She remembered her father and brother laughing as she'd proudly walked around with her new silver chain. She'd later found out that Arbor had been the one who'd bought it for her, as her parents couldn't afford such an expensive gift. He'd used some of his savings when one of the traveling merchants passed through Woods Clearing.

She'd tried to give it back, but Arbor had insisted she keep it, saying that such a beautiful young lady deserved an equally beautiful gift. Dinner that night had been amazing as well. It had been just the four of them. Her mother had made all her favorite things and had even baked a cake. When she'd gone up to bed that night, she'd made her mother a promise.

She still remembered those words as clearly as the day she'd said them. "I know you can't have any more children, and I know that you love lilies. When I have a daughter, I'm going to name her Lily."

Her mother had cried and hugged her and told her how proud she was to have such a wonderful daughter. Her memories of that night were the ones she cherished above all else.

Karria touched the spot where her necklace had hung up until she'd lost it on that fateful night. She'd been devastated to lose such an amazing gift, especially since she'd attached so much meaning to it. It had been more than just a necklace to her. It had been a representation of the promise she'd made that night.

"Kya told me that your mother loved these," Blyss answered, watching her expression carefully.

She was more than a little surprised when Karria threw her arms around her in a tight hug.

"Thank you," she whispered. "This means more to me than you can ever imagine."

The broach may not be the same as the necklace, but she would treasure it all the same. If not for what it was, then for who it reminded her of.

"You're quite welcome, my dear," the queen said, hugging her back.

They stayed like that for another few seconds, before Karria pulled away, dabbing at her eyes.

"I really should get some rest," she said, rising from her seat and looking at Kya one more time.

"Have a good night, and happy birthday."

Karria bowed to the queen, then swept out of the room, the box with the hairpin clutched under one arm. She opened the door to her room, lost in her thoughts, and nearly jumped out of her skin when someone spoke.

"I was wondering how long I'd have to wait for you."

Karria's head whipped to her desk, her heart pounding furiously. A tall man with spiky red hair and purple eyes sat in the chair, smiling at her as he played with her dagger.

"Silver? How did you get in here?!" Karria was so shocked by his appearance, that she couldn't think of a better question.

"Close the door," he said, still smiling as he placed the dagger back on her desk. "I'm sure you have a lot of questions, but it would be better for everyone if no one knew I was here.

She was dumbfounded but did as he asked and closed the door. She approached him then, her thoughts in turmoil. Silver didn't move. He sat there and smiled as she approached.

She stopped in front of him and stood there for a moment, her mind racing with a million unanswered questions. One was at the forefront of her mind and she needed an answer. "Did you really meet my brother?" she asked in a quiet voice.

Silver nodded.

"He stayed with me for a month of training. He left only a few days before you arrived."

He opened his mouth to say more, but his head was whipped to the side as Karria suddenly delivered a stinging slap across his face.

He looked at her with a bemused expression as he rubbed his cheek.

"I suppose I deserved that."

He was shocked when she then threw her arms around him in a tight embrace. He sat still for a few moments, before hugging her back and shaking his head at the oddity of women.

He'd lost count of how many years he'd been alive, but even after all this time, he still couldn't predict what they would do.

Karria pulled away from Silver and gave him a scrutinizing look.

"You have a lot of explaining to do," she said, folding her arms and glaring at him.

"Yes, I have quite a bit of explaining to do. Unfortunately, I don't have a whole lot of time. There is somewhere else I need to be right now, so I will answer three of your questions. Then, since it is your birthday, I will grant you one wish as well. Choose carefully, because once a question is asked, you will not be able to rescind it."

Karria's mind was in a whirl.

There were so many things she wanted to ask him. Who was he? What was he? Where did he come from? How did he manage to kill Eletha? And what did he mean by 'grant her a wish'? She opened her mouth to ask but stopped herself. She only had three questions, so she had to be careful.

"Where is my brother?"

She knew that this would be her first question. She'd wanted to ask him the moment he'd confirmed that he was indeed alive.

"Your brother is currently fighting a war out on the Flatlands. He is near the base of the Defiants, a rebel group, which is right next to the Great Salt Lake."

Karria felt her heart skip a beat.

"Will he be alright?" she asked before she could stop herself.

Silver crossed his arms and seemed to think for a few moments.

"Nothing is ever assured in this world, but there is one thing I am quite certain of. Arbor will survive the battle, though he is about to face a very dangerous opponent."

Karria breathed a sigh of relief at that. Though he was in danger, he would survive.

"I have answered two of your questions. You have one remaining. Choose carefully."

Karria cursed silently to herself.

The second question had slipped out before she had time to think about it. There were still two questions that she desperately wanted answered, but now she would need to choose between the two.

"Who are you really?" she finally asked. "I know what you are, but I have a feeling that you're a lot more important than you've been letting on."

Here, Silver's smile faded slightly.

"I am sorry, but that is a question I cannot answer. You will have to forgive me, but if you knew the answer to this question, you would be in immediate and life-threatening danger. You may ask me another question, as I could not answer this one for you."

That answer made her even more curious about him, but she knew if he didn't want to divulge any secrets, he wouldn't. There was still the matter of the third question.

"Why didn't you tell me that my brother was alive?"

This was one of the questions she'd wanted to ask, but didn't think she'd be able to, due to her slip-up.

"Well, the answer is fairly complicated, and would take some time to explain, so I'll give you the simple answer for now."

He leaned forward and interlaced his fingers.

"There is a war coming, a war which the likes of have not been seen in thousands of years, and you will both have a role to play in it. You were needed here, and he was needed elsewhere. If I had told you that your brother was alive, you'd never have come here."

Karria opened her mouth to ask another question, but Silver shook his head and rose from the chair.

"I have answered three questions, as I said I would."

Karria closed her mouth and glared at him.

He just smiled, a bright warm smile, and she felt her annoyance melting away.

"You still have your wish. Ask for anything, and if it's within my power, I will grant it for you."

Karria was stunned, the thing he'd said earlier finally sinking in. Could he really mean it?

"I can ask for anything?" she asked.

She knew what he was. Sylvester had explained to her that he was from the salamander race. He hadn't explained why he distrusted him so much, but Karria was beginning to see why. Silver kept more secrets than anyone she'd ever met. He had plans for her and her brother, but wasn't willing to share them. Still, he did answer her questions honestly enough when she'd asked. She now knew where her brother was, and that he would be alright.

She thought for a few minutes about the wish. If she could have anything right now, what would she want? She wanted to see Arbor, but had a feeling that Silver would deny her that particular wish. Money? She didn't really have any use for that right now.

Then it hit her – she knew exactly what she wanted.

"Can you cure Kya?" she asked, looking at him with a hopeful expression.

"I can, if that is your wish," he answered. "Are you sure that's what you want?"

Karria nodded emphatically.

"As selfless as always," he said, flashing her a warm smile. He glowed a brilliant white color for a few seconds, then he abruptly vanished.

Karria stood there for a moment, not really sure as to what had just happened. He was gone! She ran out into the hallway and looked both ways but saw nothing out of the ordinary.

What about her wish? He'd left before anything had happened!

She looked up and down the hall once more to make sure she hadn't missed anything. Her eyes inadvertently fell on Kya's door, and her heart began to pound as she slowly approached it. She wrapped her fingers around the knob, too afraid to turn it.

She wanted desperately to believe that Kya was better, but she couldn't face such a disappointment. Silver had said that he could cure her before he'd vanished, and he had glowed with magic for a few seconds, so maybe that had cured her.

She stood by the door for a few more minutes as indecision wracked her mind. Finally, she just couldn't stand it anymore. She needed to see for herself.

Taking a deep breath, she knocked once and turned the doorknob, pushing the door open.

The sight that greeted her upon entering the room was Blyss, hugging her daughter tightly as great wracking sobs shook her body. Karria felt her heart freeze as she looked on, fearing the worst.

She took a faltering step forward but stopped short when Kya turned to her, a confused look on her face.

"Karria, what's happening? Why is my mother crying? I've tried asking her, but she won't answer." She looked quite distraught and was patting her mother consolingly.

Karria stood stock still for a moment as her mind tried to process what was happening. Then she ran forward, tears already beginning to fall from her eyes. These were not the tears of sadness she'd been shedding over the past two weeks. These were tears of joy.

As Karria wrapped her arms around her friend and the queen alike, only one thought occupied her mind.

Silver truly had granted her wish.

62

"They're gaining on us!" Ramona yelled into his ear.

Arbor grunted and pumped a little more magic into his legs, feeling his pace increase only a bit. They'd been running for the last thirty minutes, and he could already make out the wall in the distance.

All they had to do was reach it.

They didn't know what the situation at the wall was, but from what he could see, it was still standing.

"They're still gaining on us!"

Arbor peeked over his shoulder to the force chasing them. Fifty gremlins on horseback, led by the general himself, were only a mile or so behind them. He allowed more magic to flow into his legs, biting back a curse as the pain intensified.

He was taking a bit of a risk, but there was no other option. He could either push himself and run faster, or they would be caught and killed. He still had promises to keep. His sister needed him, and Ramson was still among the living.

He gritted his teeth as he felt a slow burning sensation building in his muscles. He looked over his shoulder again and saw that they were slowly pulling away from the horses.

By his estimate, they were still ten miles or so from the wall. At their current speed, he should reach it in about twenty minutes. The question now was if his body would hold up until they reached it. He still had the two-minute reprieve his armor could give him, but he didn't want to use it just yet.

He ran on, pushing through the mounting pain and watched as the wall grew closer. His side throbbed where the iron ball had hit him, and his arm burned where the green lance of energy had struck.

If he were well rested, a run like this would hardly be a problem, but he'd overextended himself earlier when fighting the gremlin Mages and now he was paying for it.

His steps faltered a bit as he felt a muscle tear and was forced to slow down. Steam was pouring continually from his legs as his body tried to shed the excess heat his magic was creating.

"Come on, keep pushing! We're almost there!"

Ramona was yelling at him again.

He bit his tongue to hold back an angry retort. He was the one doing all the work, and what was she doing? Treating him like a pack animal and telling him to run faster.

He looked over his shoulder again. He'd put another mile between him and his pursuers, but they were now catching up again. He looked to the wall again, calculating the distance to see if they would make it. He felt his heart drop.

At the speed they were going, they would be run down about half a mile from the wall.

He took a deep breath and dug deep. He had to survive! If not for himself, then for his sister.

Arbor kept repeating that same line as he pumped more and more magic into his legs, feeling himself rocket away from their pursuit. Then he tapped into his armor's reserve of power. It would allow him two minutes at his current speed, but after that, it would begin to cost him dearly.

He was running nearly twice as fast as before, the ground seeming to be a blur as he flew over it. He was forced to squint as the wind whistled around him, and dust flew into his eyes. He was closing the distance to the wall at a rapid pace.

They were almost there!

Then the worst happened. His armor's enchantment wore off, leaving his body to fuel the magic once more. The strain was immediate and excruciatingly painful. He felt his muscles tearing themselves apart at an alarming rate and felt something hot begin to trickle down his legs. The pain was blinding, yet he kept on going, one thought in his mind: He had a promise to keep.

The wall was only a mile away now, just another minute and they would be there! He could see fighting further down the wall but ignored it. The wall was fast approaching now, and he saw that he wouldn't be able to stop in time. He didn't think he could stop now, even if he wanted to.

"Hold on!" he yelled and felt Ramona's grip tighten even further. He gathered up his legs under him and jumped. He rocketed twenty feet into the air, just managing to clear the top of the wall. His momentum took him further than he'd expected, and he was soon on the other side, falling towards the ground below.

They wouldn't survive a fall like this, especially at the speed they were going. They would hit the ground hard, then continue bouncing and rolling until the momentum from his run was all used up. He didn't know what to do. He needed time to think!

He slowed his perception, allowing him a few precious seconds to come up with a plan. There was only one thing he could try, but it would be extremely risky.

Closing his eyes, he reached for his second Origin. The magic immediately responded, eager, and willing. White light coated his arms as the ground approached; he could feel the magic sharpen his senses and attune him to the world around him. He could also feel it roiling against his will, demanding to be released so it could destroy everything in its path.

He gritted his teeth as he thrust his arms outward, fighting the destructive energy for control. He heard Ramona screaming in his ear. They struck the ground. An enormous explosion of dirt and debris showered them as his magic created a massive crater in the ground, the resistance greatly lessening the impact and slowing their momentum.

They came to a stop a few seconds later, and he released his perception magic as the fight for control began once again. He fought against his second Origin as the magic lashed out in all directions, destroying the ground around him and showering them in debris. He knew that if he didn't stop his magic now, they would both be buried alive.

He fought against the roiling power as it tried to escape his grasp, the white light trying desperately to escape. He heard a cracking sound from above and more debris began showering down on them.

Concentrating with all his might, he finally cut off the magic, stopping any more from escaping, then he angled his arms upward and allowed the remaining magic to discharge into open air, where it couldn't hurt anyone.

He rolled onto his back, panting for breath and wincing at the pain. Looking over to Ramona, she could see she was bleeding heavily from a wound in her scalp, and she wasn't moving.

He felt his heart seize up in fear as he watched her still and unmoving form. She couldn't be dead! Not after all they'd been through to get back. He forced himself onto his side and crawled over to her in a panic. He breathed a sigh of relief as he saw her chest rising and falling.

She was still alive.

He didn't know the extent of her injuries, so placing his hand on her forehead, he reached for his perception magic once more. He felt the blue sphere of power, pulsing at his center and allowed a small amount to flow down the stream in his arm.

It was extremely painful, especially since his body was so overtaxed, but he couldn't allow Ramona to die because of him.

His magic flowed into her body after a few moments of effort, and he forced it up towards her head. It was immediately obvious what was wrong. She must have smacked her head against something in the fall.

Her skull was cracked, and a tiny fragment of bone was poking into her brain, causing swelling and heavy bleeding. He hesitated for a moment when he saw this. Arbor didn't know much about healing, but he knew that injuries to the brain were extremely dangerous.

If he made even the smallest mistake, he could kill her, but if he did nothing, she would most definitely die.

He forced his pounding heart to calm by taking a few deep breaths. Then, he forged on, making the magic flow upward and into the injury. He watched as the magic knitted the cracked skull and began to coat the swollen tissue in her brain, but he could already see that the amount of magic he'd used wouldn't be enough.

He allowed more and more magic to flow into her, feeling the pain in his own body mounting to an almost unbearable degree. Then, it was over. The swelling in her brain went down and he knew that he had done all he could.

Releasing his magic with a groan of pain, he rolled onto his back and stared up at the lip of the crater he'd made, nearly twenty feet over his head.

This was likely the only reason they'd survived the fall. The massive hole his magic had created had greatly reduced the impact of their landing. He closed his eyes and concentrated inward.

He had to see the extent of his injuries. He knew Ramona would be alright, but he was most likely the only one in danger at the moment. He began to examine his body thoroughly. He had two broken ribs where the metal ball had hit him, but no other bones were broken. There were a whole bunch of partial tears in his leg muscles, but thankfully, none of them were completely torn through. His legs were also covered in burns, as well as small cuts.

That must have been the warm feeling he'd felt earlier. They were all scabbed over right now, so at least he wasn't losing any blood. There were torn muscles in his arms as well, but once again, the damage was far less extensive than he thought it would be.

It looked like his body was slowly building more of a resistance to his magic. He must be a lot tougher than he thought. The thought made him laugh out loud and he winced as the movement hurt his aching body.

"What's so funny?"

Arbor cranked his head to the side, to see Ramona, sitting up and looking around in confusion.

"Oh good, you're awake," Arbor groaned, staring back up at the sky above. "You really had me worried for a bit, but it looks like your head healed up nicely."

Ramona stared at him for a few moments, her mind trying to comprehend as to what was going on.

"Tell me what happened," she finally said after a few more moments.

Arbor looked to her in surprise.

"You really don't remember?"

Ramona just shook her head.

"The last thing I remember is running from the gremlin camp."

Arbor sighed.

Brain injuries were unpredictable. He hoped this short-term memory loss was all she would suffer.

He explained what had happened over the last hour, and Ramona sat quietly through the entire thing. He could feel his body beginning to heal his injuries while he spoke and was glad for his accelerated healing. There was still a war to fight, after all.

Once he finished his story, Ramona sat in silence for a few moments, allowing it all to sink in.

"It looks like I owe you my life, once again," she said in a quiet voice.

He turned his head to look at her once again.

She looked troubled, and there was something else. Something he couldn't place. She stared at him for a few moments, biting her lip and looking uncomfortable. Maybe she felt like she owed him, and that made her uncomfortable?

"You don't have to worry about owing me anything," he was quick to reassure her. "It was my fault you were hurt in the first place, so it was only right for me to heal you."

Her cheeks went pink as he said that, and she quickly looked away from him.

"No, that's not it at all."

"Then what is it?"

"It's nothing. Just drop it," she snapped and got to her feet.

He didn't know what he was doing wrong, but decided it was best to change the subject before he said anything else to upset her.

"Well, we're still technically in the middle of a battle. You should probably head back to the main force. It'll take a little while for my body to heal, so you'd best go on ahead of me."

"Don't be ridiculous," she said, coming over to sit down next to him. "I won't leave you here alone."

What was it with women? One moment she was thanking him, the next she was snapping at him, and now she wanted to stay here until he was better? He wanted to scream in frustration and rail at the Almighty for making women so confusing. Instead of doing that, he turned his head so he could look Ramona in the eye.

"They need you out there. You can't just stay here with me while your men are dying out on the battlefield. Just leave me here. I'll recover in a bit and be right behind you."

Ramona stood still for a minute, indecision clearly written on her face.

It was odd to see her like this. She was normally more decisive than anyone he knew. She looked at him for a few long moments before finally turning away.

"I expect you back on the battlefield as soon as you've recovered, is that understood?"

Arbor smiled to himself as she said this.

"Yes, Co-founder," he replied.

She nodded once, then began climbing out of the crater. He watched her go for a few seconds, before closing his eyes. He was exhausted, and the hard ground under him felt as soft as the softest bed at the moment. It didn't take too long before he was fast asleep.

Arbor woke with a start, blinking up into the glaring sun as he tried to get his bearings. Then it all came back to him in a rush.

How could he fall asleep at a time like this? Men were fighting and dying, while he was taking a nap!

He rose quickly to his feet, shaking off the last vestiges of sleep and peered up at the lip of the crater nearly twenty feet above. He still felt a bit sore but could tell that he was mostly healed up.

Measuring the distance to the top, he crouched and concentrated on pumping magic to his legs. He kept going until he felt a light strain, then he pushed off with all his strength, releasing the magic and feeling the strain drop off instantly.

He sailed neatly over the lip of the crater and landed on his feet. He winced a bit as he landed, feeling a slight twinge from his legs, but otherwise, felt completely unharmed. He turned to look at the massive crater and whistled in appreciation.

If he could somehow manage to gain control of his second Origin, he would be unstoppable! His smug feeling was short lived as he beheld what his lading had done. A huge section of the wall had splintered away, leaving the area open for attack.

Arbor had no delusions that General Sor'shin had not seen that breach. He was likely gathering a part of his forces now to circle the wall and hit them from behind.

He turned back toward the direction of the main camp. Ramona had likely seen the breach as well, and would be sending men to defend it, but right now, he was the only one here.

Arbor felt his spine stiffen as he stared at the breach. He knew what he had to do. In order for them to survive, he would have to hold it alone until help arrived.

63

Arbor watched the approaching dust cloud. He'd been working for about an hour, and even the minor twinge of discomfort had worn off by now. He had pulled some of the planks across the opening in the wall to create a funnel, so that only one or two gremlins could pass at once. This would be a hard fight, made all the harder at his lack of a proper weapon.

The sun was already beginning to set as the approaching horses grew larger and larger. He sharpened his vision and began counting. He soon gave up as the numbers grew ever larger.

There must be over two thousand of them, he thought in horror. *Why isn't Ramona back here with more forces?* She was surely back with the main force by now and wouldn't want to leave such a massive breach unguarded.

The horses were close enough to hear now and the entire ground shook at their approach. Arbor amended his previous thought then. He needed to hold the wall, but there was no way he would last if the horses came charging through.

They grew closer and closer, less than a mile away now, and not slowing down in the slightest. Arbor could make out banners flying in the wind as they rode. They were a stark white in color, with a figure holding two halves of a body overhead, while blood poured down on it.

"Looks like the general is with them," he muttered as the horses slowed down, and finally halted just a few hundred yards from the breach.

Arbor stepped right into the opening and out the other side. He could spot the General now, sitting on top of a massive black beast. These were definitely not horses, as he had previously thought. Sure, they had iron shod hooves and walked on four legs, but that was where the similarities ended.

Long shaggy fur hung in tangles from the beast's sides and deep red eyes stared back from snarling muzzles and yellowed teeth. He didn't know why the gremlins didn't just use regular horses instead of these monstrosities. They really didn't seem to be suited for the heat with all that thick fur.

One of the gremlins rode forward and stared down at him with open disgust.

"Surrender now, and your end will be swift. Stay and fight, and we will kill you slowly."

Arbor cocked an eyebrow at the gremlin.

"If I surrender, you'll kill me, and if I fight, you'll kill me." He smiled mockingly at the gremlin. "Seems like I end up dead either way."

The gremlin smiled evilly.

"That's the idea, human."

He leveled his spear at him and moved forward until the spear tip was poking his breastplate.

"So, what will it be, human?"

Arbor moved so quickly then, that the gremlin didn't even have time to blink. Then next thing he knew, he was on the ground with his own spear pricking his throat. He looked into the eyes of the human and felt his heart rate speed up.

"What was that you said earlier?" Arbor pretended to think for a second. "Oh yes, now I remember," he raised his voice so that the entire force could hear. "Surrender and die quickly, fight, and die slowly." He looked back down to the gremlin under his spear point. "So, tell me gremlin, which option would you prefer?"

The gremlin stared wide eyed, opening and closing his mouth a few times.

"I surrender! Please don't kill me!" he wailed, trying to back away.

Arbor watched the rest of the gremlin forces. They weren't moving, just watching the scene with interest.

"Very well," Arbor said, pulling the spear away from his throat. "I'll be merciful and let you go."

The gremlin stared up in disbelief. He quickly scrambled to his feet and backed away a few steps.

Arbor looked out over the army arranged in front of him and opened his mouth to speak. This was the only way to buy himself enough time for reinforcements to arrive, and he had to believe they were coming. Otherwise, the battle was already lost. Hord should be here with reinforcements by morning. All they had to do was survive the night.

He smiled, grimly at the thought.

"General Sor'shin!" His voice boomed out over the open Flatlands. "Come face me, you coward! You hide behind your forces while they fight and die for you!"

A stirring began to move through the army as the gremlins began talking in hushed tones.

"When we heard that the infamous Bloodbather was coming to our door, we were terrified. 'Surely we couldn't hope to prevail against such a mighty foe' we said. 'Surely the battle is already lost.'" Arbor sneered here, doing his best to provoke the general. "But once the battle was joined, where was the infamous general?"

Arbor paused here to let the muttering grow.

"He was hiding with the pampered Mages, and stuffing his fat face with meat and wine!"

"Liar!" A voice roared out from the center of the formation.

There was movement in the ranks as they quickly parted to allow General Sor'shin through. He was flanked on either side by gremlins dressed in fine chainmail and holding his banners aloft.

"I was on the front lines, battling with you scum all day. I've killed over five hundred of you myself!" he boomed.

Arbor saw the gremlins begin to nod.

"I saw him myself!" A cry came out from the middle of the force. "The General killed their commander this morning! Cut him right in two and bathed in his blood!"

Arbor had to smile at that. It appeared that this legendary general was all bark and no bite. He was a total fraud!

Arbor quickly allowed his vision to shift so he could see magic. It was just as he thought. The mighty general didn't have a speck of magic on him. He was just a regular gremlin with an over-inflated ego and sense of superiority.

"Oh, really?" Arbor yelled back. "It just so happens that I was with our commander this morning. *She* and I wiped out most of the Mages in your camp, while they were sleeping off last night's feast!"

The gremlins went deathly silent at that. It also wasn't lost on them that Arbor had said 'she' when referring to his commander.

"And do you know who I ran into while killing these Mages?" Arbor asked, letting the suspense build. "Why, it was the good general himself!"

He watched Sor'shin's skin go from deep red to light pink as he said this, and his beast took a step back as he shifted nervously in his saddle.

"Who are you going to believe?!" he finally yelled at his soldiers. "Me? Or this upstart human? I've killed thousands of men and bathed in their blood!"

"Really?" Arbor yelled back, cutting him off. "If you've killed as many men as you claim, why is your armor so clean? Shouldn't it be red with the blood of your enemies?"

He motioned to Sor'shin's spotless armor, then to his own, which was covered in blood, gore, sweat, and dust. He looked as though he'd been fighting all day. Sor'shin looked as though he'd just donned his armor for the first time all day.

The gremlins began looking at the General with suspicion now, and the gremlin whose life Arbor had spared spoke up.

"Why is your armor so clean, General? You don't look like you've done a drop of fighting since you've gotten here."

Angry muttering moved through the army, and Sor'shin's face went a deep red.

"I am your General!" he roared, spittle flying from his lips. "I command you to kill this human at once!"

Arbor tensed for a moment, expecting a charge, but nothing happened.

"Why don't you face me in single combat, General?" Arbor said mockingly. "After all, I'm just one human, and since you've killed thousands of men, it should be quite easy for you."

Sor'shin glared at him, then turned back to his forces.

"Are you deaf? I said, kill him!"

"Will you not fight a single human armed only with a spear?" Arbor held his arms out to the side then addressed the gremlin forces. "Your general is a coward who won't even fight to protect his own men! Why do you follow him? Do you really want someone like that leading you?"

He waited for a moment before one voice shouted.

"No!"

That was all it took, and soon the entire force was shouting at Sor'shin and calling him a coward.

Sor'shin looked around for a moment, anger and fear clouding his features. Then he hopped down from his beast and drew

Aaron Oster

a massive double handed broadsword from the sheath at the beast's side. The entire force went silent at that and watched as their general walked forward.

"I have killed thousands of men!" Sor'shin yelled, gesturing wildly to his forces behind him. "Now I will kill this one as well, and I'll do it with a single stroke of my sword!"

He ran forward then with a mighty roar, lifting the sword high overhead.

His roar was cut off when the tip of Arbor's spear punched clean through his breastplate and out his back.

He looked down in disbelief at the spear shaft protruding from his chest. Then, there was a loud clang as the massive broadsword dropped from his nerveless fingers. He tried to grab at the shaft, but his body wouldn't obey his commands. He took one last breath, opening his mouth to give one last order to kill the human, before slumping over, dead.

The force before Arbor went deathly still as he dropped their general's lifeless corpse to the ground. He looked out over all of them and took a deep breath.

"Why do you fight?" His voice echoed over the open plains.

The gremlins looked at one another in confusion as the muttering began once again. Why did they fight? They had no real reason to be here.

"The answer is quite simple," Arbor continued. "You fight because you are forced to. You fight out of fear of your commanders and fear of the king. Well, look at your commander now. He is dead, and you all saw what a coward he was. You all saw how weak he was and any one of you could have bested him in single combat. Is that really a leader to fight for or to be afraid of?"

There was no hesitation this time, and the entire force roared out with a resounding, "No!"

"Why don't you follow a commander who will respect you? Someone strong. Someone who will be loyal. Someone who would fight for you instead of hiding behind you!"

There was a loud cheer as the gremlins beat their swords against their shields.

"Follow me, and together, we will build a world where gremlins don't have to fight for some far-off king! You can do whatever you want with your lives! Follow me and you can be free!"

The cheer that followed this last statement was so loud that it echoed across the open plains.

He remembered then what Ramona had said about all the gremlins being enslaved to the king and wondered why they would bother listening to him. He'd just been hoping to gain a little time by making them doubt their general. He hadn't actually expected it to work.

He felt something warm on his chest then and reaching into his armor, pulled out the red pendant his father had given him. It was still as beautiful as the day he'd received it. The roaring lion's head gleamed on one side, and the oak tree on the other. The five diamonds still glittered in their sockets and reflected the light of the setting sun.

He had a hunch and let his sight shift to the magical spectrum. The same rainbow-colored light filled his vision as before, but now there were thousands of tiny lines stretching from the pendant to the force of gremlins stretched out before him. He stared at it in astonishment for a moment, as what he was seeing began to sink in. He looked from the pendant to the army spread out in front of him and smiled.

Even now, his father was protecting him. He remembered the promise he'd made so long ago over his families' graves and reaffirmed it once again. He would rescue Karria, and he would avenge their deaths by killing Ramson.

He tucked the pedant back beneath his shirt and motioned the gremlins to quiet down.

"Let us go and put an end to this pointless battle! Come with me!"

Arbor quickly mounted up onto the shaggy beast that had belonged to General Sor'shin and turned its head toward the distant fighting.

He heard the cheering of the gremlins behind him and quickly kicked the beast into a canter.

Ramona should have been here already, which worried him more than anything had up until this point. It could only mean that the battle was going badly for her. And with the force of gremlins at his back, it should tip the battle in their favor. He just had to hope he wasn't too late.

64

Arbor approached the battlefield at a gallop. It had taken him a bit to become accustomed to the odd gait of the beast he was riding, as it ran more like a cat than a horse, bringing its back legs between the front ones, then pushing off. As a result, it took a lot more leg strength to stay on its back, but the tradeoff was that they ran much faster than average horses.

He could now see how it was possible that the gremlins had been able to catch up to him and Ramona so quickly.

The gremlin force was about a quarter mile back. He'd asked them to ride there, as he wasn't sure what the situation would look like back on the battlefield and didn't want the Defiants attacking his new army.

Now that he was approaching, he could see that it was an unnecessary precaution. The battlefield was empty, oddly so. Arbor didn't like it, not one bit.

The air felt heavy, as though charged with power, and seemed to be growing thicker by the second. He slowed his beast and allowed Dev, the gremlin he'd spared to catch up with him. He'd decided to use him as a go between for now, until he could figure out the command structure of the gremlin military.

"What is it, Boss?" he asked, slowing his beast near Arbor and motioning the force to halt.

"Something's wrong," Arbor said, peering at his surroundings.

He could clearly see the bloodstains and disturbed ground of the battlefield. There were still corpses littering the ground, but not a soul was to be seen.

"Yeah, something's definitely not right," Dev agreed. "An attack was launched earlier this morning with over three thousand soldiers."

Arbor's brows knitted together as he heard that, feeling the air becoming heavier and heavier. He grimaced, realizing he wasn't using his head. Quickly switching over to his magic sight, the world lit up in color, and he immediately spotted what was wrong.

A massive conflagration of red energy was being pulled from all directions and was collecting about a mile away. Wherever the magic was going was blocked from his sight, due to the curvature of the wall, but whatever it was, he knew it couldn't be good.

"Did any of the Mages join today's battle?" he asked, already dismounting from the beast and getting ready to run the rest of the way.

Dev nodded.

"Yeah, all the Mages who weren't killed in the attack were sent here by Sor'shin. Don't know why, though," he said with a shrug.

Arbor grimaced, beginning to understand what was going on. The gremlin Mages *had* been planning something and whatever it was, it was massive. The amount of power only kept growing, to the point where he was forced to deactivate his mage sight so as to avoid being blinded.

"I'm going to run on ahead. The rest of you set up here. I don't know what's going on, but I don't want to risk any of you in this fight."

Dev opened his mouth to object, something which amused Arbor as the gremlin had been prepared to kill him not half an hour ago.

"Don't worry about me. If I need any help, I'll send a gremlin named Grak back for you. Until then, just set up here. There's a ton of magic being used, and I don't think any of you will be able to help."

Dev's lips turned down in a frown, but he nodded all the same.

"We'll wait for you here then, Boss. You'd better not go and die on us. Not before you fulfill all those promises you made. Freedom is something my race had never known, so don't dangle it in our faces then take it away."

"I wouldn't dream of it," Arbor said, crouching a bit and coiling his muscles.

Then, he rocketed forward, the wind whistling around his face as he ran straight at the wall. As he reached it, he put just a little extra power into his steps, then ran straight up the twenty-foot wall, using momentum and gravity to keep him going until he reached the top.

Despite the obviously dire situation, Arbor grinned to himself as he reached the top and took off running down the wall. He hadn't been sure it would work, but he was glad it had.

He breathed deeply as he ran, pouring on more and more speed. He was risking further injury, he knew, but his instincts were now screaming at him that he had to reach the place where all that magic was converging. It was a matter of life and death.

It took him a further minute until the area finally started coming into view, and what he saw confirmed his worst fears, yet at the same time confused him. The entire force of the Defiants were standing in a massive gap in the wall, all attacking what seemed to be thin air. Thirty-seven gremlins stood on the other side of the wall, all clasping hands with their eyes closed.

He couldn't see any other gremlins, but when he cast around for them, he spotted a mass of figures a good few miles away from the wall.

As he approached, he could hear people shouting orders as the archers unloaded their quivers towards the group of gremlins, sword and spearmen attacked and even a few cavalrymen, but all their weapons were stopped at the gap in the wall. There appeared to be some sort of forcefield in place, preventing them from reaching the gremlins. What he didn't know, was what they were trying to accomplish, though judging by the chanting and the massive amounts of power collecting, it couldn't be anything good.

He needed to find someone in charge, preferably Ramona or even Tenor. His eyes flicked over the forces gathered below until he spotted a flash of silver. Gathering himself up, Arbor took a running leap and cleared the front row of attackers, eliciting a few cries of alarm. Rolling as he landed, he came up to his feet and continued running, weaving his way between the panicked soldiers.

As he approached, he could finally make out what Ramona was saying, though none of it made any sense to him.

"...Attacking, don't let up! We *have* to break through!"

Finally breaking free of the crowd, Arbor came to a halt before a startled Ramona, who was sitting on horseback next to Tenor and Leron, all of whom were yelling orders.

"Arbor! You're back!" Ramona exclaimed, her face tight with worry and fear.

"Yeah, and I saw a massive amount of power being gathered by those gremlins. Can you explain what's going on?"

"They're trying to summon one of the gods of the lower planes," Ramona said. "We've been trying to interrupt their summons, but none of us has been able to break through the forcefield they've thrown up."

"They're trying to summon what?" Arbor asked, his eyes going wide.

"A god of the lower plains," Ramona repeated. "Most likely an Elemental or Greater Demon. What color was the magic you saw them gathering?"

Arbor had to close his mouth to stop himself from gaping. He'd never even heard of a lower realm, let alone gods. He'd always been under the impression that there was only one: The Almighty.

"Arbor!"

"Sorry," he said, shaking his head to dispel his whirling thoughts. "The magic was crimson. Lighter than blood, but darker than fire."

"Shit! They're trying to summon a Crimson-Ash Elemental."

Both Tenor and Leron went pale at that, something which was pretty impressive for Tenor, due to his dark skin.

"Can someone please explain what that is?"

"A minor god of ash and fire," Grak said, forcing her way through the crowd. "It's good to see that you made it back in one piece, by the way." She gave him a tight smile before turning to Ramona.

"I take it you know more about this Elemental than we do," Ramona said. "Do you know of any weaknesses? Because it doesn't look like we'll be busting through that shield of theirs before they manage the summoning."

Grak grimaced and shrugged.

"Water and Earth magic would be most effective but wouldn't do much against a creature like that. If you want my suggestion, you'll all run as far and as fast as you can. A monster like that will go on a rampage after it's summoned, destroying everything in its path until it's burned to ash."

"What threat level are we talking about?" Ramona asked. "Give it to me in terms that we can understand."

"It would depend on the Elemental," Grak said with a shrug. "But the very weakest would be at least on par with a Tier 5 Shatterer Mage."

"Damn it," Ramona cursed once again, biting her lower lip as though trying to think up some plan of action.

"Isn't there anything we can do?"

"We can hope it ignores their summons," Grak replied doubtfully.

Arbor turned his head, opening his mage sight once more. The world was painted in crimson light. It was so thick now that it blanketed the very sun, blotting out the entire horizon. On top of that, he could now clearly see a pinprick of darkness at the very center of the gremlin circle that was swallowing the power at a prodigious rate.

"Yeah, I wouldn't count on that. It looks like whatever they're trying to call is listening."

"We need to evacuate, then." Ramona came up with a decision on the spot. "If it's on par with a Shatterer Mage, it can destroy our entire army within seconds. None of us would stand a chance. Leron, Tenor, give the order."

Both man and dwarf nodded, quickly galloping away on their mounts to order a retreat.

"What are you going to do?" Arbor asked. "There's no way everyone can retreat in time."

Ramona took a deep breath, squaring her shoulders.

"I'm going to stay here and try and slow it down."

"Are you nuts?" Grak demanded. "Did you not hear me when I said it could destroy you all? Why do you think the gremlin army was moved so far back?"

Ramona just shook her head, a grim smile coming to her face.

"I have no choice. I am the commander of these men, so it's my responsibility to make sure they escape with their lives."

"Like hell!" Arbor cut in. "There's no way you're staying here alone. You made me a promise remember? To help me save my sister. Until then, I'm not going to let you die. I'm staying here with you."

Ramona opened her mouth to argue, but Grak cut in.

"If you're staying, then I'm staying too!"

"No, Grak, I need you to do something else," Arbor said, already knowing she would insist on staying with him. "There's a gremlin force about a mile to the southwest. They're working for me now. I need you to warn them about the Elemental and get them as far away from here as possible."

Grak's eyes widened, and Ramona chuckled.

"If we survive, you'll have to tell me how you convinced a whole bunch of gremlins to join you instead of killing you."

Arbor flashed her a grin in return.

"Oh, I plan on surviving, and it's a story I'm sure you'll enjoy. What do you say, Grak? You're the only one I can trust with this. Will you do it?"

Grak stared at him for a long moment, her light blue eyes piercing his.

"Do you promise you'll make it out alive?"

"I still have too much to do to die now. Yes, I'll make it out alive, I promise."

Arbor said this with as much conviction as he could muster, and he saw Grak's shoulders slump noticeably. Then she walked up to him and wrapped her arms around him and shocked him by pressing her lips to his.

Arbor stood there, stunned as the beautiful gremlin woman kissed him. Then, he returned the kiss with a passion he had not been expecting. All the guilt he'd been feeling about Florren vanished in an instant as he held Grak in his arms. Her lips were so soft and tasted of cinnamon and cloves. It was exotic, unlike anything he'd experienced with his fiancé. Before he knew it, it was over and Grak was pulling away.

Her red cheeks were flushed, and she was panting heavily.

"Just so you know, you'd better not break that promise. Otherwise, I'll kill you." Then she turned and bolted off, sprinting in the direction Arbor had indicated.

"Well, damn. Looks like she beat me to it."

Arbor was brought from his stupor by Ramona, who was watching the gremlin's retreating back with a mix of jealousy and admiration.

"What was that?" Arbor asked, still feeling quite heady from the kiss.

"Oh, it was nothing," Ramona said, waving him off and turning her attention back to the battlefield.

Most of the soldiers had evacuated already, moving into the underground base. From there, they would travel to their families living under the Flatlands, then escape through a different exit and head for a backup post in a different area. They just had to hope that they would be able to move fast enough to get away.

According to Ramona, the Elemental would only have a limited amount of time on this plane of existence, so if they held it off for long enough, it would be sucked back to its home dimension. The amount of time it could stay would be determined by how much magic it was fed.

"Why didn't you tell me that earlier?" Arbor asked, eyeing the now empty battleground.

The only ones that were left were him, Ramona, and roughly seventy others who'd opted to stay behind and fight. Through the splintered remains of the wall, they could see the group of gremlins still chanting as a black disk grew in size.

Ramona shrugged.

"Guess I just didn't think it was important. We couldn't break through the forcefield, so it was a moot point."

"But I can try busting through," Arbor said, already reaching for his glaive, which had been retrieved for him just a few minutes prior.

"No point," Ramona said. "The portal is already open. Now all we can do is wait and hope it's not one of the stronger ones."

Arbor didn't like just waiting around but nodded all the same. She was the one in command, and he wouldn't disobey her in front of her own men.

They all stood, some of the soldiers muttering to each other in low tones, as the sky grew darker and darker, beginning to take on a red tinge, even to normal sight. The portal continued to grow, until the chanting abruptly stopped, leaving an eerie silence over the flat plains.

Then a loud booming voice echoed out of the open portal.

"Who dares summon me?"

The voice sounded as much in their minds as out loud, making everyone, including the gremlin Mages, take a step back.

"Well, looks like we're about to meet our visitor," Ramona said, as a burning face appeared in the center of the black circle.

65

Arbor's eyes widened as he watched the massive creature pull itself through the black portal. It would have been impossible for a creature that size to make it through, had it been made of a solid mass. This creature was more element than a creature of flesh and blood.

Probably why it's called an Elemental, Arbor thought as the towering, twelve-foot creature of crimson flame and gray ash pulled itself completely from the black disk. The upper half of its body was roughly humanoid, with a pair of arms, shoulder and a head, complete with a set of gleaming red eyes set in a face of swirling gray ash.

Its lower half, however, was just a tornado of swirling fire and ash, leaving the creature floating a few inches off the ground. The power the Elemental exuded was immense- so immense, in fact, that Arbor couldn't even begin to fathom it.

He could feel the people around him shifting nervously and muttering amongst themselves as the monster was revealed to them. He could feel their fear as palpable as the magic swirling in the air and coating the Elemental.

"We have summoned you, Oh Great One, to destroy our enemies! Now destroy them!"

They all turned to see one of the gremlin Mages, commanding the other-planar being to do its bidding.

"Do not think to order me about as though I were some peasant worm!" the Elemental boomed.

"You must do as I command! The seal forces you to... aggh!" The gremlin's tirade was cut off as the Elemental's fiery fist slammed into it, burning it to ash within seconds.

The other gremlin Mages turned to flee at that point, realizing that the Elemental was not under their control as they'd thought it would be. But they were too late.

Arbor watched in grim fascination as the Elemental's body glowed with power. Then, an explosion of fire and ash spread out in a dome, engulfing the entire group. Their screams were cut off within seconds and the smell of charred meat reached Arbor's nose, carried to him on the wind.

The Elemental then turned glowing eyes on their group, flames collecting in its hands as it prepared another attack. A massive creature twice its size suddenly appeared before it, made of solid stone and carrying a sword made of ice.

"Do you think you can fool me with such parlor tricks, mortals!?" The Elemental boomed, sending a gout of flame straight through the illusion and right at their group.

Arbor reacted without even thinking, his magic already warning him of the attack a few seconds in advance. He shot forward, pumping magic through his body and caught Ramona in a sideways tackle, knocking her clean off her horse.

There was a scream of pain as the horse was roasted, as well as a group of six soldiers standing near. Arbor heard panicked screams then and looked up to see the others fleeing. Clearly, the sight of their comrades being cooked alive was too much for them.

"There is no escape!" The voice of the Elemental boomed, then it clapped both hands together.

It pulled them apart a second later, fashioning a lance of burning fire.

"Arbor!" Ramona yelled, but he didn't need to be told that staying in the vicinity of that attack would not be a good idea.

He was on his feet in an instant, his magic thrumming in his veins as he ran to the side, away from the fleeing group of soldiers. He felt back for what was about to happen, but they were running like cowards instead of holding their ground.

The lance streaked through the air, leaving a heat distortion as it flashed toward the group. Arbor poured on the speed, then leaped to the top of the wall in one massive jump, just as the projectile hit.

It pierced straight through the back of one of the soldiers, killing him before he could utter so much as a sound. Then, there was a massive explosion as the dome of fire spread from the point of impact. The others were swallowed within moments and the aftershock slammed into Arbor just as he was cresting the wall.

The force of the attack threw him forward, sending both him and Ramona tumbling over the wall. Arbor barely managed to orient himself, landing so that he didn't crush Ramona.

The air was knocked from his lungs as he hit the ground, and it took everything he had, to force himself back to his feet and start running again.

"Run faster, Arbor!" Ramona screamed.

He didn't need to be told twice as another explosion sounded behind him. Throwing a glance over his shoulder, he could see that a massive section of the wall was aflame, burning with such intensity that it was already beginning to blacken and crumble.

"Where do you think you're going, mortals?"

"Shit! I was hoping he wouldn't notice us!" Ramona cursed as Arbor's magic warned him to dodge to the left.

His body was already beginning to flag. The day's events had exhausted him to the point where he was surprised that he could still stand. Yet he had to keep pushing.

The ground before him exploded in flames and he leaped back with a curse, throwing extra power into one leg as he landed to avoid another attack. He landed, facing the monster head-on and watched as it clapped its hands together again. He could feel his heart in his mouth as he saw that, remembering the massive blast the last attack had caused and knew that they would not be able to outrun this.

"There's nothing to lose now!" he shouted. "Let's hope I can contain it if I somehow survive this fight!"

"What?" Ramona asked, from her place on his back. "Ow! What the hell!?" She demanded as Arbor dropped her on her ass and bolted forward, running for all he was worth, right at the Elemental.

This was probably the craziest thing he'd ever done. He'd just watched the monster torch several dozen people in less time than it took for him to blink, yet he was running right at it. But he knew he had no choice, just as he knew on the night of his wedding that he had no choice but to fight even though he stood no chance. If allowed to leave this place, this monster would rampage through the Defiants' base, killing thousands of innocent people. If he could hold it here for just a few minutes, it could mean the difference between life and death for all of them.

"Oh, what do we have here? A human with a spine?" the Elemental asked, its booming voice sounding amused as Arbor charged.

"No matter. You will burn, just like the rest!"

The Elemental's palms began to glow as it pulled them slowly apart, fashioning the lance of flames. Arbor wasn't about to give it the chance to attack. Taking a deep breath, he reached for his second Origin.

Power flooded his body in a massive rush as he fully tapped the glowing white Core in his chest and allowed it to pour from his skin. His glaive was drawn in a flash as he closed with the monster, his body – and unbeknownst to him – his eyes, glowing white. Tendrils of power curled off his skin, coating it and shielding him from the immense heat projected by the Elemental's body.

The monster pulled the lance back, preparing to throw, when Arbor's glaive, coated in white magic, sheared through its arm. The Elemental screamed as its appendage dropped to the ground, writhing and twitching and only his still active Perception magic kept him alive, warning him of the counterattack.

A blast of fire shot from the Elemental's mouth, blasting through the area he'd been occupying just seconds before. He landed on his outstretched hand, spinning in place and lashing out with his foot. Coated in magic as it was, it slammed into the creature, blasting out with immense power and showering the ground behind it in flames and ash.

Arbor had no idea how he was doing what he was. He'd never learned to fight like this, yet it seemed his body knew what to do all on its own. He sprang back, avoiding a blast of fire that erupted from the ground at his feet, his body feeling light as a feather as he danced between plumes of flame.

The Elemental was now squarely focused on him and, despite the injuries he'd dealt the creature, was already beginning to regrow the parts of its body he'd blasted away. Worse, he could feel his body nearing the verge of collapse. The white magic might have been near limitless, but his body couldn't handle the continued strain that his Perception magic demanded.

His foot twinged as he landed and a muscle tore, causing him to stumble. Only by throwing himself forward was he able to avoid being roasted. He didn't escape unharmed, as the condensed beam of fire blew through his left shoulder, leaving a searing line of pain in its wake.

Arbor crashed to the ground, wheezing in pain. He forced himself onto his back, pulling his glaive up and around in a whipping motion, then channeled the white magic up to the point and sent a half-moon blade of white power to collide with the Elemental's follow-up.

The two energies collided, and shockingly enough, the white power cut straight through the Elemental's fire, cutting right through its body as well. The monster screamed once again as it was ripped in half, but tendrils of flame poured from both halves, pulling it back together.

This gave Arbor the chance to get back to his feet. Body shaking with the effort, and shoulder burning in agony, he propped himself up using the half of his glaive to keep him upright. He could no longer keep his Perception magic going, and without it, he wouldn't be able to avoid the Elemental's massive attacks and powerful bursts of flame.

His white magic still pumped through him, curling off his skin and coating his glaive. Looking around, he couldn't spot Ramona anywhere and was secretly glad. He watched as the Elemental finished pulling itself back together and turned its burning red eyes on him. He no longer had the strength to so much as move. His mind was a fog of pain and it was taking all his strength just to stay upright.

At least he'd managed to hold the creature for a couple of minutes. Perhaps that would be enough for the others to escape.

"What form of sorcery do you command, human?"

Arbor blinked the weariness from his eyes and looked up to the Elemental, who was staring at him with its head cocked to one side.

Was it talking to him?

"Will you not answer me, human? I must admit that I am curious as to how someone of your race came to possess the Origin, but if you do not wish to reply, I do not mind. You must die either way. No one can be allowed to house such power!"

The Elemental pulled its arm back, gathering a massive ball of fire. Arbor could see the red magic pouring into the attack, knowing that the blast radius would be well over a mile from such an intense attack. He just hoped that Ramona had made it far enough away to avoid it.

He coughed, hacking up a wad of bloody spittle and sending it to one side. Then, gritting his teeth, he forced himself to stand upright. If he was going to die, he may as well do it on his own two feet.

"That's it, human! Stand and fight to the very end. That is how the bearer of the Origin should act!"

Arbor had no idea what the Elemental was talking about and he couldn't care less. Forcing his legs to widen, Arbor pulled his glaive back and began channeling as much of the white magic as he could into it. The Mythicallium blade seemed to be able to hold an almost infinite amount of power, so if he was going down, the least he could do was take the creature down with him.

As he channeled his power, he began feeling something strange, an odd tugging from his Core. He wondered if his magic was finally running out when he felt his Origin suddenly expand and new strength flooded his body. What shocked him was that the Origin that had grown was the Core that contained his Perception magic. He'd finally advanced to the 3rd Tier!

Arbor laughed as the power flooded through him, lending him new strength and he began pushing the Core to its limit, pulling the power into his body. He hadn't expected to advance now, and now that he had, he had another option aside from blasting the Elemental as he was engulfed in flames. Now he could fight back.

"You're going down, you flaming bastard!" Arbor shouted, using his newfound power to launch himself at the towering construct of flaming magic.

"You gain a few specs of power and believe yourself to be my equal? Do not be delusional, human!" the Elemental boomed, pulling back its arm to launch the nearly ten-foot sphere of boiling flames.

Arbor ignored the monster, closing the gap as he felt his body beginning to strain once more. He might have gained some new power, but he'd already been in pretty bad shape, so it only helped to a certain extent.

He knew this would be his last chance to stop the other-planar being, so he poured all he had into his glaive until it shone a brilliant white, lighting the Flatlands for miles in all directions. The Elemental launched the ball of flames right at him and Arbor brought his weapon around in a mighty swing, screaming his defiance.

He unleashed all the stored power in his glaive, just as it contacted the massive ball of fire. For a moment, Arbor was afraid it wouldn't be enough. He felt his legs beginning to buckle as he struggled against the mass of power. Then, the white Core in his chest flared and the ball of flames was blasted apart in a brilliant flash.

The attack continued, engulfing the Elemental in a brilliant flash of white light. The creature screamed as it was swallowed up, a scream of such pain and agony that Arbor's eardrums burst under the pressure.

He staggered, only just managing to catch himself as the last of the power left his body. Finally, the white Core in his chest seemed to be out, for now. He swayed on his feet, watching through blurry vision as a flaming creature emerged from the billowing clouds of dust.

Its body was pockmarked with wounds and steam rose from its body, as though it, a creature of fire, had been burned.

"Well, despite your best efforts, it seems that I have emerged victorious. You may carry the Origin but do not yet know how to use its power. But this is clear meddling of the natural order, and Lord Nilegard will have to be informed. At least I'll be able to tell him that I finished you off before I go make my report."

Arbor didn't even have the strength to move as he watched the Elemental charge another flaming lance.

So, this is it, he thought grimly, watching his death approaching with an idly detached calm. He knew he should be afraid, if not for himself, then for his sister's sake. But he now knew that even if he died, he had friends who would ensure her freedom.

He'd done all he could, but in the end, he hadn't been strong enough to kill this beast. It seemed that there were indeed creatures that were well beyond what humans could handle.

The Elemental finished forging the lance, then pulled it back, its eyes gleaming red in the dim lighting of the Flatlands.

Arbor wanted to stand straight, to face his death with dignity and strength, but he was too weak, and his body too thrashed. Even if he wanted to, he didn't think he'd be able to so much as twitch.

"It has certainly been an interesting experience trading blows with you, human. I'll make sure to…"

The Elemental vanished mid-speech, taking with it the flaming lance and leaving Arbor staring out at a once more empty but scorched patch of open ground.

He blinked a few times, his exhausted brain not comprehending what had just happened. When it finally began to sink in, Arbor started to laugh. Despite the pain, his body shook with mirth, even as he collapsed onto his back and stared up at the darkening sky above.

He might not have killed the Elemental, but he had managed to drive it off. He had no idea what would happen now, whether the battle would continue or not, but for now, he could rest.

He might not have killed the Elemental, but he had, without a doubt, won.

He could vaguely hear voices shouting in the distance but didn't have the strength to pull himself to his feet. That was fine, though. He'd fought hard all day, and now all he wanted to do was rest.

Epilogue

Silver watched from his perch atop the wall as Arbor lead the gremlin force away. He stood there, watching them go, until they were lost from sight.

His plans were moving along as expected. Arbor had a dangerous enemy to face, but was now in command of over two thousand gremlins and should come out victorious in the end.

His thoughts were interrupted when a man appeared behind him and walked to lean against the wall next to him. Silver knew him quite well and was not alarmed at his sudden appearance.

"Looks like your plans are moving along well," the man said.

Silver turned his head to look at the man.

He couldn't make out his features, as they were obscured by a heavy cloak, but he knew what the man looked like underneath, and could easily picture the disapproving look he knew he was getting.

An easy grin came to his face.

"You look ridiculous with that thing on."

"This thing, as you so put it, is the only reason I'm still alive," the man grumbled and folded his arms. "You should consider getting one, as well. You won't be able to hide from them for much longer if you don't."

Silver opened his mouth to retort, but the figure vanished, leaving him alone on the wall once more. He snorted a little and straightened to his full height. His job here was done and there was somewhere else he needed to be.

With a moment of concentration, his surroundings folded in on themselves as he vanished from the wall as well. A moment later, he stood in front of an ancient ruin in the heart of the Endless Wood.

He could hear the distinct sound of a large beast roaring from within and a smile touched his lips. The plan was moving forward nicely, indeed!

***

Two figures appeared in a clearing in the Goldenleaf Forest. One had the distinct bruised skin of an Infiltrator, while the other's features were disguised by a hooded cloak.

They looked around the clearing for a moment, before spotting what they'd been looking for. A large crater stood in the center of the clearing, with a distinct pattern of cracks radiating outward from the middle of it.

"He was here," the cloaked figure said, stooping to examine the cracks in the ground.

The Infiltrator was instantly alert. "Where is he? I don't see him anywhere."

The cloaked figure rose with a sigh. Infiltrators were great at gathering information, sowing discord, and even killing. They were not, however, the brightest of creatures.

"Do you really think he'd stick around after releasing so much power? Think before you speak, worm."

"Sorry, sir. I guess I wasn't thinking too clearly," the Infiltrator said, quickly bowing his head to the cloaked figure.

The figure looked around the clearing one more time before deciding on a course of action.

The trail was gone now. He'd most likely wiped it clean on his way out, but there was a city not too far from here. Maybe one of the locals had spotted him...

He turned to the Infiltrator and issued his orders.

"You are to go into the city and gather information. Make sure you are well disguised. I will return in a month's time, and I expect answers."

The Infiltrator bowed once again, and when he looked up, the figure was gone.

He turned his head right and left, sniffing the air. *That way.* He began running in the direction of the city.

He only had a month to come up with a lead on their quarry. Otherwise, he would be considered a failure. He shuddered, remembering the last Infiltrator who had disappointed his master. The King was not one to disappoint.

***

Ramson sat in a plush chair and stared up at the ceiling. He was sitting in a lavishly decorated room, hung with rich tapestries, and fine woven carpets. All the finery was lost on him, as he raged inwardly at being kept waiting so long.

A message had been waiting for him once he'd reached Fivora, summoning him to the city of Vergara. One look at the seal was enough. He'd immediately packed his saddlebags and ridden straight here. He was greeted at the gates by a young whelp who'd demanded he hand over his weapons before entering.

Just the memory of that made him want to scream in rage, but Ramson wasn't a fool. There may be many who feared him, but even he would be an idiot to insult one of the great noble houses of Laedrin. That was why, despite having already been kept waiting over three hours, he didn't allow even a shred of anger to cloud his features.

A door to his right opened and he sat up straight in his chair, watching as a finely dressed man came into the room.

The man bowed slightly at the waist and motioned to the door.

"He will see you now."

Ramson nodded and stood, quickly straightening his clothes, and followed the man. He felt his heart rate increase as they approached a large, ornately carved oak door.

There was only one reason he'd been summoned here, and all he could hope was that it wouldn't cost him his life.

The finely dressed man halted before the door and knocked once.

"Enter," a muffled voice said through the door.

The man opened the door for Ramson, motioning him inside, and taking one final, deep breath, he entered the room.

Rows upon rows of books greeted him as he entered. There were so many, in fact, that he almost missed the large desk occupying the center of the room. A man sat behind the desk, impeccably dressed in a fine black suit with silver buttons lining the front.

The man had steel gray hair and dark eyes. His face was lined and hard, and a short-cropped beard covered the bottom half of it. The man finished writing something as Ramson bowed at the waist. He didn't move from his position until the man had finished writing and motioned him to come and sit.

Ramson obliged and pulled out one of the chairs facing his desk.

The man looked at him for a moment, scrutinizing him with a penetrating stare.

"I assume you know why you summoned here." It was a statement, not a question.

"Yes, my lord," Ramson said and cleared his throat nervously.

"You had one task. Retrieve the pendant and bring it to me." He spread his arms to the side as if to ask where it was.

Ramson licked his lips a few times before replying.

"With all due respect, My Lord, the information I received was bad. The man named Darver said he didn't have the pendant."

"Did it ever occur to you that he would be lying?"

"Of course, My Lord," Ramson quickly said. "I held a sword to his wife's throat, but he still insisted he didn't know what I was talking about."

"And I assume that you captured him and brought him in for questioning?" the man asked in a tone suggesting he already knew the answer.

"Well, no. After his wife was dead, he ran at me, so I had one of my men cut him down."

"How very unfortunate." The man folded his arms on the desk in front of him. "There was also a son and a daughter, if I'm not mistaken. Did you at least capture one of them?"

Ramson swallowed hard. "Well, we did have the daughter, but she somehow managed to escape. The son is most likely dead. After he took my eye, he begged me to kill him, but I let him live to prolong his suffering." His mouth twisted into a cruel smile at this.

The man didn't seem to be impressed by this.

"So, what you're telling me is that everyone who might know where the pendant is, is either dead or missing. Is that correct?"

The smile slipped from Ramson's face as he said this, and he slowly nodded.

"Then tell me why I should allow you to leave this room with your life. After all, the reason I hired you is because I can't exactly have the king's men raid a village in his kingdom. The people would

Aaron Oster

revolt. That's why I paid you an absurd amount of money to attack the village and retrieve the pendant. It seems to me that since you failed in this mission, I should have you executed for attacking an innocent village in the king's lands."

Ramson shot to his feet at this, anger clouding his features.

"If I go to the gallows, I'll make sure to take you with me!"

The man only smiled, then picked up a small bell and rang it. One of his bookshelves slid to the side and a woman came out of a hidden passage behind it.

"Calm yourself, Ramson. If I wanted you dead, you would not have received a letter summoning you here. One of your men would have cut your throat and would now be here instead of you. Now sit." His voice hardened, and Ramson sat back down, trying to compose himself.

"Now I'm sure you recognize this fine woman." The man motioned the woman over, and she threw back her hood.

It was only then that he got a good look at her. She was dressed in an extremely tight-fitting and very revealing leather top with a plunging neckline, as well as a pair of tight pants with rips and tears all along her long legs. It wasn't her extremely attractive and scantily clad figure that caught his attention, though. His eyes were glued squarely on her face.

"But... You're dead!" he spluttered. "I saw you die myself, back at the village!"

The woman smiled at that and turned to the nobleman.

"I told you he'd be surprised."

"Yes, my dear. You are quite convincing when you have to be."

Ramson still didn't know what was going on. He only knew that a dead woman was standing right in front of him, alive and well.

"I see that this has come as a shock to you," the nobleman said, turning back to him. "This was the source of my information, and I can assure you that she is quite trustworthy."

Ramson stared at the woman for another minute before looking back to the man.

"So why is she here? Why did you want to see me?"

"Oh, the reason is quite simple. I have heard word that the boy of this Darver was last seen fleeing towards the Jagged Peaks. You will go and hunt him down for me. To make sure you

452

cooperate, she will be accompanying you on your journey. She knows the family quite well, the boy in particular."

The woman stepped forward and stuck out her hand, a half-crazed and quite terrifying smile lighting her face.

"Looks like we'll be working together for the next few months."

Ramson took the proffered hand hesitantly and shook it.

"You may go now," the nobleman said, waving his hand to dismiss them.

Ramson rose from his seat and headed towards the door. He was stopped as the man's voice called out to him.

"One more thing before you go. Do not think you can kill her and run. Betray me, or fail me again, and I'll have you killed in a very slow and painful manner."

Ramson swallowed once and left the room. It was as though the man had known exactly what he'd been thinking. He could hear the telltale swish of the woman's cloak as she followed him down the opulent halls of the manor. It unnerved him to see her alive and well.

He left the manor as quickly as he could, stopping only to retrieve his weapons. Rain was coming down in sheets, but he didn't hesitate for a second, running out into the pouring rain and heading out of the manor grounds. He only looked back once he was outside the gates. Through the pouring rain, he could just make out the banners of Duke Carve Gregmar fluttering in the wind.

He looked to his right and saw the woman staring at him with a raised eyebrow.

"What?" he asked in an annoyed voice.

"Oh, it's nothing," she said with a coy smile. "I heard that you lost your eye in quite a spectacular fashion. That boy is quite something." She sniggered and walked over to a small overhang where a pair of horses were tethered.

Ramson gritted his teeth and followed the woman, mounting up next to her.

This woman was clearly unhinged and more than a little crazy, but just what was she doing working for the Duke?

A question had been nagging at the back of his mind ever since he'd seen her, and now that they were alone, he just had to ask.

"How are you still alive?"

The woman looked at him, cocking her head to side.

"It would take far more than a few crossbow bolts to kill me, Mister Ramson."

She grinned again, that same insane smile, and winked at him, turning her horse and trotting off down the road.

Ramson shivered as she spurred her horse forward. It took a lot to scare him, but this woman was absolutely terrifying. He'd never seen anyone take so many injuries and appear as healthy as she did right now. If he'd had any plans of disposing of her, he would have to go about it with extreme care. For now, though, he had no choice but to follow the Duke's plans. So, turning his horse, he headed out into the pouring rain, in direction of the Jagged Peaks.

Afterword

What's up Super-People?! For reaching the end of the book, you get a good old-fashioned handshake. (Sorry, I can't afford anything else, since no one buys my books). If you want to see a book 2 in this series, please let me know by leaving a great review. I really need those. They're very important, and I'm not above blackmailing you to get them.

But seriously, if you enjoyed the book, please leave a review, every single one helps. (Except the negative ones. Those don't.) You can also help by sharing my books' URL codes to friends and family who you think would enjoy my books.

You can check out my website for all news on current and upcoming releases, blog posts, artwork on characters, and other exclusive content. You can also contact me directly through the site if you have any questions.

AaronOsterAuthor.Com

You can also support me on Patreon if you want some exclusive previews and benefits. You can also follow me on my various social media, as that is where I do giveaways and the like.

Patreon: Rise To Omniscience
Instagram: Aaron Oster
Facebook: Aaron Ostreicher
Facebook Group: RTO/Buryoku

Upcoming releases

Rise to Omniscience (Book 4) October 2019
Rise to Omniscience (Book 5) Winter 2020
Animal Kingdom Online (Book One) November 2019
Land of the Elementals (Book Two) ???

Out Now

Rise to Omniscience

Supermage: Book One
Starbreak: Book Two
Skyflare: Book Three

Buryoku

Power: Book One

Land of the Elementals

Rampage: Book One